one
split
second

Also by Caroline Bond

The Forgotten Sister
The Second Child

one
split
second

caroline bond

CORVUS

Published in hardback in Great Britain in 2020 by Corvus,
an imprint of Atlantic Books Ltd.

10 9 8 7 6 5 4 3 2 1

A CIP catalogue record for this book is available from the British Library.

Hardback ISBN: 978 1 83895 107 8
Trade paperback ISBN: 978 1 78649 923 3
E-book ISBN: 978 1 78649 924 0

Printed in Great Britain by Bell and Bain Ltd, Glasgow

Corvus
An imprint of Atlantic Books Ltd
Ormond House
26–27 Boswell Street
London
WC1N 3JZ

www.corvus-books.co.uk

Dedicated to the people
who say, 'Yes'

THIRTY-TWO DAYS AFTER THE ACCIDENT

THE MESSAGE went out to *All Staff* at the beginning of the day. It was read and passed on over and over again. Conversations were had about who could be spared and who could not. Far more wanted to attend than were able, but that was the way it was – even for this. Many of the frontline staff knew immediately that they wouldn't be able to go. Their presence was required elsewhere. When your day job is a matter of life or death, *the living* take precedence. A number of people were secretly relieved to be denied permission. It felt wrong not to want to be there, *and* wrong to be thankful to miss it.

The corridor vigil was a St Thomas's tradition that had started with Lenny Okafor. Nineteen years of age, cause of death: inoperable internal bleeding caused by falling from a roof. (The firm that employed Lenny was eventually prosecuted for its poor health-and-safety procedures, but that provided little solace to Lenny's family.) Lenny's dad, Vincent – who was a porter at the hospital at the time of the accident – was, thankfully, not on duty the day his son was brought into A&E. In fact Vincent would never work as a porter again, not in St Thomas's or anywhere else. He said he simply couldn't face doing the job any more, not after what happened. The honour guard for Lenny was a spontaneous gesture of support organised by Vincent's work mates. It felt like the least they could do to show their respects to the family and the brave decision they had made.

There were probably about twenty people there for that very first act of observance, most of them porters. They stood in clumps of twos and threes, ranged along the corridor, uncertain of the protocol, which was understandable – because there wasn't any. Robbed of their usual banter, their feet still and their hands idle for a change, Vincent's work mates shuffled and whispered quietly – until the doors of the ICU banged opened and Vincent, the bloke with the loudest laugh and the worst jokes, wheeled his firstborn out on his last-ever journey. As the gurney passed along the corridor the porters bowed their heads in absolute silence.

Now the attendees for the vigils came from every walk of life and level within the hospital. An untimely death touched all the staff, irrespective of their clinical and professional experience. They were all mothers and fathers, brothers and sisters, friends and lovers – all capable of contemplating the unimaginable, and humble enough to pay witness to it. Indeed, the corridor ritual for the organ donation patients and their families had become a touchstone in the lives of many of them; a way – not that anyone ever voiced it – of warding away the Furies from their own precious, all-too-fragile loved ones.

By 10.36 a.m. on Wednesday 3 April more than two hundred people were gathered in the corridor on Level B. Clerks, porters, nurses, cleaners, quite a few of the junior doctors, a smattering of consultants and even a few members of the general public who happened to be there and who bravely chose to stay and participate. Many of the faces were familiar: rivals, adversaries, subordinates and bosses. They whispered to each other or stood apart in quiet contemplation – just as the porters had done for Lenny.

At 10.37 a.m. two of the ICU nurses came out of the ward and held open the doors. That was the signal. The gathered crowd, which had been subdued before, now fell silent.

The wait lasted only a matter of seconds, but it felt, as it always did, much longer.

Those nearest the door heard it first – the mechanical sound of the life-support machine. The trolley emerged slowly, flanked by the attendant staff and the patient's relatives. In a wordless ripple, the attendees along the corridor bowed their heads. They did so to pay their respects, but also to avoid looking into the eyes of the grieving family.

Chapter 1

THE NIGHT OF THE ACCIDENT

PETE MCKINNON was looking for his cat when he heard the bang or, more accurately, felt it deep inside his chest. There was a moment of silence. Then the screaming started – a loud stream of noise that went on, and on. Pete froze. For a split second he contemplated going back inside his house and pulling the door closed behind him, but his better instincts took over and he set off running.

According to the police report, it took Pete less than twenty seconds to get from his small, weed-filled front garden to *the incident*.

Pete was the first person on the scene.

The first person to call 999.

The first person to try and help.

The first witness.

And he would wish, for the rest of his life, that he hadn't been.

For years afterwards he would dream about the blood under the girl's fingernails and the way she'd rocked back and forth in the moonlight before collapsing face-down on the grass.

The sirens woke more people. They peered out from behind closed curtains, felt an immediate sense of shock and an irresistible impulse to see more. Bare feet were shoved into shoes, jackets pulled on top of pyjamas, and phones slipped into pockets. They emerged from their houses and crept guiltily towards the lights – moths towards the flame.

Many would later wish that they hadn't.

The first photo was posted sixteen minutes after the crash.

The first parent to feel vaguely sick when she saw the post was Tina Walker, up with her youngest daughter: earache – again. Tina was one of the lucky ones. Lydia, her eldest daughter, answered her phone on the third ring and promised faithfully – above the noise of the party – that she was fine. Tina insisted that she stay put and wait for her father to pick her up. It was a late-night 'dad taxi' run that Liam was deeply thankful to be able to do. Having reassured herself that her own daughter was safe, Tina began worrying about other people's kids. She called Steph to double-check on Becca. Steph understandably panicked and spread the gut-clenching anxiety by texting anyone and everyone who had a son or daughter of an age to be out on a Saturday night, including Kath. Kath sent a group WhatsApp, thinking it was the quickest way of getting the word out. Cheryl saw it and immediately rang Sam and Melanie and, on second thoughts, Dom.

And so it was that the arteries that ran deep within the flesh of the community spread the fear. Even parents who knew full well that their kids were safe, and in their rooms, scrambled out of bed and went to look in on their 'children', many of whom were awake, their faces lit by the glow of their screens.

News travels fast, especially bad news.

By 1.45 a.m. the ripples of alarm had gathered force and a tidal wave of panic was sluicing through the community. The promise of instant contact afforded by modern technology became a blight. Anyone unable to reach their son or daughter *immediately* assumed the worse, many incorrectly – but not all. Those who did speak to their kids directly did so hurriedly, urgently, telling them to stay put until they could be fetched safely home.

Five miles away in the home of Alice Mitcham – whose parents were away in Crete for the week – the party came to a juddering halt. The music stopped, the drinking stopped, the fun stopped. All of them suddenly felt stone-cold sober. Someone switched on the big light and the party-goers huddled together under its unforgiving glare, hugging each other. Names were whispered, roles assigned, motivations attributed. And so it was that the story of the night took root and began to grow. There was relief when the first cars started arriving to take them home. They left one by one, two by two, quietly, obediently, young adults returned to childhood by the shock. When the last person had gone, Alice sat, on her own, amidst the remnants of the party, her phone clutched in her hand, looking at the messages, wishing her own parents home.

By 2.30 a.m. the whereabouts of most of the kids was known. Most – but not all. Because, for a small handful of parents, there was no response to their frantic calls and messages. No wordless reunions and fierce hugs. These parents – the truly unlucky ones – plunged headlong into the awful realisation that their child had been involved in the night's events.

Chapter 2

SAL REYNOLDS, Tish's mum, was at home, on her own – as she always was nowadays – when the posts started appearing. Her instant reaction was to assume that Tish was one of those hurt. The recorded message telling her that *the phone she was calling was switched off* made her feel sick. Sal had little faith in fate not to dump an unfair proportion of crap into the lives of those already struggling. And Sal was used to crap happening. It was Tish and her against the world. That's how they got by. The thought of something bad happening to her only child made Sal feel deeply, shakily afraid. She rocked, she paced, she dialled and re-dialled. Nothing. After half an hour of panic she simply couldn't stand being trapped in her small living room, not knowing, any longer. She put on her coat and set off for the crash site, compelled to go, but terrified of what she was going to find. As she hurried through the tight grid of streets that led down to the ring road, she noticed how many of the houses had lights on. Different families – the same fear.

Sal arrived quietly, unannounced, and stood behind the police cordon with the growing congregation of horrified, curious bystanders, her stomach clenched so tightly that she had to stoop to accommodate the pain.

Jake Hammond's three older brothers, Sonny, Charlie and Ed, also made their way down to the ring road. They drove – a couple of beers didn't count.

The minute they'd heard about the accident they'd felt a fizzing compulsion to find out what had happened. They'd gathered back at home, summoned by the frantic calls from their mum, Anita. As she cranked herself up into a frenzy of worry, they'd offered to go and double-check that Jake wasn't involved. Jake often stayed out until four or five in the morning; he was bound to be at a different party or in a bar somewhere. They were confident that he wouldn't be heading home this early on a night out.

They arrived at the crash site in plenty of time for the scene to have lost little of its excitement. Their hearts thumped in response to the lights, the crackle of the police radios and the frenetic, but controlled focus of the fire and ambulance crews. The brothers were glad they'd come. People were going to be talking about this for weeks. They already felt a curious pride, knowing they'd be able to say that they *were there*. Instinctively they raised their phones and started taking pictures, zooming in, zooming out, trying hard to capture the drama and the scale of the carnage. Weaned as they were on the graphic simulations of *Grand Theft Auto*, the scene in front of them was nothing new, but what they were unprepared for was the dawning realisation that this was different – because *this was real*. This was what real speed did to a real car that had real passengers inside it. This was metal smashed with a bone-breaking impact, and glass exploded by the exertion of way too much force. This was the acrid smell of petrol and melted plastic, and the weird quiet of a closed road.

The car, or what was left of it, was embedded in the wall of the Gerard's Fabrications building. A total write-off. It had once been a Seat Leon. A blue Seat Leon.

Harry Westwood drove a midnight-blue Seat Leon.

Harry was Jake's mate – had been since primary school.

Jake and Harry went out together, a lot.

Their mum's hysteria began to seem like a rational reaction.

Dom was driving back up to York from Birmingham after a long, tedious meeting and a late business dinner when Cheryl rang and told him about the accident. Dom's company was looking into acquiring a new dealership group based in and around Edgbaston. It was pricey, especially given the state of the market, and the investors they had lined up were getting twitchy, but Dom thought they were being over-cautious. It was a good opportunity. The group was currently being run, badly, by a father, two sons and a nephew combo – some sort of Brummie mafia. They were stuck in the Dark Ages in terms of marketing and IT, but the showrooms were in great locations and the dealership had a large, loyal customer base. The deal had its problems, but it also offered a lot of potential. The last thing Dom needed at the end of a long day was this – whatever *this* was. Probably Cheryl panicking. She was a 'molehill into a mountain' merchant. That said, Dom drove faster after talking to her.

He instructed his hands-free to call Harry. He kept glancing at the display as it repeatedly, automatically, fruitlessly re-dialled his son's number. Anxiety increased the pressure of his foot on the accelerator, but as he neared home he was forced to slow down. Suddenly there was traffic, which made no sense; he would normally have sailed round this section of the ring road at this time of night. The realisation that the hold-up was probably a result of the accident was sobering. Dom sat in the queue of cars and refused to allow himself to worry. Harry often ignored his phone, especially when he was out. That was the mantra Dom decided to stick to – his son's all-round slackness, his 'easy come/easy go' life of friends and having a good time; Harry's similarity to himself at that age. The phone tried again, and once again abandoned the call after eight attempts. Harry could very well have left his phone at home, dropped it down the loo – again – or just be ignoring his calls. All of which was highly likely. Dom drummed his fingers on the steering wheel and blocked out any possible connection between the crash, his son and his son's new, midnight-blue, high-spec Seat Leon.

Shazia and Nihal sat together on the sofa in their front room, taking it in turns to ring Mo, and trying to convince each other that the fact the police hadn't contacted them was a good sign, that there was still hope. But with every slow minute, their faith weakened and warped. They didn't know what to do, where to be, what to think – other than that they must try and not think the unthinkable. They hadn't wanted Mo to go the party. He had work in the morning, and he was a boy who needed his sleep. Not a boy, obviously; a young man now. University in September – all being well. Leaving home. He was not just growing up, but almost grown-up. But he was still a child in their minds, especially when he was hungry or grumpy with tiredness. And he would be more than tired by now. It was late. Later than he would ever normally stay out.

Where was he? And why hadn't he been in touch to let them know he was okay?

Half a mile away Fran and Marcus were asleep, unaware of the panic racing through their friends and neighbours. Two bottles of red wine after a hectic work week had poleaxed them both. Jess was safe and sound, round at Gabbie's – a girls' night in. As the messages piled up on their mobiles, they snored, sighed and rolled over beneath the duvet.

They were oblivious…until the doorbell shattered their dreams.

Chapter 3

AFTER THE awful conversations with the police, the dash to the hospital, the slap of shoes on hard surfaces, the voices directing them *up here, just along this corridor, through the door on the left, please* – after all the rush and clamour – the sensation of being washed up on a far-away shore, isolated from events, was deeply disconcerting. Most of them had been brought to the hospital in squad cars driven by polite but monosyllabic uniformed officers. Dom was the exception; he'd insisted on driving himself, despite the very best efforts of the female officer who'd been assigned to him. She'd stood in his hallway, her radio crackling, advising him that the shock might make driving an unwise option. He had ignored her.

Now, gathered together in this small room, they looked at each other and saw their own panic made flesh. Anita was crying and talking uncontrollably – *Jake this, Jake that, Jake, Jake*; how she could maintain such a constant flow of tears and words was beyond most of them. The recognition that they were not going to swerve this tragedy, that they were going to be hit full-tilt by it, had stunned the rest of them into silence. Tears were out of reach. To cry was a release, and there could be no release until they knew how bad it was for their child. *Their* child, not anyone else's; there wasn't space, yet, for such empathy. Their panic was too raw and personal to be shared. Hence they stood, passive and acquiescent, in their pairs or alone, as the senior policeman confirmed their place at the front of the queue for this nightmare. In a clear, steady voice he told them that their questions couldn't be answered – *not yet, not until there was clearer information about the casualties – which would be available soon. So please, if they could be patient for a little longer. The medical staff would be in to talk to them shortly.* The officer left the room, quickly, as if relieved to be away from them.

And then they waited.

Dave hugged Anita, while opposite them Shazia and Nihal sat immobile: poles of the same emotional compass. Fran and Marcus stood by the window, staring out at the orange halos of light in the darkness, trying not to imagine what might have happened to Jess, while Dom paced. And Sal? Sal sat on her own, near the door, hunched over her phone, lost in the world beyond the hospital, where the accident was a dramatic local news story, not a real event. Her croaky voice broke through their personal purgatories. 'Christ! There's so many photos.'

Dom went and sat next to her. She passed him her phone. The others watched as he swiped the screen – imagining what he was looking at. Fran couldn't bear it. 'Please, Dom, don't.' But Anita looked up and stretched out her hand. After Dom had seen enough, he passed her the phone. Anita's and Dave's faces creased and crumpled as they flicked through the images. Anita's hand went to her mouth and the sobbing started up again. Dave offered the phone to Nihal, who reached out and took it, but Shazia's recoil was so severe that he tossed the phone straight back at Dave. Dave then offered it to Marcus. Marcus's 'No!' was so loud that they all jumped. Fran turned away and closed her eyes.

She knew them all, liked them all, but she wished at that moment that she'd never met any of them. Never spent a minute – never mind what felt like a lifetime – with Dom; never got to know and respect Sal; never learnt to appreciate Shazia and Nihal's quiet humour; never found enough common ground with Dave and Anita to be around them, occasionally, for short periods without wanting to scream. In that claustrophobic room, waiting to hear just how bad it was, Fran wished, fervently, that Jess had never made friends with the children of any of these people.

Chapter 4

AS SOON as the date for the prom was confirmed, Dom stepped up and offered to host the 'pre-party'. No one put in a counter-bid. The other parents were happy to leave him to it. Marcus did jokingly question *since when had a pre-prom party become a thing* – but he got shouted down by Jess and Fran. Fran informed him, semi-seriously, that the high school prom was an important rite of passage, a step over the threshold from childhood to adulthood; and, she confessed, coming closer to the truth, that she was looking forward to seeing them all in their finery. Marcus smiled and tuned out the subsequent discussion about the pros and cons of spray-tans and whether 'hair up' or 'hair down' was the way to go.

Five months later they were glad Dom had offered to host the party. The staging was idyllic. There were clusters of silver helium balloons, platters of posh canapés and trays of real champagne in crystal flutes. The weather was just what the girls' dresses demanded, balmy and still. And the sunlight was exactly right, soft and pink-tinged – perfect for the hundreds of selfies that were being taken. It was typical Dom, totally over the top and unnecessarily costly, but at the same time all very, very lovely. As the booze flowed and the kids laughed and shimmered around on the immaculate lawn, the mood was upbeat.

They all looked great. The lads suited and pointy-toe-shoed, the girls transformed by false lashes, fake tan and imitation designer dresses. It was like watching a group of children playing dress-up and pulling it off. Fran found herself surprisingly moved to see them all together, possibly for the last time. Most of them had been friends since primary school; Jess, Harry and Jake went even further back, to nursery and playgroup. They'd shared sleepovers, chicken pox, multiple birthday parties and a seemingly never-ending round of car journeys to out-of-the-way running tracks and football fields. She knew them all, had been part of their growing up. Indeed, it was down to the kids that the adults knew each other at all. The shared experiences and responsibilities of being parents of kids who were similar ages had bred friendships that would otherwise never have flourished.

Take Anita and Sal. They were hardly bosom buddies – a world apart in attitude and volume – but there they were, standing side-by-side, both smiling, sharing the moment in Dom's sun-dappled back garden. Dom himself was 'circulating', chatting to everyone, orchestrating the mood, topping up drinks; rather too quickly for Fran's liking – they were only fifteen and sixteen, after all. Fran could hear him cracking jokes about prom-night traditions that strayed perilously close to being in very poor taste. This was a side of Dom that Fran was very familiar with, but could do without. The showman who – given an audience, and any audience would do – couldn't stop himself playing to it. It was the Dom that most people saw: brash, loud, confident. It was not the gentler, occasionally vulnerable Dom who had few real friends, but whose friendship, once earnt, was fiercely loyal.

Dave, Jake's dad – who was downing champagne like it was beer – laughed raucously at one of Dom's jokes. Another man's man.

Through the melee, Fran met Marcus's eye and smiled. It was a moment of marital understanding that made her feel simultaneously mean-spirited and understood. Jake was also laughing, horsing around as usual. He looked resplendent in a dark-red three-piece suit. Jake had always been a little sod, prone to being in the middle of any trouble, but there was such an energy, a lust for life, about him that it was hard not to warm to him. His spivvy suit was the perfect choice. Harry also looked sharp, but in a much more understated way. Harry was the cool one in the group. Popular, without having to make an effort. As he drank his beer and lounged in a deckchair listening to one of Jake's stories, Fran tried to marry this version of Harry with the little boy who used to follow her around her house.

After Harry's mum, Adele, upped and left, Harry lost a lot of confidence – understandably; it was a very confusing, upsetting time. Overnight he went from being a boisterous, scabby-kneed seven-year-old, indulged by both his parents, to a cautious child. Being caught up in the middle of a domestic war was not a good place for a little boy. Fran had absorbed a lot of the childcare responsibilities for Dom during those sticky years when his marriage had imploded. She'd seen, close at hand, how both Harry and his three-year-old sister Martha had struggled with the sudden separation from their mum, and with the acrimony that had erupted around the divorce and the custody arrangements. It had been a vicious, vitriolic mess – which Dom had emerged from, eventually, as the victor. He was fierce as a father, as well as a friend. Harry had coped, but there had been a price to pay, a new-found introspection and watchfulness that were unusual in a child.

But look at him now! What, in a little boy, had been a worrying sign of sadness and separateness had transformed into a quite distinctive breed of coolness and self-reliance. Yes, Harry had done all right, despite everything. If Fran felt a sense of pride at being part of that survival and transformation, who could blame her? She'd been his surrogate mum, when he needed her. And though their relationship was no longer as close – which was natural and as it should be – there was still a special bond between the two of them, and she hoped there always would be.

She was jolted out of her reverie by Harry himself meeting her eye, smiling and raising his beer bottle to her in mock salute. Yes, at sixteen, Harry was no longer anyone's child.

A sudden, very loud crash on the patio drew everyone's attention.

Mo got to his feet, held up his hands and started apologising. Dom made his way over and righted the fallen heater, his mouth set in a forgiving smile. To be fair to Mo, the need for three huge copper heaters on an early summer's evening was questionable, but that was Dom – 'go big or go home'. Fran swallowed another mouthful of champagne and reminded herself to stop being so ungracious. Commotion over, and apologies flapped away, Narinder, Mo's 'date' for the prom – small, bossy, resplendent in cerise – pulled him away from the tables of bottles and glasses and food, obviously not trusting him not to cause another accident. They joined the other kids down on the lawn, adding more colour, life and noise to the gathering.

Fran felt the music from the outdoor speakers enter her spine. She swayed to the beat, feeling the old urge to dance come pushing back up: a sure sign that she was relaxing, or getting gently oiled. She smiled. It was turning out to be a lovely occasion. A chance for them all to celebrate – the kids to blow off some steam at the end of exams; and the parents to take a moment to appreciate getting their offspring through high school intact.

As she breathed in the relaxed atmosphere and the general goodwill, her eyes sought out her daughter. Jess had, as always, put her own very personal spin on the proceedings. A short, dark-purple skater dress and a new pair of pristine white hi tops. She was jittery with excitement, already bopping around the garden – like mother, like daughter – her arm linked with Gabbie, her 'date' for the evening. Gabbie was rocking a 'vintage' – that is, charity-shop – confection in patterned brown and gold and a pair of sparkly Docs, which Fran knew had cost her more than a new prom dress would have done. Jess and Gabbie seemed young compared to Sal's daughter, Tish. She looked stunning. She'd opted for a fitted floor-length, off-the-shoulder, pure-white dress that clung to her figure. Jess and Tish were only a few days apart, in terms of birthdays, and yet Tish already had an ownership of, and confidence in, her body that was rare for her age. She was aware of her power and happy to use it. This evening – stunning in her Greek-goddess dress – Tish was absorbing most of the attention from the boys and, somewhat more unsettlingly, some of the dads, but at least it took the heat off the other girls. For that, Fran was grateful. Sixteen was too young. If Jess stayed this side of adulthood for a little while longer, so much the better.

On the lawn the kids drifted, coalesced, photos were taken, then they floated apart and the pattern reconfigured again. Fran felt buzzy with the booze, and it was only 6 p.m. She turned away from the party and headed back into the house, intending to stick the kettle on for a brew.

Dom's house was as lovely as his garden, remodelled after Adele's departure and redecorated every eighteen months or so ever since. Dom was never satisfied with anything for very long. The end result was chic and uber-stylish, but the thought of all that deciding on colours and fabrics and furniture, and the pressure of living 'your best life' in a virtual show home, made Fran feel tired. What Dom was still trying to prove, she wasn't altogether sure. She filled the kettle, put it on, then wandered further into the house. The noise of the celebrations followed her, muted by the soft furnishings.

'Hello there. I was wondering where you'd got to.'

Martha was lying on one of the sofas in the snug, reading *The Curious Incident of the Dog in the Night-Time*. She was twelve now, going through that gawky, awkward stage. Fran felt for her. Martha sat up and folded a corner of a page down to mark her place in the book.

'Are you enjoying it?'

Martha gave a diffident shrug. Fran should have known better than to ask such a direct question. Martha studied the front cover of the paperback as if the picture would give her the right answer. 'It's okay. I'm not sure I understand what it's going on about really.'

Fran sat down beside her. 'Give it time. It's one of those books that makes more sense when you've read it all.'

Martha pushed the book under one of the cushions, as if embarrassed to be caught reading.

Fran changed the topic. 'Aren't you going to come outside and see them all in their glad rags?'

Martha shrugged again, her collarbone moving beneath her pale skin. The vest she was wearing accentuated her thinness. Fran felt a maternal urge to make her a sandwich, but it wasn't her place, not any more. Though perhaps – she reflected – she should mention Martha's weight to Dom; another time, when he wasn't in full party-host mode. Martha wriggled her feet along the couch, bringing her toes to rest against Fran's hip.

Instinctively, Fran reached down, lifted them up and put them in her lap. 'They're cold.'

Martha smiled. 'You always used to say, "Cold feet, warm heart".'

Fran smiled, touched by Martha's reference to their shared history. They sat in comfortable silence as the sounds from the party drifted through the house. Fran could understand why Martha might prefer a book and a room on her own to a garden full of beautiful people. The role of 'embarrassing little sister' was not an appealing one. And in many ways Martha was a young twelve-year-old. Physically she was still very much a child; emotionally too, Fran suspected. Her immaturity was unsurprising. Three years old was too young to lose your mum; four, too little to be caught between two warring factions;

five, too soon to learn that people can let you down; eight, too young to barely see your mother, aside from high days and holidays. Where the divorce had toughened Harry, it had weakened Martha. She seemed to have lost a layer of protection, and that had made her vulnerable. Fran pulled the end of a throw over Martha's toes and rubbed them. She heard the kettle click in the kitchen. 'Do you fancy a cuppa?'

Martha shook her head, but when Fran stood up to go through to the kitchen, the girl followed her.

They talked in fits and starts about high school and how Martha's riding was going. She obviously still loved visiting the stables. Fran listened patiently about a new hack that Martha and her instructor had discovered, in the valley, which led down to a stream that Sable, Martha's regular ride, was nervous of crossing. Fran nodded, sipped her tea and half-listened. The draw of the laughter outside grew. Surreptitiously she glanced at the clock. The limo would be arriving soon and the youngsters would be off. She really wanted to take her tea outside and re-join the party. Deep down, a part of her resented having to sacrifice this special time with her own daughter for time with Dom's. She loved Martha, but her pre-teen shyness made conversation hard work. Fran decided that she would make a move.

'I think they'll be setting off soon. Are you sure you don't want to come outside, just for a little bit?'

Martha pulled at her lip.

Fran tried another tack, one that gave Martha the chance to hide in plain sight. 'It would really help if you could take a few photos of them all for me. I'm useless. I never seem to catch people right.' She offered Martha her phone, and was pleased when the girl took it from her outstretched hand.

They walked through the house back out into the garden. The sunlight blinded them both, so that for a few seconds they saw only stars.

They were just in time. Anita was getting everyone gathered for the big group shot. There was a lot of self-conscious silliness about who should stand next to who. Anita was insistent that they had to organise themselves into a boy/girl, boy/girl sequence. Martha went down onto the grass and took her place at the end of the line of parental paparazzi. At last the kids got themselves into an 'Anita-acceptable' formation. The girls fussed with their hair and fiddled with the straps on their bare shoulders, and the lads buttoned up their jackets across their puffed-out chests. Behind them the balloons twisted and glinted in the still air.

At last Anita shouted, 'Okay. Everyone ready? One, two, three... Shout "Prom"!'

A ragged chorus of 'Prom!' went up.

The best photos were the ones Martha took of the line dis-integrating as they collapsed into each other, laughing.

Chapter 5

HARRY HAD expected it to be crap. A party in a local hotel – the bar closed, with all the weirdos and squares from school, patrolled by the Year 11 teachers – that finished at midnight: it was never going be great. And for the first hour it had been totally awkward. Everyone sitting around in their little cliques, drinking warm Coke out of plastic cups, not eating the 'sad as hell' buffet. Harry didn't feel the remotest bit sad about leaving high school. He couldn't wait to get away from the staff, the other students, the school itself, with its petty rules and high expectations. He was done with it. Period. And then the Prom King and Queen thing! That had been totally embarrassing. All that clapping and foot-stomping, like it mattered. What the hell was he supposed to do with a cardboard crown? But Tish had insisted that he wear it, had crowned him herself, a knowing smirk on her face. She had looked smoking, as always, even with the cheapo plastic tiara plonked on top of her elaborate 'updo'.

It was all so clichéd.

But something about the spotlight and the cheering had crept up on him; that and Tish grinning and twirling and laughing with him up on the stage, mocking the whole thing even as she revelled in it, and in them. The golden couple. Prom royalty. The official seal on their position at the top of the people-pile. It was so cheesy, so naff, so childish – but also so seductive. And when the DJ started playing the bangers, it had shifted up another gear. Jess had dragged them all onto the dance floor and, before he knew it, they were all bopping around, not giving a damn. As the beat took over, Harry forgot that this was just another cheap high school prom – the scene of his last, lame moments at Raincliffe – and started to have fun.

Jake was being Jake, pogoing away quite happily in a bubble of his own sweat and excess energy – Chloe, his 'date', long abandoned. That was no surprise really, Chloe was pretty, but she was also a total yawn. Jake had only invited her for one reason, and even that seemed to have been forgotten. Then there was Jess and Gabbie – both barefoot – belting out the lyrics, daft grins plastered on their faces. And Mo – Mo was the real revelation. Watching him throwing shapes with nerdy Narinder was both wrong and totally hilarious.

It felt good to be at the heart of it.

When the DJ put on the power ballads at the end and the crying started, they all linked arms, forming a tight circle. Harry, Jake, Tish, Mo, Narinder, Jess and Gabbie. A sweaty bundle of mates, glued together by time and familiarity. A unit. And as the glitter ball twirled and they all swore allegiance to each other, for ever, they meant it. They were friends and always would be.

Nothing could tear them apart.

Apart from the music stopping.

The lights going on.

And the teachers calling, 'Time'.

Chapter 6

THE NIGHT OF THE ACCIDENT

DOM'S NAME was the first to be called. It came as no surprise to the others, but it did cause a bitter spike of resentment. Why Dom? Why not them? Why should he be the first to discover what had happened to his child? The not knowing was excruciating, the waiting a test of endurance. How come Dom got to be released from such suffering before they did? But as Dom followed the nurse out of the waiting room, the others started to rationalise. Perhaps it wasn't a good thing to be summoned first. Perhaps it was a sign of bad news. It had been impossible to deduce anything from the nurse's composed, bland expression. Either way, as the door slowly closed, Sal had an overwhelming urge to run through it and demand to see Tish. She had as much right as Dom, didn't she? This polite, humble patience was surely the wrong response. Perhaps it was time to start shouting and demanding action, and access. Wasn't that what a parent should do? Fight tooth and nail to be with their child, not sit on their hands waiting to be given permission to leave the room, like obedient school children.

But the door clicked shut, and Sal found that she hadn't moved.

The disturbance of Dom's departure over, they went back to staring into the spaces between each other.

Dom was told that Harry was on a ward up on the fourth floor. The nurse – who seemed too old still to be working – wasn't very forthcoming about what state he was in. As they waited for the lift, Dom held himself rigid.

The police arriving at the house had blown apart his refusal to think the worst. He'd had to reset. The policewoman had spoken slowly, calmly, clearly. *A car had crashed, at speed. They believed the car to have been Harry's. There were casualties. Harry was one of them. The occupants of the car had all been taken to St Thomas's.* Dom had listened, processing everything, saying little, building up resistance. Faced with the reality of the situation, he'd swapped his earlier defiant optimism for a realistic dark pessimism. It was better to be prepared. A full-on crash, into a brick wall, at speed. The driver would, undoubtedly, have come off worse. Dom had asked about the injuries sustained by the people in the car, specifically the driver, but the policewoman couldn't, or wouldn't, give him any personal information about who was involved or what state they were in. Dom had turned away from her and begun thinking through the practicalities. Martha! She was asleep. Should he wake her? And tell her what? That her brother had been in a crash, that he was in hospital, that he was injured – how badly they didn't know. Dom went up and checked on her.

She wasn't asleep. His conversation with the police officer must have woken her. Martha was sitting up in bed, looking bewildered. He minimised the news, said that nothing had been confirmed, but she still started crying. She scrambled out of bed and began searching for her clothes, sitting down and standing up randomly. Dom hugged her to a stop, reassured her – then lied to her – saying that she couldn't come to the hospital with him. The reality was that he couldn't cope with Martha and with whatever had happened to Harry, at the same time. He never had mastered the knack of parenting both his children simultaneously. He laid the blame for Martha not being able to go the hospital on the police. He promised to ring her the minute he had any news. He told her not to worry. That *Harry was big and daft enough to look after himself.* Then he said that he was going to drop her round at Cheryl's on his way to the hospital, so that she didn't have to be on her own. And, finally, he told her that she must NOT look at *anything anyone* was posting about the crash on social media. *It was all speculation and nonsense.* She nodded and promised him faithfully that she wouldn't. He didn't believe her. He made a mental note to ask Cheryl to monitor her phone use.

Daughter sorted, he turned his attention to the fate of his son.

Yet, as Dom followed in the wake of the frustratingly slow nurse, he found himself still worrying about Martha. She and her brother were close, unusually so for an eighteen-year-old and a fourteen-year-old. It made sense. When your mum abandons you, you cling on harder to those left behind. Dom hated Adele for many reasons, but top of the list was the way she'd left, the mess that followed and the impact it had had on Martha. It had turned her into a worrier. She was often anxious about small, irrelevant things, always fearful of what *might* happen. That was all Adele's fault. Christ, how was Martha going to deal with this? What if Harry really was badly hurt? Or worse? Why couldn't the nurse just tell him, one way or the other?

They came out of the lift and turned left. They seemed to be heading away from the action, into the quieter, calmer hinterland of the hospital. Dom rationalised that this must be a good sign. They were not going to A&E or the operating theatres; they were going to a ward. 'Here we are.' As the nurse laboriously punched numbers into the keypad, Dom tried hard to quell his mounting frustration. At last the door buzzed and they were through. She led him onto the ward. It was a long, old-style room with a lot of beds, many of which were filled with sleeping, unidentifiable forms. Dom spotted Harry straight away. He was sitting in one of the cubicles with the curtains open. The angled wall lamp cast a tight circle of light around him. Dom's first instinct was to shout 'Harry!', rush over and hug his son, but something stopped him – respect for the other patients, the presence of the nurse, or was it something else? He wasn't sure.

He asked the nurse if she might be able to find someone to talk to him about Harry's injuries and treatment – effectively dismissing her – then took a few moments to compose himself. Dom found that he wanted to assess the situation, examine his son, get a grip on his emotions, before he was ready to move. Harry was sitting on a plastic chair, staring at his feet. He looked in one piece. In fact he looked remarkably normal. He certainly didn't look as if he'd just been in a bad car accident. This reality shook Dom, bringing with it a rush of pure, powerful relief. He wouldn't have to smash Martha's world. Thank God.

And yet still he hesitated, processing the night's events.

Harry hadn't moved. Why hadn't his son moved? Why was he frozen to the spot?

Dom crossed the room. On his approach, Harry looked up. The expression on his face stopped Dom in his tracks. Harry's face wasn't full of relief. It didn't flood with love at the sight of him. It was blank. Totally devoid of any emotion. Instead of embracing his son, Dom put his hands in his pockets.

Perhaps that was the moment – that fraction of a second when neither of them reached out to the other in their need and shock – when it all started to go wrong.

'You okay?' Dom asked, as if it was nothing, as if the last three hours hadn't been some of the worst in his life, and Harry's.

Harry seemed to have to think before answering. 'Yeah.'

Dom leant awkwardly against the bed and looked his son over. A quick scan revealed a scatter of cuts and abrasions on his face and neck, a bandage around his right hand and dressings on both his arms. That was it. Given the photos of the crash, the state of the car, the amount of broken glass and bent metal, the lack of physical damage was a miracle. So why weren't they celebrating? Why weren't they clinging onto to each other, crying with love and gratitude?

Harry had gone back to looking at the clumpy bandage.

'Harry!'

'What?'

Dom asked the only question that seemed relevant, 'What happened?'

Chapter 7

JAKE'S PARENTS were the second family to be called.

They were escorted down to the bowels of the hospital, to the operating theatres, the place where the emergency cases were treated. The thought of her youngest being cut and stitched behind one of those frosted-glass doors made Anita feel nauseous. They walked the full length of the building, past one, two, three sealed-off areas, imagining the worst, until they were finally led into a curiously hushed and calm recovery bay. Anita ran and actually skidded across the room into the trolley in her rush to get to her son. The jolt made Jake open his eyes. 'What the hell, Mum!' His voice was gravelly. He was battered and bruised. But he was alive. After so many hours of not knowing, the reality of being with him, seeing him alive and hearing him speak, was overpowering. It was not so much a relief as a release.

He was half-sitting, half-lying on the trolley, his right leg hoisted up and attached to a complicated shiny contraption that arced over the bed. The pulleys and weights on the frame were wired into bolts that had been driven deep into his skin. Dave tried to avoid looking at his son's smashed leg, but it was hard not to. There were patches of what looked like blue felt-tip marks around the holes and bolts in his skin. The sight made Dave feel light-headed. It was better to focus on his son's top half. There was a drip in Jake's arm and monitors attached to his bare chest, which was covered in sickly brown marks, like rust stains. There were cuts on his arms – some dressed, some not. He looked like some sort of weird hybrid creature: half-human, half-Meccano.

'Oh my God, Jake,' Anita sobbed.

'Hey there, Bud.' Dave's emotions were too big to allow for anything other than small words.

'Hey, Dad. Hey, Mum. Whoa! It's okay, Mum. Calm down. I'm okay.'

Dave didn't know where to touch his son. Every bit of him seemed claimed by the hospital equipment. Anita stroked Jake's hair across his forehead and kissed his face. 'Are you in pain?'

Jake rested his head back against his pillow and actually smiled. A dopey, very familiar expression. 'Nah. They've given me the good stuff.' He did sound high. 'But I think I'm a bit fucked for the match.'

Despite everything, Dave and Anita laughed.

Chapter 8

FRAN AND MARCUS were the next to be called. They got up quietly, their hearts skittering, suddenly reluctant to face their fate.

Twenty minutes later, despite the doctor's patient explanations of MRI scans and damage assessment, Fran was still struggling to put the sharp fragments of the night together and connect them to Jess. The transition from a normal Saturday night to the intensive care ward was so abrupt and abnormal that it was hard to take everything in. But above all, what Fran felt was relief. At least they were finally with Jess, able to hold her hand and talk to her, to see her face and touch her hair. They had their baby back. And despite the showreel of horrors that had been spooling through Fran's head since the police had knocked at their door, Jess looked...okay. She was very pale and there was a nasty scrape along her jawline, but there were no dreadful contusions, no blood.

The doctor spoke of how lucky Jess had been to escape any pelvic or leg injuries. They had not had to operate, though he stressed that surgery might still be necessary, depending on the result of the scans and on Jess's progress over the next twenty-four- to forty-eight-hour period. Fran was struggling to listen. She couldn't stop looking at their daughter. Whoever had got her settled had done a good job of cleaning her up and making her comfortable. Jess looked serene. Peaceful. Not in pain. That would be the drugs – the sedation the doctor had spoken to them about. For that, Fran was grateful. She didn't want Jess to be frightened, or distressed. After the trauma of the crash it was good that she was sleeping, unaware of all the lights and activity and machines. Jess was stable. That had to be good news.

Fran laid her head down on the sheet next to Jess's hand and very lightly stroked her daughter's fingers. They were cool, but not cold. The weight of Marcus's hand resting on her own back was reassuring. They were together again. It would be all right, as long as they stayed together. The worst was over.

Chapter 9

IT WAS Sal's turn next.

The doctors gave her a choice: stay in the tiny side-room near the operating theatres or go up to the ICU unit and wait there. They stressed that Tish could be in surgery for quite a while, and that she would be very heavily sedated when she did finally emerge. How long she would be in theatre, they didn't know. How conscious she would be, they couldn't say. Sal panicked. The thought of being alone frightened her. There'd been a curious comfort in being trapped in that awful waiting room with the others. Or, if not comfort, then at least a solidarity of anxiety. They had been in it together. She couldn't face the thought of being left on her own in the underbelly of the hospital, with nothing to do but wait and pray. When they told her that Marcus and Fran were already up on the ICU unit, that decided it.

A porter with copious tattoos and a boxer's face escorted her to the unit. He was kind, chatting away to fill the void in her social skills, pointing out where she could get a cup of tea twenty-four hours a day, where the nicer visitor toilets were, how to get to the staff canteen on the ground floor – where the food was *much cheaper* – all the useful things she was going to need in the coming days and weeks. Because this *was* where she was going to be for the foreseeable future.

Tish was in a bad way. The doctors had been very clear about that. They'd used big, complicated medical words that she hadn't fully understood, but the message had been stark. They were in for a long haul. Tish had life-threatening injuries, to her face and neck. Her jaw had been broken. They were having to repair *a tear in her trachea* – which was her windpipe. There was *concern* about her left lung. A respiratory specialist had been called in. Sal had nodded and tried to listen. This was important. The most important information she'd ever been given, and yet illogically it was the sound of Tish's voice that filled Sal's head, drowning out the doctor's words. Tish singing, up in her bedroom, joyous, loud, inappropriate; nothing delicate about it, because there was nothing delicate about Tish. And that was because Tish was strong. Invincible. Sal didn't push the memory away; she welcomed it, listened to it in preference to the doctor's relentless, negative litany of what was wrong with her daughter.

The porter buzzed and pushed open the door to the ICU, but didn't come onto the ward with her. That Sal had to do on her own. It was scary, like voluntarily walking into a fire with nothing to protect you. Had it not been for Marcus looking up and seeing her arrive, she might have stayed in the entrance hallway for ever, too frightened to venture any further. He stood up and came straight over, put his arms round her and held her tight, squeezing hard. His ferocity helped to ground her. The sense of something shared gave her strength.

'Any more news?' Marcus asked.

'She's still in surgery. How's Jess?'

They both looked over at Jess. Fran was leaning over the bed, her hands fluttering above their daughter's sleeping form as if performing some type of ritual healing.

Marcus said, 'She's stable. They've sedated her. They're doing tests. Lots of tests. She has a fracture behind her left ear, and some sort of wound at the back of her head. But no other broken bones. It's the impact on her brain that they're concerned about.'

Sal nodded, though she didn't understand what that meant, or where it put Jess on the scale of suffering and damage. Regardless, she returned his kindness by squeezing Marcus's arm.

'Have they told you much about Tish's injuries?'

Sal nodded and swallowed, then found that she couldn't say anything in response to his question. But Marcus was sensitive enough not to expect an answer.

'It's a *good* hospital, Sal. Expert, professional staff. I'm sure they're looking after her.' They were hollow words, but they were well intentioned. They clung onto to each other for a few more seconds before separating; Marcus to go back to his daughter and wife, and Sal to present herself at the nurses' station.

An hour and a half later and the bed next to Sal remained empty. Tish was still somewhere else. The wait was excruciating. Sal couldn't stop thinking about the surgeon, in the basement of the hospital, dressed in green scrubs, his rubber-coated fingers digging around inside her daughter. Cutting and stitching, stretching and suturing, mounds of red-and-white swabs on the metal tray next to him. She'd seen enough hospital programmes on TV, watched through splayed fingers as they hacked and hurt, in their attempts to heal. She'd shed tears for complete strangers, prayed for their survival; and she'd waited, on the edge of her sofa, for the weepy, post-surgery reunions and the 'two months later' miraculous transformations.

Now it was her turn. But this time there was no way it was going to be neatly resolved in the next hour; and there was no audience to shed tears of relief, or sadness, for her and Tish. Sal looked across at Jess again. Fran and Marcus were curled around her, forming a protective barrier. Sal sat alone, fearful that she wasn't going to be enough.

Chapter 10

SHAZIA AND Nihal were the only ones left in the room. They felt as if they had been there for days.

'It's because he's dead.'

Nihal took hold of his wife's arms. 'Shazia, stop it. Please.'

But Shazia wouldn't or, more accurately, couldn't be comforted. 'But this doesn't feel right, does it? Why keep us here for so long without telling us anything? Everyone else has been taken off to be with their kids. But not us! He must be dead. That's the only possible explanation. That's why we're the only ones left. They want us to be on our own when they tell us.'

In the absence of anything to contradict her, Nihal closed his eyes, raised his hands to his face and started to pray.

At last, as if summoned by Shazia voicing the unthinkable, the door opened. They turned and braced themselves, but it wasn't a nurse or doctor who came into the room, it was the police liaison officer, accompanied by a woman. The officer looked at them, registered the panic on their faces and made a strange, air-patting gesture with his hands. Wired as they were, the gesture gave them a sliver of hope. The officer wouldn't have signalled that they should calm down if Mo had died in the crash. This wasn't going to be the worst day of their lives. They weren't about to be led into a room and asked to identify the body of their son. The relief was intense, but short-lived. Because if Mo wasn't dead, what then? Why were they being kept separate from everyone else?

The officer tugged at his jacket and actually cleared his throat. 'I'm sorry to leave you sitting in here for so long. It's somewhat hectic out there, as you can imagine.'

Neither of them sat down. They waited for him to deliver whatever fate he held for them.

'I'm afraid...' Nihal reached out for his wife, 'that we've been working on the basis of some inaccurate information about the identity of the young people in the car. There have been quite a number of conflicting reports coming in, from various sources, and it's taken some time to verify these different statements. But I can now confirm, with a degree of certainty, that your son wasn't recovered from the scene with the others.'

'What?' they asked in unison.

'We've checked and double-checked, but he isn't in the hospital. He wasn't brought in by the ambulances.' The officer watched them, waiting for the news to sink in. Which it did, rapidly, bringing with it waves of confusion. He continued, 'Mohir was reported, by a number of eyewitnesses at the party, as getting into the car that crashed; and given our – and your – inability to contact him, an assumption was made that he'd been involved in the incident. Hence you being asked to come to the hospital. But after checking the IDs of the other casualties, and now that the other parents have provided positive identification of their children, it's become clear that Mohir is not among the injured.'

'Are you sure?' Nihal asked. It was hard to swap one narrative for another so quickly.

'Yes. We're sure. That's what we were checking. Hence the delay in speaking to you.'

The following silence was a barren one.

'So where is he?' Shazia's confusion echoed Nihal's own. Where was their son, if he wasn't at the hospital? He'd been with the others. He'd been in the car. He'd been involved.

The officer couldn't tell them. 'That's what we're trying to ascertain.'

Again neither Nihal nor Shazia could compose a response that was adequate. Eventually Nihal said, 'So what do we do now?'

The officer paused. 'We'd advise that you go home – wait for him there. He will, we have to assume, come home eventually. He was seen leaving the party, and a couple of witnesses are adamant that he got into the car, but that's the last confirmed sighting we have of him. We're obviously continuing our enquiries. Has he ever dropped off the radar before?'

'No.' They put up united front. What was he implying?

'And you don't have any ideas about where he might be?'

'No.' Again in unison.

'Okay.' The officer didn't add anything. They all just stood there, in middle of the room, wrestling with their own thoughts and questions.

It was the woman who broke the impasse. 'We have your contact details. Obviously if we hear anything we'll contact you ASAP, and you must let us know if – *when* – he gets in touch with you or returns home.'

Shazia reached for her bag. They had to leave. There was nothing for them here. Mo was elsewhere, lost to them, and seemingly to everyone else.

As she reached out to push open the door, the officer said, 'We'll obviously want to talk to him when he does turn up...' After a beat he added, 'as a witness.'

Chapter 11

DOM WAS discovering that time moved at a totally different speed in hospital, dictated by medical priorities, not chronology. The doctor – who the ancient nurse had said *would be along shortly to speak to them* – had still not put in an appearance. The wait, in the dark, trapped in their tiny cubicle on the slumbering ward, had been interminable. Once he'd phoned Martha to tell her that her brother was okay, Dom had had nothing to do but sit and stew. Initially he'd been patient and polite, grateful even, but as the minutes crawled by he grew restless, then exasperated. After three hours of waiting he was angry.

Harry had been tight-lipped, which Dom supposed was understandable, but it was also deeply frustrating. When he'd tried to get details about the accident out of him, Harry had said very little, other than that the car had crashed when he'd swerved to avoid something in the road. He volunteered nothing else and, when Dom pressed him, he said he had a headache, lay down on the bed and closed his eyes – a *piss off and leave me alone* gesture, if ever there was one. Left to his own devices, tired, stressed and irritated, Dom had felt like a caged animal, hemmed in by a flimsy curtain, the cast-iron hospital protocol and an awful feeling of being totally out of control.

By dawn he had had enough. As Harry slept, or pretended to sleep, Dom went to the nurses' station and demanded, rather than requested, that they be allowed home. The senior nurse repeated that Harry had to be seen to eat, without vomiting, and had to have had a normal wee and to have opened his bowels – and be signed off by one of the doctors – before they would be permitted to leave. Dom promptly went and fetched a can of Coke and a cereal bar from the vending machine, woke Harry up and supervised him as he consumed them. Then he pointedly took the evidence of consumption to the nurses' station. He was told, again politely, but this time even more firmly, that they still had to wait until the full observation period had been completed.

And so they waited.

By late morning Dom was at his wits' end with his son, and with the wait. He resorted to going out into the corridor. His in-box at least provided a distraction. Life went on. Time pressures and deadlines remained. He responded to a couple of enquiries, then composed what turned out to be a long email to the solicitor handling the Birmingham deal about the issues that had emerged during his visit. Before he knew it, nearly an hour had passed. Faced with the option of going back onto the ward or staying in the corridor working, he chose the latter. It was, he reasoned, better for everyone.

Harry was relieved finally to be left alone. He'd not spent this long with his dad, in such a confined space, for years – not since their camping holidays in Wales when he and Martha were kids. That felt a lifetime ago, in the dim, and increasingly hard to remember, post-'Mum walk-out' days. He and his dad were not good at being together at the best of times, and this was not the best of times. They needed other people around to act as a buffer. Harry didn't normally give his relationship with his father much thought, but marooned in the hospital, his body and soul in shock and his dad sitting at his bedside vibrating with frustration, it was hard not to. The momentary relief of seeing a familiar face and hoping that his dad would somehow make it all go away had vanished within seconds. Dom was not the indulgent, loving type. Never had been...at least not with Harry. Their relationship had always been spiky, competitive, lacking in any emotion other than flashes of anger and, much more rarely, pride. Perhaps it was because, deep down, they didn't really like each other that much. Who knew? Who cared? Normally.

Martha! She was the one who cared. She'd cried when Harry had called to tell her that he was okay; tears of disbelief, to start with, then of relief. She'd not asked what had happened, just how he was, what hurt, whether they were looking after him, when he would be coming home, if he *really was all right*. Harry could hear the fear in her voice and felt terrible for being the cause of it. When he'd said that he had to go – as if he had something urgent to attend to – Martha had insisted that he pass the phone back to Dom. Harry had been able to tell, by his dad's whispered responses, that she was checking that he wasn't lying to her about being okay. Harry watched his dad change as he spoke to Martha. His posture, his voice – everything about him – became softer and calmer. That hurt. But he was used it to. His dad ended the call and sprang back into his normal coil of repressed energy.

And so they had settled in to wait.

With every passing minute the pressure inside the tiny cubicle had built. He could feel his dad's impatience pulsing off him. The nurses were patient with Dom's rudeness and were kind to him, which only made Harry feel worse. They brought him cups of tea, which he accepted, to show willing, and offered him paracetamol, which he declined. There wasn't enough pain. Nowhere near enough pain!

When Harry asked about the others, which he did repeatedly and increasingly desperately, they smiled sympathetically and said they were sorry, but they didn't know anything. His dad had been equally unforthcoming. He claimed to know nothing other than that Jess, Tish and Jake were being treated somewhere in the hospital – for what, and how bad their injuries were, he couldn't, or wouldn't, say. Out of habit, Harry's hand kept reaching for his phone, only to flop back onto the bed. His lifeline was gone – taken by the coppers at the scene. Evidence? The thought made the sinews in his neck tighten. He thought about telling his dad about the blood sample the police had taken from him, but decided not to. It would all come out soon enough.

It was unbearable. The not being able to leave. The not knowing what he was going to have to face.

And yet after the seemingly never-ending wait, when they finally told him he could go home, Harry was floored. They were sending him away from the hospital, away from his friends. He did not require any further treatment – unlike them. He had been lucky – unlike them. Harry watched the doctor as she spoke, wanting her to look suddenly concerned and say they were very sorry, but they'd found something wrong, something serious, that had shown up on an X-ray. He was in fact badly hurt, and it was imperative that he stay. But that didn't happen. He was discharged, with nothing more than a photocopied letter that had to be dropped off at his GP's, *when he got the chance*. No medicines, very few wounds, no limp, no crutch; indeed, very little to show that he had even been in a car crash, except for the scatter of cuts on his arms, his aching, stitched hand and the scream in his head that no one else could hear.

Chapter 12

THE JOURNEY home was somehow worse than the drive to the hospital – the dark dread of imagining Mo injured having been replaced by the muddy confusion of him being missing. Nihal concentrated on his driving, very aware of the traffic and of the shocking normality of an ordinary Sunday taking place outside the thin shell of their car. Shazia was silent, her face turned away from him, staring out of the window. He knew what she was doing: she was looking for Mo. Illogical as it was, he 'got' that she was trying to spot their son at bus stops and amongst the people out walking in the cold sunshine. Her felt her body tense when they saw a young lad with dark hair waiting to cross at the lights on the high street. Even as they approached home, and the number of pedestrians thinned to near zero, she didn't come back to him. She remained rigid with concentration, her shoulders tight.

As they turned into their road Shazia suddenly shouted, 'No!', causing Nihal to brake and stall.

'What?'

She turned to him. 'We can't go home. We have to check.'

'Check what?'

'That's he's not still there.'

'What are you talking about?' Nihal restarted the car and drove the last few feet to their house. They parked up. This simple act seemed to tip Shazia over the edge.

'Nihal! No! We can't just go home and sit there waiting. We have to go and make sure that he's not still there. They could've missed him.'

Realisation dawned. Nihal looked at his wife. 'You want to go to the crash site?'

'Yes. We have to. We have to make sure.'

'Shazia. That doesn't make any sense. He won't be there. We should do what the officer said – go in, wait for him to come home.'

But Shazia simply stared at him, the look in her eyes steely.

Reluctantly, Nihal put the car back into drive and pulled away from the house.

They parked on Brayton Road and walked to the ring road.

It felt such a strange thing to do, to go looking for a Mo in full view of the passing traffic, but Shazia was adamant.

The scars in the verge were visible from quite a distance away, the muddy car tracks looked black against the grass. Both Nihal and Shazia shuddered to think of the car leaving the road and literally ploughing its way into the wall. The blue-and-white police tape twisted in the breeze. By unspoken agreement, they didn't go up to the actual site of the impact. Instead they paced beside the road, looking for anywhere that a hurt, confused or concussed Mo could have crawled away to. That's what Shazia was thinking: that he had somehow got out of the car after the crash and slunk away like an injured animal. It made no sense to Nihal, but there again, he couldn't come up with any credible, alternative explanation for where their son was and why he hadn't been in touch with them. Mo had been seen getting into the car. The officer had confirmed that much.

They weren't the only ones on the side on the road. At regular intervals small knots of people arrived, many of them teenagers. Nihal watched as they bowed their heads for a few seconds, in actual prayer or just as a sign of respect, then stood with their arms linked around each other, staring at the physical scars left by the accident. The solidarity of friendship. As the cars whooshed by, the exhaust-laden air was filled with the sound of their whispered speculation.

Shazia and Nihal made three passes of the verge. It was pointless and upsetting, but when he suggested they return home, Shazia point-blank refused. She was not done searching, not yet. *Mo had to be out there somewhere. It was their job to look.* So, for no rational reason that Nihal could discern – other than Shazia's maternal compunction to keep going – they left the ring road and made their way along to the park. Once there, they proceeded to conduct a bizarre version of hide-and-seek, looking behind trees and under bushes, for a child who was long gone.

Chapter 13

WHEREVER PETE went, he couldn't relax. The front of the house was the worst – obviously – as the windows provided a clear view of the crash site, but even in the back room he felt uneasy, unable to settle. He was clear-sighted enough to know that his restlessness was caused by lack of sleep and adrenaline, but this sudden self-consciousness in his own home was unnerving.

He'd called into work as soon as the gym had opened and explained, very briefly, why he couldn't come in. When Ellen started asking questions, he'd somewhat brusquely cut her off, saying that he'd see her on Monday morning as normal; and to get Rhys, the deputy manager, to call him if he needed anything. After Pete got off the phone, he ran a bath, wanting to be clean. He lay in the tub for a long time, poaching his tired body, watching the condensation trickle down the walls into the grubby grout. The previous night's events jittered through his mind like one of the cartoon flicker-books he used to make when he was a kid; isolated images that, when strung together, created a jerky story that unfolded at double speed. In reality, each moment had felt painfully long.

He only got out of the bath when the tank could no longer yield any more hot water. Body scoured and hair washed, dressed in shorts and a T-shirt, he went downstairs and put some washing in the machine. He watched it swish around for a few minutes, the detergent lifting the grass and bloodstains out from his once-favourite pair of trackie bottoms. He made a coffee – drank it; made toast – left it. He had no idea what to do with himself. Pete was not used to having time on his hands, especially at the weekend. Sundays were one of their busiest days, with people swimming or treadmilling off the excesses of the night before. For the first time in Pete's life the quiet and his own company, which he usually cherished, felt like a pressure.

He flicked on the radio, switching his usual news channel over to a music station. He washed Cleo's bowl and put down fresh food and water, though where she'd got to was anyone's guess. Cleo was no biddable TV pet, purring and entwining herself around his legs, simulating love in exchange for sachets of expensive cat-gloop. She was independent, largely indifferent to him, almost feral. Perhaps that's why they were such a good fit. The loner divorcé and his lone-wolf cat; both of them quite happy to coexist as long as there was no expectation of anything more than the convenience of having another soul present in their lives.

The radio announced that it was 9.30 a.m. Pete contemplated walking up to the shops, but swiftly discounted this as a truly dumb idea. They'd all be buzzing about the accident by now, picking over the events, swapping tales of what had happened, who was involved and who was to blame. As much as he didn't want to be alone, he didn't wanted to be part of that particular feeding frenzy, either.

The rap of the door knocker made him jump. Through the glass panel he could make out two figures. Both male. Pete opened up and was relieved to see that it was an official visit, rather than a concerned neighbour's knock. The coppers presented their warrant cards and he let them in. Immediately his house seemed to shrink. They made stilted small talk as they went through to the front room.

All of them glanced outwards, across the road with its now-flowing traffic, before quickly taking their seats.

Over tea they took Pete's statement, starting with *the moment he realised that something had happened.*

'I was looking for my cat. That's why I opened the front door. She stays out late sometimes, then whines to be let back in after I've gone to bed. It's really irritating.' He paused, wishing that was it: the beginning and end of a very boring, very short story.

Neither of the coppers said anything. They knew what came next, but they needed his version – his unique perspective on what happened.

'That's when I heard the noise. A really loud bang.' He looked down at the rug, concentrated on the pattern and thought himself back into his front garden in the dark, cursing Cleo, impatient – just another normal night. He'd been about to shut the door, leave her outside to her own devices. 'It was a crump, like a bomb going off. I looked up and saw the car. I could tell it was bad, straight away. Then the screaming started.'

The copper with the glasses asked, 'A male or female voice?'

Pete closed his eyes and heard it again: that high, compressed scream, full of pain and panic. But whether it was one of the girls or the lads, he couldn't say. 'I don't know.' All he knew was that it was enough to galvanise him into action. 'I had my phone in the pocket of my trackies. I dialled nine-nine-nine as I ran over.'

'Did you see any other vehicles on the road at the time?'

'No.'

'Are you sure?'

'Yes. It was quiet.' In truth, Pete hadn't checked; he'd just set off running across the Tarmac, his phone clamped to his face, his words echoing back inside his head. The closer he got, the worse it had looked and the tighter his chest had become. It was a miracle he'd managed to tell the operator anything. 'It looked like the car had smashed into the wall, then spun round. It was facing the wrong way.'

'Which wall, Pete? Sorry, but we need as much detail as possible.' The other copper this time.

'The Gerard place.' He paused, picking the facts out of the messy awfulness of it all. He wanted to make sure what he told them was accurate. 'The passenger side had taken the worst of it. '

'And what make was the car?'

'It was a Seat. A dark-blue Seat. There was a strong smell of petrol – and something else. A scorched smell. The grass was all churned up on the verge where it had run off the road. But to be honest, I don't think I noticed that at first. I think I saw that later, when we were waiting for the lad in the back to be cut free. I remember thinking the car must have been travelling at a hell of a lick to end up where it had.' He checked himself. 'Sorry. That's not for me to say, is it? I don't know what speed it was going. I didn't see the actual crash.'

'It's okay, Pete. You're doing a grand job.' The comment made him feel pathetically grateful – for the kindness, and the praise. 'And the casualties...the people involved in the crash. Can you tell us about them? Where they were? What kind of state were they in?'

Pete nodded. 'The first person I saw was the young lad. He was crouched down on the grass near the car. He didn't seem to be that badly hurt. He was shouting, but not making much sense. I asked him if he was all right, which was a bloody stupid thing to say, in the circumstances, but he ignored me. When I put my hand on his shoulder to try and get him to come away, he lost it. Started yelling at me to "fuck off". He was hysterical, frightened.'

'Did he say anything else, apart from the abuse?'

Pete tried to remember, but although his brain still echoed with the visceral sounds of the crying, and the noise of the car creaking and straining like a trapped animal, the lad's actual words wouldn't come to him. He took a few breaths, and the coppers waited. They didn't prompt him or ask anything else, but the atmosphere in the room shifted slightly, and Pete suddenly realised the importance of what he was saying. This was an official statement to two police officers, about a crash in which people had been very badly injured, possibly killed. The lad on his knees was the driver, or so Pete had assumed. As the driver, he would be in the frame.

He shook his head. 'No. It was just *to leave him be* – he was more focused on the girl in the front seat than on me. And it wasn't "abuse" as such; he was in a state. Anyway, I decided to see if I could get into the car. That's when I saw that the doors on the passenger side had been ripped off, and I noticed there were other people in the car. There was a lad. He was flopped against the back seat. Upright, but not right. What I mean is...I could tell he was in a bad way. For a minute I thought he was dead, but then he kind of rolled his head towards me and opened his eyes. He was quiet. He looked at me like he didn't understand where he was, or even that he was injured. I cleared some of the glass off the back seat and climbed in next to him. That's when I realised his legs were pinned. There was no way I was going be able to drag him out. I didn't think I should try to move him anyway. I don't know what I thought I could do for any of them really, apart from let them know I was there – that help was on its way. I could see the back of the girl's head, the one in the front seat.' Pete stopped. The officers waited. 'There was a lot of blood. Did she...? I mean...?'

The younger officer glanced at the other, as if confirming some sort of protocol. 'I'm afraid we can't release any details about the people involved, Pete. We're sorry—'

But the older guy cut him off. 'There've been no fatalities reported yet. The casualties are all being cared for at St Thomas's. You ringing for the ambulances made a difference, Pete. If they'd been there longer, it would've been worse.'

Pete didn't believe there was any way it could have been much worse, but again he was grateful for the effort to reassure him.

'Are you all right to keep going?'

'Yes, sorry.' He took himself back to the crash. To the sounds and the smell. To the sense of utter helplessness. 'That's when I heard this really awful noise. It was like an animal in pain. It wasn't the girl in the front. She was unconscious, I think.' He paused, uncertain if he was remembering everything accurately. 'I climbed out – there was nothing I could do for the kids in the car – and I followed the noise, in the dark. That's when I saw the other girl. The one I'd missed. I swear I never saw her at first. She was about fifty feet away along the verge. I don't know how she got out of the car. She was on the grass, sort of kneeling up, rocking. She had her hands – both her hands – on her face, like this.'

He lifted his own hands and cupped his chin, his fingertips resting against his cheekbones, just as she had. It made him remember her eyes, or at least one of her eyes. The other was lost in a black, messy pulp.

'I went over. Crouched down next to her.' He paused again. 'She was making a lot of noise. It sounded like a pan bubbling over. I couldn't make out anything she was saying. It sounded like she was choking. There was blood all over her hands and her clothes. I tried to...I tried, well...I tried to help. But she kept swaying back and forth. I couldn't get her to stop. I don't why I wanted her to keep still. She must have been in so much pain. I took my sweatshirt off and put it around her shoulders. It seemed to go on for ages: the rocking, the choking noise, the lad being hysterical over by the car. Then she suddenly pitched over. I didn't have time to catch her. Maybe I was looking for the ambulances, I don't remember. She didn't put her hands out. She sort of fell forward, a dead weight. I'm assuming she blacked out. She was kind of splayed on her front, with her head skewed to one side. I didn't dare move her.'

Pete swallowed; his throat was still dry from the smoke and the trauma.

'I bent down, checked that she was still breathing. She was, but my God, her face. It was…well, it was such a mess. I sat on the grass next to her. One of her hands was poking out from underneath her body. I held her fingers, really carefully. I didn't know what was broken and what wasn't. I kept talking to her. I just thought that if she was even a tiny bit aware, then at least she would know she wasn't on her own.' He stopped and waited, desperate for them to tell him something – anything – about how she was doing.

The older officer took pity on him, but only so much. 'Like I said, they're all being well looked after.'

That could mean anything. Pete wanted to know more, but realised it was none of his business – other than that he had been there, in the darkness, on the side of the road, before the fire crews and the police and the lights. He'd been there when it was lonely and frightening. He'd talked to her and held her hand, willed her to cope, to keep breathing, to hang on in there. After the ambulances arrived, he'd watched her being worked on by the paramedics. He'd been shocked by the seeming brutality with which they manhandled her, turning her over, taping her jaw in place, pumping something into her slim arm. He saw her being hoisted onto the stretcher and slid into the brightly lit interior of the ambulance. He'd watched it drive away, bumping down the kerb with a thud that had made him wince. He'd looked after the flashing lights long after they disappeared.

It was a natural point to take a breather. Instinctively all three men glanced out of the window again to the road, the endless traffic and, beyond that, the damaged wall.

But they're weren't done with his statement yet. 'You stayed on the scene for quite a while, didn't you, Pete?'

'Yeah. One of the officers asked me to stay, to give an initial witness statement. And anyway, I couldn't leave. I needed to see them get the lad out. What I mean is, I needed to see them all into the ambulances.' Because for that brief, seemingly endless period, between hearing the bang and the police arriving, they had been his responsibility.

Both of the officers nodded. Then the older one asked, 'Is there anything else that might be of use to us? Anything you saw that might have contributed to the crash. Anything at all? The road conditions, the weather, the traffic?'

'No. It was a really calm, clear night. I like I said, the road was quiet, empty.'

'Okay.'

Pete suddenly felt tired, but they still weren't finished.

'Can we just get you to circle back a little bit, Pete? Thinking about the young man again – the one who was kneeling next to the car.'

'Yes.' Pete added nothing else.

'Any observations you want to make about him?

'Such as?'

'His behaviour? His level of coherence? His breath? Was there anything to indicate that he might have been drinking or taking drugs?'

Pete paused, gave it real thought. *They were all young. It was late. The girl was wearing party clothes. They'd probably been drinking. Two girls, two boys. Testosterone swirling. The temptation of an empty road. A Seat Leon – the 'go-to car' for boy racers.*

He opened his eyes and shook his head. 'No.'

He'd been young himself once, a lifetime ago.

Chapter 14

SHAZIA PULLED the door closed behind them and immediately knew the house was empty, because it *felt* empty. They often chided Mo for being noisy, complaining about his music and his big feet stomping around upstairs. It was the family joke – Mo, the klutz, an accident waiting to happen. Shazia stood in their hallway and made a pact with herself that she would never again moan about his crashing about, if he would just walk through the door, unharmed, with a credible explanation of where he had been for the past fourteen hours.

Nihal was, once again, on his phone. She turned away, unable to watch his distress, and wearily climbed the stairs. At the top she stopped, her breathing laboured. The fear of losing Mo had aged her, overnight. She crossed the landing and went into his room. It was the usual mix of mess and manic tidiness. His clean clothes – all ironed by her – were, as always, carefully folded away in his wardrobe; he liked to look smart, 'sharp' in his terminology. But his worn stuff was strewn around the room, some on his chair, some on the floor, more on the end of his bed. It looked like a hurricane had passed though. In contrast, his expensive, deeply cherished trainers were all lined up in a neat row against the skirting board, laces tucked in. No, not at all of them. There was a gap. A pair was missing. His new Nikes.

Shazia turned away. On the desk his *daada* had bought for him was Mo's college work, a slew of papers, printed sheets and textbooks, all neatly annotated in his small, precise handwriting. Chaos and control in one revealing snapshot. It was odd that a boy could be made up of so many contradictions.

Even in his room, surrounded by his things, Shazia found that she couldn't cry – she wanted to, but she couldn't, because she didn't know what she was mourning. She picked up one of Mo's sweatshirts; underneath were his only pair of smart black trousers and the branded polo shirt that he had to wear for work. Shelf-stacking at Sainsbury's: minimum wage, hard work, good life experience. Clothes that should have gone straight into the linen basket. She scooped them up as well, along with a couple of stray socks and a towel. The towel was still damp from his shower the previous evening.

She decided to get his uniform washed and ready for him. He would need it for his shift on Tuesday evening. She was sure they would understand about him missing today, as he was normally very diligent. He was never late; he worked hard; never, normally, dropped a shift, even if he wasn't feeling well. He was a good employee. He was a good son. She had to have faith.

Holding the bundle of washing to her chest, Shazia walked back downstairs, along the now-empty hallway. Nihal had had the extension built as a twenty-fifth wedding anniversary present for her three years ago. He still hadn't lived that one down. *The romance! Who needed a weekend in Paris when they had extra space for a tumble dryer and an ironing board?* Her friends had teased her about it, whilst at the same time revealing glimpses of envy.

Instinctively Shazia looked left into the kitchen as she made her way towards to the back of the house. Mo wasn't there; of course he wasn't, because he wasn't anywhere. Her chest felt cold, the damp from the towel had seeped through her shirt. She unlocked the door into the utility room and that's when she saw them – a pair of Nikes, no longer pristine, sticking out of the gap between the dryer and back wall.

Chapter 15

IT TOOK Shazia and Nihal a few minutes to wake Mo. When he did eventually come round, he was groggy. He struggled to his feet, stiff from having spent so long curled up in such a small space. He cracked his elbow against the dryer on his way up, but he didn't seem to notice. They both studied him, looking for signs of injury. There were none. He was just rumpled. Close up, Shazia could smell the sweat on him, an acrid tang that reminded her of the homeless man on the bridge who she sometimes said 'hello' to on her way to work.

'Why on earth didn't you call us? We've been frantic.'

He hung his head. 'I'm sorry. I didn't have my phone. I had to walk home, and it was really late. I came in the back, but the inside door was locked. I didn't want to wake you, so I decided to kip down in here. I'm sorry – I thought you were in bed.'

'We've been at the hospital all night. We thought you were in the car.' As he said it, Nihal realised that his son didn't know what had happened. He and Shazia exchanged a look of concern, and confusion. What the hell was going on?

They shepherded Mo through to the kitchen. Wanting to be somewhere safe and warm before they broke the news to him. Habit dictated that Shazia put on the kettle and Nihal fetch the cookie jar. Once the water had boiled, Shazia passed them each a mug of hot, sweet tea and they sat round the table, as they had thousands of times before.

Calmly and clearly Nihal told Mo about the crash, the police and the dreadful night they'd spent at the hospital, thinking he was one of the casualties.

Mo looked like he was going to cry. 'How badly hurt are they?' His voice wavered.

Nihal shared what little they knew. Most of their information was coming from Anita's texts.

'Harry's okay – apparently. Minor injuries, cuts and bruises. A bit of a miracle actually. Jake's been more badly hurt. His right leg took a lot of the impact. Multiple fractures. Some broken ribs as well.'

Mo looked wild. 'And the girls? What about Tish and Jess?'

Shazia gently touched his sleeve. Nihal spoke softly, as if whispering would somehow lessen the blow. 'They're both in intensive care. We don't know any more than that.'

For a while the only sounds were the hum of the fridge and Mo's uneven breathing. They waited, watching their son struggle to absorb what had happened to his friends.

The tale, when he did eventually start talking, came out in a series of disconnected chunks, which was confusing, but they knew their son well enough to follow his circuitous route to the truth. It was a rush of stumbled words and emotion, which began with, 'We were having such a good night.'

'At the party?' Shazia prompted. The frustration of not knowing what had happened was eating her up, but Mo's glazed expression worried her. She didn't feel able to demand answers; not like she would normally have done.

'Yeah. At Alice's. It was the usual crowd.'

'Were you drinking?' Nihal shot Shazia a warning look, but they needed to know.

'No.'

They wanted to believe him – Mo wouldn't lie about something like that, though an unfamiliar flicker of doubt rippled through Shazia.

'We were just hanging out, dancing, talking.' He even swayed a little, as if the music still echoed through him. 'I got hot…with the dancing. I went out into the garden. Harry was there, with Jess, chilling. It was nice. I don't know how long we were out there. It was Harry who decided we should leave. I don't know why. It wasn't late.'

'What time was it?' It was Nihal this time, edging the story forward.

'I'm not sure; about twelve, maybe earlier.' Not late in the teenage play-book. 'We went back into the house to find Jake and Tish. Jake was going for it – jumping around like a loony. Tish kinda appeared from somewhere. I don't really remember. Jake wouldn't come at first. He was having too much of a good time. He had a bit of a stand-off with Harry, nothing major. Just the usual banter, but he was being a bit of a prat. In the end Harry said we were going, and if Jake didn't come, he'd have to get home on his own. That got through. Jake followed us out and we all got in the car.'

At the mention of the car Shazia's stomach knotted. So Mo had been *in* the car. 'Then what?' she asked.

'We drove to McDonald's.' They both blinked, thrown by the banality of his answer. Mo went on. 'That was Jake, again. He said he was starving. Once he'd started banging on about cheeseburgers, we all wanted something.'

It was called 'the munchies'; Shazia wasn't stupid, she knew the effect alcohol – and drugs – had on appetites. Mo experimenting with drugs? No. He wouldn't. Would he? But he would always – normally – text, to let them know where he was and what time he'd be back. He was a good like that. Normally. Mo and drugs? No. It didn't compute. She decided to stick to the chain of events. 'The McDonald's near the roundabout, on the ring road?'

'Yeah. Harry wouldn't do the drive-through. Said he didn't want his car stinking of food, so we parked up and went in.'

'At that time of night?' Shazia wasn't sure why she was questioning his story.

'Yeah. It's one of the twenty-four-hour ones.' Mo stopped and looked round the kitchen. He registered his tea, picked it up and drained it in a series of long, deep swallows. Without a word, Nihal swapped the empty mug with his own full one. Mo drank half of that as well.

Why was he so thirsty? Drinking made you thirsty. This doubting Mo's word was a new and wholly horrible feeling. Shazia tried to concentrate on listening to, not mistrusting, her son.

'Harry said he'd do the order. Tish and Jake stayed with him, at the self-serve machines. Jake kept changing his mind about what he wanted. Me and Jess went and sat down. It was all fine. Me and Jess talked about the party. Then I went to the loo.' He stopped.

'And?'

'And when I came back, they'd gone.'

'Gone?'

He nodded. 'Gone outside. I could see them in the car park.'

In Shazia's mind's eye, she saw her son standing, abandoned, in the middle of the brightly lit McDonald's. She felt his confusion and his sense of humiliation. Later she would feel some small bitterness at them excluding her son, but at that moment, deep within her bruised heart, she was grateful. But for their cruelty, Mo would have been in the car. He would have been in the crash. He would, at this very moment, be in hospital. Or worse. 'They drove off and left you?' Shazia's voice held both her anger and her relief.

Mo took another drink, then glanced at her, his expression unreadable. 'No, not straight away.'

Chapter 16

IN THE hospital lobby Dom pushed his credit card into the machine to pay for his parking. He was tired and – though he didn't want to admit it – stressed. He wanted to pick up Martha, get home, shut the door, then sit Harry down and get him to talk properly. They needed to talk. Silence was not a normal reaction, nor probably a wise one in the circumstances.

As Dom entered his PIN number into the keypad, he got a call. He glanced at the caller ID, expecting a work call. It wasn't. It was the police. With his phone clamped under his chin, Dom dealt with the payment, grabbed his validated ticket and stepped to the side. He turned his back on everyone milling around the lobby, not wanting his conversation to be overheard.

They enquired after Harry, but that was only the warm-up. The real reason for the call was to ask – in fact, to insist – that Harry come to the station to be interviewed, as soon as possible. Dom wasn't surprised, but he immediately went on the offensive: pointing out that Harry was badly shaken, sleep-deprived, and that his son needed some time to recover. As he talked, Dom started skimming through his mental Rolodex of friends and contacts, thinking who might be best to ask for advice about solicitors, and who, just as importantly, he could trust to handle such a request with discretion. He was so distracted by his thoughts that he nearly missed the comment about the test results.

'Sorry, can you repeat that?'

The officer didn't react to his sharper tone. 'I was saying that the blood-test results should be back in about a week.'

'You took blood? From Harry?'

'Yes. With his consent.'

Dom's heart rate kicked up a notch. The idiot! 'Surely you should have waited for me to be present?'

'No. There was no need for a parent to be present. Harry is eighteen.'

'He was injured and in shock. He can't possibly have given informed consent, in the state he was in.'

The officer chose to ignore Dom's objections and carried on regardless. 'It is standard practice, Mr Westwood. Anyway, as I was saying, we need to book a time for the interview. I also want to remind you that Harry is still under caution.' It went from bad to worse.

The act of straightening his shoulders helped Dom recover some of his usual authority. He pushed back, in defence of his son. 'I'm afraid I can't confirm a time right now. Besides, it sounds like we need to sort out legal representation before we attend any interview.'

The tone at the other end of the line remained resolutely professional. 'That's your call, Mr Westwood. But it is a matter of some urgency that we speak to Harry again, to take a formal statement. We've scheduled the interview for one p.m. tomorrow.'

Dom refused to allow them to bounce him into agreeing anything. 'You'll have to leave me a number, and I'll call back to let you know.'

A number was provided, goodbyes were exchanged, then the officer repeated the time and the address of the station, and their expectation of attendance at the interview. The call ended.

Dom took three deep breaths before turning round. They needed to get home, now. They needed to start preparing a defence, and the first step in that defensive strategy was going to be Harry telling him *exactly* what had happened.

But Harry was not standing by the lifts, as they'd agreed. Dom's heart rate ticked up another notch as he set off in search of him.

Chapter 17

HARRY WAS drifting aimlessly through the waves of patients, staff and visitors. When he came across a block of largely unoccupied plastic chairs near the cafe, he sat down. He didn't want to leave, felt he couldn't leave – not without knowing what was happening to the others. He would refuse to go. His dad couldn't actually drag him away from the hospital, could he? Harry looked up at the boards listing all the different wards and wondered where his friends were. They were 'badly hurt', that's all he'd been told. Where would they be being treated? Orthopaedics? Thoracics and General Surgery? The Intensive Care Unit? Major Trauma? It was a long, long list of terrible-sounding places.

'Harry?' He recognised Fran's voice instantly.

He had just enough time to stand up before her arms were around him, hugging him tight. So very tight. It was good to be held. He bent his head low and rested it on her shoulder. She smelt of sweat and stale perfume and something else – a medical, antiseptic smell. The wave of emotion that washed through him was strong and, for a moment, such a relief, after all the anxiety that had been coursing through him since the accident. He hid in her embrace, letting her take the strain. It was so good to feel love. But it only lasted for a few moments, then the balance shifted and she gently pushed Harry back onto his own two feet. She held him at arm's length, studying him intently, and immediately the shame returned.

'My God. I'm so glad that you're all right. Are you? All right, I mean?'

He nodded and felt his face flush red. She noticed. Of course she did. Fran was the one person who could see straight through him. That's why he'd been staying away from the house lately. He hadn't wanted her to look at him and see the lies; hadn't been able to bear the scrutiny. Now it was a hundred times worse.

Fran smiled, fleetingly. 'I'm so relieved. The police wouldn't tell us much.' She made him meet her eyes, reassuring him that she meant it. 'Where's your dad?' she asked.

Harry pointed across the lobby. Dom was on his phone, his back to them. The question was pressing against Harry's skull, but now that he had the opportunity to ask it, he found that he couldn't. His dad turned, phone in hand, and started scanning the concourse. Harry didn't wave. Dom spotted them and starting walking over. Harry had to ask his question now, before his dad steam-rollered his way into the conversation. In his panic, it came out bluntly. 'What about Jess? How's Jess doing?'

Fran let her hands drop from his arms. She sat down abruptly. Harry sat beside her. 'She's...' She seemed unable to get any words out.

Harry's fear sharpened.

Fran tried again, 'She's...'

Dom arrived and broke into her answer. 'Jeez, Fran. Are you okay? What's going on with Jess?' He laid a hand on her shoulder.

Fran wilted in her seat. 'She's stable.'

'That's good.' Dom asserted, far too quickly. Harry was ashamed of his father's brashness. It was the tone, as much as what he was saying. Dom was in business mode. Brisk. Polite. Assertive. 'And she's being properly looked after?'

Fran shrank another few millimetres. 'Yes.'

Harry needed more, but his dad plainly thought that his social duties had been fulfilled. He obviously wanted to be off – as he had for the past fourteen hours. 'Well, send her our love. And to Marcus, of course. We'll keep in touch. If there's anything we can do, let us know?' He started edging away, looking at Harry, silently *telling* him to stand up.

Harry stayed put. This was *not* adequate. No way. It was not enough. 'How is she really, Fran?'

Fran reached out and rested her fingertips on the top edge of his bandage, lightly, carefully. 'She's very poorly, Harry. They're doing lots of tests. The damage is hard to assess apparently. So it's just a case of waiting, and praying.' Fran forced herself to sit a little taller. 'But she's calm and she's not in any pain. I promise.' Jesus, she was trying to make him feel better.

Dom cut in again. 'You are all in our thoughts. We'll keep in touch. But I really think I need to get this young man home. It's been a very long night, and day.' As he bent down to kiss Fran on the cheek, Harry had the urge to shove his father away from her.

'Can I come and see her?' Harry asked.

Fran said, 'Maybe in a few days, Harry, when we know more. I'll text you.'

'You promise?' He sounded like a child.

'Yes, Harry. I promise.'

Still Harry couldn't leave. He had other people's blood on his hands. 'Have you heard how Tish is doing? And Jake? They wouldn't tell me anything. They kept saying they weren't allowed to, because of patient confidentiality.'

Dom started running the parking ticket through his fingers. Harry tried to block him out.

'Tish is on the same unit as Jess. I can't lie, Harry; she's not in a good way. There's a lot of damage to her face and neck. Her jaw was broken in the crash. They've had to pin it back together. And she's been having some breathing problems.'

Harry thought he might as well curl up there and then on the floor.

Fran looked at him, her face pale and drawn with tiredness, but then she did what good mums do – she tried to make it better. 'They're doing everything they can for them both. We have to trust in their skills. Give it some time. It's amazing what people can recover from, Harry. We all just have to keep the faith.'

He made himself smile in the face of her bravery.

'And it is better news about Jake. Anita messaged me to say that the surgery on his leg went well. Apparently he's already being cheeky with the nurses.'

Dom was shifting from foot to foot. 'Well, that's good to hear. I really don't want to be rude, Fran. But if it's okay with you, we need to be going. We've got to get back...for Martha.'

Fran ignored Dom and instead looked straight at Harry. A flash of the old Fran. He steeled himself; he knew what she was going ask. He had prepared himself for her asking it, thought about nothing else all night. She had the right to know. There was a beat of silence. 'Harry, what happened?'

The words clotted in his throat. 'I'm so sorry. It was an accident.'

Fran touched his arm again, sympathy and pressure in one gesture. 'I know that, but I need to know what actually happened – what caused the crash.'

A cacophony of images and sounds bubbled up inside Harry – too many, all clambering and competing, scrambling over each other in their awfulness. He struggled, trying to compose his answer into something as coherent and as close to the truth as possible, but before he managed to settle on one fact to begin with, Dom leapt in. 'Fran. I'm sorry. But now really isn't the time. He's still in shock. He's had virtually no sleep. None of us have. We're all strung out by what's happened. We will speak soon, I promise. But we really have to go now.'

And, like the coward he obviously was now, Harry allowed himself to be dragged away – because he couldn't face telling Fran the truth.

Chapter 18

FRAN WENT back up to the ICU shaken by her chance meeting with Harry and Dom. She was relieved that Harry had escaped with so little damage, but their encounter had rattled her. Their conversation had been so pressurised, so full of emotion, yet at the same time so devoid of information. She knew no more than she had fourteen hours ago. And Dom had been weird – itching to get away, seemingly anxious to stop Harry talking. But as she stepped out of the lift, Fran pushed the stirrings of disappointment and resentment to the back of her mind. She had other priorities. She buzzed to be allowed back onto the ward, wishing, with every fibre of her being, that Jess was anywhere else in the hospital or even – as Harry was lucky enough to be – going home with barely a scratch.

For all the efforts of the staff to be compassionate and supportive, the ICU was an alien, frightening environment. White, bright, harsh – full of complex, high-tech machinery and inexplicable noises. The best of everything, staffed by the most qualified medical professionals, designed to care for the most critical cases.

Jess and Tish were now two of those cases.

The contrast between the two girls was profound.

Jess looked unnervingly unchanged, except for the machine that was breathing for her and the absolute stillness of her body. A sleeping beauty: her face glacial, her eyes, beneath their paper-thin lids, motionless. The wound at the back of her head was neatly dressed. Her skin was clear and unblemished. She looked like she looked every evening when she came down to say 'goodnight': make-up free, their little girl once again. But it was what they couldn't see – what was being scanned and measured by the sophisticated machines, minute by minute – that was the problem. Jess's bruising and swelling and damage were all internal. It was her tender brain within her fragile skull that they were worried about.

The damage to Tish's body was much more obvious. Shockingly so. She looked like she'd been viciously beaten. She was barely recognisable beneath all the dressings and tubes. Only her hair and her hands seemed to have escaped being crushed. Though even from right across the room Fran could see the thin rims of black blood under her fingernails. Tish was not fighting her injuries quietly or calmly, like Jess. Despite the huge quantity of pain relief they were pumping into her, she was restless, her breathing loud and raspy, as she tried to vent the pain that had hold of her body. Every time they had to move her or re-dress her wounds, Fran and Marcus heard Tish cry out in protest. Sal – mirroring her daughter's restlessness – was up and down, out of her seat every few minutes, stroking Tish's hand, straightening her sheets, trying desperately to provide some comfort to the tiny slivers of her child that were still available to her.

Every half-hour or so both women would walk the ten steps across the ward to meet each other in the middle; to touch base, to ground each other's panic, to say 'I'm here' by a hand on an arm or simply by standing vigil by the girls' bedsides while the other went to the toilet or to fetch a drink. Neither of them asked any direct questions about how each girl was doing any more. It was unnecessary, and it would have been cruel.

Their daughters were in the ICU.

Both girls were critically ill.

Nothing could change that, except time.

Chapter 19

IT WAS gone 4 p.m. by the time they eventually got home, having picked Martha up from Cheryl's. Dom had been deft and assertive in defending Harry from Cheryl's understandable questions about the crash, insisting that the priority was to get his 'children' home. Walking into their house and pulling the door shut was a relief. No more strangers, no more noise – the feeling of having stepped outside the nightmare back into mundane normality was calming.

But of course things weren't normal. Martha was wired, fizzing with a desperate, oppressive need to offer affection. As they made sandwiches and drinks, she kept giving Harry little pats and squeezes on the back of his neck or top of his arm, touches that Harry knew were designed to be comforting, but in reality made him feel claustrophobic. And every time he looked up, Martha's big eyes seemed to be there, following him around, pleading, worrying, seeking reassurances that he couldn't give. He didn't want touching. He didn't want someone fussing over him. All he wanted was to be left alone.

When he snapped and told her to give him some space, Martha froze, blinked and disappeared up to her room. Harry felt bad, but he hadn't anything to offer her. He couldn't tell her everything was going to be all right, because it wasn't – it probably wasn't going to be all right ever again. Dom had disappeared 'to make some calls', so he, thankfully, wasn't around to witness Harry's insensitivity towards his sister. God, it was such a mess: Martha upstairs, on her own, probably crying; him alone in the kitchen, not knowing what to do with himself; and his dad ensconced in his study – doing whatever it was that he found so much more interesting than his own kids. They really weren't up to much, as a family.

Harry was just about to escape to his room when the study door opened and his dad emerged. 'We need to talk.'

Harry desperately wanted to keep walking up the stairs, but Dom's tone stopped him. 'Dad, please, not now. I'm knackered.' He went up another step.

'No, Harry, this can't wait. We need to have a conversation, and we need to have it now. You have the interview with the police tomorrow.' Harry felt cold. 'You'll have to answer plenty of questions at that. It was a bad crash, Harry. People have been hurt. It was your car. You were driving. They're going to blame you.'

'I know that, Dad.'

'Good. Because I was beginning to think you hadn't grasped how serious this is.'

Harry stared at his father. Dom really was clueless sometimes. 'I know how bad it is, Dad. I *was* there. Those "people" are my best friends.'

'Exactly. So sticking your head in the sand and hoping it will all go away isn't going to work, is it? Harry, look at me.'

Harry did and saw a familiar sight. His dad, impressive, implacable, intimidating.

Dom went on, 'I have to know what happened last night if I'm going to be able to protect you. You have to tell the truth – to me and to the solicitor.'

'What solicitor?'

'The solicitor I've spent the last hour sorting out. The solicitor who's coming to the house first thing in the morning, as a personal favour to me.'

Christ, even with something as awful as this, Dom's ego muscled in. Harry felt a flicker of anger stir beneath the heavy layers of guilt and shame. He mustered up some defiance. 'Well, if you've arranged an appointment with this solicitor buddy of yours for the morning, we can talk about it then, can't we? There's no point going over it all twice. That's simply not an efficient use of everyone's time, is it now, Dad? I'll see you in the morning.' He didn't wait around to hear his father's reply.

Chapter 20

BEING IN a police station was very unnerving, but Mo's parents had insisted that they needed to go as soon as they could, to clear up his involvement in the events of Saturday night. So instead of his normal Monday morning – upper-sixth biology with Mrs Lowe – Mo found himself in an interview room with his parents and a harassed-looking police officer, who didn't seem overly interested in taking his statement.

'So you're saying they drove off and left you at McDonald's?' she asked.

Mo's heart rate had settled enough so that he could concentrate a little better – at least the distracting pulse in his ears seemed to have subsided. Getting through the first half of the story without stumbling too much had helped; that, and his mum and dad's reassuring presence. They kept nodding, urging him on. In a corner of his soul, Mo felt ashamed of needing them there, for relying on them so much – it was like being little again, running to his *amii* because he was scared – but a far bigger part of him was grateful for their help. He still felt very rattled.

The officer was waiting.

Mo got back on track. 'Not straight away. I followed them outside into the car park. There was an argument going on. The atmosphere had changed.'

'How?'

Mo remembered Harry's voice more than anything else – the anger. The memory was sharper now, brought into focus by what he now knew came afterwards. 'Harry was leaning into the car, trying to talk to Jess, but she didn't seem to want to hear him out. Tish was involved as well.'

'How?'

'Well, I'm not sure. But she seemed part of the row.'

'And what was Jake doing at this point?'

'He was dancing.'

'Sorry – what?'

'He was dancing around, waving his arms about, in his own little world.'

'Was he drunk?'

Mo hesitated. Jake was drunk or high most weekends. Saturday night had been no different, but somehow saying it to the police felt like a betrayal. 'I don't know. I wasn't with him much at the party. He'd had a drink, but I couldn't say whether he was drunk or not. Jake doesn't need a drink to be daft.' This last bit was true, at least.

The officer changed tack. 'What was the argument between Harry and Jess about?'

'I don't know.' The memory that he had been on the edge of things, yet again, made Mo feel embarrassed. 'Harry had my phone in his hand. That's where the music was coming from – the music that Jake was dancing to.'

'Harry was playing music on your phone?' The officer sounded confused, and slightly irritated.

Mo felt the sweat prickle in his armpits. 'I think – I'm not sure – that it was the party.' The officer's expression grew even more clouded. Mo tried to be clearer. 'I think it was some of the video that

I'd filmed at the party, but I didn't see, not properly, because when I walked up to the car, Harry stopped talking to Jess and he turned on me.'

'Sorry, Mo. We need you to clarify what you mean by "he turned on me"?'

'He started shouting.' They waited. His mum gave a tiny nod. It still felt wrong. 'He told me to *fuck off out of it. That I'd...caused enough fucking trouble for one night*. Then he rushed me. And I ran, and Harry came after me.'

'Was there physical contact?'

'Yeah. He shoved me in the chest.' Again the heat of embarrassment crawled through him. 'I fell. Landed on my backside. He leant over me.' And Mo had thought that Harry, his friend since primary school, the person who'd stuck up for him with the inevitable, brainless dickheads who had an issue with Pakis, who he'd never seen raise his hand to anyone – even on a football pitch – was about to smack him in the face. Yes, Mo would have sworn that, in that moment, Harry was readying himself to punch his lights out.

'And then what happened?'

'That's when Tish starting yelling at him.'

'Yelling what?'

'For him to stop. She said something about it *not being my fault*.'

Mo remembered seeing Jake doing his weird, spaced-out dancing around the bin, and Tish storming at Harry, shouting, her vest top shimmering in the street lights.

'What did she mean by that?'

Mo took a breath. 'I don't know. Harry kinda stopped. He looked like he didn't know what to do next.' The option of thumping him had still been on the table, Mo was sure of that. 'He suddenly seemed to remember that he had my phone in his hand. He lobbed it across the car park. Really launched it. I heard it hit the concrete and slide.'

'And?'

And…Mo had still been braced for a punch. Harry still had a wild look in his eyes. 'Harry turned round and ran back towards the car. I got up and went to look for my phone. He'd thrown it towards the containers on the far side of the car park. It must have gone under one of them, because I couldn't find it.'

'And while you were hunting for your phone?' There was a hint of derision in the policewoman's voice.

'There was some more shouting, then the car drove off.'

'And they left you there, in the car park?'

'Yeah.'

There was a beat in which Mo felt certain they could hear the sweat dripping down his sides. Threatened by his mate – for doing something he didn't have a clue about – defended by a girl, left stranded in a McDonald's car park, miles from home, his phone gone: yeah, that was his Saturday night. But had it not been for that catalogue of disasters, he would have been in the car when it crashed, and he could be dead.

Chapter 21

HARRY WAS hiding. He knew it and was ashamed, but it seemed the only sensible thing to do. He hadn't slept well. On the occasions that he had managed to nod off, he'd fallen headlong into horrible dreams that soon woke him – nightmares full of screaming, and an overwhelming sense of Jess and Tish and Martha being near, but too far away to reach. By 6 a.m. he'd given up on sleep and switched on his PS4; the mindless distraction was comforting in a way that nothing else was. As he machine-gunned his way through enemy combatants, he heard Martha getting ready for school, but he didn't get up to say goodbye. Another fail. His phone was still blowing up with messages, but they weren't from the people he wanted to hear from.

The solicitor was scheduled to arrive at 10 a.m. Time for *the truth, the whole truth and nothing but the truth.* If only he could.

He paused the game and threw down the controller. He studied the scrapes and cuts on his arms, seeing how close they came to the veins. Only the gash on his right hand had come anywhere near an artery. It made no sense that he'd escaped so lightly. He started picking at the corner of the dressing, lifting it with his nail. Once he had a firm grip, he ripped it off. He welcomed the sudden, intense burning sensation. The stitches were already beginning to scab over. His hand looked ugly, but his injuries were nothing really, not in comparison to the others. As he lay back on the bed, tracing his fingers over the stitches, he remembered a day in college when they'd been messing about predicting each other's futures. Jess had got him to curl up his hand, so that she could count the folds of skin near his little finger. She claimed it was a sure-fire way to predict the number of children you were going to have. Based on this foolproof method, the prediction had been: Jake – three, or at least three he'd know about; Tish – none, she'd been pissed off about that; Jess – two; and for him – four. He'd laughed and discounted it as nonsense, but deep down the thought of four kids had made him happy.

The memory of feeling happy made Harry feel worse, which made him feel guilty, which…et cetera, et cetera. Self-pity. He was drowning in it.

It was only his dad coming into his room and telling him to get up, showered and dressed that hauled him back up to the surface.

The solicitor was already sitting at the dining-room table when Harry got downstairs. He stood up as Harry entered and extended his hand. The only time Harry ever shook hands with anyone was at cricket or football dos, usually when he was collecting a cup or a plate: 'Players' Player', 'Best Innings by an Opening Batsman'. This was not that. The man controlled the handshake, a firm grip. 'Ross Glover. Nice to meet you, Harry. Sorry it's in such difficult circumstances. How are you holding up?'

Harry shrugged. He could sense his dad already gearing up for a comment, but the solicitor got in first, 'Take a seat.'

Dom chose the chair next to the solicitor, leaving Harry alone on the other side of the table. Was that deliberate? Harry was too tired to know. The man sounded 'expensive'.

'Now, as I'm sure your dad's explained, my role in this situation is to protect your best interests, with regard to the police investigation.

And to do that, we need to get to the bottom of what contributed to, and ultimately caused, the crash that resulted in the injuries to yourself and your friends. We obviously don't know, and we probably won't for a while, whether there will be any charges in relation to the incident, but we have to be prepared. It's always better to be over- than under-prepared. Any accident of this magnitude is subject to a lot of scrutiny and, sadly, a lot of speculation, so until *all* the facts are established, my first piece of advice to you – and this is important, Harry – is that you are very careful about who you talk to, and what you say. The best policy, really, is to say nothing. Of course I'm not including your dad in this...' they had obviously had a conversation about Harry's unwillingness to 'share' with Dom, 'but with anyone else – and I do mean anyone, even people you might class as close friends – it's best to keep your own counsel.' He pinned Harry with his stare.

Harry watched his lips moving. What a pretentious arse!

His dad was the one to provide the requested reassurance. 'I'm sure Harry knows that he's got to be very careful what he says, and to who. Don't you?' Dom could never just leave it at one instruction; he always had to hammer it home.

Harry gave the lawyer the nod his father was demanding.

The posh guy went on, 'That includes – in fact, it's even more important in this day and age – social media. Post nothing. Comment on nothing. "Like" nothing to do with the case,' he paused, 'or anything else really.'

What did he think Harry was? A fucking idiot? A fucking insensitive, heartless zombie? And what the hell did he mean by *anything else*?

The solicitor opened his briefcase and pulled out a yellow notepad and a pen. 'What we need to do this morning is prepare for the interview this afternoon. So what I want is for you to talk me through exactly what happened. All of it. Warts and all. In your own words.'

Harry blinked three times, but there could be no further delay.

An hour and a half later it was all written down, in black ink on the yellow pad, with some words underlined for emphasis. A script that Harry had to stick to in the police interview.

According to Ross Glover:

- It was fine to answer questions about his relationships with the people in the car – that was a good place to start...*It really wasn't.*

- It was okay to talk about his actions on the night: to describe the journey to the party, the party itself, driving to McDonald's, stopping to get something to eat, et cetera, but he must keep it simple and factual – it would demonstrate a clear memory of the events, which was beneficial...*He didn't want to remember what had happened.*

- It was okay, in fact it was good, to tell them about Jess shouting about the cat in the road; it would set up a cause for the accident and counter 'driver error' arguments, which was essential...*He couldn't bear to think about his role in the crash.*

- It was okay to tell the police what he remembered of the crash itself: how the car spun, the impact, et cetera – this would highlight Harry as a victim, as well as the other casualties, which was useful...*No, he had got off way too lightly.*

- It was good to go into as much detail as possible about staying with the car and how he had tried 'so desperately' to help his friends – this would feed into Harry being 'of good character' – which might, if they ended up in court, be influential...*The thought made him feel sick.*

What Harry must *not* answer any questions about, at this stage, was his alcohol consumption. Ross said it would, undoubtedly, be a line of questioning. He instructed Harry to pause, as if thinking about his answer, and let Ross intervene. He promised to 'handle any and all questions' about Harry's drinking on the night, at the pub and at the party. He stressed that he needed time to explore the circumstances of the taking of the blood sample, to see if the results could be ruled out, on the basis of consent.

It was all very thorough, and decisive and depressing. When they'd finished, Ross capped his pen and actually smiled. 'Great. Well, that's me up to speed – if you'll pardon the pun.'

If Harry hadn't him hated before, he did after that comment.

Chapter 22

AS ALWAYS, when any of the staff approached the bay, Fran tensed. They'd only been on the unit for three days, but already they'd become wary and defensive. Although they hung on every word from the doctors and nurses, Fran and Marcus both dreaded their attention. Time at the bedside always meant more tests, more physical interventions, more treatment of the girls as objects that required maintenance and correction, rather than as human beings. None of which had led to any breakthroughs – yet. Being asked to step outside, or invited to stay, while they did whatever they had to do, was always bad – neither option felt right. They were way past the point of respecting the girls' privacy.

This time it was the ward manager, Adam, who approached them, not a member of the medical team, which was a relief. On the other side of the room Sal looked up, alerted by the soft crackle of Adam's tunic. When you're on edge, you're aware of everything that might signal a new problem. Seeing Sal look up, Adam beckoned her over.

'Thanks. I might as well speak to you together. Now, please, you must feel free to take a bit of time to think about this. There's no need for an immediate reaction.'

What now? was all Fran could think.

'I wanted to let you know that we've had a request from one of the young men who was in the car. He would like to come and visit the girls. Just a very brief visit.'

Simultaneously Sal and Fran said, 'Harry?'

Adam checked the piece of paper that he had clipped on his board. 'No. A Jake Hammond.'

Fran looked at Sal, and Sal looked at Marcus.

'I thought he was laid up with his leg,' Marcus said.

'His consultant has said it's okay to come for a short visit. And his family have agreed. One of them, or a member of staff if you'd prefer, would bring Jake across from the orthopaedic ward – with your permission, of course. But as I said, you don't need to decide now. Have a think about it, and let me know when you're ready. Apparently he's been asking, a lot.'

They deferred to Sal, who said, 'I'm not sure Jake seeing Tish like this is going to help.'

In the end they agreed to give it another twenty-four hours, to see if there was any change. None of them voiced whether they meant for the better or for the worse.

In the morning, after another restless, noisy night for Tish and another silent night for Jess, they agreed to the visit. At the last minute Sal asked that Jake be brought down by a member of staff. 'I just can't face Anita. Not at the moment. Is that awful of me?'

Fran reassured her that it wasn't. The thought of Anita's full-wattage emotion was too much to contemplate amidst the cautious, considered atmosphere of the ICU. Here calm was the commodity that held desperation at bay.

That said, the prospect of Jake's visit added a curious air of expectation to the day. It was something different to 'look forward' to as the minutes crawled by, measured by the bleep of the machines.

Sal had a soft spot for Jake. Despite her daughter's frequent, less-than-complimentary comments about his many shortcomings, he seemed a decent enough lad at heart – a bit daft, but harmless. He reminded Sal of a couple of her early boyfriends. Like mother, like daughter: they both seemed to have a weakness for cheeky chaps who weren't the most reliable boyfriend material, but were fun and funny.

She looked at Tish, lying trapped in a web of wires and tubes, drugged to high heaven. Tish kept drifting in and out of consciousness. By now Sal didn't know which was worse – the periods of wakefulness, which seemed to signal the hope of recovery, but came with the distress of seeing her daughter panicked, in pain and unable to talk, because of all the wires and pins in her jaw; or the patches of deep sleep when, although Tish was calm, she was gone. Sal cleared her throat, set her mind to positive and started to tell Tish about Jake coming to visit her. Behaving as if life was normal – it was the only thing she could do to make it so.

Sal apologised for allowing the visit. Tish wouldn't usually let anyone see her without her 'full face' on, her hair fixed and something stylish 'just thrown on'. She would hate people seeing her like this, so stripped of her identity and her defences – but these were special circumstances. As a token gesture on the appearance front, Sal fetched her hairbrush from her bag and very gently began brushing the edges of Tish's hair, taking infinite care not to go anywhere near any of the dressings that were obscuring her daughter's once-beautiful face. When Tish opened her eyes and blinked a few times, before closing them again, Sal chose to interpret it as permission for the visit.

She had agreed to Jake's visit, for a number of reasons.

The first was the sliver of hope that Jake's presence – his voice, his touch – might somehow help to coax Tish back permanently from the tumultuous twilight world of pain where she currently seemed to be trapped. Sal had seen and read enough *woken from a coma by a favourite song* or *saved by the kiss of a lover* stories to be prepared to give it a try. She suspected that Jake wasn't the love of her daughter's life, but it had to be worth a shot. Didn't it?

Secondly, Sal was honest enough with herself to admit that she just wanted to see Jake. She needed all the moral support she could get, even if it came in the shape of her daughter's boyfriend.

And lastly, as Fran had pointed out, Jake was the only person – other than Harry – who could tell them what had caused the crash. They had heard little more from the police; the online speculation was upsetting and wild, and the press coverage lacking in detail. Jake would know. He was there. It was important that they found out what he could tell them.

Sal dabbed Tish's dry lips gently with a damp sponge and told her that she looked as beautiful as ever. Well-meaning lies were all that she could give her daughter in advance of Jake's visit.

Fran watched Sal chattering away to her daughter. It made her feel inadequate. Sal knew that Tish was unable to respond, other than with cries and moans or silence, and yet she carried on talking to her, all day and long into the night. Somehow she managed to keep up a steady stream of cheerful reassurances and anecdotes; and, when those dried up, Sal read celebrity gossip aloud from the dog-eared glossies left behind on the ward by previous patients' families. Fran and Marcus had been given the same advice: to talk as normally as possible to Jess, tell her anything and everything about what was going on in their lives, keep her connected with the real world beyond the confines of the hospital. But the sad truth was there was nothing in their lives, other than the stark white walls of the ICU and the never-ending medical procedures, which resulted in no change whatsoever.

So it was no surprise that Fran was finding it nigh on impossible to chat to her daughter. Anything she did manage to say sounded false or utterly irrelevant. Life went on for others, but not for them, or for Jess. Her own and Marcus's self-consciousness was acute in the face of Jess's silent inertia. Yet try she must. It was part of Jess's 'pathway to recovery'. Fran turned her attention away from Sal and back to her own daughter. Conscious of the shake in her voice, she began telling Jess about Jake's impending visit.

Jake was Jess's friend by default; he 'came with' Harry, like a free gift stuck to the front of a magazine. He and Jess had never had much in common but, regardless, Jake had become a permanent fixture in their tight little group. From what Fran and Marcus had seen of Jake over the years, he was the least mature of the group, not the brightest tool in the box and – if the truth be told – a bit wayward. Not Jess's usual type of friend at all.

But there had undoubtedly been a friendship there. Fran had heard the affection in Jess's voice when she'd talked about Jake; the mix of exasperation and amusement. Fran suddenly remembered the time Jake climbed the drainpipe on the side of the house and succeeded in ripping off a whole section of guttering, in a foolhardy attempt to deliver a Valentine's card to Jess. Not a serious one – a joke. He said he'd heard that Jess hadn't got a card, and he thought that was a shabby reflection on the whole of mankind. Fran reminded Jess of the escapade now, injecting some warmth into her voice. Jess lay still – listening or not, Fran couldn't tell, but at least it was something to 'talk' about.

In fact as they waited, they all found themselves pinning their fragile hopes on Jake's arrival. In the midst of so much sorrow and seriousness, they craved his lightness and energy.

But when Jake was finally pushed around the corner by a porter, the sight of him quickly dispelled any naïve hopes of an upbeat, uplifting visit. It wasn't so much his physical state – they had been told about the damage to his leg – it was the change in *him*. Joker Jake had left the building.

While Fran and Marcus held back, Sal went over to greet him. She stooped down, kissed Jake's forehead awkwardly, and started chatting away. As she talked, Fran could see Jake's eyes scanning the ward, orientating himself, but – though he was obviously taking in his surroundings – his eyes studiously avoided stopping at either Tish's or Jess's bed. He looked scared. Who could blame him?

Sal's voice was painfully, falsely bright. 'It's lovely to see you. Not lovely, of course. But good. Good to see you up and about. Well, nearly. Have they been looking after you?' At last – a good, direct, simple question.

'Yeah. Yeah. I'm okay.' Jake said.

'Pain under control?'

'Yeah. I'm on some super-strong stuff.'

'Good.'

The conversation dried and Jake's eyes raked the room again, snagging on Fran and Marcus, then bouncing off.

'Do you want to come and see her?' Sal prompted. That was the purpose of the visit, after all.

Fran heard Jake swallow from way across the other side of the room. 'Yeah. If that's okay.'

'Of course it is. It's good of you to come.' Sal took hold of the handles of the wheelchair. 'She's still very poorly, Jake. She's a bit in and out, in terms of knowing where she is. And you mustn't be too upset by the way she looks. Every day she's getting a little bit better.' As she pushed him carefully towards Tish's bed, Fran saw his face freeze. Sal kept talking, as if words could help to soften the blow. 'You know Tish. Tough as nails.'

She positioned Jake's wheelchair alongside the bed, which was awkward, because of his raised leg.

Her voice dropped a level, grew softer and yet somehow more insistent. 'Tish, honey, look who's come to see you. It's Jake.' The room quietened. 'He's doing fine, aren't you, Jake? On the mend. Just like you.'

Even the staff at the central desk seemed to hold their breath, waiting to see what he'd say. The silence went on. At the point where it became painful, Tish made a guttural noise.

Jake started talking, in a rush. 'Hiya, Tish. It's just me. I'm sorry I didn't come sooner. I wanted to. Kept on nagging about it to the nurses. The docs wanted to keep me away, but your mum said it was okay.' He looked at his hands, as if they held the key. He swallowed and dug deep. 'Your mum says you're doing well. It's good to see you. I've been so worried about you. But I needn't have, need I? I should've known better. Your mum says you're doing well. Real well. Sorry, I'm talking shit.'

Then, as if the effort had been too much, his shoulders slumped and his words stuttered to a stop. Despite their own sorrows, everyone felt for him. Aware that he had nothing more to say, Sal sat between her daughter and Jake, holding both of their hands, trying to absorb their pain, and picked up the burden of the 'conversation'.

From her prime position across the ward, Fran watched the awful awkwardness of it all. Jake's distress was obviously genuine, and the sight of a broken young man was upsetting; but more than anything else – more than her sympathy with Jake and her empathy with Sal – what Fran felt was frustration. Jake was a witness, after all, and Sal seemed to have forgotten that she was supposed to be asking about what had caused the crash. So when the nurses came to change Tish's catheter, and Jake had said his goodbyes and had been wheeled into the hallway to wait for a porter to take him back to his own ward, Fran followed him.

'Hey there, Jake.'

He smiled. 'Hey, Mrs Beaumont. I'm sorry I didn't come over to say "hello". I didn't know whether I should or not. I didn't want to intrude.'

'It's okay. You were here to see Tish.'

'How's Jess doing?'

Fran felt torn between the truth and protecting his feelings. She chose the truth. 'There's no change – which isn't a good sign.' Jake looked uncomfortable, but she ploughed on. 'Jake. I want you to tell me what happened? We can't get a clear answer from the police, and obviously neither Tish nor Jess is able to tell us anything – at the moment.' That was harsh, but she had to know – something, anything, that might help to explain why her daughter was lying in a bed, a few metres away, being monitored for signs of brain activity, instead at college living a normal, happy life.

Jake grimaced. 'I would. If I could.'

'Meaning?' Fran's slender hope thinned.

'The crash. I really can't...' He tried to shift position in his wheelchair, but found that he couldn't, because of his leg. 'Mrs Beaumont, I'm sorry, but I really haven't got much to tell you. I remember being at the party; we were all having a laugh – Jess and Tish as much as everyone else. It was a good party. I remember us leaving, then stopping at McDonald's, and after that we got back into the car. But that's it. The next thing I knew I was waking up in hospital. I don't remember anything else. I'm sorry. I really am.'

Fran stared at him. 'You must remember more than that. Anything at all.'

Jake looked genuinely distraught. 'It was just a normal night out. We were all having a good time.'

'So you've said. Were you drinking?'

'Well, yes, I was. I don't know what the others did or didn't drink.'

'But Harry...was he drinking?'

'Look. Like I said to the police, I don't know. We're weren't together at the party much. People were spread out in different rooms. I'm really sorry. I'm not covering anything up, I promise. I'm really not. I understand that it must be awful for you and Jess's dad and Sal, but I don't know what Harry drank at the party, and I honestly don't know what caused the crash. I don't know whose fault it was. What I mean is...whether it was anyone's fault.' His eyes kept flicking past her. He was looking at the ward doors, hoping that a porter would appear and take him away. But he was out of luck.

The next few minutes were painful for both of them, but no matter what Fran asked about that night, Jake was of little use. All he kept saying was that it had been such a good night, until it had all gone wrong – as if that made any difference.

Chapter 23

THE FOLLOWING day Adam, the ward manager, came to tell Fran and Marcus that there was policewoman waiting for them in the family suite. It was nice description for a nasty, faded box of a room down the corridor from the ICA unit, with a stained tea tray and two sofas that were just too short to sleep on. God only knew how many desperate conversations had been held inside it.

The police officer said nothing until they were seated. 'Thank you for agreeing to meet me. I'm sorry to have to take you away from your daughter at this difficult time. I'll keep this as brief as possible.'

Marcus and Fran simply sat and looked at her, waiting for information. They hadn't the energy or the inclination for social niceties any more.

'As you know, investigations are proceeding and a considerable number of interviews have been conducted about the events of the night of the accident.'

Fran wondered what they had got out of Harry, but wasn't naïve enough to ask directly. Both she and Marcus were by now very aware of their irrelevance to the process. Their own repeated attempts to get any response from Harry or Dom had been consistently blocked.

The policewoman opened her notebook – such an old fashioned, low-tech approach. 'I just have a few questions for you, if that's okay?'

More questions, but no answers. Fran wanted to stand up and walk out, but the thought they might learn something about the results of the investigation stopped her.

'Could Jess drive?'

It wasn't what they were expecting. *Can!* a voice in Fran's head screamed.

'Well, yes she *can*, but she hasn't passed her test yet,' Marcus said. 'She's been learning for about six months.'

The officer blinked, point taken, but not fully grasped. 'Whose car did she drive? I mean, before the accident.'

Marcus answered. 'Mainly her instructor's, but I've taken her out a few times.'

'Might she have driven anyone else's car ever?'

They both shook their heads, but they sensed there was something behind the question, because she kept pushing.

'But among her friends, a number of them had access to cars, didn't they?'

'Only Harry and Jake have passed their tests, I think.' Marcus looked at Fran, seeking confirmation. 'But Jake doesn't have a car. Well, not that we're aware of.'

The police officer wrote something down. Fran watched, thinking how neat her handwriting was, how laborious. 'Why do you need to know whether Jess can drive?' she asked.

'Oh, nothing, really. It's just routine. Establishing the facts.'

'Relating to what?'

She smiled. 'It's clarification really. Discounting alternative scenarios.' They waited for her to elaborate, but she didn't. Her smile faded as she geared up for her next question. 'Now, I wonder if you could help me by telling us a little bit more about Jess's friendship group – specifically the people she was with on the night of the crash?'

Marcus cleared his throat as if searching for a start point, but Fran cut in. 'Why are you asking this again? We've been through all this. You know who they are, and that they've been friends for years. You know who was in the car. You know who was driving. I can't see what else you need to know.'

The officer answered her. 'It helps to build up an accurate picture of the events leading up to the incident. I appreciate that it can seem tedious, but such information can be very useful, in terms of understanding the behaviour and motivations of everyone involved. For example,' she glanced at her notes, 'Mohir Akhtar. Was he a close friend?'

'Why are you asking about Mo? You said he wasn't even in the car.' Fran could feel a small, tight kernel of anger forming inside her. This was all irrelevant. What they should be doing was establishing why the car crashed. 'He's just a friend. They're at college together. In the same biology class. They got on.' As she said it, she remembered the confusion on the night. The mistake that had landed Shazia and Nihal in that bloody awful holding room. The fact that Mo had been missing then had suddenly reappeared.

'Was Mohir friends with everyone in the group?' the officer asked.

'Yes. Why is any of this relevant? Was Mo involved in the crash somehow, after all?'

The officer shook her head ever so slightly, dismissing the question, and moved on, working down her list. 'We're trying to work out the dynamic on the night. Were you aware of the actual relationships in the group? Boyfriend/girlfriend stuff, past or present? Any jealousies? Anything that could cause any tension?'

'What's been said?'

'Mrs Beaumont, we're just trying to clearly establish what happened, and why.'

But the niggle wouldn't go away. The officer looked at them, still waiting for anything they could tell her. She was obviously fishing, but for what? Maybe there was something the police knew that they didn't. Perhaps it wasn't down to them to decide what was relevant or not. Fran spoke: the truth, as she knew it.

'Tish and Jake are together. It's on and off, from what we can tell, but they're an item at the moment. Jake's been in to see Tish…and Jess. The rest of them are just good friends. They've known each other since primary school. There weren't any problems between any of them. We've known Harry since he was born. We've been close with the Westwood family for years. We used to spend a lot of time together when the kids were younger – holidays and stuff. He and Jess were like brother and sister.'

'Right.' She nodded.

Fran waited, her frustration growing. After a few more minutes of the painstaking note-taking, Fran had had enough. She stood up.

The officer took the heavy hint and closed her pad. 'Well, thank you very much for your time. It is appreciated.'

She had one foot out of the room when Fran said, 'Our daughter is still in a critical condition. On a ventilator. Unresponsive to stimuli. They can't say with any certainty the extent of the brain damage.'

The officer looked ashamed.

Fran was glad. She swept past her. 'Thank you for asking.'

Chapter 24

THE SOCIAL MEDIA activity around the crash was still frenzied. It was like people couldn't get enough of it. The local neighbourhood Facebook page had got the most hits so far. Friends and neighbours and random strangers – they'd all piled in. Maybe it was a 'parent' thing, the fear and fascination with bad stuff happening to their kids. That generation didn't seem able to accept that sometimes *shit just happened*; they had to blame someone or something.

Sitting with his leg resting on the pouf – glad to be out of hospital and back in the loving clutches of his mum – Jake scrolled through the posts. He recognised many of the names, but not all of them. There were some surprising standouts. Gayle Hessle, for example. It took him a second to work that one out; it was the first name that threw him, but his brain cogs finally clicked into place: their old headmistress at middle school. There was also a long post from Trevon, Jake's football coach. A man who'd spent four years yelling at Jake, telling him, in no uncertain terms, what a lazy twat he was and how, if he didn't get his arse to training on time, he would be on the bench for the whole match. Trevon had gone to the effort of putting up an old photo of Jake and Harry when they were playing in the under-thirteens, and he'd written – at length – about wasted talent and the lack of youth opportunities, as if the crash had been the symptom of some much bigger issue.

Most of the posts were sympathetic, but in among the expressions of shock and support, there was a pulsing vein of speculation about the cause of the crash. The party was mentioned – a lot – along with some very unsubtle comments about drink, drugs, fast cars and spoilt kids.

But, fascinating as the gossip and the gushing were, of greater interest to Jake were the posts by people who'd been there on the night of the accident – the ones who'd actually gone down to the ring road with their phones held in their sweaty hands. His brothers included. These were the posts that Jake studied the closest, looking for clues, alert to any glimpse of himself. He'd missed most of it first time around, but his awkward conversation with Jess's mum had prompted him to go back and look through it all again.

There was a lot of material to spool through, plenty of blurry photos and shaky video in which he 'starred'. After all, his rescue had been the most dramatic, the most filmed, the most touch-and-go operation. The photographs and footage were of very variable quality; some people really did need to discover the zoom on their phones. Irrespective of that, it all fascinated him: the fire crews working on the wreckage; the cutting equipment; the arc lights; the sizeable police presence; the ambulance waiting for him to be freed. In many of the shots his face was visible, and it was odd to be able to look back at himself in the middle of the action. In most of the shots he looked ghostly pale, but oddly calm. You could tell that he wasn't shouting or carrying on, which made no sense, given what he knew now. How his body had been pinned by the crushed car. How there had been multiple shattered bones in his right leg, and cracks in two of his ribs. And how the act of lifting him free would break more.

Jake looked at the images closely, trying to will himself back into the scene, but he couldn't. He had told Jess's mum the truth. He really couldn't remember anything. Not even the pain. Oh, sure, he could feel the pain now; whichever position he shuffled his carcass into, and no matter how many ibuprofen he chewed, he couldn't escape the bite of the screws in his leg, or the cage chafing the skin on his calf red-raw. His leg was well and truly fucked – there was no forgetting that. But of the crash that had caused his injuries, Jake had absolutely zero recall.

In truth, most of the night was lost to him. It was simply a collection of sensations and pictures that floated randomly to the surface of his memory every now and again. Whether they were from the night of the crash or from every other night out he'd ever had, he couldn't say. All he could muster was a flicker of images: the same faces as always, the classic Saturday night cocktail of booze and dope, the joy of dancing and not giving a fuck, the darkness pocked with bright lights and loud music. Just another night out.

The frustration was almost as bad as the pain in his leg, and in his hips, his ribs and his wrist. He really was good for nothing. All he could do was talk, but even that was proving to be a strain. All anyone asked him about – all anyone was interested in – was the crash. His family, his mates, the police, the press, that's all any of them wanted: the drama, the horror, the gore, the heart-rending awfulness of it. But he was running on empty. The biggest experience of his life…and he couldn't remember a sodding thing about it.

So who could blame him for needing a little bit of help filling in some of the blanks.

He went back to the threads from the night of the crash and began weaving together a better story to tell, when next somebody asked.

Chapter 25

FRAN WAS in the hospital canteen when she saw Jake on the local evening news. He was laid up in his front room, his battered leg on display, his mum sitting alongside him, patting his arm as he spoke, a balled-up hanky in her hand. Fran had never been inside the Hammonds' house. There had been no occasion that had warranted it. She and Anita had nothing in common. Their sole connection was Jake's friendship with Jess and Harry. A detached, pre-accident part of Fran noted how small and cramped the house looked, much too small to accommodate so many grown boys. From memory, she thought they might actually have five kids, one of them working away. What an excess of offspring!

Such bitterness – it was a nasty thought, unlike her. But…a swapped seat in the car, Jake riding up front with Harry, and it could all have been so different.

Fran stood and watched the soundless images, oblivious to the obstruction she was causing. The interview was interspersed with photographs. She should have been immune to them by now, but she wasn't. There was a night-time shot of the fleet of ambulances, a snapshot of lights and frozen urgency. Another one of the wreck being winched onto the back of a flatbed truck, in the following day's bright sunshine. Then one of the kids all together at their prom. A head-shot of Tish looking like a supermodel. One of Jess, looking young; the photo they'd supplied to the police was the one she'd used when she applied for her provisional licence.

An overpowering sense of the worst and the best of their lives being stolen away from them washed over Fran. On the screen, Jake's lips kept moving, the rendition of a testimony that she couldn't hear, but which thousands of voyeuristic strangers could. She wished she could hear what he was saying. Not that it would help. He had been unable, or unwilling, to tell her much when they spoke on the ward. The girls were still in no position to tell them. And Harry was maintaining a resolute and total silence.

The crash was a mystery, a tragedy, a news story.

People skirted around her, carrying their food to their tables. A chance to take a break and refuel, the TV nothing more than a backdrop. She'd done it herself, often; had half-watched and half-listened to the local news round-up – with its litany of personal calamities and desperate families – while cooking a meal or chatting with Jess. Now Jess had become nothing more than a prop in one of those stories.

Fran let slip the tray from her hands. It dropped on the floor with the loud clatter. She was glad. She wanted her despair to have witnesses.

Dom was cobbling together some tea for himself and Martha when the item came on the local news. Thankfully, Martha was upstairs. Harry was out – where, he hadn't specified.

Jake! Living proof that even the best car money could buy for a newly qualified driver, with the best NCAP ratings in its class, was only a partial defence against speed and a brick wall. Dom scrabbled for the remote and succeeded in knocking over a bottle of soy sauce. A dark, salty river spread across the work surface. He let it flow. Jake was talking shite, nothing unusual in that; but Jake talking shite on television: that was a new and potentially damaging development.

'It's just so hard. We were' – a hesitation – 'we are best mates. Harry and me, and the girls. We've been friends since primary school. We've always been tight. And Tish…' He made a gesture that implied he couldn't bear to speak about her without breaking down. 'I still can't believe what's happened.'

Dom knew that Harry had had couple of text exchanges with Jake – content not revealed. Dom had had to reiterate that Harry should, in no circumstances, say anything about the crash. Harry, of course, had blanked him. There had also been an envelope pushed through the letterbox. A 'Thinking of You' card, with a rambling message inside from Anita about 'shared pain and recovery'. Dom had thrown it away. He hadn't wanted it in the house. And there was Anita now, sitting by Jake's side, nodding and murmuring, 'It's been dreadful. A tragedy for everyone.'

Jake shifted in his chair, and the camera zoomed in as his face rippled with pain. Dom felt a flare of anger, rather than sympathy, stir in his belly.

Anita breathily fluttered on, 'That's why we're talking to the council about traffic-calming measures on that section of the ring road. We need some good to come out of this…for the families involved, and for the community. Because this *has* shaken the whole community. It could've been anyone's child, any family's tragedy.' So many clichés.

The camera stayed on Jake as his mum spoke. He looked, for all the world, like a little boy who had taken a bad tumble. Tears balanced on the rims of his eyes. The interviewer's next question was designed to get Jake's tears to flow. 'And what about you, Jake? How are you doing? We gather that before the accident you had a promising football career ahead of you?'

He'd been a very average defender, often too hungover to be much use until the second half. Dom's anger sharpened.

Jake swallowed a couple of times. 'I can't think about that now. It's going to take me a long time just to get walking again. As for my football, well, I doubt that's an option any more.' There was a beat of reverential silence, then Jake stoically lifted his chin. 'But that isn't what matters. I know I'm one of the lucky ones. Poor Tish and Jess.' At that point the tears started sliding down his cheeks, unchecked. 'That's who I'm thinking about.'

'For fuck's sake!' The sound of his own voice startled Dom.

The segment ended, and the presenter went on to a report about the decline of the local high street. Dom looked out at the garden. It was sunlit. For a moment prettily dressed and besuited ghosts flitted in and out of the dappled shade, laughing, flirting, taking endless selfies. Dom felt cold. Everything was tainted by the crash: every memory, every thing, everyone. Jake had mentioned Harry at the top of the piece, but not at the end. The omission was glaring – had it been deliberate? Even if it hadn't, it had still been noticeable. And Anita's mention of traffic-calming measures hinted at a speeding car. That could be damning?

Dom was fully aware, even if Harry wasn't, that lines were being drawn and judgement passed on who deserved the most sympathy and who deserved the least; even, perhaps, who deserved no sympathy at all. If there were victims, there had to be a perpetrator. Jake's interview left very little room for any conclusion other than that the person responsible for the crash was Harry. Fear for his son made Dom feel anxious and out of control. They were uncomfortable, unfamiliar emotions.

The sound of Martha coming downstairs forced him to plaster on a smile. He reached for a dishcloth and mopped up the soy sauce. His voice sounded normal when he said, 'Stir-fry all right?'

'Yeah.'

'School all right?'

'Yeah.'

Did he detect a hesitation? 'You sure?'

'I said…"yes".'

'If you get any trouble, you will tell me, won't you?'

For a second Martha looked at him, and it was as if Adele had walked back into his life. It was the same sense of being judged and found to be wholly lacking. Then she blinked and his daughter was back. His daughter, not Adele's.

'Five minutes, then tea.'

'Okay.'

She walked off and Dom went back to slicing peppers. The story of the crash was getting away from them. It was time to pull it back.

Chapter 26

IT WAS two weeks to the day since the crash. It felt longer, but that was because Harry's normal life had stopped the moment he lost control of the car. He hadn't gone near college, couldn't face the thought of it; and, perhaps surprisingly, his dad hadn't pushed him. So aside from his trip to the police station and his occasional night-time walk around the block, he hadn't been far. He'd been living like an OAP, shuffling round the house, watching crap TV, spending hours on his PS4, snacking, dozing, never really settling. That was the way he was now, unable to concentrate on the thing in front of him, never mind the rest of his life. That was just dark. There wasn't going to be a future – not one he wanted to live anyway. Whether he was charged or not, it made little difference. When a little old lady on the news started talking about what it was like having dementia, how she would walk into a room and simply stand there, Harry understood. It was how he felt. Rootless. Lost. Confused.

But then on Saturday morning his dad walked into his bedroom and sat on his bed.

'I've been thinking. Do you feel up to going to the hospital?'

Harry pushed himself up into a sitting position. Suddenly alert after days of foggy inertia. 'Yes. I've told you over and over again that I want to go in and see them. But you said I couldn't.'

Dom nodded. 'I know. I'm sorry. I think I took what Ross said too literally…about it being best if there was no contact. That was wrong of me. Do you want to go?'

'Yes.'

'Okay then. If you get up and grab a bit of breakfast, I'll drop Martha round at Emily's house, then I'll drive you over.' Dom stood up.

'Thanks, Dad.' Harry meant it, but the thought of setting foot on the ward filled him with dread. 'Shouldn't we contact Fran first? Check with her that's it's okay – me going?'

Dom answered as he walked out of the room. 'I'm sure it'll be fine. Fran has been asking to see you all week. I'll see you downstairs.'

The hospital car park was already filling up when they arrived. They had to drive up to the third floor before they found a space. Dom parked and switched off the engine. Harry went to open the door, anxious to get going, but Dom stopped him.

'Just a minute, Harry.' Harry sat back in his seat. 'Are you okay?' Dom asked.

He was taken aback by the question, surprised at his dad asking it, but it felt too complicated to spit out an answer in the car in a few minutes. In that moment all he wanted to do was get inside the hospital and see Jess and Tish.

'I'm all right.' When he saw the disappointment in his dad's face, he relented a tiny bit. 'I'm coping, Dad. Honest. I don't want to talk about it now, if that's all right. Can we go?'

'Okay.' His dad had to take what he was being offered.

But as Harry started walking away towards the exit, Dom called him back to the car. Harry retraced his steps. Dom popped open the boot and there, lying in the trunk, were two very fancy-looking bunches of flowers. Harry had lived with his dad long enough to know that not all flowers were the same. He knew that how they were tied, and how big and exotic the bouquets were, mattered more – when you were trying to impress – than how pretty they looked. Dom reached into his jacket pocket and took out two small rectangles of card and his pen. He held the cards out to Harry. Written on them, in curly gold writing, was 'In Our Thoughts'.

'Really?'

'It's just a gesture – for Sal and Fran, as much as for the girls.'

'But what the hell am I supposed to write?'

'Something simple. Heartfelt. Something that lets them know you're thinking of them.'

Harry took the pen and stared at the five centimetres of pure-white card that needed filling. It felt impossible. His dad was waiting. He grasped the fat, slippery pen and wrote on both of the cards: 'There are no words. Harry x.' At least that was true. His dad glanced at the messages, nodded his approval and tucked a card into the top of each bouquet. Then he stood back, forcing Harry to pick them up.

As self-conscious as he felt, carrying the flowers over to the hospital entrance, far more pressing and unnerving was the thought that he would finally get to see Jess and Tish. Harry knew they were both still seriously, critically ill. Because of him.

Memories of the crash were with him all the time. Jess strapped in the front seat of the car, her face perfect apart from its utter, abnormal stillness. His despair at her stubborn, heartbreaking silence, despite him shouting her name, over and over again. The reality of her being there, right in front of him, but at the same time totally unreachable. And Tish, her face unrecognisable as they lifted her into the ambulance. Blood everywhere. The loop of awfulness never stopped playing inside his head. The enormity of what he was about to walk into made him feel ill, but he wanted to be there, alongside them, once again – where he should be – even if it meant facing Fran and Marcus and Sal. He owed them that.

In the lobby they went over to the information boards to check which floor the ICU was on. As they were standing there, looking up, the woman sitting at the reception desk gestured at them to come over. She smiled. 'Can I help?'

'Yes please. We're just checking where the ICU is,' Dom replied.

'Floor B,' she confirmed. They were about to walk away when she said, 'I'm very sorry, but you do know that flowers aren't allowed on any of the wards, don't you?' Harry felt such an idiot. She stood up and leant across the counter. 'Such a pity – they are really beautiful. Very unusual.'

As she admired the bouquets and Harry stood there like a chump, not knowing what to do with them, he heard the sound of a camera shutter. He turned round and was shaken to see his dad taking a picture. More than one, in fact. Harry didn't know why on earth his dad was taking photos. Dom slid his phone into his pocket, with no explanation offered, and approached the desk.

'Oh, that's my mistake.' He smiled, going into full charm-offensive mode. 'I don't suppose we could leave them with you then, could we? For the front desk. Somebody might as well get the benefit of them.'

The woman went into a weird type of flutter. 'Oh, thank you. That's very kind. They really are beautiful.' Harry handed the flowers over, but the woman wasn't finished. Her smile became tentative. 'I'm sorry you're going think I'm being dreadfully officious, but I'm afraid that you can't go onto the ICU until after two p.m.' The clock on the wall showed 10.14 a.m. 'And even then, visiting is strictly limited to close family.'

Harry closed his eyes. What a nightmare. He waited for Dom to explain, to say that they had permission from Fran, to sort it out, but instead what he heard his dad say was, 'Really? Again, how remiss of me not to check.'

There was something in Dom's tone, his immediate acquiescence, that bothered Harry. Dom hated being told 'no' – normally. Harry opened his eyes and caught an expression of satisfaction on his dad's face. It disappeared a split second later, to be replaced by a look of concern.

'Harry?' Dom's hand on his arm, attempting to usher him away, was the trigger.

Harry shrugged it off and walked over to the lifts. He had no intention of leaving.

Dom followed him. 'Harry, you heard the lady. I'm sorry we've had wasted trip. We'll come back later or arrange it for another day.'

There it was again, that greasy tone. Harry felt he was being manipulated, though he didn't know why. He studied his dad. The sudden offer to come to the hospital, the showy flowers, the messages on the cards, the photos, the mix-up about visiting times – something was off.

'I'm going up to the ward anyway. If I ask to see Jess Fran will let me.'

Dom's expression shifted to something less conciliatory. 'Not now, Harry.'

'Yes. Now. You spoke to her. She knows I'm coming. It'll be okay.'

Dom put his hand on Harry's arm again. 'Actually, she doesn't know. I couldn't get hold of her this morning. I left a message asking her to call me back, but she hasn't yet.' He made a show of getting his phone out and checking. 'No. Nothing yet. Let's leave it for now, eh, Harry? Today maybe isn't a good day. They'll get your note. The lady said she'll send them up to the ward. They'll know we were here.'

'No.' The lift doors opened and Harry got in. Dom had no other choice but to follow him.

The presence of others put a stop to the argument for a minute and, when the doors opened, Harry didn't waste any more words on his dad. He hurried along to the entrance to the ICU and, before Dom could stop him, pressed the buzzer.

Dom pleaded twice more for him to *leave it*, and twice more Harry pushed the buzzer. He had to see them. He had to get inside. On the third buzz a disembodied voice answered. Harry began to explain who he was, but the voice from inside the ward cut him off. 'We aren't open to visitors at present. Please ask at reception for details about how to arrange a visit.' A crackle, and that was it.

Harry wanted to cry, or hit something, hard. Instead he turned on his dad. 'Why did you lie about talking to Fran? Why bring me here, if you knew I wouldn't be allowed in? Why?' Dom went to hug him, but Harry shrugged him off. 'Why?'

Dom finally spoke up. 'I honestly didn't know we wouldn't be allowed in.' His expression grew more belligerent – a sure sign that he knew he was in the wrong, but also that there was no way he was going to admit it. 'And besides, I thought it was important to make the gesture.'

'An empty gesture. You never really wanted me to actually see them, did you?' Harry shouted.

Dom sighed. 'You think what you want, Harry. You always do. But believe this: I have your best interests at heart. I always do. I'm your dad.'

Harry turned and started walking away towards the lifts, not knowing whether his dad having his back was a good or a bad thing.

Chapter 27

MARCUS AND Fran were taking it in turns to go home every other night in order to break down the fatigue and, more pragmatically, because the hospital simply did not have the facilities for more than one of them to stay.

The surprising thing was that Marcus was sleeping, deeply and solidly, during his nights at home. His routine was always the same. He would let himself into the house, scoop up the piles of cards from friends and complete strangers and go straight through into the kitchen. There he would microwave a portion of whatever had been left by the neighbours. He'd stand by the back door, cradling the ballistically hot bowl with a tea towel, shovelling the food into his mouth with a spoon until it was all gone. As everyone kept saying, *It was important to keep his strength up*. Then he would climb the stairs, get into bed and fall into a deep pit of sleep. No nightmares, no sudden waking up bathed in sweat, no heart-crushing dreams of Jess, whole and happy. Nothing. In the morning the alarm would wake him. He would shower, then eat a bowl of cereal, aware that the quicker he ate, the quicker he could get back to the place he least wanted to be.

Fran looked up from her phone as he approached the bay. 'You're late back,' she said. He wasn't. Not really. He didn't greet or kiss his daughter. Neither of them spoke or touched Jess much any more. Precisely when they'd stopped, he couldn't say for sure. The physical distance between them was the same, a hand-span between bed and chair, but emotionally the separation was much wider and deeper.

'Has something happened?' He shrugged off his jacket.

Fran nodded, stood up and walked away from Jess's bed, indicating that he should follow, which he did, his mouth sawdust-dry. They picked a spot near the noticeboard in the corridor. 'Harry and Dom came to the hospital yesterday.'

'What?'

'I had a message passed on to me from some woman downstairs, saying a man and his son had brought some flowers to reception and that they'd left a message.' She passed him an envelope. Inside was a florist's card, and written on it was, 'There are no words. Harry x.'

Marcus didn't know what to say, but he knew why Fran was upset. His response was cautious. 'At least it's a sign that Harry must be willing to come in and talk to us.'

Fran's agitation increased. 'So you'd have thought. But no. Look!' She thrust her phone at him.

Marcus found himself looking at a photo posted to the local Facebook group thread about the crash. The photo clearly showed Harry handing over a huge bouquet at the hospital reception. There was a comment underneath from Dom, expressing their fervent wishes for Jess's and Tish's recovery. Marcus felt his head begin to thud. It was a crass thing to do, but he really didn't care – couldn't care.

'Please, Fran. Does it really matter?' Marcus didn't have any energy left over for anger. 'We have far bigger problems than what Harry and Dom are, or aren't, doing.' He immediately regretted his comment, but it was too late. He saw Fran flinch and move away from him, a tiny retraction, but a noticeable one.

'It matters,' Fran gathered herself, 'because Dom is more concerned with how Harry *looks* than with what Harry has *done.*' Blotches of red mottled her cheeks. 'It was his car. He was driving.'

Marcus was weary, but he forced himself to speak his mind. 'Fran, it was a horrendous accident.'

She stared at him. 'Are you telling me just to accept it?' She struggled to compose herself. 'Accidents happen! Is that it? Is that all we are going to get? Look at Jess, Marcus. Look at her!' She gestured back towards the ward. 'Look at the state she's in. Harry was driving.'

'That doesn't mean it was his fault.'

Fran stood completely still. 'Well, if it wasn't his fault, whose was it?'

Marcus had no answer for that. They had reached an impasse.

After a few awkward moments he said he needed to go to the toilet. Fran went back to Jess's bedside without him. It was a lie, he didn't really need the loo; what he wanted was a moment on his own. Time to breathe and for Fran to calm down.

In the Gents he depressed the tap and held his hands in the stream of water. Five seconds of release. He allowed himself another press. It was a tiny comfort. Liquid warmth, the smell of soap, a fraction of a pause from the harsh imperative of watching and hoping and worrying. When the water stopped, Marcus looked up and studied his reflection in the mirror. He looked shocking. Old. Grey. He rested his head against the glass, just to take the weight off the stretched sinews in his neck for a few moments. It was an accident. They had all been hurt. Jess and Tish took the brunt of it. It was unfair. Life was. It was cruel and arbitrary, but blaming others wouldn't change that. It would only add another huge weight to the burden they were already having to carry.

The door opened and someone entered the bathroom, but Marcus didn't move. He could tell, by the slowing of the footsteps, that whoever it was, they were curious, concerned about him even.

Then one of the toilet doors banged – so not concerned enough to say anything. He wasn't surprised. Distress didn't invite company. He peeled himself away from the mirror, straightened his spine and headed back to his post.

The minute he came through onto the ward he could tell that something was wrong. The energy was different. In the place of careful concentration there was a sense of urgency and action. He ran on to the ward.

They were gathered in the bay, a swarm of white coats and busy hands. Instructions were being issued and acted upon with an efficiency that didn't seem human. One voice dominated; the others assented, quickly, with the minimum of words. The moment after the doctor shouted, 'CLEAR', there was a millisecond of nothing and Marcus felt his heart stop.

Then the violence of the shock.

The jerk and rise of her inert body.

The collapse back onto the bed.

The awful quiet.

The urgent queries.

The second 'CLEAR!'

The application of the second shock.

Marcus stood rooted to the spot, as the battle between life and death raged in front of him – nothing more than a bystander.

There was a suspended moment, then the mood shunted.

The staff started moving around the bed, as professional and efficient as ever, but the tension had changed. The instructions were softer now, though no less urgent. Something was injected into her drip, and the spaghetti of wires were reattached to her chest. There were a few moments of collective stillness as the heart monitor was studied – time stood still, again – then the doctor confirmed, in a calm, firm voice, that she was stable.

They had succeeded in yanking her back over the line.

She had gone, but they had brought her back.

Crisis over.

Marcus felt the blood slam back into his heart and his pulse surge, but the rigidity in his muscles remained. The scene in front of him blurred and swayed, but he could do nothing but stand and stare. This was too much.

As he watched, one of the nurses realised that Sal was standing motionless at the end of her daughter's bed. She left her colleagues to their tasks and came to Sal's side. Cautiously, and with a tenderness they had not afforded poor Tish, she put her arm round Sal's shoulders. The nurse didn't say anything – what was there to say? – but just stood there, anchoring Sal, as death took a small step backwards away from her daughter.

Marcus turned away, too shocked to offer Sal any comfort. His eyes met Fran's. She was standing beside Jess's bed, her hand pressed against her mouth in horror. He rushed over and pulled his wife close.

Please, God, he prayed, *let that never be us.*

Chapter 28

SIXTEEN DAYS after the crash a small team of council workers in hi-vis jackets turned up to make good the damage. They collected up the last remnants of police tape and threw it away. Then they replaced the two smashed kerbstones and shored up the factory wall. It was a bit of a bodge, but at least it was safe. The factory owner was supposed to be sorting it out properly, once the insurance came through. The workmen left the grass alone, other than stomping on the worst divots in their heavy boots – grass was resilient stuff. It would recover soon enough. Job done, they bumped their van off the side of the road and went on to their next job.

When Pete got home, he was pleased to see that the view out of the front of his house no longer looked like a crime scene. In fact unless you knew what you were looking for, you might very well not have noticed the scars left by the crash.

It was good that things were getting back to normal.

The press had stopped contacting him about his involvement in the accident, and there'd been no further follow-up from the police, other than a letter of thanks from the PCC. The letter praised Pete's swift actions and *his attempts to comfort the injured on the night of the incident.* Pete had stuffed the letter away in a drawer in the kitchen. It had made him flush with embarrassment. And besides, even had he wanted to, there was no one to show it to.

Work was as busy ever. He was glad. It was better to be occupied.

There was one spot of sunlight amid the daily grind. A new woman had started with the Community Inclusion Team, and the two of them were spending quite a bit of time together, working on a strategy to promote the gym to a broader demographic. The woman, Claire, had the nicest laugh Pete had ever heard.

Yes, life was back to normal. Eat, sleep, work, repeat.

That didn't mean Pete didn't occasionally, in a quiet moment – often when he was letting Cleo back into the house last thing at night – pause, look across the road and see himself back on the verge, in the dark, holding the hand of the girl with the sparkly top, praying that she would hang on in there.

Chapter 29

LIFE WAS supposed to getting back normal for Mo, as well. He was back at sixth form – expected to crack on and focus on getting the grades he needed, as if nothing had changed. Although, with all the anxiety still churning around inside him, respiration and photosynthesis were the last things on his mind. An A in biology and two Bs in his other subjects were what he needed, if he wanted to get into Liverpool. His heart had been set on going away to university, before the accident. Now he wasn't so sure.

Harry had not returned to college, though there was plenty of gossip about him doing the rounds. There were two schools of thought: one that he was so upset by what had happened that he was having mental health problems; and the second, that he felt so ashamed that he couldn't face anyone. Mo defended Harry as best he could, but it was difficult, given that he'd not seen or spoken to him since the night of the crash. Harry's silence – he hadn't responded to any of Mo's texts or calls – was worrying. Mo kept replaying the night in his head, trying to make sense of it, but he couldn't. He still didn't know what he'd done to make Harry so mad; but he did worry that it was Harry's anger that had led to the crash. In desperation, Mo texted Jake and arranged to call round. Perhaps Harry had talked to him.

Jake was getting better, slowly, but it was a long haul. He was not the same; nor were people's reactions to him. On the few occasions he'd managed to get out of the house, people had stopped him and asked how he was doing, offering sympathy – the wheelchair prompted that – but what they actually wanted was to know was…*what really happened?* They always got round to that eventually. A brush with death wasn't an everyday occurrence. They were fascinated, wanting to know what it felt like to be involved in something *so awful*. The rumours about charges being brought against Harry came up a lot, but Jake always said he thought that wasn't going to happen, implying that the police didn't have either the grounds or the evidence. He was *confident about that*; as confident as someone could be who couldn't remember more than a blur of bright lights, dancing and shouting…then nothing.

He said the same thing to Mo, when he turned up on the doorstep. His request to call round had come out of the blue. Jake couldn't remember every really being on his own with Mo for any length of time, despite them knowing each other for so long – certainly not when he was sober anyway. Harry was normally there, the glue in their relationship.

After the standard questions about his leg, Mo went quiet. Jake was tempted to turn the TV back up, indeed was about to, when Mo blurted out his real reason for coming.

'You heard anything from Harry?'

Jake hadn't, not a dicky bird for weeks, but some pathetic sense of rivalry with Mo for Harry's friendship made him lie. 'A bit.'

'How is he?'

'Stressed, but who wouldn't be, in the circumstances?'

'Is he not going to come back to college?'

Jake shrugged; what did he know?

'Do you know if he's still pissed off with me?' Mo asked.

Jeez, what did that matter, given everything else? Jake didn't feel he owed Mo any reassurances. He had dodged a bullet, after all. 'I'm not sure he's thinking about you at the moment, mate. He's got other priorities.'

Mo took the hint, though he looked disappointed. Then he asked, 'You heard any more about how the girls are getting on?'

He really was beginning to tick Jake off. 'The girls' – as if they were shared property. Tish was *his* girl. No one else's. 'It's touch and go. Jess still hasn't woken up, and Tish has had to have another operation on her face. A skin graft, to cover up where they had to wire up her jaw.' Anita had told him. It had made Jake feel sick.

Mo blinked and didn't ask anything else. They stared at the TV in silence. It was totally awkward. Jake was glad when his mum – who had no doubt been listening in the hall – came in and announced that Jake needed to take his meds. Mo stood up, politely said his goodbyes and left.

After he'd gone, Jake swallowed his pills and he told his mum he felt rough. She helped him through to the back room, where they'd made him up a bed. When he was settled, Anita kissed his forehead, despite it being covered in a sheen of sweat from the exertion of transferring himself onto the bed. She left the door ajar on her way out – *just in case he needed her.*

When she'd gone, Jake pushed down the duvet and looked at the damage. His leg was well and truly fucked – the question was whether it would ever get back to normal. The puckered skin, the screws, the pain that pulsed inside his bones. The sheer ugliness and uselessness of his body frightened Jake. Going back to work at the golf club was a distant prospect – he wasn't going to be mowing the hilly seventh tee anytime soon; kicking a ball was a pipe dream; getting it on with a girl, ever again, a fantasy. And he'd been lucky. Not as lucky as Mo and Harry, obviously, but very lucky – compared to the girls. The image of them lying in their hospital beds, like pieces of meat, haunted Jake. A horror film, but real. He couldn't imagine there was any way of coming back from that type of damage. And even if they did, what sort of shape would they be in? He couldn't bear to think about it.

He knew he should arrange to go in and see Tish, the next time he went back to St Thomas's for his outpatient's appointment. He really should. He'd let Mo think he was in the loop, acted as if he'd been in to visit her again. Jake wasn't sure why he'd done that. It was low.

He shifted and his leg throbbed. A wave of self-pity washed over him. The truth was that he wasn't strong enough. He couldn't face it. It wasn't only the physical state of Tish. It was the pressure of dealing with Sal. And Fran and Marcus. All that emotion, all that worry and pent-up love. It was too much. He lay back, closed his eyes and listened to his mum singing along to Freddie Mercury on the radio in the kitchen as she crashed about making tea. It was soothing. Just for now – he decided – he was going to take his mum's advice, which was to concentrate on getting himself better before he tried to think about anybody else.

Chapter 30

FRAN PUT her arms round Sal and hugged her. People moved past them, barely paying attention. They were in the hospital canteen, the place where relatives came for a break and the staff came to refuel. Crying, hugging, napping, arguing, beeps going off – it was all part of a normal lunchtime.

'Sorry.' Sal pulled away and scrubbed the tears off her cheeks with the heel of her hand. Sunlight washed the room. Someone ordered a large portion of chips.

'Don't be silly,' Fran said.

'No. I am sorry for losing it.'

Fran understood. After the endless weeks of waiting and worrying and stress, with every muscle in your body tensed, it was understandable that when the release came, you fell apart. A change of scene, that was what they needed. 'Shall we go outside?' There was a garden with planters and benches that ran alongside the canteen. Sal nodded.

They chose a bench at the far side and sat down. Sal took Fran's hand. 'I couldn't have got through this without you. You know that, don't you?'

'Same here.'

'I mean it.'

'I know.'

'I feel bad.

'For God's sake, why?'

'For leaving you and Jess, and Marcus. In there...in that bloody awful place.'

Fran turned to face Sal. 'It's fantastic news that Tish is being moved off the ICU. We're so happy that she's turned the corner. Look at her now. Drinking on her own. Talking. It's lovely to see.' Sal teared up again. Fran chided her, 'Don't you dare.'

Sal launched into a frenzy of words. 'If I think back to when she crashed,' she swallowed, 'and now. It's amazing what's possible. Once they got on top of the infection...I will keep praying for the same for Jess. You know that, don't you? Just because I won't be there, right across the way from you, don't think that you won't be in my thoughts. And I'll text you. All the time. I'll probably drive you mad. You will text me back when you can, won't you? I'll need to know what's happening. Please, I can't bear the thought that I won't know what's going on with Jess. And be honest. If you need me to come up, I will. I'll come anyway, to visit, if they let me.'

Fran put her hand over Sal's. 'I promise. And I know you'll be thinking of us.' She took her hand away. 'Now, don't you need to get back upstairs? You've got some packing to do.'

Sal stood. Fran didn't. 'Aren't you coming?'

Fran forced a smile. 'I'm going to have another five or ten minutes of fresh air, then I'll head back up.' Sal hesitated. 'You go. I'll see you up there.'

Fran watched Sal walk back through the doors and travel the length of the dining room. Even from a distance there was a noticeable change in her gait. She was walking taller, her head up, looking forward – there was a lightness of step that had not been there before. Fran waited until Sal was gone, before letting her head drop into her hands.

There was no lifting of the weight for Fran. Her soul was heavy.

With her eyes closed, she felt the cool breeze on her skin. People walked past her. She kept her head in her hands, trying to reduce herself to a thing without thoughts. Not a mother. Not a wife. Not anything. She concentrated on the sounds – a burst of laughter, the scrape of a chair being pulled out in the dining room, the occasional bleep of the doctors' pagers, something crashing on the serving hatch. She wished she could stay there for ever.

She couldn't.

She lifted her head and opened her eyes. With one last glance up at the clear blue sky, she stood up.

Jess lay silent and unmoving up on the ward.

Marcus was sitting beside her, waiting.

They had a decision to make.

Chapter 31

THE MESSAGE went out to *All Staff* at the beginning of the day. It was read and passed on over and over again. Conversations were had about who could be spared and who could not. Far more wanted to attend than were able, but that was the way it was – even for this. Many of the frontline staff knew immediately that they wouldn't be able to go. Their presence was required elsewhere. When your day job is a matter of life or death, *the living* take precedence. A number of people were secretly relieved to be denied permission. It felt wrong not to want to be there *and* wrong to be thankful to miss it.

Sal didn't want to attend the vigil, but she felt she had to be there – she owed it to Fran and Marcus. When she emerged from the stairwell onto the corridor she felt very exposed, conscious that there were hundreds of pairs of eyes on her. Thankfully, Aiden, one of the nurses that she recognised from Tish's time on the ICU, was there. He beckoned to her, creating a space between himself and a colleague, into which she slotted herself. Aiden smiled, his eyes kind. He asked how Tish was getting on. Sal reassured him, briefly, that she was doing well, then they fell silent.

As she stood waiting beside Aiden, on the hushed corridor, Sal's decision to honour Fran and Marcus's bravery began to feel like a terrible mistake. She was too close to this. Much, much too close. Their decision could have been hers. It could have been Tish – had very nearly been Tish. Would she have said 'yes'? It was not a hypothetical question. It was real. Fran and Marcus had sat in a room while their daughter lay in a bed on the ICU ward only metres away, and they had been asked by the medical staff to switch off the machine that was keeping her alive.

How did you make such an unbearable decision?

How could you bear to let them go?

Really. How?

Your own daughter. Your flesh and blood. The person you love more than anyone else in the world. The person you can't face life without.

And then. Once that impossible decision had been made – on the basis of the best available advice, and after days and nights of agonising contemplation – the doctors had asked the next question. Could the hospital take her organs? Would Fran and Marcus consent to their daughter being cut open and her heart, her lungs, her liver and God knows what else – Sal had heard that they could take the corneas from people's eyes now – would they give permission for *that* as well?

How could you agree to such a thing?

Really. How?

If it had been Tish, would she have agreed? Would she have nodded and signed the paperwork, knowing the good it would do, the comfort that was supposed to come from it? Could she have found it within herself to accept that her grief might lead to someone else's joy? Knowing all that, would Sal have been that brave?

How did you do that?

Really. How?

At 10.37 a.m. two nurses emerged from the ICU and held open the doors. The already hushed corridor fell absolutely silent. Sal leant back against the wall for support, her heart thudding.

They heard the rattle of the trolley first, then the 'suck, tick-tick' of the ventilator. Sal glanced down and saw the skin on Aiden's fingers whiten as he squeezed his hands together. As a medical professional, he must have seen it all before, but he was still human – they all were. The trolley emerged from the ward, flanked by four nurses and a phalanx of machines. Sal recognised the pale-blue blanket that had been keeping Jess warm for weeks. She concentrated on that, saw the outline of her feet beneath it. Instinctively Sal's eyes travelled up the blanket to Jess's face. It was uncovered. Of course it was. She was still alive. Her features were obscured by the clumsy ventilation tubes, but it was still Jess, pale-skinned, her lovely blonde hair – the object of Tish's envy – a delicate fan around her head. Someone had obviously washed it specially. That's what was so unbearable: it was still Jess, and yet it was not.

How do you force yourself to go through with it?

Really. How?

When the entourage drew level with Sal, she found herself stepping forward, compelled not to let them pass without some gesture of love and support. The trolley halted. She hugged Marcus, then Fran. Brief, wordless, fierce hugs. They received her affection, but didn't respond. They felt like solid blocks of grief in her arms. Then the procession moved off again. As it made its way down the corridor, borne forward by the silent prayers of those in attendance, everyone bowed their heads.

Sal didn't let herself cry until after the lift doors closed.

Chapter 32

THERE WAS no honour guard down on the surgical floor. It was empty.

They moved along the corridor slowly, encumbered by the equipment and the awful awareness of what was about to happen. Halfway down they turned into a side-room – the antechamber to one of the operating theatres. The porter positioned the bed in the centre of the room, and the nurses sorted out the machinery that was keeping Jess's body functioning – physiologically functioning, but not alive. It was an important distinction. Jess was not living, in any meaningful sense any more; she hadn't been for weeks. That's what the counselling team had told them to hold on to. It was the only way. They'd been advised to move the dial back on the horrendous events of the past month – to retrain themselves to accept that Jess's death had really occurred sometime during the forty-eight hours after the crash, when the aneurisms caused by the trauma of the car smashing into the wall had destroyed her brain.

They had been keeping vigil over an absence, not a presence.

But it didn't feel like that. This was still their daughter.

The nurses slipped away quietly. As they departed, one of them whispered, 'Goodbye, Jess.' That left just Marcus, Fran and the donations coordinator. Marcus looked across at his wife. She was rigid, her hands gripping the guardrails on Jess's bed. Her face shuttered.

The coordinator's voice startled them both. 'I'll leave you alone for a few moments. But I'll be outside, should you need me.' Her shoes didn't make a sound as she left.

Marcus and Fran stood on either side of the bed. The ventilator worked away. Jess lay waiting.

'I can't,' Fran said.

'We can,' Marcus replied. Fran started shaking her head. Once she'd begun, she seemed unable to stop. Marcus heard himself say, 'We have to. She's gone.' As if it was as simple as that.

'But she's right here, Marcus.'

They both looked down at Jess's face. She was still, so obviously, their daughter. Jess had Fran's cheekbones and nose; her lips and hair she'd inherited from Marcus; and the rest – as she'd like to proclaim, loud and proud – 'was pure Jess'. Their daughter. Seventeen years old. Loving. Kind-hearted. Fierce, despite her delicate looks. Bad-tempered when she was hungry. Articulate. Fit. Funny. Bright.

Gone.

'She's not, Fran.' Marcus hated himself for his brutality. 'This isn't Jess. Not any more. We have to let her go.' He was ashamed that he had no comfort to offer Fran, other than clarity. They had to stick to what they had agreed. They had to go through with this. They had to honour Jess's wishes. Why? For the people waiting to have their lives transformed by Jess's donation? No. He didn't care about any of that. Not now. Not in this moment. They had to do it because he couldn't go on waiting and watching – not any more.

'I can't.' Fran was still shaking her head and swaying. Marcus knew that she was on the verge of collapse.

'We have to.' He was shocked by the certainty of his own voice.

Fran stopped shaking her head. She lifted her chin and stared at him, her face raw. 'I know.' A sob stuck in her throat.

Neither of them moved.

Neither of them reached out to touch their daughter.

Neither of them spoke words of love to her.

Because it was impossible.

It was purgatory.

After what felt like an eternity or perhaps no time at all, the door opened and the coordinator came back into the room. She spoke softly, but firmly, forcing momentum upon them. 'The team's waiting. When you're ready, I'll take you up to the office and we can talk through the next steps.'

More silence, more excruciating inaction. Marcus caught her look towards the frosted-glass door and give a nod, some sort of signal. Two people in scrubs entered the room. They went to the workbench and began quietly moving equipment around. Part of the retrieval team? The reality of that word – its literal, violent meaning – hit Marcus in his stomach. There was no 'not knowing' what they were about to do. It had been explained to them, in detail – all part of the process of briefing and counselling that had led them to this point. They must leave Jess with the surgical team. They must let them take what they wanted. It was what they had agreed.

No.

Yes. They must. Jess was gone, never to come back to them. She was dead. This wasn't her. It was a body.

But it was all they had left.

It was agony.

It had to end.

The coordinator moved to stand beside Fran. 'Fran. Shall we?' Her voice was kind, but firm. She placed her hand near, but not on, Fran's arm – respect and insistence in one tiny gesture. It worked. Fran bent over the bed and gently kissed Jess on the forehead. She let go of the bed rails and stumbled backwards. The coordinator put out her hand to steady her. Fran leant against her and allowed herself to be half-guided, half-pushed out of the room.

Then there was just Marcus and Jess. Alone, together, at the end. Choking on a goodbye he couldn't bring himself to say out loud, he touched his daughter's hand, for the last time, ever, then turned and abandoned her.

Chapter 33

THE FIRST bunch of flowers was already there on the grass, in
the lee of the factory wall, when Pete set off for work the following
morning, but he didn't notice them. He was in a rush. Claire was
coming round to the house for the first time that evening. Calling
in before they went off to the cinema – just a casual arrangement,
nothing special. He had, however, spent two hours thoroughly
cleaning the kitchen and the bathroom, just in case she had time for
a drink before they set off.

When he returned that evening, early – time for a shower and
brush-up – there was no missing the mound of flowers, teddies
and candles that were piled up against the wall. He parked and got
out of his car with a clenched stomach. Across the road a group
of youngsters were adding their own tributes. One of the boys was
obviously crying. His friends threaded their arms round him in
support as they read the messages on the cards that other people had
left. Even with the noise of the traffic, Pete could hear the cellophane
on the bouquets crackling in the breeze.

So one of the girls had died. After all this time.

Pete let himself into the house and closed the door, but that didn't
stop the swill of bitter memories. A quick search online confirmed

that it was the blonde girl who was in the front of the car. The article gave scant information. It just rehashed the details of the crash, confirmed her death and gave her age. She had been seventeen years old. At the top of the article there was photo. A close-up. In the photo the blonde girl was laughing, full of life. Her name was Jess Beaumont – someone's daughter, sister, girlfriend.

Pete sat on the sofa and felt cold. He should have done more.

He rang Claire and cancelled – said he felt he was coming down with something. Then he stood by his lounge window and watched as the pile of tributes grew.

Chapter 34

THERE WERE a couple of casseroles on the doorstep when they arrived home. Fran picked them up and brought them through to the kitchen. She put them on the side – they would never eat them. She could sense Marcus standing behind her. The longer the silence went on, the harder it became to say anything. The pressure built. Fran's headache worsened.

'I'll walk to the shop and get some basics.' Marcus grabbed his keys and fled. The relief of getting away from each other was profound.

With Marcus gone, Fran was released. She walked through the rooms, touching the dusty surfaces, absorbing everything. Jess's jacket on the back of one of the chairs in the kitchen; her college bag on the floor in the hall; the book she was halfway through reading in the lounge. Fran took the stairs slowly. On the landing her courage failed her. She turned and went into the bathroom, purely because it had a lock on the door and only a small, frosted-glass window, with no view. The bathroom was the closest thing to a safe room or a cell that they had. She pushed the lock across. She scanned the room slowly. A tube of Clearasil, her hairbrush, a pair of hoop earrings, her retainers on the shelf by the sink. Clear plastic moulds of her teeth. Two years of braces – worth all the cost and the effort. Her teeth had become much straighter, nearly perfect. She'd been happy with the result, more willing to smile in photos.

Fran looked around again, checking that she had noted everything. This was what she was going to have to do with the whole house: map every single thing in order to neutralise the power of the hundreds, maybe thousands, of everyday items. Only then might she be able to breathe in the space that her daughter no longer inhabited. The sudden need to pee caught Fran off-guard. She debated simply standing there and wetting herself, but the imperative to actually do something, however basic, won out. She tugged down her trousers and her knickers in one clumsy move and used the loo. Then, on a whim, she stripped off the rest of her clothes and stepped into the shower. The water was cold. She gasped. As it warmed, she heard her breathing gulp and swoop around the small room. The water pooled in the bottom of the shower, swirled around her feet, a fragile tether. It took quite a while before her breathing settled.

Marcus let himself back into the house and was relieved that Fran wasn't still in the kitchen. He put the bread and milk away, went through to the lounge and flopped down. He stared over at the corner of the room. They had all had their favourite spots. His 'space' was on the far right; Fran's on the left; Jess normally sat on the floor. The lead for her laptop was still plugged in at the wall socket. She used to sit there all the time, shopping online, watching hours of mindless videos that would make her smile and laugh unselfconsciously, filling in forms for college, uni open-days, temp jobs: all the steps for the next stage of a life that she would never get to live.

The realisation shook him upright.

It was here in this room that she'd done it, sitting with her laptop on her knee and a plate of toast and blackcurrant jam next to her on the carpet. And Marcus had seen her. He'd watched her, blissfully unaware, as she'd completed her application for her provisional licence. He remembered thinking that she'd get the keyboard sticky, and being irritated with her.

'Done!' She'd closed the lid and picked up a doorstep of toast.

'God help us!' he'd said.

'Thanks.' She'd chewed and swallowed, before announcing, 'I think I'll be a good driver.'

'Based on?'

'On the fact that I'm quite calm.'

He'd laughed. 'Calm!'

'I am, most of the time.' She'd licked butter off her fingers. 'Compared to my friends. Think about it – who would you rather have pulling up behind you at the traffic lights: me or Jake or Harry?' She'd made a balancing gesture with her hands, taken another bite of toast and spoken with her mouth full. 'Will you take me out? Once I've had some lessons?'

'Yeah, sure. After about a hundred or so.'

'Very funny. I'm being serious – will you? I'll need to practise if I'm going to pass first time.'

'And that's the plan, is it?'

She'd yawned and stretched, upending her plate in the process, sending crumbs all over the carpet. He'd suppressed a comment. 'Whoops. Sorry.' She'd started picking up the specks of toast and rubbing at the butter-and-jam blobs on the carpet with the cuff of her sweatshirt. 'Yep. By the middle of the summer.'

'You mean just in time for your birthday?'

'Well, if you did feel the urge to buy me a nice little Mini – a red one – that would be lovely. It would save you having to pick me up all the time.'

And he'd said, 'In your dreams, young lady.'

That's when she must have done it, with him sitting on the sofa, in exactly the same seat, obsessing about sodding toast crumbs. That's when she must have checked a tick box on the application form and agreed to donate her heart, her lungs, her liver and anything else they wanted, in the event of her death.

And she hadn't even mentioned it.

Chapter 35

FIVE DAYS later Sal was preparing for another, very different departure.

Tish was being discharged. They were going home, at last. But the mood in the room wasn't one of celebration. It was one of tension. Tish was jittery, a bundle of nerves. Sal understood. After weeks inside the sterile walls of the ICU, then in the safe side-room on the plastic surgery ward, the long-awaited news that she was about to re-join the world had come as a shock. Jess's death had hit Tish hard. Initially she'd got very, very upset – crying, agitated, sobbing like a child. That her breathing was still affected by the scarring had only made things worse. Then she'd become angry, pacing around the room, talking a lot, but making very little sense. Because her speech was still affected, it had been very hard for Sal to make out much of what Tish was saying. It was like watching a toddler having a meltdown: upsetting and stressful. Everyone was a target for her raging: the doctors, the nurses, Sal, Jake, Harry. Especially Harry. Tish seemed to be casting around for someone – anyone – to blame for Jess's death. She found plenty of candidates. The storm had gone on so long that Sal had had to summon help. She'd been frightened that Tish was going to rupture something. Expecting sedatives to be offered, Sal had been surprised when the nurse had simply taken hold of Tish's hand and told her to 'let it all out'.

Since that initial breakdown, neither of them had mentioned Jess. Her death was still there, in the ether, but they both edged around and over it. Cowardice or self-protection? It was hard to say. Either way, Sal had no intention of bringing it up herself, because Tish was still unpredictable: one minute elated to be going home, the next mad about something and nothing. There had been tears, on both sides, already that day, tiredness making every tiny little thing seem like yet another mountain to climb. They'd been tied together too tightly, for so long, that they were both short of breath – and it wasn't about to end. There were months of recovery and healing to come.

Their current wrangle was over the helium balloon that Mo had sent. At first it had bobbed around Tish's room, tight as a drum, bip-bopping against the ceiling, driving Sal to distraction. But over the past few days it had lost air, drooping lower and lower. Now it was drifting round the room, trailing its ribbon behind it like a sulky drag queen. Sal was tired of it – of all of it.

'Just pop the damn thing and stuff it in the bin.'

Impeded by stitches and thickening scar tissue as she was, Tish managed a defiant, mumbled 'I'm taking it with me.'

Sal sighed and gave up. They were ready to go, had been for the last hour; they just needed the discharge paperwork. She made herself ignore the sound of Tish unzipping one of the holdalls, yet again, and the huffing and puffing as she pulled everything back out. In truth, Sal was as anxious about leaving as Tish. Once they stepped outside the security of the hospital, it would be up to her: the dressings, the ointments, the routine of facial exercises, the discipline that the doctors had stressed over and over again *was essential to deliver the best possible outcome* – it would all fall on her. They had prepared her, given her some basic training, explained it all very carefully, so

Sal hoped she would manage the practical care side, but it was the other stuff she was more worried about. Tish's readjustment.

She knew that her daughter's re-entry into the world was going to be difficult. How could it not be? People were going to respond to Tish very differently, because she *was* very different. No longer a pretty, confident girl, but a scarred, nervous one. Even within the confines of the hospital, Sal had seen the double-takes, the shock, the unconscious fascination with Tish's disfigured features. It was proof, beyond doubt, that human beings only feel comfortable with the familiar and recognisable. Heartbreakingly, it was going to be a long time before Tish fell inside the margins of 'normal'. The surgeon had said the skin that was pulling the whole left side of her face down, like a stroke patient's, would relax with time, and that more dentistry would improve the shape and look of her mouth, but Sal knew that Tish would never look the same. The thought made her stomach twist.

Tish was still fussing with the packing, undoing what had already been done. Sal refreshed her smile and made a comment about the weather.

Two hours later they stepped out of the lift into public for the first time. Sal led the way, not looking back, making a beeline for the main doors and the taxi rank. A quick getaway. She felt anxious, but pushed on, forging ahead, her arms full of bags. One hurdle at a time. They needed to get home, back to the safety of their small house, into a routine. They needed time for Tish's wounds, physical and emotional, to heal. But there were no taxis. Just a ragged queue of people waiting. Sal joined the back of the line. She turned to say something to Tish, hoping to reassure her, but she wasn't there.

Sal panicked. She scanned the concourse. Saw her daughter immediately.

Tish was standing just outside the hospital entrance, getting in the way. People streamed past her, many of them turning for a second look. Bastards! People were bastards. She was stranded, frozen by other people's cruelty. The only thing moving was the damn helium balloon. It drifted and twirled prettily around Sal's once-confident, beautiful daughter.

Chapter 36

SIX PAGES of high-grade, pale-cream vellum paper. Copperplate script. Nine hundred and fifty-three carefully chosen words. Not an eighteenth birthday, a graduation ceremony, an engagement or a wedding invitation; not the announcement of the birth of their first or second grandchild. The order of service for Jess's funeral.

Fran ran her fingertips back and forth across the staples, the sharp edges catching her skin. A flimsy anchor.

It had been a beautiful service. A fitting celebration. Everyone said so. Friends, neighbours, work colleagues, the three nurses from the ICU ward who'd spared the time to attend, the legions of Jess's mates. There were a lot of people she didn't know. It didn't seem to matter. Irrespective of their individual connection with Jess, they all seemed compelled to offer their condolences – in person. They grasped her hand, kissed her cheek, hugged her unyielding body. Fran endured it, dry-eyed, straight-backed, holding herself in. It was all part of the tradition.

She had planned the funeral meticulously. The appointment of the celebrant, Joan – caring, non-religious. The eulogy, which had been funny and heartfelt. The choice of Gabbie – calm, mature Gabbie – to do the reading. The wicker casket. The careful selection of the songs from Jess's favourite playlist. The flowers – a simple, modern, hand-tied spray of long-stemmed white roses with spurs of orchid. Even the weather was as 'ordered': benign, light, bright shafts of spring sunshine falling between the trees. Fran had discovered that funeral-planning played to her strengths. Organisation, budgeting, meticulous time- and people-management. It helped, of course, that she had an in-depth knowledge of her subject. Her daughter. Marcus had let her have free rein, assenting to her choices with little comment.

Now for phase two. The wake. An open bar at the local rugby club, chosen because it was big enough to hold all the mourners. Fran had opted for non-traditional catering – curries and samosas from Jess's favourite restaurant. Everyone had been invited back to send her off *in style*. Well, not everyone. Dom and Harry had been asked not to come back to the club. It was only at Marcus's insistence that Fran had agreed to them coming to the funeral. She hadn't wanted the pressure of their attendance, the inevitable speculation it would cause. This day was for Jess. And Jess alone. In reality, Fran had seen Dom and Harry only briefly when Jess was carried into the chapel, two tall, dark shapes in the back row – Harry's shoulders shaking and Dom standing unwavering beside him; but that was it, a glance. It was all she could cope with.

The bottleneck outside the crematorium didn't seem to be dispersing. The relief at getting the service over and done with was palpable, the mood strangely upbeat. Conversations sprang up, ties were loosened. Many of the mourners tilted their faces up to the sun, a few even closed their eyes. Fran and Marcus were trapped amidst the sea of bodies. As yet another relative pulled her into an unwelcome embrace, Fran looked over their shoulder and saw the ushers moving through the crowd, trying to encourage people to make their way back to the car park at the bottom of the drive. Another service was due to start, presumably. A conveyor belt of grief. Their efforts seemed to be having little effect. The wodge of bodies remained solid. There was a slight pressure on her elbow, another demand for attention. She turned. It was the undertaker.

'Perhaps if you made your way to the car, Mrs Beaumont. People might follow suit.'

Fran nodded and passed the request on to Marcus. He seemed relieved to be asked to make a move.

By an unspoken understanding, a pathway opened up to let them through and the crowd grew silent once again, the same ripple of respect that they had endured in the hospital corridor. The undertaker led the way. Fran and Marcus followed his slow, measured steps, the object of pity. Everyone was sympathetic and supportive, of course – sharing a tiny portion of their pain – but, in truth, Fran knew that many of them were secretly counting their blessings. She would have been the same. Unable not to think, 'Thank God it wasn't my child.' A glimpse of Sal, with Tish at her side, standing under the trees, on the far side of the crowd, only served to underline their fate.

With the wake in full flood, Marcus excused himself and headed to the Gents, not because he needed to go, but because he wanted a break from the distress of other people. Jess's friends were the worse. Their beautifully made-up, bewildered faces haunted him. And his mum, Karen, pouring tea, passing around the food, comforting others with such kindness and dignity, it hurt. Marcus felt guilty for bringing so much grief into her life. He had failed to protect them all. Failed to protect Jess.

But there was only so long a fully-grown man could hide in a toilet cubicle. Eight minutes felt like the maximum. He tugged his shirt straight, glanced at himself in the mirror and headed back down the corridor towards the melee.

Based on the noise alone, you would never have guessed it was the funeral tea for a seventeen-year-old girl. The clink of glasses, the volume, the requests for *another G&T and half of lager* – it sounded like a party. As he neared the room he slowed. He wished they would all just go away. He wanted to go home, shut the door, lock it, go upstairs, take off his suit, lie on the bed and stay there. He couldn't face having to talk again, to absorb the inarticulate struggles of these people, all of whom he knew, many of whom had loved Jess in their own, individual ways, but none of whom had loved her as much as he did.

Marcus stood, unobserved in the corridor – invisible for the time being. The gathering had a life of its own now, fuelled by food and drink and relief. The tension from earlier at the crematorium had dissipated. The worst bit was over, for them.

He searched the room, looking for Fran.

She was on the far side, sitting with Teri and Chris, their next-door neighbours. At least she was with good people. Teri, especially, had been stalwart in her support. She'd been round to the house most days, bringing food, offering to shop or run errands, trying to help Fran with the funeral arrangements – though Fran had been very resistant to that. He understood. The funeral was the last thing she was going to be able to do for Jess. Hence the obsessive attention to detail on everything from the exact shade of purple for the ribbons on the casket to the appropriate number of poppadoms for each person.

From his vantage point, Marcus watched them, gathering enough momentum to propel himself across the room. Fran was talking, her hands carving shapes in the air – a noticeably frantic spot in an already-busy room. The repressed energy that had been crackling through her in the build-up to the funeral was obviously, finally, finding an outlet. In response to her deluge of words, Teri and Chris seemed to be nodding – a lot – and saying very little.

Marcus worried about what was going to happen when Fran's mania ran out; which it no doubt would, when they returned home, alone, with nothing to do. He set off, weaving through the throng, saying 'Excuse me' often and swerving the many attempts to stop him and draw him into a conversation or buy him a drink. He acknowledged the sympathetic smiles and tried not to flinch away from the pats on his arm and his back, but he was determined to keep moving. He needed to be with his wife.

The area near the food was packed. A lot of people were still eating, many appeared to be on their second 'fly-by' of the buffet. Fran, Teri and Chris were trapped at a small table in the corner, cut off from him by the queue for the lamb bhuna. Marcus edged through the line, making his apologies, and very nearly made it. The celebrant, Joan, proved to be the last obstacle. She turned, saw him and put down her plate.

She'd conducted the service beautifully. She'd spent a lot of time with them beforehand, 'getting to know' Jess, making notes, recording anecdotes, asking gentle but probing questions about the glory that had been their daughter. The resulting eulogy had been written with great care, and delivered with sensitivity and humour.

'How are you holding up, Marcus?' Joan rested her hand on his arm. Painted nails. That surprised him.

He shrugged. 'You know.'

She smiled. Because of course she did. She did this for a living. 'I thought Jess's young friend, Gabbie, did an amazing job. Such maturity. But there again, people often underestimate the young, especially at times like this. In my experience, they can actually be the best at processing and expressing their emotions. It's a different generation. A different approach to feelings and loss. And all the better for it, if you ask me.' She went on, 'There are a few practical matters that I could do with discussing with you. If that's all right.'

A beat.

'The collection. I've got that locked safely away in the boot of my car. I'm happy to take it back home with me and count it up, if you'd like? It's one less thing for you to think about. I'm guessing that the charity...' she successfully covered up not remembering what the charity was, 'meant something to your daughter?' Marcus didn't respond, which didn't seem to bother Joan in the slightest. 'I've also gathered up some of the Orders of Service from the chapel. I know that families are often asked for copies by relatives and friends after the event, as mementoes.'

Marcus was no longer listening, not to Joan at least. He was listening to Fran, which wasn't difficult, given the rising volume of her voice. He began to understand why Teri and Chris were looking so uncomfortable.

'They test for a "response to pain". We were asked to step out while they did it, but I couldn't leave her. Not on her own. Not when they were deliberating hurting her. But as they explained and, as we saw, the fact that Jess didn't register any pain was indicative of the scale of the damage. A badly injured brain doesn't process the messages from the nerves. It's one of a battery of tests they do. They also injected something into her neck, which is supposed to raise the heart rate.'

Teri glanced at Chris, and Marcus saw the panic in her eyes. Joan seemed to have moved on to complimenting the food.

He cut across her. 'Sorry, Joan. You'll have to excuse me.' He moved past her. The relief on Teri and Chris's faces was obvious. He grabbed a spare stool and sat down. 'Fran.'

She looked at him and continued. 'It didn't work. Nothing worked. Or I suppose it did – from their point of view. They established that she wasn't just brain-damaged, but brain-dead. It was very thorough. They have to repeat the tests over a specified period of time. It's all very tightly controlled. That's why the final decision wasn't taken until the end of March. They obviously have to be absolutely certain.' Marcus put his hand on Fran's and guided it down. He had to press quite hard. That secured her attention.

He spoke quickly, trying to acknowledge her testimony while

deflecting her from saying anything more. 'It was dreadful, as you can imagine. But the staff at the hospital were...' He was about to say 'kind', but found he couldn't. What they'd been was respectful and professional, and brutally clear that Jess was dead. 'Supportive.'

Teri's eyes filled and she swallowed loudly, ashamed of her show of emotion. Marcus looked away. This was agony. He wanted to leave. He didn't want to think back to the trauma of the donation.

'Fran, can I get you another cup of tea? Or are you ready to go home?'

She slid her hand out from under his. 'No. Not yet. There are still a lot of people I haven't spoken to.' She stood up and walked off.

Teri and Chris looked after her with pity – Marcus with deep concern.

Chapter 37

SAL OPENED the door, expecting it to be Jake. He'd said he'd call round, when they saw him at the funeral. That had been more than a week ago. But it wasn't Jake; it was Mo, holding a bunch of tulips.

'Hello, Mrs Reynolds. I was wondering if Tish is in.'

Sal didn't tell him that Tish was always in.

'Yes. She's here.' She didn't move. Sal knew she was being unhelpful, but her job was to protect her daughter, even if it included making Mo feel uncomfortable.

'Could I maybe say hello? Just for a few minutes.' He seemed to remember the flowers. 'And give her these. I've also brought her a book that she might like.'

The incongruity of a book as a gift for Tish struck Sal, but at the same time the kindness of the gesture softened her. 'Okay. Come in. Go through to the front room. I'll go and see what she's up to.' Sprawled on her bed, looking at her phone, odds on. 'I won't be a minute.'

Sal was right. Tish was lying on her bed, still in her PJs. She didn't look up from her screen when Sal entered. 'Who was it?'

'Mo.'

'What did he want?'

'You.'

'You did tell him that I'm not seeing anyone, didn't you? I don't want him thinking it's just him.'

'No. I didn't tell him that. I invited him in for a chat. He's downstairs in the front room.'

'Very funny.' Tish still hadn't looked up from her phone.

Sal turned to walk out. 'Suit yourself. It'll be nice for me to have someone to talk to for a change. And if you don't want the flowers, I can always have them.'

'You let him in!' Tish scrambled off the bed.

Sal nodded. 'Yes. Because you can't hide in here for ever. And the lad has made the effort to come and see you, and bring you presents. Which is sweet of him. So it's up to you. You can leave him in my tender clutches for the next half hour, or you can put a bra on and come downstairs.'

Sal went to the top of the stairs. The sound of Tish spraying deodorant and pulling open her underwear drawer was music to her ears.

Mo didn't sit down. He didn't feel he should.

He'd never been inside Tish's house before. Their friendship took place at college and at parties. He hadn't even been sure of her house number. He'd had to text Jake to double-check her address. That had been awkward. Jake's 'Why'd u want it?' had been hard to answer. Mo had messaged back to say that he had a Get Well card from his family that he needed to drop round. It was nearly the truth.

The living room was small. A bit shabby, but cosy. There were a lot of photos in different frames, singles and triples, and individual snaps propped up on the shelves. Tish from babyhood to the present day. Well, very nearly. There were quite a few of Tish with her mum. They definitely had a look of each other. It felt odd seeing Tish as toddler, round-faced and square-bodied – she'd been a proper little chubber; even stranger to see her at about twelve in a pair of chronically untrendy trousers and a terrible blouse with a big floppy collar.

A noise upstairs frightened Mo back into the middle of the room. If she caught him looking at the photos, she'd have his head off. He couldn't hear their conversation, just the buzz of words. Tish was at least definitely in. What wasn't as obvious was whether she wanted to see him. He switched the bag with the flowers. The cellophane felt slippy in his hands. He really didn't want sweaty palms. Though no one would know. He wasn't likely to be shaking hands with Tish or her mum.

Footsteps. Tish's mum re-entered the room. 'Do you fancy a cuppa?'

So he was staying. 'Yes please.' He would've preferred a Coke, but was too embarrassed to say.

From the kitchen Tish's mum shouted, 'Are you all right with dogs?'

Again he said 'yes', although the thought of an Alsatian or a huge Labrador bursting into the room was a bit unsettling. He heard the back door opening and the scrabble of claws.

'This is Harley.'

A lump of curly black fur with four loopy spaghetti-legs cannoned towards him. The puppy jumped around and sniffed at his trainers while Mo stood stock-still, terrified that he was going to stand on it. Thankfully, Tish's mum came into the room carrying three mugs. One of the mugs had a straw in. The sight of it worried Mo. Sal misinterpreted his anxiety.

'He doesn't bite. Or bark. Or do much at all really, except pee. You can sit down, you know.' Sal went to pass Mo his tea, but his hands were full. 'Pop them on the side, love.' He did as instructed, then took the only single chair. The dog immediately leapt up onto his lap. 'Get down, Harley.' The puppy ignored her, turned a full circle then collapsed on Mo's lap and snuffled its nose against his fingers. 'Just shove him off if he's being a pest.' Sal took a drink of her tea. 'Tish won't be long.'

'Thank you.'

The dog was actually chewing Mo's fingers. It had small, needle-sharp teeth. He surreptitiously pulled his fingers free and reached for his mug, before realising that there was dog-drool on his hand. He left his mug on the table. He was beginning to regret coming.

Sal gave small talk a go. 'How's college going?'

'Okay.' Certainly not good. Mo was lonely at break times. Self-conscious in the cafeteria. Glad to get through his lessons, focus on his upcoming exams. The whole of his life Mo had got by, quite happily, by flying under the radar. That wasn't possible any more. He was 'famous' now. *The one that got away.* Conversations stopped when Mo walked into rooms or appeared around corners, whether it was because they were implicating, criticising or pitying him, he didn't know. Not that the gossip really mattered, in the grand scheme of things. He knew he'd been lucky, but it was still difficult.

Footsteps. Tish.

At the sound of her, the dog pricked up its ears, its little body quivering, then it launched itself off his knee. Tish entered the room, bent down, scooped up the dog and held his furry, wriggling little body close to her face. Mo saw a flash of Harley's pink-and-brown mottled belly. As distractions went, it was a welcome one. Mo stood up, then sat back down again, totally awkwardly.

Sal smiled, picked up her mug and said, 'I'll be out back, if you want anything.'

The 'dog love-in' went on for a few seconds. Eventually Tish put Harley down and he ran out of the room after Sal. Mo wished that he'd stayed. A focus of attention.

'Hi.'

'Hi.'

'Mum made you a drink?' Her words sounded odd, like she was talking through clenched teeth.

'Yeah. Thanks.'

Tish sat on the sofa. 'It's nice of you to call round.' It seemed such an effort for her to get the words out. Mo was worried that it was hurting her.

'Yeah. Well.' His mouth furred with anxiety. 'Oh, I brought you these.' He stood, reached for the flowers and passed them to her.

He hadn't seen Tish to talk to at Jess's funeral. She'd stayed out of the way, giving the impression that she wanted to be left alone. He had respected that. She and Sal hadn't come back to the rugby club after the service. He understood why. Close up, her face was a shock. Mo saw the line of dark stitches embedded in the puckered skin on the left side. They ran all the way round her chin up the side of her cheek. Her left eye also looked wrong, kind of tight and droopy at the same time. The eye itself was badly bloodshot.

Tish lowered her face into the flowers and breathed in. And, like the totally inadequate human being he was, Mo made it worse by saying, 'Sorry, I'm not sure they smell of anything.' He wanted to take it back, but it was too late.

She looked up and made him meet her eyes. Her right eye was okay. Unhurt. She let him off his crassness. 'So what's in the bag then? More stuff for me?'

He fumbled with it. 'A book and a card.' He pulled out both. 'From my mum and dad...and me.'

'Cheers.' She took them from him, but didn't open the card. Why should she? What use was a card. 'Get well!' Or a helium balloon, for that matter. The memory of it made him cringe. He really should ignore his mum's advice more often. What a stupid thing to tell someone in Tish's position. It was like saying 'Get Over It.' There was no way he was giving her the oil that his mum had sent, but his attempt to stow the bag behind his back must have been too obvious because Tish said, 'Hey. Is there more?'

He reached into the bag and took out the little bottle. 'It's from my mum.' Blame her. 'She said it's really good.' He sounded like he was bigging up his mum. That wasn't it at all. He was trying to explain why he'd brought Tish something so bloody insensitive.

She took the little brown bottle from him and studied it. *Restorative Oil.* The name made it worse. She didn't say anything.

'Tish. I'm sorry. I didn't mean to upset you. I'll be going.' He turned to leave, tangled in too much embarrassment to stay.

'Stop being such a wuss! It's nice of her.' He turned back round. 'Though I think it's gonna have to heal some more before I can use it.' She was actually reading the label on the back of the bottle. She patted the sofa next to her.

Mo went and sat beside Tish, on her damaged side. She kept reading, letting him look at her face. And the more he looked, the more it upset him and the more it made him want to do something – anything – to make her feel...not better, that was going to take a long, long time, but at least okay.

Tish was still reading the instructions on the oil. 'I thought your mum was a midwife.'

'She is.'

'Ah. Stretch-marks and scars. Buggered skin! I get it.' Tish put the bottle on the table and picked up her coffee. The straw in it swung away from her and she had to chase it around the mug. 'Once the last of the stitches and clips come out, I should be able to talk and drink like a normal person again.' She sucked up a little coffee.

Mo could see how difficult it was. 'What about eating?'

She put her mug down. 'No Big Macs – unfortunately. I'm on a pulped diet. It's like Slimming World, but worse. Everything tastes the same when you mash it up. Proper pukey!' She did look thinner, fragile in a way that just wasn't Tish.

Mo's face must have given him away.

She mustered up some old-style Tish defiance. 'Hey. I'm okay. I needed to lose some junk.'

'Yeah.' He didn't believe that for one second.

'I am okay, really.' She lifted her chin, as much as she could, given the scar tissue. 'Or I'm gonna be.' After her attempt at bravery, she went quiet.

'Sure you don't want me to go?' Mo asked. Part of him wanted to get out. She shook her head. He took a drink of his cold tea as a signal of his commitment to stay.

'Thanks. I've not had many visitors, apart from family.' She touched the top of his hand with her fingertips for a second.

What to say? His mind was a yawning blank. College gossip. The stuff Tish used to thrive on. Not that he had his finger on the pulse, but he could elaborate on what snippets he had observed and overheard. 'So do you want me to tell you what's going down at college? Who's having hysterics about the exams?'

She pulled a blanket across her knees and snuggled down, settling in. 'Yeah. Dish the dirt.'

And so he did.

In the kitchen Sal listened to them, feeling the first tiny, but very real lift in her spirits for weeks.

Chapter 38

THE POLICE rang to say they needed to come to the house. Dom asked why, though in his heart he knew. The investigating officer said they would prefer to explain in person.

What Dom didn't understand was why police officers always travelled in twos, like animals entering the Ark. Out of nowhere, he suddenly remembered that Harry used to have a Noah's Ark play set when he was little: elephants, zebras, camels, even a pair of green-and-yellow snakes and one tiger. The tiger had lost his mate early on – gone the way of so many toys, into the inner recesses of the car, or into the rubble of small pieces of plastic at the bottom of the toy box. When the set was handed on to Martha, she'd insisted on pairing the tiger up with a spare lioness, she hadn't liked it being on its own.

What the fuck was he doing, thinking about toys at a time like this? He really needed to focus. The senior officer was looking serious. It *was* serious. It felt wrong having the police in the house. Dom's life was not one that was supposed to have criminal investigations and statements and defence lawyers and big, chunky coppers with their kit-laden uniforms in it. He had worked hard to make Harry and Martha's lives comfortable, insulated from hardship and unpleasantness; safe – or so Dom had thought – from the general nastiness of the world. But since the accident, nothing had felt secure. The good life that had taken him so long, and so much effort, to build after Adele's departure was under threat. It made him anxious. It was Harry who had brought all this into their home. Harry who sat next to him now, chewing at the skin alongside his thumbnail and staring through the patio doors.

The officer said, 'As you know, the file has been with the CPS for a while, but they've now made a decision.'

Pause. Why did people pause? Why not just spit it out? Too much TV drama.

'They *are* bringing charges.' Harry didn't react, but carried on worrying away at his thumb. 'The key factors are the presence of alcohol in Harry's bloodstream, the estimated speed the car was travelling when it left the road, and the injuries the passengers suffered.' Nothing from Harry, not a comment or a flinch. 'The formal charge is going to be...causing death by dangerous driving, with an additional charge of driving under the influence. Do you understand what I'm saying, Harry?' the officer asked. They all waited.

Harry let his hand drop, nodded, but not a single word of denial or defence emerged from his mouth.

What the hell was wrong with him? It fell to Dom to respond. 'It was an accident, for God's sake. It could've been any of them driving that car. You're telling me that Harry's the one who is going to be punished for taking responsibility that night. He was the most sober of all of them. Jake was off his head! Both the girls had been drinking! Was it Jess dying that tipped the scales?'

The senior officer adjusted his jacket. 'No. That's not influenced the decision to prosecute, though it has had a bearing on the charge. As with every case, it's down to the evidence.'

Dom felt the panic building up inside him at the police officers' solid, assumptive, wrecking-ball presence in his house. How dare they sit there so impassively, hiding behind their uniforms and their supposed impartiality? They were acting as if this was nothing to do with them, while all the time it had been they who had been building the case. They were the ones who had passed the 'evidence' on to the CPS; they who must have made an application for a prosecution.

'So, you're saying that even if Jess had survived, you'd still be hounding my son.'

Harry had gone back to gnawing on his thumb.

'Mr Westwood, we're not "hounding" anyone. We are duty-bound to investigate every incident and ascertain responsibility and culpability, in the public interest. And in this case there is evidence that Harry's behaviour on the night in question was a substantial contributory factor in the car crashing, and the subsequent serious injuries suffered by those involved and in the death of Jess Beaumont.'

Dom made a disgusted noise.

The officer sat up straighter, chest out, shoulders back. One alpha male fronting up up another. 'Mr Westwood! Please. This isn't personal. It's the law. I suggest that you calm down a little.' He continued, 'The reality is that things could be worse. The CPS could have gone for the more serious charge of manslaughter, for which the penalties are much stiffer. "Dangerous driving" often does carry a custodial sentence, but any mitigating circumstances will be taken into consideration.' The implication that Harry was somehow getting off lightly did not help to placate Dom. 'We advise that you speak to your legal representatives, now that the case is going to trial. They will be able to explain the process and advise you on the next steps. You will need to enter a plea, in response to the charge.'

Dom cut across him. 'Oh, don't you worry. We'll be taking advice all right – and we will be fighting the charge. I won't have my son's life ruined by this, not if I can prevent it.'

'That's your decision to make.' The officer looked pointedly at Harry as he said this. The officers stood – bomb dropped – ready to leave, but before they did, the older guy deposited one final piece of unwelcome advice. 'We want to be clear,' a last loaded pause, 'this prosecution *is* going ahead. You need to prepare yourselves for that, practically and emotionally. We'll be in touch.' He was experienced enough not to offer his hand in farewell.

Dom showed them out without another word. His brain had already moved on, scrolling through the implications of the charge becoming public: for Harry and Martha, and for his business. Because it would get out – and soon. 'They' were going to have a field day with this. Final confirmation that they could pin it all on Harry. Action, not words, that was what was needed. He went into his study to retrieve his phone. First step, call the solicitors, put a fire under their arses. He insisted that the receptionist put him directly through to Ross. He wasn't going to be fobbed off with some note-taking junior. When Ross came on the line, Dom explained the situation, stressed the need for proactivity and booked a meeting for the following day.

It was only after he ended that call that he noticed Harry had left the room without saying a single word.

Chapter 39

HARRY SLIPPED through to the garage, intending to drive away. It didn't matter where. Just away – from the police, from his dad, from everything. Dom's BMW was parked in the space nearest the door, low-slung, bright red, six litres. No hybrid, planet-hugging eco-awareness for his dad – at least not outside the confines of his work. Next to Dom's M5 was a Seat Leon-sized gap. His car was gone. For a second, Harry was shocked. But of course it wasn't there. He hadn't really forgotten. How could he? It was simply that driving was – correction, *had been* – such a natural, enjoyable part of his life that his brain seemed unwilling to accept it was over. Not that he wanted his car back. He never wanted to see it again. It was too stained by the memories of that night. Even if it hadn't been wrecked by the crash, it could never have been just a car again. It was apparently locked up in some police compound somewhere – evidence in the case against him. A case that was now definitely going to court.

He let himself out through the side-door and set off walking. The cop car was turning at the end of the street. It slid out of sight, with a blink of its indicators. Harry felt no relief at seeing it go. He knew this was only the beginning. The long weeks of waiting had been bad enough, but he knew it was going to get worse. He'd been expecting the police to charge him. The conversation with them had gone exactly as he'd imagined. The laying of guilt squarely at his feet. The direct request for him to pick it up. The temptation to do exactly that. Then the full-throttle response of his dad. Dom believed that attack was the best form of defence. And he was right, when it came to dickheads on a football pitch; but in real life it was a crap philosophy, and it clearly hadn't gone down well with the police. Watching the senior copper and his dad square up had been depressingly predictable. As they'd butted heads, Harry had sat there, mute. He might as well not have been in the room. Their machismo performances had underlined how much the accident had taken away from him. Not least, any sense of who he was any more.

Harry walked aimlessly. He had nothing to do, no one to see, nowhere he'd be welcome. Not now. Not after what had happened to Jake and Tish and Jess. At the end of the avenue he turned right, at the junction right again, then left, then across the road, then second right. By now he knew where he was heading, knew it was stupid, knew he shouldn't, but he kept going anyway, aware of how pathetic it was, and how risky. He'd been told to go nowhere near Marcus and Fran's house. He understood why, but his feet kept moving and his destination grew ever closer. It was a route he'd walked so many times he could have done it with his eyes closed. In fact, he used to. When he was a little kid – walking back to Fran's house from school – he used to pretend that he was blind. He would hold Fran's hand and shut his eyes, squeezing his eyelids tight to ward off the temptation of peeping. Jess would sometimes play along, too. Fran used to get involved with the make-believe, warning them when they were coming up to a kerb, asking them if they could hear the cars, the birds, the ice-cream van, and so on. Harry remembered the edge of fear that came from walking along with your eyes closed, but he trusted Fran – she would never have let him walk into a lamp post or onto the road. Years later, when he and Jess were trading childhood memories, she'd laughed at Harry, saying that she'd never done it properly, but had kept peeking, to make sure she didn't bump into anything.

The house was visible as soon as he turned the corner. Halfway up the hill. A red-brick box slotted into a row of very similar boxes. Solid, square, not special. A blue front door, a white porch. Fran's old Audi parked up behind Marcus's Renault out front. So they were home on a midweek morning. No one, and nothing, was back to normal.

Harry slowed, wanting to get closer, but afraid to. Jess's bedroom faced onto the back. It didn't matter that he couldn't actually see her window; he could imagine her room easily enough, he'd been in it hundreds of times. Her pinboard of mementoes – she was a believer in all that 'making memories' mush. Her collection of cacti – such a Jess thing. *They're cute, but spiky. Like me,* she'd joked. Her 'hurt your eyeballs' choice in duvet covers. Psychedelic, hippy-dippy patterns – she called it having *eclectic tastes.* The smell – a nice, girly, fresh scent. Her bedroom door that didn't quite shut properly, because it caught on the carpet. A safe, Jess-styled haven.

He'd tried to summon up Jess so many times since the accident, wanting desperately to travel back in time to a point of ordinary happiness, but he'd always failed. Now, walking towards the one place where he'd always felt safe, Harry could. It was as if being near her house had unlocked the part of his brain that had been stubbornly, resolutely closed off to him.

Jess. Alive and whole. And full of it. Lying crossways on her bed, on her stomach, her feet jigging around in the air behind her. Jess talking. Always talking. Enthusiasm for *this*, passion for *that*, indignation about something or other. Full of energy. He hadn't always listened. How many times had he sprawled in the chair, looking at his phone, flicking through mindless crap that – at the time – had been more deserving of his attention than her? He'd sometimes laughed, at the wrong moment; offended Jess with his indifference or his mockery. He'd had slippers, rulers, pillows – any missile that came to hand – hurled at him in his time. Her hairbrush once caught him slap bang in between the eyes. She'd been horrified. Scrambled off the bed in a panic as he faked concussion. He'd hammed it up, claiming to feel dizzy, seeing stars, demanding sympathy. She'd laid him down on her bed, fetched a damp flannel for his head. Happy times.

Seduced by his daydream, Harry hadn't been paying attention. He found that he'd drifted up the road and was standing right outside her house. It was not what he'd intended. Yet it was so hard to walk on by. He stood still, swaying slightly. More than anything he wanted to open the gate, walk up the short path, knock at the door. Have Fran open it, welcome him in, offer him a snack – she knew Harry was always hungry. Have Jess bounce downstairs, smiling, then lead him upstairs to the one place he'd always felt 'right'. If only that could happen.

As if summoned by his thoughts, the door opened and Harry heard her. 'I'll see you later. Bye.' The same inflection, the same voice – coming from Fran.

He bolted. Broke into a run. Kept going until he was off their street.

Was he a danger to others? A threat to their happiness and wholeness?

Yes. Guilty as charged.

Chapter 40

SAL WAS very reluctant to agree to the police coming to the house, but the alternative was a trip to the station, and that was out of the question. Their refusal to say why they needed to see Tish was worrying.

When she told Tish the police wanted to speak to her again about the accident, she swore, slid back down the bed and pulled the duvet up around her. But given that refusing to get up, not washing, hardly eating or talking in single-word sentences was still normal behaviour most days, her reaction didn't really surprise Sal.

At least it meant that on the morning of the visit Tish had to get up and dressed, after a fashion. She appeared downstairs in sweat pants and a T-shirt, hair tied back – to Sal's surprise – emphasising the damage to her face. Her mood was, as ever, low, with an edge of nerves. They both stared at the TV, waiting for the police to arrive, neither of them really watching, but it was better than silence.

Eventually there was a knock at the door. The officers came in and sat down. Sal didn't offer them tea. They weren't welcome guests.

'Thank you for letting us come and talk to you again, Tish. How are you getting on?'

Sal felt a sudden, strong impulse to intervene and actually answer their question with the truth. They hadn't been near for weeks – very few people had. This woman didn't really want to know whether Tish was coping; it was one of those stepping-stone questions they put down, in order to tempt you to cross the river.

Tish touched her face self-consciously. 'Okay, I suppose.' That was all she was going to give them. Good on her.

'The reason we needed to come and speak to you is that we want to ask a few more questions about what happened the night of the crash.'

Though Sal had known this was why they'd come, the thought of reopening old wounds made her anxious. Rehashing everything wasn't going to do Tish any good. How could it?

'She's given her statement. Twice. And she's checked through the written version of it. You said that would be it!'

'I know. I'm sorry. But I'm afraid we need to revisit a few things, in the light of some additional information that has emerged.' The officer turned her attention to Tish. 'Before we get started, can I check that you're okay with your mum staying with us while we talk?'

Sal was taken aback. She'd been at Tish's side throughout this whole nightmare, and they had the cheek to suggest that her daughter might be uncomfortable talking in her presence. They hadn't a clue. She and Tish had gone past the point of having any secrets from each other a long time ago.

'Look, we said you could come and ask your questions. We didn't have to agree to it. Tish still isn't fully recovered, and this isn't helping. I really think that—'

Tish quietly but firmly interrupted her. 'Mum, please.' She shuffled in her seat, composing herself. 'What do you want to know?'

The officer dived straight in. 'Firstly, we'd like you to go back to before the crash – to the party at Alice Mitcham's house. We want you to think again about what was going on. It is important. Are you sure you can't recall any disagreements, any arguments, Tish? Any tensions between the five of you? I mean, before the altercation at McDonald's.'

'No.'

'Are you sure? Other people who were present say differently.'

Tish said nothing.

The officer pressed on. 'So, as far as you are aware, nothing happened at the party? Nothing that might have caused any trouble?'

Tish said 'No' again, but more quietly.

'Okay.' The woman moved on, seemingly reluctantly. 'Can you tell us anything more about what Jess and Harry were fighting about in the car park?'

'No.'

'You're sure?'

'Yes.'

She referred to her notes. 'And you said in your statement that you didn't know what *set Harry off*, with regard to his fight with Mo?'

'I wouldn't call it a fight?'

'What would you call it?'

'I don't know. A bit of a ruck.'

'A ruck...which was caused by what?'

'Like I said before, I don't know.'

Sal didn't like the shift in tone in the questioning.

The officer went on. 'Are you sure, Tish? The thing that's troubling us is that you seem to have been oblivious to everything that was going on that night. And yet you were there. These people were your close friends. You seem unable to remember very much at all.'

Tish shifted in her seat. When she next spoke, her voice sounded strained. 'I didn't say I couldn't remember. I said I wasn't involved.'

This comment seemed to prompt a change of tack. The officer put her notepad aside. She bent down, pulled a laptop out of her bag and rested it on her knee. Sal concentrated her attention on Tish, aware of something shifting. She saw a change in her eyes, a flicker of some new, different anxiety that had not been there before.

The woman looked up. 'Okay, Tish,' but she said it as if she meant the exact opposite. 'There's something we'd like you to see.' She tapped at the keyboard. 'Mo's phone was eventually retrieved from the car park at McDonald's. There's some video footage on it that we feel may be relevant to the case.'

Tish stiffened so much that Sal heard her spine crack.

'We'd like you to take a look at it. Is that okay with you?'

Tish mumbled 'Yes', but her body language said 'No.'

The officer passed the open laptop to Tish.

She glanced at the screen and said, 'Mum, do you mind?'

Sal didn't get it. *Mind what?* Then she did. Her face burnt as she got up and walked out of the room, pulling the door closed behind her.

Chapter 41

THE DOORBELL went at 7.15 a.m. Dom opened up, expecting it to be the postman, a cup of coffee in one hand and a piece of toast in the other. Fran was standing on the doorstep. They stared at each other.

Dom swallowed, 'Fran.'

'I just want to talk,' she said.

Neither of them moved. Impasse.

One, two, three seconds. It felt longer. Dom waited, blocking her path. He did not invite her inside.

That seemed to infuriate Fran. She brushed past him into the house. Dom was so shocked that he didn't try and stop her. She went straight through into the kitchen, Dom in pursuit. It was empty.

'Fran, what is it that you want?' Dom kept his voice low, pitched at 'calm'.

'I need to know what's going on. I need you to tell me what Harry's said to you? I need the truth.'

'You know I can't discuss anything to do with the case with you.'

She glared. 'Can't! You mean "won't"! Ignoring my messages, my texts, keeping us at arm's length, refusing to let us speak to Harry – it's not right! Did you think we'd give up and go away, once she died? Is that what you were banking on?"

'Fran, please.' Dom searched her face for the friend he used to know, the woman who had helped him more than any other human being on the planet; who had hauled him out of the pit he was in, after Adele left; the Fran who had helped him be the best dad he could be. That Fran, who was warm and full of good advice, and humour and love. But she wasn't there. All those weeks in hospital, Jess's death, the funeral and now the decision to charge Harry – it had changed her, it had erased the woman she used to be.

It was tragic. It was awful. He got that. But imagining that he would choose her over his son! That wasn't rational. Dom tried to placate her. 'I know this whole thing is an appalling mess. That it has screwed everything up between us. And for that, I am truly sorry. But you know Harry can't talk to you, Fran. Not now there's this prosecution pending. I'm sorry, but that's the way it is. It's a legal matter now, which Harry is caught up in the middle of. I have to think of him. I think it's best if you leave.'

'No.' One word. Spat out.

Dom's tone hardened. 'Please, Fran. Don't. This is only making a bad situation worse. I don't want to fight with you.'

'You don't want a fight!' she mocked. 'You don't want an upset.' Her voice rose. Loud enough to wake Harry and Martha? Dom hoped not. 'What about what *I* want, Dom? I want some answers. No one is telling us anything. Can you even imagine what that feels like? Can you imagine knowing that everyone else knows more than you do, about your own child's death? Harry, Jake, Tish, the police, the lawyers, you! I'm her mother, for God's sake!' Her voice was raspy with grief, and resolve. She turned her back on him. 'If you won't tell me anything, then I'll have to ask him myself.' She made a move, as if intending to go upstairs. Dom grabbed her arm, gripped it tightly, holding her back. They struggled, locked in a tug of war that neither had any intention of losing.

Dom's patience finally snapped. 'Fran, stop it. You're not seeing

Harry. You have to leave him, and us, alone. It's up to the court now.' She twisted in his grip. The last time he'd held her had been at the hospital, the day after the accident, when they'd hugged and he'd felt the grief washing through her. Now all he could feel was sinew and rage. 'Fran. You can't talk to him.' He hated having to say it, but she needed to know there was a barrier, and that she'd crossed it by coming into his home in such a rage. 'And I wouldn't let you, even if I could. Not in the state you're in. You need to calm down. And leave. If you refuse, I will call the police.'

Suddenly Fran stopped struggling. The tension between them went slack. Dom held on, uncertain of her intentions. She was breathing erratically. Calming or gathering herself? It was impossible to tell. Then she looked up at him. Her face uncomfortably close to his. He waited for her to say something. Saw the turmoil in her eyes. Felt for her.

'This is unbearable,' she whispered. Her voice was old, stripped of every shred of hope.

'I know.' He loosened, but didn't let go of his hold on her.

'What am I supposed to do, Dom?' she asked.

He was fighting for his son. He had no idea what Fran had left to fight for. 'I don't know, Fran. I'm sorry, but I don't know.'

'Is everything all right?' Martha's voice startled them both.

Dom did his level best to sound normal. 'Yes. Everything's fine. Fran called round to have a word with me about something. She got a bit upset.' Fran seemed transfixed by Martha. Dom didn't like it. 'You go and get dressed. Fran's just leaving.'

Martha half-turned as if to leave, but then she did something totally out of character. She defied Dom and faced into, rather than away from, the awkwardness of the situation. In other circumstances Dom would have been proud of her. She came into the kitchen and walked over to the kettle. 'At least let me get Fran a drink before she goes. A cup of tea?'

Trapped by Martha's insistence on kindness, Dom had to acquiesce. Fran said nothing, but continued to track Martha's movements as she moved round the kitchen, getting out mugs and teabags and milk. Holding onto Fran became too uncomfortable, so Dom let her go. But he stood poised, ready to react, watching Fran watching Martha like a hawk. There was something very unsettling about the intensity of her focus.

Tea made, they moved into the conservatory and sat down.

There followed the most uncomfortable fifteen minutes of Dom's life. Martha tried to fill the void with chatter about school, while Fran sat on the sofa, gripping her mug with white-knuckled fingers. Dom just wanted Fran out of his house – the woman who had babysat for his kids more times than he cared to remember, fed them their teas, wiped their noses and their backsides, read them bedtime stories and kissed them goodnight – he wanted her as far away from his family as possible. Martha valiantly moved on to an anecdote about one of the ponies at the stables. Dom wasn't listening. He was too on edge, alert to any signs of life from upstairs, or movement from Fran. He was also busy contemplating whether he was going to have to speak to the lawyers about some form of restraining order.

Suddenly Martha's face drained. Fran had said something that he hadn't heard. There was a beat, then Fran delivered her follow-up blow. 'Didn't your dad tell you? Your brother's been charged with Jess's death?'

Martha recoiled. Tea spilt from her mug all down her PJ bottoms, but she didn't seem to notice. The look of distress on her face galvanised Dom. He scrambled to his feet and grabbed hold of Fran. This time there was no hesitation.

'Out! Now!' He dragged her, stumbling and resisting to the door, fumbled it open and pushed her through it. 'If you come near Martha, or Harry, or this house ever again, I will call the police. Go away and stay away, Fran. There is nothing for you here. Nothing.' He slammed the door shut and went to comfort Martha.

The windows in the whole house rattled. Harry felt the reverberation travel up through his spine. He waited on the landing, keeping watch, out of sight. Fran emerged. She walked quickly down the drive, turning round every few steps to look back at the house, her face a blur of emotions.

He'd heard it all.

He'd heard her arrive. Heard her demand to speak to him. Heard his father block her. Then the ominous quiet. He hadn't realised, until it was too late, that Martha had joined the 'party'. He'd been *so* close to walking downstairs, into the room and presenting himself for Fran to take a swing at – as many swings as she wanted. She was right, he did owe her some answers, but he'd bricked it. Totally, humiliatingly, bricked it. He'd hidden upstairs, too afraid to face Fran's condemnation, and her questions. Instead he'd let his little sister step into the firing line. What a coward!

Fran used to love him.

Now she hated him.

He understood that.

He deserved it.

But he didn't know how to handle it.

Chapter 42

THE MEETINGS with the solicitors were held in their offices now, the time for informal chats at home long gone. Theirs was an active case. The billed hours were racking up, as Harry's defence was honed and polished.

Fenwick and Milling's offices were on St Saviourgate. The parking nearby was awful, but Dom had driven into the city centre regardless. He had meetings afterwards. As they waited to be shown into the conference room, he glanced at Harry. He was sitting, totally immobile, staring into space. Dom looked away. There was no point speaking to him until they were in the room. Harry had always rationed his words, even as a child, but since the accident this trait had grown worse. Dom was tired of having to tease and cajole anything out of his son. And besides, it was largely pointless. He no longer expected any of the scant words that did emerge from Harry's tight lips to bear much relationship to what he was actually thinking or – God forbid – feeling.

When they were all settled, Ross explained that the purpose of the day's meeting was to explore the factors the team were planning to put forward *in mitigation*. They were past the point of *denial*; they were into *minimising, challenging* and *reframing* the contributory factors that the prosecution was intending to present. Harry might not have expanded his legal vocabulary, but Dom certainly had.

One of the assistants dealt out a stack of documents. The binders slid across the tabletop like cards on a poker table. They all opened their packs and turned to page eight, as instructed – everyone, that is, except Harry. He didn't pick up his folder, but merely stopped it skidding off the edge of the table with the palm of his hand. The binders were substantial. Dom was both impressed and horrified by the volume of work the solicitors had done. There were bold headings and bullet points, and photographs and statements, all divided into colour-coded sections.

Ross began speaking, fluently, quickly and totally unemotionally. 'One of the biggest problems we have is the video from the traffic cop's vest-cam. To a lay person, it does look very much like Harry is drunk...or high. For those who haven't seen it yet, I think it's worth reviewing the footage.' He clicked a remote device, and a hidden system somewhere threw the footage from the night of the accident up onto the wall.

Instantly the room was filled the noise of sirens. The world of expensive suits and measured words receded, replaced by the loud, messy aftermath of the crash, projected onto the pristine white walls. They all watched transfixed as Harry – the driver, the person who had just caused so much damage and pain – swayed in and out of the frame, his face sometimes visible, sometimes not. The officer was moving around a lot as well, the camera picking up the crashed car, the emergency services on the scene, even the shadowy crowd gathered in the distance. But the focus kept returning to Harry. A sweaty-faced, bloodstained, wild-eyed, incoherent Harry. The crackly, discordant audio bounced around the conference room, hurtful to their ears. Harry was rambling – by turns aggressive, then pathetic. A flood of guttural panic gushing out of him, unmoderated, unchecked. The officer kept telling him *to stay put, to leave it to the professionals*, that *there was nothing he could do.*

Dom tore his horrified attention away from the screen and looked at his son. Harry was staring at the wall. Catatonic.

On the video the officer asked, 'Who was driving, Harry?'

'What?' Even that small word sounded slurred.

'I want to know who was driving the car, Harry? Look at me, lad! Was it you who was driving?'

At this point in the footage Harry turned away and started shouting again, a jumble of words, some of which were discernible. 'Be careful with her. No! Please!'

The officer persisted. 'Leave them to it, Harry. They know what they're doing. I want you to answer my question. Were you driving the car, Harry?'

Harry's face swung back into frame, in close-up. He looked terrified. 'Yeah. It was me. Me driving. It's my car. Oh God. Oh God. I'm sorry. I'm so sorry.'

A click.

The images disappeared from the wall, but not from Dom's mind. It had been like being there, on the ring road, trapped inside his son's panic. The footage brought home to Dom just how much of a nightmare the crash had been. He felt a sudden urge to reach out and touch Harry, offer some comfort, but the presence of the lawyers stopped him.

Ross picked up again, smoothly. 'There's no need to view any more of the tape, as that's the salient section they'll be submitting in court.' He referred them back to the binder. 'This is where the toxicology report comes in. Clean for drugs, as we expected. And for alcohol: ninety-eight milligrams per hundred, on the blood sample.' He tapped the page. 'Less, or none, detected would obviously have been better, but ninety-eight – that's not disastrous. The issue for us is Harry's behaviour on the tape. Unfortunately it plays into the reports of him being drunk on the night, though on this we can show the undue influence of Jake Hammond's behaviour at the party. There is a case to be made that Jake's drunkenness had a halo-effect on witness testimony. They tarred Harry with the same brush, et cetera.'

He waved his hand expansively. 'In fact I'm not overly worried about the party hearsay. Most of the witness statements can be challenged, due to the generally high levels of intoxicants consumed by nearly everyone present. But the tape remains damaging. We need to put it into context, and for that we need to talk about the impact that shock can have on a person, in terms of behaviour, speech and clarity of thought. For this, I'd like to draw your attention to the expert witness statements in Section F, pages twenty-four to thirty-two. We intend to show that what we're seeing on this video is a young man in profound shock. We need to get the court to realise that Harry's demeanour is evidence of someone who is acutely distressed about what is happening to his friends, in front of his eyes; not proof of intoxication and guilt. Our expert thinks that isn't going to be that difficult, given the impact of the crash, Harry's closeness to the people in the car, the trauma...'

They all looked at Harry. His eyes flicked round the table, settling on no one. His expression was impossible to read.

Ross went on, 'The second factor the prosecution is relying on, to get the charge to stick, is "excessive speed". This is where it gets technical. The angle and depth of the skid marks on the road, and the tracks on the grass, are the basis for evidence here; and the good thing is that, with road analysis, there's always leeway for interpretation. We're on that, aren't we, Mia?'

The silent, note-taking assistant nodded. Dom wondered how much of the legwork she was doing, and how many of those long hours were being charged as Ross's expensive endeavour.

'There are, as we know, no witnesses from the night, other than passengers in the car.' This time he referred to his notes. 'The only person to make any comment about the speed the car was travelling was Leticia Reynolds, and her perception can be presented as unreliable, given her consumption of alcohol and' – here he actually smiled – 'cannabis. Apparently she was very forthcoming about smoking a joint before going out that evening, and that she shared another one at the party.'

Dom was impressed with their thoroughness. Ross wasn't finished.

'Road conditions are of no help. Too benign. So we'll leave that alone. There's no point fighting battles you can't win. It tends to weaken your case. But there is one other thing I wanted to raise.' More paper-shuffling and page-turning. When he looked up, Ross focused exclusively on Harry. 'I want to return to your claim that there was something in the road that caused you to swerve, but that you couldn't say what it was. I know we've raised our concerns that this statement is too vague and unsubstantiated to be helpful. That it is, in fact, harmful, as it feeds into an argument about lack of attention, which, in turn, supports the prosecution's contention of "dangerous" driving. But I wanted to check: do you have anything more to add, Harry?'

The pressure in the room built. At last Harry responded. 'Like I said...Jess suddenly shouted to watch out.'

'And you still have no idea why she shouted?'

They all stared at Harry, waiting for more.

'She just shouted. I guess I reacted. Pulled the wheel a fraction. I don't know. Maybe that's what made us crash. I don't know.' He folded his arms.

Ross, suave as ever, made a note on his folder. 'That's honest, but doesn't help us, I'm afraid. No matter. We'll put a pin in it for now. We can always circle back to that another time.' He flipped over some more pages in the folder. 'The last issue we want to discuss today – and it is a critical one, when it comes to mitigating factors – is "character". It's an amazingly influential area, when it comes to trials. We need to make sure we maximise the fact that – up until this incident – Harry has been an exemplary young man. Well liked, a good student, hard-working, responsible, trustworthy. As you'll see, we have ample statements from his tutors, his employers at his holiday job at the showroom, some of your family friends. It builds a solid picture of Harry being "of good character". All of which will be presented. As you know, the issue of the footage from Mohir Akhtar's phone has been contentious, in terms of its relevance. Teenage relationships are hardly a matter for the courts to have an opinion on, and we are still challenging its admissibility. Overall I think it's fair to say that we're in a strong position when it comes to Harry's character.'

Harry stiffened in his seat. Ross straightened in his.

'We are, therefore, almost there, in terms of putting forward a strong defence case for the barrister to present. But – and I have to stress that this is your choice, not mine – there does appear to be another option open to us. One that would avoid a court case.'

He paused, checking that he had their attention. He had.

'We had a meeting with the CPS yesterday, at their request. While we were there an interesting line of discussion opened up, which I want to walk you through. The prosecution has come back with an offer that could take all the evidence out of the public domain and negate the need for a trial.' Dom leant forward. 'They have asked me to ask you to consider the nature of your plea.'

'Meaning?' Dom asked.

Ross held up his hand to still Dom's impatience. 'They're willing to discuss the option of the charge being reduced to "careless driving".'

'And that's good news because...'

'Because "careless driving" carries reduced penalties. Or, to put it another way, there's an increased chance that we might be able to minimise any custodial sentence. And there is a less stigma. "Careless" implies more error of judgement; "dangerous" speaks for itself.'

'Why would they offer a lesser charge, after all the effort that's gone into pinning this on Harry?'

'Well, the honest answer to that is cost, and to obviate the need for a trial. Trials are expensive, and the system is backed up. The other argument is that it reduces the trauma and stress for the victims' families.'

Dom winced at the use of the word 'victims'.

Ross went on, 'But here's the rub – the offer is contingent on Harry entering a guilty plea.' He stopped talking. Glanced from Dom to Harry. As expected, it was Dom who responded.

'So Harry gets dumped with the responsibility. After all this…' He pushed the file away angrily, 'after all this effort to prove that he's not to blame, you're advocating that we fold and he puts his hands up?'

'I'm not advocating it. I'm presenting you with the option. There's a gamble with any trial. We are ready and able to present our case as clearly and forcefully as possible, but there are no guarantees. A guilty plea removes the element of uncertainty. And, as I said, it avoids the trauma and cost of a court case. It can be in everyone's interests. Hence them offering it.'

'But Harry will serve time and he'll have a criminal record.'

'A custodial sentence, yes – that's unavoidable because of the alcohol, the severity of the injuries incurred and Jess Beaumont's death. A criminal record is also unavoidable.'

Dom squared his shoulders. 'I say we fight it. Harry has his whole life ahead of him. Prison, a record: it will screw it all up. No. That's not happening to my son.'

Ross nodded in acknowledgement, but not necessarily agreement, then switched his attention to Harry. 'What are your thoughts, Harry?' Everyone else looked at him as well.

Harry ran his hand over his face. 'So you're saying that if I plead guilty, there's no court case?'

'Correct. The court moves straight to a sentencing hearing.'

'And neither of the videos would be shown at that?'

'No. Not in open court.'

'And Tish and Jake and Mo, they wouldn't have to give evidence at this sentencing thing?'

'No. They will be asked to submit impact statements, and they'll be able to present these at the hearing, if they so wish, but they'll not be asked to give witness testimony.'

'And I wouldn't have to stand up and say what happened?'

'You'll need to confirm who you are and enter your plea formally. Whether you want to say anything "in mitigation" is up to you.'

'Look, wait a minute,' Dom started flustering.

Harry stared at the file on the table. They all waited. 'In that case...I'll plead guilty.'

As Dom imploded with indignation, and Ross responded with cool professionalism, Harry sat stoically amidst the storm. A decision had been made. Whether it would be in everyone's interests, including his own, remained to be seen.

Chapter 43

FRAN WAS in the park, watching the drifts of cherry blossom. She went there often. It was the *only* place she found any respite. The compulsion to keep moving and doing was getting worse; day and night her brain whirled and raced, but never tired enough to let her sleep. Only in the park was she able to switch off. It was a relief do nothing except sit and let the hard screw of grief that propelled her through each day ease a little. Droplets of other people's lives fell on her as she sat under the trees, swaddled in her sorrow. She observed the older couples going about their daily routines, and the young mums with their children killing time. She smiled at the sprightly progress of the old folk and the make-believe games of the families. As she sat, unobserved, she caught snippets of conversations: humour, patience, kindness and imagination – a world of caring that was lost to her.

Occasionally she was recognised. Reactions varied: some people pretended not to have seen her and took a different route across the park; others smiled and came to sit beside her. The 'sitters' invariably asked *how things were going*. Meaning well, but wanting a reassurance she couldn't give. Their sympathy always forced her to move on. She became adept at creating fake appointments and pressing commitments. She'd walk away, take a turn round the neighbourhood until she was confident they'd gone, then she'd return to her bench.

Today the park was busy, the nice weather drawing people out, so there were plenty of other lives to watch and ponder. The burr of her phone in her bag broke her reverie. She thought about not answering it, but knew it would be Marcus, concerned about her whereabouts. He worried. But it wasn't Marcus; it was Joe, their police liaison officer. The peaceful sadness that she'd been lost in evaporated.

He explained. She listened. He ended the call with a promise to 'keep them posted'. Such a casual phrase.

Outrage flooded through her bloodstream.

'Careless driving!'

It was an insult.

Careless was dropping a glass, or dinging someone's car door in a supermarket car park. Careless was doing something through lack of attention, a lapse in good judgement, a mistake. It was something small and inconsequential. Harry had not made a mistake! He'd got drunk, climbed behind the wheel of his boy-racer car – bought for him by his indulgent father – driven too fast, lost control, crashed and killed their daughter.

Fran stood up and set off walking, fast steps, blood pumping, anger brewing inside her. There was to be no trial. It would be 'unnecessary'. Joe had actually had the temerity to suggest this might be 'better' for everyone in the long run. 'Less painful.' He obviously knew nothing about pain, about its capacity to mutate and bloom, bruise, cut and nag in turn. No trial. Less cost. A quicker resolution. 'Better all round.' It was *not* better. It was an affront to Jess. Her death was huge and of consequence. It needed to be recognised, and prosecuted as such.

She left the park and headed along the road, closing in on home. Joe had gone on to clarify what she knew already, that a charge of

183

'careless' rather than 'dangerous' driving carried a lesser tariff. Less punishment. Less censure. Less justice. This was Dom's lawyers at work. Throwing money at the problem. It was Dom's answer to everything, and this was no different. But it *was* different. It was Jess. If she hadn't got into that car with Harry, she would be alive.

Fran fumbled for her door keys. She let herself into the house, full of indignation. She needed to speak to Marcus immediately. She needed him to share in her rage, formulate a response, sanction her plans to appeal. They must fight for the more serious charge, insist that Harry was prosecuted properly. They *had* to.

But Marcus wasn't there. She looked in all the downstairs rooms. She yanked open the back door and looked out at the garden – he spent hours out there most days – but there was no sign of him. His car was parked outside. Where was he? Upstairs. She took the stairs at a lick. He would be as shocked as she was.

'Careless!'

She saw him before she made it up onto the landing. He was in the bathroom, sitting on the floor, his legs outstretched, his head bent, inert. The sight stopped Fran in her tracks. The shimmering bubble of bitter words in her head popped. He looked wrong. As she reached the top stair, Marcus looked up and stared, without seeing her. She walked slowly into the bathroom and crouched down beside him. His trousers were wet. He was holding something in his hands. Her brain was scrambling to decode what she was seeing. Marcus was crying, softly, steadily, unceasingly.

'Marcus?'

Beside him on the floor was his tool box. The lid open. The top tray was 'Marcus standard' neat: the various screws and nails all appropriately stowed in their different compartments, his tools lined up precisely, his secateurs, a collection of different-sized screwdrivers, a Stanley knife. A pulse of panic went through her. But there wasn't any sign of injury. No blood on the tiled floor. His colour was okay. His breathing was shallow, but he was obviously getting enough oxygen. Besides, Marcus would never do anything like that. Never. He wouldn't ever leave her – even if he wanted to.

'Marcus?'

He seemed finally to register her presence. 'It wasn't draining properly.' He meant the shower. It hadn't been. The water had been taking ages to empty. Now she could see that he had unscrewed the drain cover. The grubby trap was lying on the floor near his hip. She knew, before he opened his hands, what he was holding; knew what was soaking into his trousers, what had broken down his defences.

Jess's hair.

His hands were full of clumps of their daughter's hair.

Fran slid down on the floor next to him and leant into his shoulder. She didn't try and take the sodden clump out of his hands. She couldn't bring herself to touch it, and she knew that he wasn't ready to let it go. Jess's hair. Shiny after a shower. A bird's nest in the mornings. Hair that drank conditioner. The bottle in the shower was always empty. Hair that stuck in winding strands to tiles and got clogged in the drain. Jess's lovely, long blonde hair – reduced to a handful of grey, gunky matter.

She leant her head on Marcus's shoulder and listened to him cry.

Chapter 44

THEY HAD taken Harley for a walk. It was grey and damp, not like late-May weather at all, but their evening walks had become something of a habit. A nice one. Mo wasn't going be put off by a bit of drizzle. Harley had 'made friends' with a cocker spaniel. The two dogs were excitedly chasing each other across the playing fields, ears flapping, tongues lolling. Mo and Tish watched, easy in other's company.

Her face was looking a lot better, the skin healing. She was using the oil Shazia had sent her; she claimed it was helping. And, to her delight, the doctors had finally given Tish permission to start using make-up again. It made a difference. But the change was not just in her appearance; it was also in her mood. Her confidence was coming back and, with it, her willingness to go out. There was talk of her coming back to college for the last few days of term before the summer break began – not to take any of her exams, but simply to see people, and to make the thought of returning in September to redo her upper-sixth year more palatable.

Mo was pleased for her. He knew how much being able to hide the worst of the scars meant to her, but it was also making him feel anxious. Tish was beginning to look and sound like the old Tish again. Which was good. It was what he wanted for her. How could he not? How could any reasonable person not want that for her, after all she'd been through? But at the same time he was very aware that the more Tish starting feeling and behaving like her old self, the less of a role he would have in her life. They'd never really been close before. They'd hung around together, but Mo had always been on the edge of things. It was the accident that opened a door for him to squeeze through. Tish getting better would narrow that tiny gap. Mo heading off to uni in September might very well slam it shut. He couldn't imagine what it would be like to lose her. No, that wasn't right. He *could* imagine it, and that was what was worrying him.

She touched his arm. 'You're quiet.'

'Sorry.'

'You don't have to be.' She pulled her jacket collar up around her neck. 'Is something up?'

'Nah.' He gave himself a metaphorical shake. 'I'm just getting wet.'

'You wuss! Come on, let's walk over to the basketball cages.' She slid her hand through his arm and set off.

His mood immediately lifted. It was stupidly old fashioned, but having Tish next to him, touching him, was as good as it got for Mo. It was the *rightest* feeling in the world. He felt proud, though there was hardly anyone else around to see them. That didn't matter; wherever they were, he felt proud to be with her. He admired her strength and her sense of humour and her loveliness. She was beautiful.

Harley spotted that they were on the move and pelted over, his new best buddy hot on his paws. The dogs raced around them three times, then shot off again, boomeranging across the grass.

Tish talked and Mo listened, and the street lights came on and Mo wished they could keep circling the playing fields in the drizzle for the rest of their lives.

Chapter 45

THE THEME tune caught Marcus unawares – a trailer for a series they used to watch together, a cringey comedy that had made them all laugh. He glanced across at Fran, but couldn't tell whether she'd registered the relevance of the music, connected it with Jess and felt the same swoop of fresh sorrow as himself. That was the problem. Not knowing at what level each other's grief was set, at any given time. And it seemed to be getting harder, not easier, with time.

The screen changed and they were back to the detective drama. He wasn't sure he could remember if it was the one with the Albanian drugs cartel trafficking girls or the one with the Deep South sadist who was killing young women in alphabetical order. Saturday nights in: brutality and cruelty in *beautifully* shot, grimy locations. Fran wasn't paying attention to the TV. She was sitting on the floor on the far side of the room, looking at her laptop. In Jess's spot.

The 'floor sitting' was a new development. It made Marcus uncomfortable, but he knew he couldn't say anything. There were so many off-limits topics between them now. The only time they actually talked about the accident, and Jess, and the impending court proceedings, was with professionals in harshly lit rooms, with strict protocols and written agendas. Agendas that were designed to keep emotions in check. The recent victim impact statement session they'd attended had been excruciating. Never before had Marcus had his life so ruthlessly eviscerated in front of strangers. Never again did he want the differences between his own and his wife's feelings so brutally explored, recorded, annotated and circulated for 'approval and sign off'. Better not to go there – though he knew that was no answer, either. The date for Harry's sentencing was approaching. Marcus wished it over. Perhaps then Fran would be able to let some of the anger go; perhaps then his wife would resurface from beneath the dark waters that were drowning her.

He stared at the detective on the TV, not bothering to follow the dialogue. He lifted his glass and took another mouthful of wine. Fran had a mug of tea on the carpet beside her. No alcohol for her. That was another recent development – a decision taken unilaterally, and stuck to, unwaveringly. This he did understand. Alcohol had played its part in the crash. He got the link. He understood the logic. But opening a bottle and pouring them both a glass was a ritual that Marcus missed – like so many other things.

The detective was now in a strip joint, seeking information from some doe-eyed pole-dancers in glittery thongs and high heels. Marcus took another drink. Two empty seats beside him. He stretched out his hand and stroked the fabric, rubbing the pile back and forth, dark–light, dark–light. His loneliness was physical, an ache that worsened with every day that passed. The kindness of strangers and colleagues – and there had been a lot of kindness and consideration shown – was appreciated, but it did little to lessen the pain of not being held and hugged. The weight of Fran's bare feet in his lap as they watched TV, the unsought spontaneous hug of greeting or goodbye from Jess, the briefest of touches from either of them as they waltzed around each other, getting on with their lives – he missed and craved that physical contact. But Jess was gone, for ever, and although Fran was in the same room, not ten feet away, she was sealed off from him. They needed each other, but whether they could help each other was a different matter.

'Fran?'

'Yeah?' She didn't look up.

'What are you looking at?'

'Oh, nothing.' But she didn't stop, didn't close the lid and come to sit beside him. Marcus didn't expect any more than a flicker of her attention, but he did want her to hear him and acknowledge his presence. He took a bigger mouthful of wine. He could guess what she was looking at, and she knew it. That's why she'd hadn't told him. More research into other cases of death by 'dangerous', 'reckless', 'careless' – did it really matter which word they used to describe it? – driving. It was becoming an obsession. Grief and retribution. Death and demands for justice. Appeals. Challenges. The 'voice of the victim'.

Only yesterday he'd walked in and caught Fran on YouTube, watching a video about the family of a man with a drug habit who had crashed a car with three of his family members in it, killing all of them. When she'd sensed Marcus standing behind her, she'd closed the lid of her laptop, ashamed, or perhaps unwilling to let him witness her obsession.

He took another slug of his wine, swallowed, put down his glass and continued not really watching the TV. For ten minutes.

He couldn't stand it any longer. He stood up and walked out. Fran didn't notice him leave.

He went upstairs, into Jess's room, and closed the door behind him as quietly as he could, putting another barrier between himself and his wife. He was spending more and more time in Jess's bedroom. Fran had her videos and her research; he had this.

With each visit he grew in confidence. Initially he'd felt like he was intruding. Jess's bedroom was her personal space. When she was alive, he only ever entered it at her invitation. Now there was no need to knock. She would never again shout, 'Come in.' He hadn't dared touch anything, to start with. He'd stood just inside the door. He certainly couldn't bring himself to sit on her bed. He hadn't opened a drawer or moved anything. But with time his self-consciousness had faded. He'd gone from standing by the door, to sitting on her chair, to perching on the edge of her bed, to sitting on it, to lying down. But lying on his dead daughter's bed had been no good for him. Not at all. It had been an indulgence, a weakness that had led him to lose hours as he drifted in the darkness. And the one thing Marcus had decided, as he stood in the crematorium looking at the casket while Joan delivered Jess's eulogy, was that he was *not* going to give up and go under. So he had sat up and started his quest to get to know his daughter better.

Her room was now the only place where he felt he could still function as her father.

He had started small, by opening Jess's wardrobe and taking out all her shoes, toughening his hands and his heart. That first afternoon, with the sun coming in through the window warming his back, he'd simply counted how many pairs she had. He'd committed the number to memory. She'd have liked that – his nerdiness being put to good use. That was the day he'd discovered his first new thing about his daughter: she'd owned nineteen pairs of shoes, most of them in need of a clean. The next evening he'd taken the shoes out again and set himself the challenge of putting them in order, according to how often she wore them. As he moved them around on the carpet, he tried to think of specific occasions when Jess had worn each pair. It was harder than it sounded. It was a knowledge test of his daughter's tastes and habits.

After her shoes, he moved on to Jess's clothes. Her clothes were more of a challenge, there were so many of them, but he found the exercise equally fruitful. There were her 'hundreds' of tops, her selection of identical-looking jeans, a tangle of Lycra sportswear and, most heartbreaking of all, her stuff for bed: her PJs and her old, wash-worn T-shirts. It was time-consuming and difficult, but that was good – because that's what being her dad had been like. With every item Marcus held in his hands, and with every trawl through his store of everyday memories, he felt like he was strengthening his connection with Jess. It comforted him.

This evening he was glad he'd had a drink before returning to his labours. He even reasoned, somewhat fuzzily, that Jess would've understood his need for Dutch courage. Because he'd completed all the obvious tasks: her clothes and shoes, her bookcase and her college bag. He'd even gone through her make-up, smelling the various lotions and potions and picking out the lip tint that he thought she wore most days. But he was apprehensive about what awaited him. Her bedside cabinet.

The small set of drawers with its handles draped with necklaces, the front papered with stickers, seemed a much bigger step. A step that took him over the boundary of her right to privacy. He sat on her bed and spoke to Jess: in his head; he couldn't bring himself to try it out loud – the lack of response would've been too much. He explained his reasons and asked her forgiveness, and tried to convince himself that she would've given him permission, but still he hesitated. The police investigation had muddied the waters. Marcus was honest enough with himself to admit that his compulsion to know everything he could about his daughter wasn't driven purely by his need to hang on to her; it had also been triggered by the police's questions, and their implications.

Marcus pulled open the drawer. Swift, decisive.

It was crammed with stuff. A phone charger, hair bands, lip balms, some tablets. On closer inspection, the tablets turned out to be contraceptive pills. This was no surprise to Marcus. He knew she'd been taking them to ease the symptoms of her periods. He and Fran and Jess had discussed it, quite openly. Dinosaur-parenting was not their style. But holding the packet in his hands, he wondered if Jess's motivation for going on the Pill had been as straightforward as he'd chosen to believe. He put the box back. Shut the drawer, moved on to the next.

It was full of stationery bits and pieces. A flutter of Post-it notes drifted to the floor as he worked his way through the Biros and notepads and elastic bands. The third drawer was more organised, as if care had been taken with the items in it. It was here that Marcus started to detect brief glimpses of the Jess he didn't know – the young woman with a private life. A notebook, a few mementoes, a perfume spray; for some reason, a children's book about seahorses.

He lifted the purple notebook out first and placed it on the bed, not ready – yet – to face what was inside: Jess's handwriting, and her secrets. Beneath the book was a small black drawstring pouch, the type that jewellery came in. It felt soft to the touch. He loosened the ties and eased open the mouth of the bag, then shook it. A handful of silver coins fell out onto the duvet. They were smooth, with words engraved on them. Not real coins, more like tokens. He picked one up. It was cool to the touch. '*A kiss in the moonlight*'. The second said, '*A back scratch*'. The third, '*A massage*'. The fourth, '*A roll in the hay*'. Tokens five and six were more of the same. A cheap gift, with tacky sentiments, that had meant something to his daughter. He put the tokens back into the bag and pulled tight the string, wondering how many – if any – she had redeemed. He felt confused as to whether he wanted the answer to be none, or all of them.

In the same drawer there was a bulldog clip, holding together a wodge of papers. He chose to look at that next. It was a stack of receipts and tickets: Nando's orders, bus tickets, e-tickets from the festival they'd all gone to as a group the previous summer; there was even a scraggy end of till roll from Sainsbury's for the purchase of two meal deals. The story the receipts told was indecipherable, at least by Marcus.

There were sounds downstairs. The click of the lights in the kitchen being turned on. Fran was on the move.

He returned the token bag and receipts to the drawer. Alone, they formed an incomplete story. He pushed the drawer shut, stood up and slid the notebook into his back pocket. His eyes swept the room, looking for clues. A sea of faces stared back at him from the myriad of pictures pinned to Jess's noticeboard. Marcus didn't know, yet, which of them had been special, which had mattered more than the rest.

He turned off the light and pulled shut the door, Jess's secret safe with him – for the time being.

Chapter 46

MO TEXTED to say that he couldn't make it; apologised, twice; said he'd message her later; sent an emoji. He was blowing it out of proportion. It was only a poxy dog walk, after all. Like it was going to bother Tish that he couldn't find the time, in between college and his job, and his obviously demanding family, to fit her in – as he had been doing so loyally for the past few weeks. But her day seemed to drag more than normal without the thought of Mo rocking up on her doorstep at 7 p.m., give or take two minutes, and dragging her out to walk and talk. Sal was at work, so it was down to Harley to keep her company. He did his best, but he wasn't much of a conversationalist.

When Mo called at lunchtime, Tish deliberately didn't pick up. She looked at his name on the screen, waited while her messaging service kicked in, saw the voicemail alert, but even then – on principle – she didn't click on it straight away. Tish had her standards, and relying on a lad, any lad, was not one of them, not any more. She had enough of her mojo back not to be that much of a doormat. A minute later a text arrived from him. After five minutes she relented and listened to his message. He sounded dorky on the phone, the hesitancy more obvious. It suddenly struck her that his 'phone voice' fitted her old impression of Mo – nice, cute, but nothing more.

'Hey there. I didn't get a chance before. To call, I mean. I had a thought. You might not fancy it. But you know I said I can't come round tonight? Well, I wondered...do you want to come round to mine? Just for a change. Mum and Dad will be out. Not that that makes any difference. Anyway, I'll text you the address. In case you can't remember it. Any time after half six is fine. Bye.'

The text was his address, as promised. Tish was ashamed to admit to Harley that she wouldn't have remembered it, without his prompting. Not that there was any way she was going round to his.

She stood outside his front door and messed with her hair. It was 6.32 p.m. She thought about going for a walk round the block before knocking, but before she had a chance to run away, the door opened. Shazia smiled and covered her surprise, badly.

'Tish, how lovely. How are you doing? Well. Obviously.'

Tish blushed and nodded, as Nihal appeared at Shazia's shoulder.

'We're just on our way out. Go on through. They're in the back.'

They? Mo's parents edged past and made their way to their car, leaving the door wide open for her. Tish didn't step inside. It seemed rude. She waited, waved them off. Only after the sound of their car had faded did she walk into the house. She crossed the hall following the noise, feeling like she was trespassing.

'No!' a child shrieked. 'Me. Me. Me.'

'Hi!' she shouted. There was no answer.

They were in the sitting room at the back of the house. Mo was crawling round the room on his hands and knees, a small boy clamped onto his back like a limpet. On the floor next to him stood a stocky little girl, who was yanking at the boy's T-shirt.

'Hi,' Tish said, louder this time.

Mo finally registered her presence. He pushed himself up onto his knees, unsteadily. The boy clung on, throwing Mo's balance off. The little girl eyed Tish for second, an appraising stare, then threw her arms around his torso – a clear indication that Mo was hers and that Tish had best 'back off'! Mo swayed, encased in his child sandwich, and grinned. 'Hi. You came.'

She nodded at this obvious statement of the truth. 'I can see you're a bit busy.'

Both of the kids were competing for his attention. 'Again. Again!' the boy shouted, obviously worried that Tish's appearance was going to put an end to their game.

'It's my go. You promised,' the little girl wailed.

'This is Fatima and her brother, Fahad. My cousins,' Mo said apologetically. Tish shrugged, indicating that it was fine with her for Mo to continue with his babysitting duties. She perched on the sofa. Mo peeled the boy off him and resumed the correct 'horsey' position for the little girl. Fahad, disgusted at being ousted, stomped off into the corner, where he sat cross-legged, his back to the room, muttering to himself.

The little girl was shorter than her brother, and this made it more of a challenge for her to get up onto 'the horse', added to which Mo kept deliberately dipping and arching his back. Her frowning frustration was funny, but Tish could see that she was beginning to get genuinely upset. Though she didn't like kids, and had little desire to touch this small, sweaty, ferocious square of a child, she went over and hauled the little girl up onto Mo's back. Once there, Fatima grabbed fistfuls of his T-shirt, trying to steady herself. When she was settled, she slapped her chubby thighs hard against his torso. In response, Mo snorted like a thoroughbred and set off around the room.

The child immediately slipped sideways. Her face froze in panic – which forced Tish to spend the next twenty minutes walking alongside her, holding her safe in her imaginary saddle.

Half an hour later the kids finally let Mo bribe them into submission with biscuits, juice and cartoons – though they refused to sit on the same sofa together, sibling rivalry extending as far as the seating arrangements. Mo and Tish stood in the kitchen, keeping an eye on them through the open door.

Tish sipped her juice. They were all on the blackcurrant squash. How much her evenings had changed! 'You're good with them.'

Mo pushed his hair back off his forehead. 'They're here quite a lot. Mum helps my Auntie Saima out. She works shifts.'

'And tonight you got the short straw?'

'Mum and Dad had to go to a "thing", at the council. Something about the new housing estate they're building at the back of the house. I didn't listen, to be honest.' He drank half of his glass of juice in a few swallows. 'I don't mind them coming around. It's kinda nice. It livens the house up. I think my mum misses having little kids around.' He turned away to rinse his glass.

'Your sisters are older, aren't they?'

'Yep, Aisha works for a marketing company down in Leicester; and Laila is in her last year at uni – on for a First. Mum and Dad are "so proud".' He made air quotes with his fingers.

'I'm sure they're proud of you as well.'

Mo looked away, focused on the kids. The twang of the cartoon soundtrack filled, but didn't cover up his lack of response.

'Mo?' Tish reached out and touched his bare arm, uncertain why the mood had changed.

He smiled at her, but it wasn't the usual full-beam grin that he normally gave her. 'Not so much lately – given what's been going on. The crash. All the publicity. The police. It's not been good. They don't say anything, but I know how uncomfortable it all makes them. But at least there isn't going to an actual trial now. My mum and dad would've hated that. Me having to give evidence…Us, I mean. Right in the middle of the exams. Not that's it's especially bad for me. That's not what I meant.'

'I know what you meant. I'm glad we don't have to take the stand, either. But even if we had been forced to, it wouldn't have been too bad. We are all just caught up in it. And you – you weren't directly involved.' He didn't look convinced. She ploughed on. 'You've got nothing to be ashamed of. Nothing to feel bad about.'

'So you said.'

The echo of the fight at McDonald's shimmered between them. He looked her full in the face.

'It wasn't anything to do with you,' Tish repeated.

'But it was. Whatever was on my phone...that's what set Harry off.' Mo paused. 'I've never seen him like that before.' He faltered, not wanting to upset her, but unable to stop, now that he'd finally said something. 'Tish, what did I film that I shouldn't have? I still don't know. The police won't tell me. They say it's part of the evidence. And Harry won't talk to me. But it's driving me insane. And I do feel guilty. Whatever it was that got into Harry that night – and whether it made any difference to how he drove or not – it did start with me. Do you know what was on my phone?'

'Don't, Mo,' Tish warned.

At that moment the cartoon in the other room changed and the kitchen was filled with the sound of an elephant trumpeting. Mo reached across Tish and pulled the door nearly shut. 'Tish? Please?'

Her voice, when she did eventually speak, was brisk, dismissive. 'Mo. You have to trust me. I'm telling you...it wasn't your fault. You've got to forget about it. Put the crash behind you. Use that huge brain of yours, concentrate on your exams and pass with straight As. Then you can bugger off to Liverpool and leave all this mess behind.'

As much as he wanted to drop it – to climb back inside the haven of their weird, out-of-hours, separate-from-everything-else friendship – Mo couldn't. He had loyalties, and not just to her. 'But what about Harry?'

Tish's face lost some of its softness. Her mouth tightened. 'He was driving, that's why it's coming down on him. There's nothing we can do about that. Even if we wanted to.'

'But he never meant for it to end the way it did. You know that. You know Harry better than I do.' She stiffened, but Mo pushed on, risking it. 'He wouldn't hurt anyone deliberately. It was an accident.' Her harshness was confusing.

'Mo, there was no one else on the road. No one crashed into us. He drove off the road, slap bang into a wall.' Tish touched her jawline, whether consciously or unconsciously, it was hard to say. Her scars were reminders that would never go away. 'Besides, it's the police who have decided to prosecute him, not us. They must think he was to blame, or they wouldn't be going after him for it. I refuse to feel bad about Harry, on top of everything else. You mustn't, either.'

Mo hated the pull of sympathies in his gut, and the shade of doubt that crept over him every time he thought about Tish and Harry. Her avoidance of talking about anything to do with that night, or about Harry, only served to sharpen his ill ease. He really wanted to leave it. But he didn't. 'Was it drugs? At the party?'

She pushed away from the work surface. 'Mo. Please. I don't want to talk about it. I'd best be off.'

He didn't want her to go. He wanted to snatch back all his questions, go back to the light-hearted silliness of horsing around with the kids. 'Stay. Please. I'm sorry, I didn't mean to upset you.' But he'd blown it and he knew it.

'Nah. I'm gonna head home.'

He saw Tish to the door and watched her walk away, without looking back. Then, because what else could he do, he went back to his babysitting duties.

Chapter 47

MARTHA DIDN'T recognise the person who walked into their kitchen on the morning of the court hearing, though she knew it was her big brother. 'Suited and booted.' She didn't know why that phrase popped into her head. Yes, she did. It was a Fran phrase. It was from the last time she'd seen Harry looking so smart. Prom night. Fran had used it as they stood together on the patio, watching Harry and his friends swanking around in the back garden in the sunshine. Harry had looked sharp that evening – the best-looking by far. Mr Popular, surrounded by his friends. Confident. Relaxed. It was the day Fran got her to take the photos, a perfect moment captured, for ever.

Harry made himself a coffee and drank it, without speaking. They listened to their dad moving around in his study, on the phone. He was always on the phone. Martha was aware that these last few minutes with her brother were important. They could be their last alone together for a long time, because, much as she wanted to be, she wasn't convinced by her dad's reassurances. This might very well be Harry's last taste of home and freedom, and therein lay the pressure. She didn't know what to say to the stranger that Harry had become – the man in an expensive jacket and dark trousers; a stranger with blank eyes who was about to go to court for killing one friend and maiming two others. She desperately needed Harry to help her. But he didn't.

'Are you all right?' It was a pathetic question, but it was all she could manage.

'Yup.'

'Sure?'

'Yup.'

She couldn't leave it at that. 'It'll be okay. Dad's confident you'll be coming home with us. Afterwards.'

He looked at her, finally. 'Yeah. Let's hope so.'

Martha could hear the lack of conviction in his voice. It frightened her. 'I love you,' she blurted out.

Harry smiled. 'I love you, too.' He put his mug in the sink. Walked over to her. Hugged her as if he was trying to break her ribs, then said, 'Tell Dad I'll see him in the car.'

Harry sat in the front and Martha in the back. She had insisted on coming to the hearing, despite Dom trying to dissuade her. That had necessitated an excruciating phone call to her school to inform them that she would be absent for the day. They hadn't needed to ask the reason; they already knew. The secretary had the cheek to inform Dom that it would have to go down as an 'unauthorised absence'. Dom had almost laughed. Almost, but not quite. There was nothing funny about the situation they found themselves in.

They were meeting Ross and his team in the lobby at the courthouse. Dom had phoned the solicitor one last time before setting off. To his credit, Ross himself had taken the call. But there was nothing he could do at this late stage, other than reiterate to Dom that everything was in order and that, from the indications he'd been getting – he didn't clarify from whom – leniency was going to be shown.

As Dom drove, he didn't speak. He and Harry had gone too many rounds over his decision to plead guilty to have anything left to say, but that didn't mean Dom had let it go. Today could have been the start of Harry's defence, the fight to exonerate him. Instead it was going to be a public sanctioning of his guilt, and a meting-out of his punishment. A done deal. No opportunity for a different result. They would never know what the alternative could have been, because Harry had refused to roll the dice. He'd caved. That display of weakness or fear – whatever it was – was eating away at Dom. It ran contrary to every instinct within him, to let other people decide your fate. His son had obviously inherited very little from him. It was as if Harry wanted the humiliation and the punishment. He really didn't seem to care about what his guilty plea meant for himself, or for anyone else. Dom couldn't even blame Adele – and, sitting on his own with a whisky many a night, he had tried.

They drove down the ramp into the underground car park, trading bright sunshine for grey gloom. It seemed an appropriate transition.

Chapter 48

IT WAS what Harry expected, but the speed with which he was sentenced and removed from the court was a shock.

In the weeks leading up to the hearing, his legal team had talked him through what would happen. They had prepared him for a number of different outcomes – a suspended sentence, a driving ban, community service, reparations to the families of the victims, a custodial sentence – with 'optimistic' minimums and 'worst-case scenario' maximums. They had also explained that, because he had turned eighteen, any custodial sentence (should one be handed down) would have to be served in a prison, rather than a young offenders' institution.

Well, a custodial sentence was no longer 'a possibility'.

It was a fact.

He'd been sentenced to four years. Six months had been taken off his term, because of his cooperation with the police investigation and his guilty plea. With good behaviour, it would be less. Ross had said they normally halved the tariff. So that would make it, *optimistically*, a two-year sentence. It was doable. It was going to have to be.

Was it appropriate? Was it fair? Or was it a travesty, given the damage he had caused? Harry didn't know. But as they led him out of the court room, away from the blur of faces and the raised voices, his overwhelming emotion had been shame. Fran had been shouting; his sister crying; Dom already raising objections. There was such a confusion of reactions that no one seemed to pay much attention to him being 'taken down'.

They put him in a holding cell somewhere in the rabbit warren basement of the building. Harry sat on the bench and waited. He was going to prison. Now. This very afternoon. This cell was his first taste of what his life was going to be like for the foreseeable future. Harry knew that if he thought about it too much, he would panic, so he chose not to. He counted the whitewashed bricks instead. They brought him a ham sandwich, a bag of crisps and a bottle of water. He ate his lunch without tasting it. He'd heard that prison food was bad. This thought, popping into his head, made him snort out loud. His capacity to still bother about irrelevant, selfish things, at the same time as his life imploded, really was quite staggering. The quality of the food inside was going to be the least of his worries.

As the afternoon wore on, he heard others being brought down. With each set of footsteps, his anxiety increased. When one of the sets of footsteps ended outside his cell, his mouth went dry, but when the door swung open, it was his dad standing in the doorway. The officer accompanying him nodded and walked away.

Seeing his father step into the cell was a surreal experience. The officer left the door open. Harry must not have been considered a flight risk. Dom's eyes swung round the tiny space. The only place to sit was on the ledge next to Harry. Dom picked up the sandwich wrapper and the empty crisp packet and sat down. There was no bin. He cleared his throat, but didn't say anything. For the first time in his life Harry realised that his dad was at a loss. There was nothing Dom could do: no calls he could make, no one he could bawl out, no higher authority he could appeal to – that would make the slightest bit of difference to what was about to happen. He eventually summoned up a question. 'How are you holding up?' His voice was loud, ill-suited to such a confined space. Harry worried that the other prisoners might hear. Privacy, that was another thing he had sacrificed.

'Not bad.' Harry said, putting on a brave face. It was the only way to go – the only way he was going to get through the next couple of years.

'They said it was okay for me to come in to have a word with you, just for a few minutes. It's not normally allowed.' His dad, swinging his dick – old habits died hard.

'Yeah. So I see.' Harry, being a dick back to his dad – another old habit.

Dom didn't bite. He compressed the rubbish in his hands. 'Bit of a shock, the sentence. Especially after everything Ross said.' It hadn't been a shock to Harry. 'The judge obviously decided to make an example of you.'

'I was expecting it.'

Dom chose to ignore Harry's comment. 'Ross has reassured me that they'll reduce it. He said they want people like you out pretty quickly. If you keep your nose clean and your head down.'

'People *like me*?'

'You know what I mean.'

'Do you know what, Dad – I'm not sure I do.'

'Please. Harry. Not now. They'll be taking you away soon. I don't want our last conversation to be an argument.'

'You still don't get it, do you? Prison *is* for people *like me*. What were you expecting? A slap on the wrist? A fine? This isn't something you can tidy away.'

'It was an accident.'

'Which I caused.'

'Oh, for fuck's sake!' Dom got up, but there was no space to pace. 'Stop! Just stop with the martyrdom, will you? This whole time – this hair-shirt routine. It's so sodding self-indulgent. While you've been wallowing, it's been me who's been fighting on your behalf. Me who's been spending time and energy, and a considerable amount of money, trying to keep you out of prison.'

'Well, that's not gone to plan, has it?'

Dom paused, blinked, looked down at Harry. 'Tell me, Harry, how come I'm the enemy?'

Harry, as so often, when confronted by his father's impatience, hunkered down behind his old defences: defiance and stubbornness. It left them trapped. For a few seconds they both said nothing. Further down the corridor a door banged. They both flinched.

'Is this it, then?' Harry asked.

'What are you talking about?'

'You said "our last conversation". Aren't you going to come and see me when I'm inside?'

Dom looked at Harry and slowly shook his head. He seemed about to say something, but decided against it. There were more footsteps and voices out in the corridor – another defendant being brought down from the afternoon session. Possibly the last one? The officer reappeared at the cell door. Time for the wagons to come and take them away.

'Of course I'll come. You're my son.'

It wasn't the sort of statement for which there seemed an appropriate response. Harry stood up. Time to say 'goodbye'. They faced each other.

'Take care of yourself. Don't let anyone push you around, but keep out of stuff as much as you can. It's just a case of getting through it and coming out the other side. You'll be okay. I'm sure you will. I'll be up to see you as soon as I can.' Then – if ever – a hug would have helped them both. Instead Dom stuck out his hand. And even in those last few seconds together, after all that had happened, his dad still couldn't resist asserting his dominance. When they shook hands Dom's grip was the firmer of the two.

Chapter 49

MARCUS NOTICED the burn on Fran's hand when they were in the car. He didn't mention it. It wasn't fresh. The skin was already healing. But it must have hurt when she first did it; the skin on the top of your hand is thin. Fran drove silently, cautiously, changing up and down the gears with laborious thoroughness. The trip had been at his instigation. They needed something to mark the end of the court process. After the endless months of waiting, it was finally over, the case against Harry made, the victim statements submitted, the judge's deliberations delivered, the sentence handed down. It was at an end. Harry was in prison. But Marcus knew it wasn't going to be that easy, especially for Fran.

Fat splats of rain started hitting the windscreen. Fran switched on the wipers. The blades smeared back and forth across the windscreen, making the visibility intermittent. He should have noticed that she'd burnt her hand. He would've done in the past. But they were so rarely in the same room at the same time any more. They were losing track of each other, literally. What they needed was time together, if there was any chance that their relationship was going to heal. Hence this trip to a place where they were guaranteed not to be disturbed or observed. No one else they knew had cause to be in the cemetery on a wet Saturday morning. They parked and walked up the path side-by-side, the only noise the sound of the rain hitting their coats. Jess's plot still struck a raw note amongst the mellowed dead.

They both knew Jess wasn't really here, but it was all they had as a destination. They stood and stared at the block of expensive marble. White, with black lettering. Marcus had known he would struggle to think of the right thing to say. That was the way it was between them now. They couldn't talk about Jess and, because there wasn't anything *but* Jess, they barely talked to each other at all. His attempts at even everyday conversation seemed to irritate Fran. It was as if his ability to notice that they were out of milk, or that the car was due its MOT, revealed a lack of respect. Weeks back, when he'd been foolish enough to risk a comment about his Year 10 classes being difficult, it had been met with not just a blank stare, but a look of hostility. Fran's furious mourning brooked no normality. That had to change. The court had punished Harry. It was enough for Marcus; it had to be, he couldn't face any more grief.

They had to move forward. There was nothing else hanging over them – except the rest of their lives. Marcus desperately wanted things to change. He'd never felt this degree of loneliness before. It was like suffocating, a plastic bag wrapped round his head, while Fran sat and watched. Hence his hope that a quiet moment, facing the tangible evidence of their shared loss, might help to unite them.

The rain grew heavier, but neither of them moved. Marcus looked at Fran, willing her to look at him, but she blocked him and continued staring at the headstone. His commitment wavered. This had been a bad idea. A grave, in the rain, was not the place to start to rebuild.

She surprised him by speaking first. 'Do you ever think about the recipients?'

Marcus knew instantly what she meant – the people who had received Jess's heart, her lungs, her kidneys and other tissues. The Donation Service had sent them a letter thanking them and confirming the number of 'procedures' that had been made possible by Jess's death, and their sanctioning of Jess's decision to donate. The letter sat in the rack in the dining room. Proof of life beyond death.

'Sometimes.' Marcus rationed such thoughts. They were too painful.

Fran wiped rain from her cheek. 'I try and imagine what it must be like to be on the other side of the equation...Being close to someone whose life has been transformed by what we allowed. I think about them getting the call to say that an organ has finally been found. The joy, the relief. How it must feel if it's your child who gets the chance to survive. I always visualise someone young. Someone good. Someone deserving. Most often I think of a girl. Jess's age, with her whole life ahead of her. I know that's not likely to be true, but it's what I imagine.'

Marcus watched the rain slide down the headstone, the drops catching in the chiselled cuts of Jess's name and the dates of her birth and her death. 'She would've been proud of us, I think. That we supported her decision and that we managed to go through with it. She wouldn't have wanted to waste what she had to give.'

'I know.' Fran reached out and took his hand. 'It's the only good thing to come out of all this misery.'

He held her hand, gently, conscious of the burn. 'Not just one good thing, Fran. Eight amazing things. Eight desperate people – and their families and all their friends. Hundreds of people's lives transformed by our Jess.' She turned into him and he put his arms around her, and they stood in the rain paying homage to their daughter.

Chapter 50

SAL WAS surprised to see Mo walk into the shop. Most eighteen-year-old boys didn't have much call for DIY products.

'Hi.'

'Hi.' He didn't say anything else.

'Can I help you with something?' She smiled to prompt him. His relationship with Tish puzzled and fascinated Sal. Chalk and cheese. But he was good for her, there was no denying that.

He gathered himself. 'I wanted to ask your permission for something. I'd like to take Tish out for the day.'

The old fashioned formality of it made Sal want to laugh, but she smothered the instinct when she saw that he was serious. 'Okay.'

'It's just...I'd like it to be on her actual birthday. That's why I thought I should ask. I didn't know what you might have planned. Tish hasn't mentioned anything.'

They hadn't anything special planned. How sad was that? Tish's eighteenth birthday and there wasn't going to be a party, no 'rite of passage' night out in town, buying her first legal drink. Tish hadn't even asked for anything specific as a gift. Sal understood.

'No. We were going celebrate at home in the evening when I got back from work.'

'Oh. Okay. So might it be all right for me to take Tish out during the day?'

He really was a kind lad. 'Sure.'

But Mo wasn't finished. 'The trouble is…it would probably end up being for most of the day.'

'Well, it's up to Tish really. You'll have to ask her. It's fine with me.'

He hesitated. 'The thing is…I wanted it to be a surprise.'

'Okay.' Sal was touched by his thoughtfulness, but at the same time she was worried. Mo was such a serious lad. Tish might not want a full day with him and whatever he had planned.

'I'd have to call for her at eight-thirty a.m.'

'In the morning!' Sal exclaimed.

That's when he did smile, a proper full-on grin. 'Yeah, I know, she's going to love me for that, isn't she? That's why I thought you might be able to help.' He screwed up his face – comic contrition. 'Maybe pretend that she had to be ready for something?'

'You want me to wake her up early, tell her to get ready to leave the house by half-eight, on her birthday?'

His smile wavered. 'Yeah. Sorry. But I know she'd want to have enough time. It would spoil it, if she felt rushed and not ready.'

Sal knew what he meant. It took Tish twice as long to do her make-up these days. Mo's awareness of her daughter impressed Sal. 'And what do you suggest I tell her?'

'I don't know.'

'Thanks for that. So I get the joy of coming up with a credible excuse for dragging her out of bed at the crack of dawn, and you get to arrive and whisk her off for her birthday treat, like her knight in shining armour!'

Mo grinned. 'Yep.'

He was hard to resist. 'Sounds fair enough to me.'

'Thank you. Oh, and I don't think we'll be back until about eight p.m. Is that okay?'

'Looks like it's going to have to be, doesn't it?' They were both smiling by now. 'So, where are you planning on taking Tish for her big birthday surprise?'

When Mo told her that he was going to take Tish for a day at the seaside, Sal gave up masking her feelings and had a little cry. For a change, they were happy tears.

Chapter 51

FRAN WAS making an effort and cooking a proper meal. When Marcus got in from his parents' evening they would sit at the table, eat together and have a conversation about their respective days, exchanging snippets of news and bothering to tell anecdotes. It was all part of their new commitment to get 'back on top of things'. Work, the house, their relationship – the day-to-day stuff they'd been neglecting for months – focusing their energy into something constructive. She had promised Marcus, and herself, that she would try; and so she was.

It looked like beetroot juice, spreading across the chopping board. She traced her finger through it, creating patterns. Who knew that scraping carrots could be so dangerous? On automatic pilot, she walked over to the sink and ran the cold tap. After a few minutes the numbness in her fingers began to hurt. She kept her hand under the stream of water. The blood continued to seep through her grated skin.

She had been knocking and chopping chunks out of herself a lot recently. It was careless of her. There was still an ugly bruise on her left shin, which she'd got from banging into the edge of the bed when she was changing it – another positive chore, stripping and washing all the bedding, except in Jess's room. That she hadn't been able to face. Fran turned off the tap and reached for a square of kitchen roll. She wrapped it loosely around her finger. Instantly it flushed a light, wet pink. The bleeding would stop when it stopped. Skin was like that; it healed in its own time. She left the dinner prep and went through to the lounge. While she waited for the scrape to stop seeping, she decided to permit herself a small indulgence. Even good wives, who were working really hard on their recovery, were allowed to spend some time on the treasure trove that was YouTube.

She clicked onto the next film in the series. It was fascinating to see how the confrontations played out. The uncomfortable clashes between the victims and their families and the people who had committed the crimes. Fran watched each film all the way through to the end of the credits, sucked into the drama, the anger, the excuses, the sense of unfairness, and the very different reactions of the victims to the perpetrators' remorse. Many of the videos were re-enactments based on the transcripts of actual meetings. What she was listening to was real dialogue, real emotions. Sitting with the laptop open on her knee, in her spot on the carpet, in the corner of the room, Fran felt alive in a way that she seldom did any more. The people in these films had more in common with her than anyone she met in day-to-day life. They knew and echoed her pain. Time flew as she watched their stories. And it never normally did that.

The film she'd chosen today was about a manslaughter case, where a young lad had died after being punched in the head on a night out – one drunken punch and that was it: a life snuffed out. The footage ended, and the contact details for the Restorative Justice Service appeared on the screen. Fran pressed pause. It took her a few seconds to re-root herself back into her own front room. The calmness of the victim's mother, her willingness to listen and, ultimately, to forgive the brutish-looking older man who had killed her son, was awe-inspiring. Fran sat and contemplated the strength and depth of character that it must take to respond like that.

Unconsciously her fingers sought out the patch of damaged carpet. They had told Jess time and time again not to paint her nails in the front room, or at least if she was going to do it there, to put the polish down somewhere safe. But, of course, in one ear and out the other. 'Iridescent Indigo' was not an easy colour to get out of a pale grey carpet. The nail polish remover that Jess had unwisely used to lift the stain had only served to fuse the carpet fibres together, making the damage even more noticeable. Why she needed her toenails painting in January in the first place, Fran hadn't understood. It wasn't as if anyone was going to be looking at her bare feet in the middle of winter. Fran ran her fingertips across the carpet. The bald patch was now one of her anchor points in the house.

The details for the Restorative Justice Service were still onscreen. She fetched a pen and paper and copied them down. She put the scrap of paper away in her purse, closed down YouTube, went back into the kitchen and picked up her carrot peeler. The scrape on her knuckles had stopped bleeding.

Over dinner, she and Marcus talked about work and the weather, like two people who had a normal life. She supposed it was an achievement that, to a casual observer, it might look as if they actually did. They watched TV and went to bed. And in the morning they got up and started all over again.

The contact details stayed hidden away in her handbag. They whispered to her every time she went to pay for something or took out her car keys. But she was disciplined, committed to weaning herself off her 'addiction'. She had promised Marcus. She kept herself busy and on-track – for three whole days.

She sent the email from her work computer on the Friday afternoon – as she'd known she was going to do, from the moment she wrote down the contact details. No, that wasn't true. She'd known she was going to reach out to the service from the very first day she'd stumbled across the videos and discovered there was a way to get in to see Harry. Once she'd made that discovery, there had been no chance that her promise to Marcus, and herself, was going to survive.

She asked the Restorative Justice Service to contact her by email, not by phone or via any correspondence to the house. She was only making initial enquiries, after all. There was no need for Marcus to know. Not yet. That awkward conversation would come only if – only when – she succeeded in setting up her own version of restoration.

Chapter 52

MARCUS SAW that he had a missed call from Joe, their liaison officer, in the middle of his Year 9 class, but had to wait until break time to call him back. Joe had done his job well, been considerate and conscientious in his dealings with them, but Marcus associated him with all that was bad, so putting a call into Joe made him feel anxious.

Joe asked after them both, and Marcus gave the appropriate answers. Then Joe explained his real reason for phoning. 'I wanted to let you know that Jess's personal effects have been passed on to me. They've released everything now. I was wondering if you would like them returned?'

The answer, of course, was 'yes'. Marcus's inventory of his daughter was incomplete. 'Yes. We want her things back. Why has this taken so long?'

Joe sighed. 'As we've spoken about before, Marcus, a police investigation prioritises the collation of evidence to secure a prosecution. I'm afraid that means the feelings of victims and their families aren't always taken into consideration as much as they should be. Jess's things were catalogued and bagged as potential evidence at the hospital – it's standard procedure. In the end, even though her belongings weren't deemed relevant to the case, we still had to wait until there was a resolution before releasing them. Hence the delay. I'm very sorry.'

Marcus brushed away his apology.

Joe went on. 'Marcus, I also wanted to speak to you directly, to warn you about the condition of some of Jess's belongings.' He stopped, obviously considering his choice of words. 'I just want you to be prepared. There is quite a lot of damage to her clothing. I thought, perhaps, that you might prefer us to keep the clothes. Dispose of them for you?'

Marcus listened to some kids racketing down the corridor outside his classroom, crashing through the fire doors. Their shouts had faded away before he replied. 'Be specific, Joe.'

He heard the crackle of a parcel. Jesus! Joe had her things there, in front him.

'The dress is the worst. They had to cut it off, and there is some blood staining. Though it may not all be Jess's blood.' Marcus felt clammy. 'I'm sorry, Marcus, but I thought it best to tell you. And I'm anxious that Fran isn't exposed to any more trauma. Though that is obviously your call.'

Marcus heard himself say, 'Yes, quite.' He took a breath, composed himself. 'I want it all.'

'Okay. If you're sure.'

Joe left a gap, presumably for Marcus to change his mind. He didn't.

Joe went on, 'I can send everything over, or I'd be happy to drop the parcel round on my way home after work one night, if that suits you.'

'No!' Marcus realised he had been too brusque.

Joe went all stuttery. 'Sorry, I didn't put that well, Marcus. I obviously didn't mean "happy".'

Marcus made a colossal effort. 'There's no need to apologise, Joe. We appreciate everything you've done for us. You have been a great help, but I'd prefer to come and collect her things myself, if you don't mind. I'll call round to the station tonight after work, if I can.'

'Oh. Okay.'

Marcus was about to end the call when Joe stopped him.

'Marcus.'

'Yes.'

'Don't forget to bring some form of ID with you.'

Marcus sat, unmoving, too battered by the experiences of the past few months to be shocked any more. So he could finally have his daughter's possessions back, but first he would have to prove that he was her father.

Chapter 53

TISH'S MUM had been as good as her word. Tish was ready and waiting, and grumpy as sin, when Mo arrived.

Not any more.

It was fab. Even better than he'd hoped...and he'd had high hopes. He'd not seen her this happy for weeks – no, for months, not since before the accident – which had been the plan all along. To make Tish laugh, make her forget everything, just for one glorious day. That was his birthday gift. The fact that it was working was making Mo feel good as well. More than good. He felt relaxed, high, giddy.

The wind blowing in off the sea was keeping most of the other day-trippers off the beach, so they had it almost to themselves. He hadn't run and laughed so much since he'd been little. Now they were lying on the sand, chests heaving, recovering. And this was only the beginning. They had all day in Scarborough; another eight hours together, on their own. As they lay watching the seagulls being flung around the clear blue sky, Mo felt a glorious sense of freedom. For the first time in his life he understood the appeal of running away, buying a ticket to somewhere and leaving everything and everyone behind – his family, uni, the weight of expectations, everything. It might be possible, tempting even, if...if you had the person you cared most about in the whole world with you.

'Now what?' Tish asked.

'Whatever you want. It's your day.'

She rolled onto her side and he matched her. They created a cave against the sea breeze. 'Thank you.'

'You're welcome.'

'No, I mean it. Really. For organising it all.'

'It's not over yet.'

'That is very true.' Tish used her free hand to brush a strand of hair away from her face. It took all of his control not to lean forward and kiss her. He wanted to *so* badly, but he didn't want to screw it up, and kissing her could – probably would – totally wreck the mood. They looked at each other for a couple of seconds.

'How about I give you your present now?' He had been saving up giving it to her for the right moment.

Tish laughed. 'A present as well!' She sat up, excited.

He sat opposite her, their knees touching. Mo's heart thudded. He reached into his bag and took out the carefully wrapped little box.

'You're spoiling me!' She untied the ribbon that he'd spent ten minutes tying into as close an approximation of a decent bow as he could manage. He was pleased to see her wind the ribbon around her finger as a keepsake. When she opened the box he couldn't see her face, but her body went still.

The pressure of wanting her to like his gift got to him and he started blabbing. 'I know you wear the one you've got on most of the time, but I thought it was pretty.'

She looked up, and for a moment he was worried that he'd upset her because she looked tearful. 'It's lovely, thank you.' She lifted the silver chain out of the box, the crystal twisting in the breeze. 'Here, hold it for me.' She passed him the chain, then lifted her hands behind her neck, unfastening the necklace she was wearing – the one with the little silver seahorse charm.

Mo felt flustered. 'It's okay. You don't have to put it on now.'

But she'd already unfastened the chain and dropped it into the box. Then she turned round and lifted her hair clear of her neck. 'Put it on for me.'

With fumbling fingers, Mo fastened the fiddly clasp. It took him a few attempts, his fingers brushing the tiny hairs on the nape of her neck, sending shivers down his spine.

Necklace fastened, she leant back against him, looking down at his gift. 'Thank you. I love it.' She rested her head against his shoulder.

'Happy birthday, Tish.' Mo hugged her, wondering if she could feel his heart thumping against her back.

She stared out to sea, and Mo was happy just to be there, his arms around her – her windbreak. After a few minutes the energy in her body changed and she turned to him. The wistful mood was gone, replaced by childlike excitement. She grinned. 'Okay. As it's my special day, this is what "Princess Tish" wants. She wants – in this order – to paddle.'

He pulled a face. 'It's gonna be freezing. It's the North Sea.'

'No arguing. We paddle and, ideally, you fall over in the waves and get soaked. We skim stones, and I get mine to bounce further than yours. Then we go and get fish and chips with mushy peas and loads of salt and vinegar. Then we go to the arcades, and I win the jackpot on the fruit machines. Then we play bingo, like an old couple, and we stay until I get to shout "House". And I pick something really crappy out of the cabinet that's full of prizes that haven't changed since 1970.'

She continued her list, counting out her demands on her fingers like a six year old. 'And, being the bountiful princess that I am, I'll give my fabulous prize to a little old lady in a straw hat who hasn't had a win all afternoon. Then we'll walk along to the funfair near the harbour – arm-in-arm, I think – and we'll go on whatever rides I choose. The Waltzers are compulsory. Possibly twice, depending on how sick we get. Then we go on the bumper cars and we take out a couple of snotty kids who look at us a *bit wrong*.' She grinned and put up her hand to stop any interruptions. 'No! They'll have asked for it. You're never too young, or too thick, to learn that it's rude to stare. Then – and this is where you actually get a say in something – you pick either a shooting gallery or one of those grabber things with the claws that never work properly, and you win me an enormous cuddly toy that I carry around for the rest of the day.'

He loved her. It was a simple as that. 'Okay.'

'Okay.' She laughed. 'Come on then.' And she scrambled to her feet, put out her hand, pulled him up and they set off running down to the sea.

'How could I forget candy floss?' They were leaning against the railings, eating spun sugar. At least Tish was eating it. Mo was pulling off the smallest lumps he could manage. The stuff had the texture and taste of fibreglass.

It was chilly now. The sea was crumping on the sand. The light above the bay was tinged pink. Tish's shoulder was touching his. Mo felt happier and sadder than he had ever felt in his life. They had to go. Their train was in half an hour.

Tish stretched and dropped the remains of the candy floss into a nearby bin. She licked her fingers. Mo thought his heart was going to burst.

She smiled at him. 'Thank you. It's been perfect.'

He forced a smile back. 'You're welcome.'

She held his gaze, leant forward and kissed him.

His heart didn't burst, but it felt like it might.

Chapter 54

THEY WERE spending more time together, eating meals, talking about work, watching TV, doing the weekly shop and the chores around the house. All the normal stuff that couples did, which was good, but it didn't make it better. The two of them simply weren't enough. What frightened Marcus was his growing certainty that they never would be; that he and Fran would never be able to fill their life on their own. There was such a strong sense of unreality about it. They were both self-conscious in their own skins. It was if they were play-acting their marriage, their jobs and their lives. And it was so tiring. When one or the other of them cautiously suggested time apart, the other always agreed, immediately. And the relief he felt on the weekends when Fran went out on one of her long walks or chose to shop alone was depressingly acute. When she left, he was free. Today that relief was even more acute than ever.

He had, as arranged, gone to the police station after work on Thursday evening. He'd presented himself and his ID to the woman at the front desk and, after a delay of ten minutes, had been handed a bulky parcel with his name written on the front in black Sharpie. The parcel was passed over to him without any ceremony or comment. He walked out carrying it under his arm, put it in the boot of his car and drove home. He didn't bring it into the house, though he lay in bed, sleepless, thinking about it for hours that night. The guilt had been terrible – not that he hadn't said a word to Fran, but because Jess's belongings were outside, in the dark, in the cold boot of his car.

He fetched the package into the house the following morning as soon Fran left for work. The dilemma of where to put it was easily resolved. Jess's things needed to go in Jess's room. He pushed the parcel under her bed, just to be on the safe side. Not that Fran ever went into Jess's room. She couldn't bear to. It was his domain.

The minute Fran left for the library on Saturday morning – another of her new habits, all part of her 'research' – Marcus went up to Jess's room and pulled the parcel out. He sat down on the bed with it on his knee. He took a few deep breaths, then he said 'Hello' out loud. The first few words were always the hardest, but with practice he had got better. He no longer felt as shy as he once had, talking to Jess. He had found that it helped to begin with everyday stuff: the weather, the news headlines, a bit of politics always loosened him up. He and Jess arguing the same point endlessly, for the hell of it, was one of the thousands of little things he missed about her not being around. He spoke about Fran sparingly, just enough to reassure Jess that her mother was coping, but not enough to require him to actively lie. Of course Marcus knew that his one-sided conversations with his dead daughter in her bedroom weren't real; that Jess could no more answer him and give her consent to his snooping than she could rise up from the dead, walk back into their lives and yell at him for being such a mushy mess.

He also knew that the contents of the parcel were not going to help with his emotional state, but he believed they might help him better understand the secrets of Jess's private life. Up until this moment he'd been dealing with fragments. All he had was a small pile of things that might, or might not, have significance: a notebook that was not a diary, but a scatter of random jottings and doodles, and a load of photos of the people in her friendship group, only some of whom he knew. Some small gifts and the receipts that she'd so meticulously stored. It was a collection of hints and glimpses that had taken on huge significance because of the questions the police had asked, and repeated.

Marcus took another breath and spoke to Jess. 'The police got in touch a couple of days ago, sweetheart. They said we could finally have your things back.' He paused. 'From the night of the crash. They had to keep everything up until now, because of the court case. I hope you understand, but I am going to look through your stuff. You know that I wouldn't, normally, but now I feel I have to. I'm sorry.'

Wanting it to be over with, he pulled open the parcel. Inside the brown paper wrapping was a large evidence bag, which was sealed with a row of big staples. They made a tearing noise as he yanked the flap free. He upended the bag and Jess's things slid out. Each item was individually sealed in a plastic Ziploc bag. For a few moments he didn't touch anything. He felt hot with shame and dread. Nervously he picked up the bag with her clothes in. There was a tangle of pale blue fabric and white lace. Her dress and her underwear. The colours of her last night out, stained brown with patches of blood. He pushed the clothes back into the evidence bag. He couldn't bear to look at them.

He turned his attention to her shoes, her white Vans, no longer clean, but normally blemished, lived-in. These he liberated from their plastic prison. He held them to his chest for a few minutes. The last shoes she ever wore, except for the pair of green Converse that she'd been cremated in. Carefully and lovingly, he added her scruffy trainers to the collection in the bottom of her wardrobe. Home at last. With tears sliding silently down his cheeks, he carefully returned everything else to its rightful place. The hairbrush, still clogged with strands of Jess's hair, to the shelf near her mirror; her lip balm to her make-up bag; her purse and an open pack of tissues to the top drawer of her bedside cabinet; her bag to the hook on the back of the door. Which left him with only one Ziploc wallet to open. The bag with her phone inside. The real reason he'd asked for her belongings back.

Marcus knew that Jess's life was stored on her phone and that, if he looked through it, he would read and see things she'd never intended for his eyes, or anyone else's. But he also knew that her phone was the key to his daughter's secrets. The need to know was stronger than the shame. He wiped his face with his sleeve and cleared his throat. 'I hope you understand why I'm doing this, sweetheart. I know it's wrong, invading your privacy. But we never got to speak, did we? We never got to say anything to each other at the end – not even goodbye. I never got to tell you how much I admire you. And that I will always love you. And that's not right, is it, love? I would never normally look at your messages, but now…well, now it's different. I can't not. I'm sorry. Please forgive me.'

He picked up the bag with her phone in and opened it. Her life lay in the palm of his hand. Pandora's box.

But it remained closed to him. Because even as he went to press the On button he knew the battery would be dead. The screen stayed dark. Of course it did. What was he thinking? He leant down, caught hold of Jess's charger cable and plugged in her phone.

Chapter 55

JAKE WAS in town, shopping for a new top – he was going on a night out with his brothers, and he couldn't have Sonny looking sharper than him. He felt better than he had for ages, physically and in other ways. He still liked having a good moan about having to drag himself out of bed at 5.50 a.m. every morning, but being back at work with the other lads was proving good for his soul and his bank balance. And – much as he appreciated what a rock his mum had been through the long months of his recovery – it was a relief to be away from her. His limp was still quite pronounced, but it was proving to be a good talking point. It certainly helped to get conversations started in bars, especially with the girls. They were always interested to hear about the crash and how awful his injuries had been.

He was just coming out of TK Maxx when he spotted Tish. She was standing outside WH Smith, looking at her phone. At the sight of her, Jake felt a stir of emotions. Tish had been his 'best' girlfriend – not only in his estimation, but in everyone else's. She was the hottest girl who'd ever let him get close, though not as close as he would've liked, and people assumed...not that anyone needed to know that. She'd been, if truth be told, a bit of a tease, happy to date, go out, have fun, flirt, snog, let him have a touch and a taste of her, but the moment he'd tried taking it further she'd always cut him off. If she hadn't looked the way she did – the way she *had* – he would probably have ended it with her, eventually. But he hadn't. And her looks weren't the whole story. Tish had also been good company; that's what had made it worthwhile. As Jake watched her scrolling through her phone, he remembered how funny she could be, how up for a laugh, a good night out – more like a mate really, except a mate with a hot body.

The accident had changed all that, of course, and he didn't just mean Tish's appearance – he wasn't that shallow a bastard. It was the whole painful, awful, messy aftermath. They'd both been too bashed up in the first few weeks after the crash, and by the time he'd started feeling better and Tish had got out of hospital, it had been too late. A few DMs were all they'd managed after Jess had died. Jake really hadn't known what to write. What was there to say about something so terrible? By the time they met up at Jess's funeral, it had been chronically awkward. At Harry's sentencing, they'd actively avoided each other.

But now, seeing Tish again, oblivious that he was watching her, Jake felt a strong urge to go over and say 'Hi'. Maybe he could see if she fancied going for a coffee. The thought of being able to give her a hug, talk to her, hear her laugh at one of his jokes appealed. Being normal together, it seemed possible, desirable. Friends again. That would be good. They'd known each other for so long. She looked up, scanned the crowds. Tight jeans, heeled boots. God, she looked good. Back, nearly, to the girl she'd been. A couple of guys walking past Tish checked her out. She didn't notice. Jake decided. Yep, he wanted to talk to her. Wanted her back in his life, as a friend – at the very least.

He ran a hand over his hair, double-checking it wasn't sticking up at the back, and stepped out of the shop doorway, intending to go over, reconnect.

He never got the chance.

Out of nowhere, Mo appeared. Tish saw Mo and, with a lift of her chin and a widening of her beautiful brown eyes, she smiled. Mo walked up to her and, to Jake's shock and dismay, they kissed. Not a peck on the cheek, either, but a full-on proper kiss. Then they turned and headed off, hand-in-hand, down Coney Street. Jake watched them, acutely aware that in all their time going out together, Tish had never once held his hand.

Chapter 56

MARCUS WAITED. The thought that the handset was one of the last things Jess had touched before she died haunted him, but there was no going back. He had to know. The screen came back to life. All her passwords and codes were written down on the inside cover of her notebook – neatly listed. He was 'in' within a few seconds. Where to start? He opted for a simple test. He scrolled through her messages to see who she'd been in touch with the most.

There were hundreds and hundreds of texts and photos. Marcus felt like he was travelling back in time. Jess's life and loves unravelled in front of his eyes in one endless, frantic, taunting loop.

After only a few seconds he knew who her boyfriend had been.

He sat back and let the confirmation sink in.

Harry.

Jess's lifelong friend, the kid who had been part of their lives for so long that he was like another member of the family. The boy who been on holiday with them, eaten countless meals in their kitchen, joked with Marcus, wound Jess up, turned to Fran for advice – *that* Harry – had, at some point, become more to Jess than just a friend. He had become the object of her passion and affection. Her jealously guarded secret.

Harry had been the love of her life, and the person who had killed her.

Fran! Christ! He pushed the thought away. He couldn't deal with that nightmare. Not yet.

Randomly he picked one of the messages and read it. It was daft nonsense about a teacher at college. He selected another. It was an exchange about some coursework. The next, a terrible joke about a frog. Had he got it wrong? Were they simply closer friends than he'd thought? No. The next message he read contained arrangements for meeting up one evening, including details of the lie they agreed she should tell, to cover up where she really was. He scrolled back in time – more 'hook-ups', more lies concocted. The sign-offs to each text left no space for doubt: Missing you, can't wait to be together; love you, love you back; thinking about you, can't wait till I see you again...And more: Sorry you were sad today, you can always talk to me. I'm here for you, I always will be. And worse: I want you, I need you, I love the feel of you, I want to—

He stopped. He couldn't read any more, didn't want to, but at the same time he did. He felt shoddy for invading Jess's most intimate thoughts and feelings, but couldn't put the phone down. He went to her photo gallery. There were thousands of images: people, food, drinks, clothes, places she'd visited, lots of shopping and laughing and hanging out and partying. Plenty of photos of her friends, many of whom he'd last seen at her funeral. But as he trawled through the gallery, he saw one face above all others – Harry. Harry and Jess, arms around each other. Harry on his own, looking broodingly handsome and absolutely a fully grown man, not the young lad of Marcus's frozen recollection. Harry in action, playing cricket. Since when did Jess ever go and watch cricket? Harry posing. Harry smiling. Harry goofing around. Harry serious, his eyes looking directly at the camera, and at Jess, and now – through the scratched phone screen – at Marcus.

Jesus! How had they missed it? How had they not noticed the change in her? How had they loved their daughter and not realised that she was in love? Sleeping with Harry. Lying to them.

'Why, Jess? Why didn't you just tell us?' Marcus's voice startled himself. Her room absorbed, but couldn't answer, his questions. He was left to guess. Embarrassment? Fear of their judgement, their disapproval – of her having a boyfriend, of her having sex, of her being with Harry? Did he disapprove? Would he have? He hadn't ever thought of Harry like that, as the choice of his lovely, sparky, opinionated feminista of a daughter. He couldn't say what he felt about the thought of them being together. The ache in his heart expanded. He missed her so badly. He had let Jess down. She obviously hadn't felt able to be herself around him or Fran.

Not giving himself time to reconsider, Marcus switched her phone to loudspeaker, dug his own phone out of his back pocket and pressed her number. The ringtone clattered around the room. He waited. Six rings, then the buzz as it went to voicemail. Her voice – loud and joyous – spilled out of the phone: *'Hiya. You've reached Jess. I'm either busy or actually ignoring you, but you can leave a message either way and I'll get back to you when I can.'*

The silence went on for what felt like for ever, then the screen faded.

Marcus re-dialled and listened to her voice four more times, before gathering enough courage to leave his daughter a message she would never get.

Chapter 57

SOME MORNINGS Harry woke with an erection, which surprised him. Being locked up with three hundred and fifty other men, suffocated by the overpowering smell of testosterone, was not conducive to feeling horny; neither was being lonely and depressed, but try telling his body that. When it happened, he turned his face to the wall and jerked off quickly, keeping his mind blank. A mechanical act, his brain not engaged. He didn't want Jess or Tish – or any of the girls he'd slept with – involved. Not here. At least he'd been put in a single 'bunk'. The shame was bad enough as it was, without an audience.

His days inside were regimented, controlled by the buzzer and a series of very clear instructions – which was actually okay. There were worse things than being told what to do all day. He was told when to shower, when to exercise, when to eat, when to work and study, when to socialise. It gave a structure to his days, and that was a relief compared to the desolate period after the crash and before he was sent down. Of all the injunctions, the pressure to socialise was the most wearing. The rec room in his wing was a minefield of shifting allegiances and antagonisms that were hard to read and navigate. Hanging around on your own was regarded with suspicion by the other lads, and by the guards. The latter tried to encourage him to participate, by suggesting that he join in with the poker games or by starting loud conversations about football, demanding that he voice an opinion – like that was going to endear Harry to anyone.

He preferred to sit and watch the old-fashioned TV in the corner. It was sealed inside a Perspex box, a sensible safety measure – people had been known to take vehement issue with the decisions of the judges on talent shows. He'd watch whatever was on, anything for a quiet life. There was a preference among his fellow TV addicts for wildlife programmes – no irony there. They especially seemed to like the shows where antelopes were chased down by lions, or water buffaloes got snapped up by crocodiles. They'd pick sides and cheer and holler, as if their passion could somehow influence the outcome. Though it wasn't all blood and chewed sinew. They had their softer side. One evening they'd watched a film about a baby penguin that had lost its mother in a blizzard. That had reduced most of the room to a silence filled with throat-clearing.

After rec, it was lockdown.

They were put to bed early, like naughty children. Most of them accepted it with grumbles and dragging feet, again like little kids. Harry didn't mind being sent to bed. Though he hated the sound of the doors being locked, it was always a relief to be on his own. At least in his room no one was watching. The rest of the time he was very conscious that the staff were monitoring him. He knew that concerns had been raised about him by more than one of the screws. He guessed that Jim had been one of them. Jim was older than most of the other officers and more tattooed than most of the inmates. An old-school officer – ex-army, Harry guessed – Jim had a mean-looking face and hands like Wreck-It Ralph, but most of the blokes afforded him some respect, and that was a rare commodity on the inside.

The interest in Harry, and the inside of his head, by the officers had come as a surprise. He had not expected prison to be about his state of mind. The only person who had ever expressed much interest in that, before now, had been Jess. Keeping them out was proving exhausting, especially during the one-to-one sessions. Talking. What was the point? Yet there was no denying that there was a pressure building inside him, which was getting worse. The routine, the smell, the noise, the sense of being part of a herd, the confinement, all that was as bad as he'd expected; but the need to keep his thoughts and his feelings to himself was far harder. He wanted *no one* inside his head. He tried his best not to go there himself.

But at night, when his cell door was locked, there was nowhere else to go.

He prepared for the mental onslaught by taking the toothbrush from the tiny shelf above the sink, smearing a small amount of toothpaste on it and sitting on his bunk, holding it, ready.

Shutdown was announced by yet another buzzer – the last of the day – followed by darkness. Well, not true darkness; even in the middle of the night there was some illumination. It seeped in from the corridor, and from the irritating blink-blink of the smoke alarm. There was always some light being shed on them. You can't keep an eye on people in the dark. But at least the shift from bright, harsh light to the monochrome of night was a relief. There was nothing worth seeing inside a prison; nothing beautiful, nothing nice, nothing green, nothing but concrete and metal and wipe-clean surfaces.

Harry sat on his bed listening to himself breathe, his eyes adjusting to the gloom, holding the toothbrush in his hand. Only when his heartbeat had slowed, and the noises on the corridor quietened, did he allow himself to think about Jess.

They had never spent a whole night together. They'd planned to – one weekend when Dom was due to be away on business, and Martha was supposed to be on a school trip. They'd been looking forward to it for weeks, but Martha had got tonsillitis, so that had buggered everything up. There'd been some afternoons, though, when they'd had time to go to sleep afterwards, or at least lie close to each other, talking. That's what he conjured up, when the lights went out and he was finally alone. The memory of his hand stroking the dip above her hip, or scratching her back. Her pale skin, its texture so different from his own. Her smallness, and yet her strength. Her Jess-ness. The seductive, reassuring cocoon of being together.

It had always been Jess who got up first, wriggling out of his grasp, shielding her body with her hands. She would scoop up her clothes and go into the en-suite to shower and Harry would lie under the duvet, wishing her back into bed, and at the same time feeling slightly offended by her urgent need to wash him off. But when she came out, her T-shirt mottled in dark patches where her skin wasn't quite dry, smelling of lemon shower gel, he'd been turned on all over again by the way she smelt – clean, fresh, edible – and he'd be aware that he was lucky to have even a fraction of her.

The third time they'd slept together, Jess came out of the bathroom rubbing her gums with her finger. The smell of mint had filled the bedroom. It's what they used to do as kids when they were camping – they'd pass Fran's family-sized toothpaste between them, fill their mouths with nose-fizzing toothpaste, then use their fingers to 'clean' their teeth. He had laughed. 'Use mine.'

She shook her head and continued to rub at her teeth. 'No. It's okay.'

He sat up. 'So you'll share bodily fluids with me, but you can't face using my toothbrush?'

She licked her finger. 'Using someone else's toothbrush goes against everything I hold sacred. Plus, it's gross.'

He remembered how she'd knelt on the bed, stretched across and kissed him, her lips and teeth fresh with mint.

A few days later he'd slipped the present into her bag. She found it when she was digging around, trying to find her purse at the end of the day. Her saw her do a double-take, but with the buses after college, if you weren't quick you got trampled, so Jess prioritised her pass. They all piled on, scanned their passes and headed up to the top deck. There weren't enough seats for them to sit together, so Jess and Shamika went and sat near the back, and he and Navin had to grab a couple of individual spare seats.

He'd watched as Jess took out the parcel and turned it over in her hands a few times, talking to Shamika. Then she started pulling at the Sellotape. He had bound it quite tight – gift-wrapping was not one of his strengths. The only person he ever bought presents for was Martha, and even she had got to the age where he could just bung some money in a card. The Sellotape wasn't budging. Jess put the present to her lips and used her teeth. At last she got an end free and proceeded to unwind the tape. Halfway down, it dawned on her what it was. She looked at him and grinned. A purple toothbrush – her favourite colour – with glitter embedded in the plastic handle. It had cost him all of £1.89 in Superdrug. One thing he had learnt from Jess was that small things mattered.

The bristles on the toothbrush were now splayed and ragged from use. He walked over to the tiny sink in the corner and ran the water. The smell of mint filled his cell. He closed his eyes and began to brush his teeth.

Chapter 58

IT WAS the fact that she couldn't text Harry that upset Martha the most, almost as much as him not being around. It had been a part of her existence: sending him daft messages and GIFs and, even better, him sometimes messaging her back. The banter had been their way of saying, 'I'm here, if you need me.' Well, she needed him now, but he wasn't there. It was just her and her dad, and it felt less than that.

Dom's approach to Harry's absence seemed to consist of not talking about any of it, unless forced to. That and being falsely cheerful – all the time. It was business as usual, as far as he was concerned – namely, fake it to make it. The pressure to 'be okay' added to the stress for Martha. The scheduled landline calls to the prison were perhaps the worst. Harry and her dad literally seemed to be unable to talk to each other. It fell to her to chat and laugh and ask questions, like it was perfectly normal to only be able to speak to your big brother once a week, at a set time, presumably with people listening in whenever they wanted to. She had pinned all her hopes on a visit to see Harry, but when Dom returned from his first trip up to Darlington, that hope had taken a battering.

'Well? How is he?' Martha needed Dom to tell her everything.

'He's doing okay.' She waited. 'He looked fine. He's lost a bit of weight. His face is thinner. Like he said on the phone, the food is garbage. But he's been going to the gym, so he's keeping fit. They have a decent one apparently, and they can access it most evenings.'

Martha's frustration fizzed. She should have known that her dad would default to hard facts in a bid to avoid uncomfortable emotions. 'But how is he really? How is he coping with being locked up?'

Dom rubbed his stubble. 'Fine, I think.'

'You think? Didn't you ask him?'

'Well, not in so many words. I asked how he was, and Harry said "okay". He said it wasn't anywhere near as bad as he'd been expecting.' Dom's tone was defensive.

'What about the other prisoners?'

'I only saw the ones who had visitors as well today. It was hard to tell anything from that, really. They were what you'd expect. There were a lot of shaved heads and tattoos, but there were plenty who looked normal. A mix of ages. Quite a few older blokes. Some had kids.'

Martha saw her opening and went for it. 'So it would be okay for me to come with you next time?'

Dom bought a few seconds by repositioning a pen pot on his desk. It was a penguin one that Martha had made when she was in primary school.

'Dad?'

'I said it went "okay". But it isn't a nice experience, Martha. You sit around waiting, for ages. They search everyone. And I mean everyone. A full-body search. You have to be buzzed through all these security doors to get through to the visiting hall. And the other visitors…well, you can imagine. It's really loud.'

She stared at him, waiting for him to say it.

'The tables are squashed together. You don't have any privacy. And it smells. Bad.'

'So?'

'I really don't think it's the type of environment you should have to be in.'

'But that's the only way I'm going to get to see him.' She crossed her arms.

Dom ran a fingernail under the rims of his nails, cleaning out imaginary dirt. 'I'm worried about you going. The noise, the intensity of it.'

The old anxiety card. She flushed. 'But I want to go and see him.'

'And I'm not saying you can't.' He sighed. 'I'm just asking you to think about it – about what it will be like, being in that room with all those other people; a room that you can't just get up and walk out of, if you're feeling…a bit off. It really wasn't the easiest place to be in for me, never mind you. Besides, you don't need to go all that way. You can have a much more private conversation with Harry on the phone. He really is okay. It isn't like on TV. He has classes and the gym, and there's a library. What I mean is, it's not awful.'

'So I should be able to go.'

'Martha.' Dom rasped his hand across his face. 'Please. Can you leave it, for now? Trust me, he's okay. I'm not lying. He's keeping his head down. Getting through his days. You'll be speaking to him at the weekend. Let's talk about it then. Now, sweetheart, if you don't mind…I have a few things to catch up on for work.'

They'd argued about it, on and off, for most of the following week. Dom was understanding, protective and so very rational, but totally implacable. Martha was not going to be allowed to go and see Harry, and that was that.

Chapter 59

THEY ALL did it: counted down the days between visits. Family wasn't what they talked about in the gym and the rec room; there it was all screwing and going to the match and big nights out, and takeaways and cars and muscle definition; but everyone, without exception, looked forward to getting visits. The system cranked up the ante: the paperwork, the strict rules, the restrictions on numbers, the infrequency of visiting days. But they all put in their requests for permissions on time and as stipulated, with the more literate helping the illiterate. It didn't matter how long your stretch; everyone needed time with someone who cared, to keep them going.

Harry waited in line with the other lads. The atmosphere – as always, on the way in – was upbeat. There was a lot of banter amongst the guys, and with the screws. At last the door up ahead opened and they were allowed to file through. The inmates went into the room first. They made their way to their allocated tables; numbers were given out while they queued up, to avoid potential flashpoints between certain prisoners and certain family members. It reminded Harry of a weird version of an exam hall, except that here the invigilators weren't someone's auntie earning a few extra quid; they were prison officers with eagle eyes. But the buzz in the atmosphere and the tension were very similar. DeeAnne, who worked in the little tuck shop and was one of the few women they saw week in, week out, smiled through the hatch at many of them as they took their seats. Once settled, they all looked at the clock. Any delay was met with frustration. Time was precious when it came to visits, and they resented being deprived of even a second.

The searches and processing must have gone smoothly that day, because the door opened on time and the relatives flooded in, bringing with them a colour and an energy that were normally so lacking in their day-to-day lives on the inside. At that point, each inmate had eyes only for his visitors. It was a powerful mix of anticipation and anxiety, because there was always a risk – until your visitor set foot in the room – that they hadn't come. Nearly every time there was one poor sod who waited, watching everyone else being reunited with their loved ones, only to realise that the last visitor had entered the room and the seat opposite them was going to remain empty. That was a long walk.

The noise levels in the room rose as the visitors flooded in. The kids and the mums were always the loudest, the most demonstrative. Harry had been surprised, the first few times, to see how much physical contact was allowed. Of course some of the lads pushed it when their wives and girlfriends came to visit, but more often than not it was their partners who pulled away, rather than the screws who had to intervene. Because although the inmates could kiss and hug and lift kids onto their knees and fist-bump their mates, there was absolutely no privacy. It was a big, impersonal room, full of people sitting at tables crammed too close together, patrolled by officers and filmed by the numerous cameras.

It was not the sort of environment that Harry's dad felt comfortable in – not at all. It was obvious that Dom hated the close proximity of other people, their crisp-munching and laughing and swearing. As everyone around them chatted away and shared news from home, they sat opposite each other, struggling to find things to say. Harry often caught himself thinking, *If only Martha was here*, but Dom had said, from the outset, that was *not* going to happen. They had their regular phone conversations and, in a recent special concession, the occasional Skype call, so a visit was, in Dom's eyes, unnecessary. And besides, he'd lectured – looking around him with barely concealed disgust – this was not the environment for a fourteen-year-old girl. The fact that Martha wanted to come, pleaded to, every time they spoke on the phone, held no sway with their father. She would not be visiting, and that was the end of the matter. As a result, his dad's visits were more of a trial than a pleasure, for both of them. The fact they were also a rarity was almost a relief.

The last batch of visitors was coming through. The prospect of the empty chair loomed large for Harry, but suddenly there was Mo, smiling and waving like he was out on the town on a Saturday afternoon. As he made his way through the maze he crashed into the back of a woman's chair, jolting her forward. Potential for a flare-up. Harry saw his friend go into a classic Mo apology mode, all waving arms and teeth. Just the sight of it made Harry smile. And, as so often with middle-aged women, even the mother of one of the hard-case inmates, she seemed amused rather than annoyed by Mo's clumsiness. Words were exchanged that were clearly friendly. She laughed, and Mo finished the last few steps over to Harry's table without incident.

'I'm such a klutz.' Mo dropped into his seat, obviously pleased to have made it across the minefield of the visitors' room without triggering a riot. 'How are you, man? It's really good to see you.'

'I'm okay. You?'

'Me. I'm good. Before we start, Mum gave me some spending money so that we could buy sweets.' He pulled a face. 'She still thinks we're twelve! She sent in some food as well, but they took that off me. Said you'd get it after it's been checked.' He grinned. 'They're obviously searching for blades in my mum's samosas.'

'Veggie?'

'Of course.' Mo stood up and fished a tenner out of his pocket. 'I'll be back in a minute. Anything particular you want?'

Harry shrugged. 'Whatever. Tell her "thank you" from me.'

'Will do.' Mo headed over to the serving hatch, made his selection, then wandered back bearing a carrier bag. 'Go on then. Open your beautifully wrapped present.'

Harry pulled the bag towards him and looked inside. It was stuffed full with chewy sweets, chocolate bars and soda. The thoughtfulness of it touched Harry. He picked out a pack of Haribo, opened it and took a moment making his selection. Three fried eggs, followed by some gummy bears and an engagement ring, for starters. He looked up, his mouth full of gelatine sweetness. 'You wouldn't believe how crap the food is in here.'

He offered the bag and Mo grabbed a handful. They chewed in companionable silence for a few moments. Mo glanced round and smiled at the kids racketing around the room; he even nodded at Saleem, the one Asian officer on duty. Saleem was leaning against the wall, overseeing the interactions at DeeAnne's serving hatch, checking that it was only cake and coins being exchanged.

Harry cracked open a Coke. Took three big gulps. It was heaven.

'You really all right?' Mo asked. 'Not having any trouble?' His eyes raked the room. Taking in the flab and the muscles, and the tattoos and the screws.

Harry took another pull of Coke and felt the caffeine and sugar careering into his system. 'Yeah. Fine. Really. You learn who to avoid, early on. Most people keep themselves to themselves outside of work and the canteen. There's some aggro, but not much. There's bound to be, with everyone banged up together.'

'No trouble...in the showers?' Mo fake-leered.

'I have my admirers, but no one that I can't handle.'

Mo cackled 'The one near the door?' He'd deliberately picked out the biggest, most brutish-looking guy – who happened to be called Gabe and was one of the nicest guys on their unit.

'Not my type, darling.'

Around them the initial rush of greetings had subsided. A low hum of conversation filled the room, not all of it easy or light-hearted. Life went on; tensions and resentments came into prison with relatives, as well as chocolate and kisses. Watching the couples, Harry felt compelled to ask Mo the questions that his dad was unable, or unwilling, to answer.

'You still see Jake around?'

Mo cartoon-stretched. 'Nah. Not for ages. Paths don't cross no more. I'm not "out out" much these days. Saving my pennies. He's doing okay, though, I think. He put up a picture of himself back at training.'

'Really?'

'Yeah. In goal.'

'God help 'em.' The next question hovered. 'And Tish?'

A gear-change. Mo went from laid-back to leaning forward in a split second. 'Yeah. She's good.'

'Really?' This time Harry genuinely wanted to know.

'Yeah. She's doing good. Really great.' He didn't elaborate.

'Do you see much of her then?'

'Yeah, you know. Around.' Mo paused.

'She seeing anyone?'

Mo shrugged, non-committal.

Harry felt a pain in his chest that could have been indigestion from eating so many sweets, but could have been something else. 'Tell her I was asking after her, will you? Next time you see her.'

Mo picked up one of the wrappers from the table and twisted it in his hands. 'Yeah. Will do.'

'So, are you looking forward to starting uni?'

'Yeah.'

'Make the most of Freshers' Week. I'll want to hear all about it.' The awkwardness of not knowing when that would happen struck them both.

'I could try and call you,' Mo said. God, life without texting was impossible.

'Nah. Don't bother, it's a hassle to set up.'

'Well, I'll book to come in again. Tell you all about it.' There was no getting around the difficulty of being a mate in these circumstances.

Harry was the one to fight the depressing turn of their conversation. 'Seriously. I hope you have a great time.'

Mo nodded, but not with confidence.

The awareness that this was the last time he was going talk to Mo for at least a couple of months struck Harry. If he wanted to apologise, he had to do it now. 'Mo. That night. In the car park. I'm really sorry. I was a bit of a mess. Jess...' his voice wobbled, 'and me, we'd had a row, and I took it out on you. I shouldn't have. I wasn't ever gonna hit you. You know that, don't you?'

'Apology accepted,' Mo said. Harry breathed a little easier. 'But, Harry...' Mo looked pained, 'what I still don't understand is why you lobbed my phone, and why everyone has been really cagey about what was on it.' He lowered his voice and leant across the table. 'Was it drugs?'

Harry's mouth felt furry. 'No. I swear, Mo. It was some footage of me behaving like a dick at the party. When Jess saw it, she got upset with me. I took it out on you. It's not logical. I know that. I was just on one. In that split second I wanted to smash something – anything – up. Unfortunately for you, I happened to have your phone in my hand.' The lie stuck to his teeth worse than the sugar from the sweets.

Mo fiddled with the Haribo bag. 'You know, Harry, you can tell me what really happened, if you want to. I know there was something going on between you and Tish and Jess. I won't judge you. I honestly won't.'

Harry looked at him and was sorely tempted, but what good would it do? None. There was no undoing that night.

As if complicit in ensuring that his burdens remained his own, the bell rang, signalling the end of the visit, and the moment for sharing passed. They fist-bumped goodbye – a hug would have been too much, a handshake not enough – and Mo got up and left, to get on with the rest of his exciting, expanding life on the outside, while Harry stood up and walked the fifty or so steps through the barred door back to his lonely, contracting life on the inside.

Chapter 60

THE ONGOING pretence made Sal smile. They were all in on it. Mo staying over 'to study' with Tish. As if! She didn't mind. The atmosphere in the house was lighter, more positive than it had been for months. If there was a slight awkwardness when they encountered each other on the landing in their dressing gowns, and if her food bill had gone up, so be it. They were small prices to play for seeing Tish so happy. They were, she reckoned, managing the etiquette of this somewhat surprising development okay – all things considered.

She'd bumped into Shazia in town a few weeks back and had been thrown by her suggestion that they go for a coffee together, thinking that their conversation was going to be truly awkward, but as they'd sat eating cake, it had become clear that her own and Shazia's subtext were the same. *Are you okay with this?* It was amazing, really, that you could have a conversation about your child's love – and sex – life without mentioning either. Shazia had set the tone, before even a forkful of chocolate brownie had been consumed, by saying how much she admired Tish. How strong she'd been. How much of a credit she was to Sal. How much Tish's 'friendship' with Mo had helped him get over the incident and all the trouble afterwards. How he seemed far more sure of himself now around other people.

It had been nice to hear. Really nice. Praise. It was a rare commodity in Sal's life. There had also been the joy of being able to respond with absolute honesty about Mo. What a decent young man he was. How important he had been, and still was, in Tish regaining her confidence and her happiness. What a polite, well-mannered boy he was to have around the house. After ten minutes of this sort of mutual love-in, Sal had been reassured that Shazia was happy that their kids were close, but that still didn't tackle the recent shift from close to...well...hooked up, sleeping together, in love? And the influence that had had on Mo's choice of uni.

Sal decided to tackle it head-on. 'And it's good to see how much Mo seems to be enjoying uni.'

Shazia nodded. 'Yes. And he's working hard.'

'You weren't too disappointed when he decided to stay in York?'

There was only a fraction of a hesitation. 'No. York is a good university, and the course is the one he wanted.' Shazia divided the last of her brownie into small pieces. 'And of course he wanted to stay around, to be near Tish.' She ate a lump of cake. 'He isn't making a nuisance of himself, is he – coming over to your place so often? Because if he is, you must say.'

Sal smiled. 'No. It's nice having him around. And he's no trouble.' She paused. 'As long as it's all right with you and Nihal?'

Shazia paused and chased the last chunk of brownie around on her plate. 'It is. To be honest, it's the best of both worlds for us. Mo growing up, coming into his own, being much more independent, but still being around, some of the time. Before all this happened, we were worried that he was too much of a home-bird. A bit lacking in confidence, compared to his sisters. Not any more.'

'They've helped each other,' Sal said.

'Yes, they have. And he is very, very...fond of her.'

'It shows.'

'Good.'

They'd laughed then and gone on to talk about other things.

Looking at Mo now, making himself and Tish toast in her small kitchen, Sal smiled. He would curl up into a ball of embarrassment if he knew that she and his mum had discussed his relationship with Tish.

Mo must have sensed her attention, because he looked round. 'Sorry, am I in the way?' He made to move away from the counter.

She shook her head. 'No, love, you're fine where you are.'

He buttered the toast, added jam, piled it on the plate, hooked the two mugs with his fingers. 'Is it all right to take this upstairs?'

He really did need to stop being so polite – but it was still nice to be asked. 'Of course, love. Say 'bye for me – I'm off to work.'

'Will do.' He stepped over Harley and disappeared back upstairs.

Sal scratched Harley's head for a minute or two before heading off to work, glad to her core that the accident had brought Mo into their lives.

Chapter 61

HARRY HAD been surprised to get her request to visit, but he'd agreed to it straight away.

Now here she was, weaving her way around the tables towards him. She'd never been able to walk into a room without causing a stir; Tish had always had the capacity to attract attention. It wasn't just her looks, it was the way she carried herself – her ability to feel comfortable with the attention. She was happy to be admired. But the Tish who came through the doors into the visitors' room was different. Now she didn't so much own the space around her as pass through it. She slid in between the tables and chairs as if trying to create the least disturbance possible. The other men checked her out, but she kept her eyes down, avoiding their attention until she made it over to his table. Only then did she look up.

Harry made himself smile. Tish met his eye, but didn't smile back. Harry felt on edge. There was too much history between them, and at the same time not enough. He didn't know why she'd come, after all this time. When she sat down and shrugged off her jacket and said nothing, neither, it seemed, did she.

'Hi.'

'Hi.' Around them greetings were being exchanged and conversations picked up where they'd been left a week, a fortnight, a month ago.

Tish swallowed and, despite his best intentions, Harry found himself looking at the scar on her jawline. She looked good, but not the same. Conscious of his gaze, her hand travelled to her face.

He felt ashamed. 'Sorry.'

'It's okay. Everybody looks. You get used to it.'

'How are you doing?'

'Okay.'

'Good.'

She looked away at the couple next to them. The woman was leaning across the table, her big breasts filling the small space, sucking the face off her man. A proper, full-blooded snog. Across the room one of the prison officers stood watching their display, poised to intervene, but either through indifference or kindness he let them have their moment.

When Tish looked back at Harry, there was a spark of something that was more like the old Tish in her eyes. 'Good to see that romance isn't dead after all.'

Harry just about managed to compose a second small smile, but it was a feeble attempt. He knew what she was reminding him of. But there was no point going there. Not now. That was another life – a life that was long gone for both of them. A wave of pity, for himself and for Tish, rolled over Harry. He hung his head.

'Hey,' she prompted. He looked up. 'I've not come to cause you grief. Well, not much. I came because I want to ask you some questions. And I need you to be straight with me when you answer them.'

'Okay.' He owed her that.

She shuffled in her seat, drawing herself more upright, making herself more present. 'First off, I want to know why you never said anything about us.'

He had known this was probably why she'd come. His promise mattered. No more lies. That was the deal he'd made in the dark, long hours of the night in his cell. It was one of the measures of him as a man – his own man, not some watered-down version of his dad, ducking and diving and coming up smelling of roses. And suddenly here was Tish, asking him for a truth that was complicated and that reflected badly on him. It was a test he had to pass.

'I did. I told the police that Jess saw the video of us kissing.'

'Is that all you said?'

Harry looked at her and couldn't *not* remember. The memories were stuck fast inside him, corroded with a thick layer of shame, but still so strong. The attraction, the excitement of sneaking around, the fierce pleasure of the sex. Perhaps that was the way it would always be with Tish – that spike in his gut, which ran straight down into his groin. They could never just be friends. 'Yes.'

'But you didn't tell the police about us...being together?'

Harry understood her hesitation. For two years they'd been circling each other, coming together for intense, short bursts, then pretending nothing had happened, until it did again. Friends with benefits. What a fucking stupid phrase that was.

'No.'

'And you only told the police?'

'What do you mean?'

'Harry. I want to know who else you told about us?'

'No one.'

'You never said anything to your dad?'

'He knows about the video. But he thinks it was just a snog at a party.'

She flinched, then asked, 'Martha doesn't know?' His expression was enough for that question not to require an answer. 'And you never told any of your mates? No snide little comments?'

He shook his head. 'No. Well, I wasn't going to, was I?' Cheating with your best mate's girl – classic scumbag behaviour. Jake, or one of his brothers, would probably have smashed his face in. He would've deserved it.

255

'What about Mo? He visited you, didn't he? Last month. Did you talk about me?' Her face flushed.

'You mean about us?'

She nodded.

'Course not.'

'Good. Don't.'

'I won't.'

'Don't.'

Once again Tish raised her hand to her face. Gently she ran her fingers across her chin, her fingertips coming to a stop when they touched the deep seam of the scar. There had, according to his father, been a flap of skin that had been hanging down beneath her eye. They had had to stitch it back onto her cheek in order to reconstruct her face. The thought made Harry want to die. When he steeled himself to look at her again, he found her searching his face.

'Did you never say anything because you were ashamed of going with me?'

'Tish. Please. There's no point going over this. Not now.'

She stiffened and straightened up even more. 'There is, for me. I want to know. Were you ashamed you'd slept with me? That you were sleeping with me?'

He sighed. 'Tish, what difference does it make? Once we crashed... once I crashed the car, it was all over. Everything was fucked. What we were doing before – what any of us were doing – it doesn't matter.'

Tish stared at him. 'Maybe it doesn't matter to you, Harry. But it does to me!'

The truth. His pact with Jess's memory. The measure of his journey back. Okay, so be it. 'All right, if you really want to know: yes, I felt guilty. I still do. I was cheating on Jess and she deserved better than that. It was a shitty thing to do.'

Tish blinked, and for an awful moment Harry thought she was

going to start crying, but he should've remembered – Tish was made of sterner stuff. 'So I was just a grubby little secret.'

'Tish. No. You know that's not how it was.'

'Yes it was. It's exactly how it was. You always thought you were better than all of us, didn't you, Harry? But you're not. That's why you kept quiet, isn't it? It wasn't to protect me. You didn't want to admit you were shagging me. You and your precious reputation. Dom Westwood's fucking golden boy. Even when you were facing prison, even then, you wanted to avoid looking bad and...' she gulped, gearing up for her finale, 'and being shown to be the lying, cheating bastard you are!'

Harry reached across and risked putting his hand over hers. 'Tish. That's not it. Christ, I promise that wasn't it. I thought I'd done enough damage. I didn't say anything because I thought it would fuck things up between you and Jake.'

They stared at each other. Tish was still breathing hard. 'Well, you needn't have worried. He didn't stick around for long. You might have noticed, I'm not as photogenic as I used to be.' She lifted her chin, defiant. There was so much of her that was still so impressive. 'Besides, he's been a busy boy – plenty of sympathy-shags to be had. He didn't want me around cramping his style.'

The waves from the crash just kept rolling in, eroding everyone and everything that had once seemed so solid and permanent. Harry kept quiet and let her vent. There seemed nothing he could say that would make any difference. He watched her struggling with the rush of old and fresh passions. She was so fierce and lovely.

When she'd finished talking, she leant back in her chair as if exhausted. Harry glanced around the room. They weren't the only ones to have run out of steam. Some of the couples were silent, looking at the wall clock, waiting for 'Time's up' to be called.

Tish's next question brought him back into focus. 'You really did love Jess, didn't you?' The tone was still spiky, challenging.

'Yes.' Love and lust. Not the same thing. A lesson learnt the hard way.

'I knew that all along, really. I always knew it was Jess and not me.' Tish looked so sad. The pause was a long one, stuffed full of memories. 'The night we crashed – do you think about it a lot?'

The change of topic jolted him. 'Yeah. It was so bloody awful. I'm never going to forget it.'

'Me neither.' She was quiet again for another few beats. 'Do you know what got to me, more than anything else? More than even this.' She gestured at her face.

'No,' he said nervously.

'That you chose her. Even with me screaming in pain, crawling around on my hands and knees, blinded by all that blood, when I was more frightened than I'd ever been in the whole of my life – you stayed with her.' The couple next to them were arguing now, the passionate snogging of their greeting long forgotten. Tish's voice dropped. 'You didn't even come and check on me. If it hadn't been for that random bloke who turned up to help, I could have crawled into the road.'

Harry hung his head. She was right. He hadn't for a second considered leaving Jess's side. The sounds of other people's conversations only amplified the silence between them.

She spoke first. 'Harry?' He looked up. Some of the tension seemed to leave Tish's body. She said quietly and calmly, 'It's okay. Or at least it is now. In the long run, you did me a favour. That night made me face up to the fact that you never really loved me. I suppose I always knew that, in my heart, but I didn't want to accept it. I do now.' They both swallowed. A lump of grief each. The silence that followed was kinder, less full of recrimination. Tish's eyes filled. 'I miss her so much.'

Harry closed his eyes for a few seconds, grateful for the acknowledgement of something shared – at last. 'So do I.'

'I've got something to give you.' Harry opened his eyes just as Tish slid an envelope across the table. 'I was going to keep it, to remember her by, but it doesn't belong to me.' Before Harry had even moved his hand to pick it up, he caught sight of one of the officers rushing across the room. He left the envelope where it was. He knew the rules. The last thing he wanted was a sanction.

'Do *not* touch that!' The officer's voice was loud. People around them looked, curious. Tish started to protest, but the screw stopped her. 'In no circumstances is it acceptable for visitors to pass gifts to inmates without prior permission.' He picked up the envelope and opened it. For a second he stared inside it. He looked at Tish for an explanation.

She flustered. 'Sorry. I didn't think. I've not been inside a prison before. I didn't mean to do anything wrong.'

The officer upended the envelope onto his palm. He poked around with his meaty fingers, examining the contents. Harry sat and waited. He was used to his life being determined by someone else.

Tish, used to life outside, was less compliant. 'I'm really sorry, Officer. Please. It's something I thought Harry might like.'

To Harry's surprise, the officer suddenly cracked a smile. 'Okay. But I'm warning you, young lady, you do that again in front of an officer less chilled-out than me and you'll find yourself in proper bother.' He dropped the contraband into Tish's cupped hands.

As he turned to walk away, Tish said, 'So, can I give it to him?' She flashed him a smile – a full-wattage 'Tish in her glory days' grin – and the officer, caught in her beam, grinned back.

'Go on then. But just this once. You've got two minutes left.'

Tish placed her gift onto Harry's outstretched palm.

It was the seahorse necklace he'd given Jess for her seventeenth birthday. He looked up, confused.

Tish said, 'I stole it. One day when we were up in her room. I wanted to take something from Jess, something that she cared about. I knew you'd given it to her. You never were great at keeping secrets, not really.'

The buzzer went.

Tish stood up. 'I'm sorry. I hope you're going to be all right, Harry, with everything, but I won't be coming again. See you around – some day.' She shouldered her bag, turned and walked away, without looking back.

Back in his cell, Harry looked at the necklace. An image of Jess sitting up in bed, her face so open and happy, the wrapping paper caught in the folds of the duvet, filled his head. The seahorse thing had started as a joke. Jess had made a comment about what odd-looking creatures they were, and he'd Googled them and discovered that *they ate about fifty times a day...like Jess*. She had countered with facts about their exoskeleton: *hard on the outside, soft on the inside...just like you*. And it had gone on from there. *Hippocampus hippocampus*. Poor swimmers with excellent eyesight, able to change colour to match their environment. Creatures that paired for life. Jess's favourite fact was that the female seahorse always went into the male's territory every morning, where they would greet each other with an elaborate spiralling 'dance'. He and Jess had taken to circling each other at least once every time they met, a secret gesture of their togetherness.

The necklace chain slid through his fingers. It had lain against Jess's pale skin and Tish's. Jesus, what a mess!

Chapter 62

SAL REFUSED to lie to Mo. If that dumped Tish in it, so be it. Sneaking around, arranging the prison visit behind his back, then lying about where she was going: Mo deserved better than that. Sal's frustration also lay in her confusion over Tish's motives for suddenly wanting to see Harry. Why go backwards, when life was finally going forward? Sal couldn't see any earthly benefit that could come from her daughter going on some crazy mission to confront him. She was also concerned that there was more to the trip than the desire for a showdown. They'd been here before, with Harry Westwood. His hold over Tish had been strong. Sal had thought – had hoped – that Mo had cured her of that obsession. What if she was wrong? What if her daughter really was doomed to repeat her own self-destructive behaviour with men, picking the bad boy instead of the decent one?

Mo turned up at the house about two hours after Tish left for Darlington. He made out as if he'd just been passing, but he wasn't daft. He must have sensed something was off. After a few minutes of awkward small talk, he asked Sal straight out where Tish was, and she told him. He looked at the floor for a second, then back up, composing himself. There was no outburst of justifiable anger, no swearing, no calling Tish out, only a shiver of disappointment. Sal was the one who felt a flash of pure frustration. After all that Mo had done for Tish, after his kindness and all-round loveliness, Sal was ashamed of her daughter.

'I'm sorry, love. She should've told you. I don't know why she didn't.'

Mo flipped his phone over in his hands. 'It's okay. Thank you for telling me.' He was so reserved. Maybe that was the problem; maybe Mo was too nice, too much of a pushover for Tish.

'I'll tell her – when she eventually gets back – that you came round, and that she needs to call you. It'll be this evening. She's gone up on the coach.'

'Thanks.' He turned to leave.

Sal felt compelled to say more, to encourage him to stand his ground. 'I didn't know she was planning it, Mo. I promise. Not until yesterday. She's out of order. You've every right to tell her that. I'm sorry, love. I really don't know what she's playing at.'

He just shrugged. On his way out through the kitchen, Sal saw him stop, crouch down and stroke Harley. She hoped it was a 'goodbye for now' rather than a 'goodbye for ever'.

Chapter 63

WHEN TISH stepped out through the last set of prison gates into the cold, grey November afternoon she felt free – released of her debt to Jess, and of her ties to Harry. Despite the wind knifing through the shelter and the long wait for the shuttle bus, her mood was upbeat. She had been right to come. When she noticed that one of the kids waiting with his mum was staring at her face – blatantly, open-mouthed – she wasn't bothered. She stuck out her tongue and the kid looked away.

Her positive mood evaporated the moment she looked through her messages. What the hell! Her mum had no right getting involved. Tish had planned to speak to Mo about seeing Harry face-to-face, so that she could explain properly. This was not the way it was supposed to play out.

Settled in her seat, she tried to compose an appropriate message to Mo. She came up with some words – a few okay sentences, even a whole paragraph – then deleted them all. She redrafted the text again and again. None of her attempts sounded right. Mo had always respected her privacy, but she knew he had his suspicions about her and Harry. A sudden prison visit – which Mo would know took time and effort to organise, and therefore must have necessitated weeks of lying – hardly helped to allay those suspicions. Why the hell hadn't her mum covered for her? A text wouldn't cut it. But the thought of Mo being mad at her, thinking she'd betrayed him, wasn't bearable, either. She couldn't ring him from the bus; it was too public for such a private conversation. Knowing that she was going to be trapped on the coach for at least the next couple of hours, she resorted to sending him one short message. 'I can explain.'

For the rest of the journey Tish sat with her phone in her hand, waiting for a reply that never came.

He didn't answer her calls or respond to any of her texts that evening, either. Sal was unsympathetic; in fact she seemed pleased that Mo was holding out on her. That only made things worse: judgement on top of judgement. Tish and her mum had words. Shouted ones – like in the old days.

The following morning Tish got up early. She got ready quickly, but carefully. At the last minute she decided to take Harley with her. A shameless ploy, but she was prepared to use anything. Mo's dad answered the door, in his dressing gown. She said she'd wait outside for Mo – *because of the dog.*

Mo took his time. When he did finally appear, she noticed that his sweatshirt was on inside out. She didn't make a joke of it, like she normally would.

'Thought you might want to come for walk.'

He shrugged on his jacket. 'Did you?' He was sulking.

'No, not really. I came because you're obviously mad at me. And I want to explain why I went. You've got it all wrong!'

'*I've* got it wrong!'

'Yeah.'

'So tell me, Tish, what part of you lying to me and going to see Harry behind my back have I got wrong?' Sarcasm didn't suit him.

'The part about why I went,' she replied.

'Go on then.' He pulled his jacket around him, keeping his distance.

Harley was whining, straining on his lead, wanting to be off, not hanging around outside Mo's house. 'Let's walk.'

'Okay.'

Tish hoped it was going to be easier to say what she had to say without Mo looking her full in the face. Perhaps not. There were very few people out this early on a Sunday morning. A lone jogger. A few cars. A cat, which Harley nearly pulled her arm out of its socket trying to chase. 'I'm sorry. I should have told you that I was going.' Mo didn't say anything. 'I wasn't sure, until the permission form came back, that I was actually going to go.'

'But you did. I presume that's why you asked all those questions about how the process worked. I'm glad I was useful.'

'It wasn't like that.'

He made a humphing noise.

'I decided I needed to see Harry. I had things I wanted to say – things that have been bothering me. He never got in touch after the crash. Not once. Not a single word or a message. Nothing.'

When Mo next spoke, his tone was still guarded and brusque. 'And you wanted him to?'

'Yes. I did.' He flinched. 'Because I was still a schmuck back then. I still thought I meant something to him.'

'Then?'

They'd arrived at the park. Tish bent down and unclipped Harley. He raced off like a bullet, falling over his feet with excitement. 'Yes... then.' She decided that nothing but the whole truth would do. 'We have a lot of history, me and Harry. You know that.' Aware that she could very well be blowing it totally, she went on, 'But what you don't know is that we were sleeping with each other, on and off, for quite a while before the accident.'

Mo just nodded miserably.

'When I was with Jake, and before, when I was with Lewis.' The look on his face was awful. Not anger, but hurt. It made her feel terrible. 'That's the sort of person I am, Mo. That's what was on your phone. That night at the party – I was with Harry. You filmed me trying get him away from Jess, the only way I knew how.'

He didn't ask the questions she was expecting – about her betrayal – but that was one of the reasons she was in danger of loving him. He simply asked, 'But why go and see him now, after all this time?' What he meant was: *after sleeping with me; after getting me to stay in York when I should've gone to Liverpool – the place I had my heart set on, until I got mixed up with you; after pretending you cared and that we had a future, when in reality you were treating me like rubbish, as badly as Harry treated you.*

'Because I wanted to look Harry in the eye and know for certain that he didn't matter to me any more.'

'And does he? Matter to you?'

'No.'

'Just "No"?'

She pulled him to a stop, made him look her. 'It's not a small thing, Mo. It's taken me a long time to realise that Harry isn't worth it, and that I'm worth more.'

'No. That's probably not a small thing.' He watched Harley, stony-faced. 'But neither is not trusting me enough to tell me what you were doing, and why.'

'I was embarrassed. I didn't want you knowing my past and thinking I was…easy.'

He shook his head. 'What? Is that what you think I'd do? Judge you, because I'm some uptight Asian?'

'No! What are you talking about? I didn't want to spoil what we had…have. I didn't tell you because I didn't want you to think I'm a whore.'

'Is that what *you* think you are?'

Harley reappeared and danced around them, a big stick in his mouth. Neither of them paid him any attention.

'No. But I let Harry use me, and I've let other lads...get what they wanted.'

'Including me?'

'That's different.'

'Is it?'

'Yes.'

Harley dropped the stick and started barking with frustration. Mo bent down, picked it up and hurled it. It flew a long way, over towards the trees, powered by his anger. He watched Harley chase after it, his ears flapping as he ran. Tish looked at Mo, waiting for him to say something.

'Have you cheated on me?' he asked.

'No.'

'Would you?'

'No,' she answered, honestly.

Harley crashed back into their orbit, barking, wanting to play. Mo bent, picked up the soggy stick and threw it again. Patience – one of his many strengths, and his weakness.

'Why?' he asked.

'Why what?'

He turned to face her, squaring up, readying himself for her reply. 'Why wouldn't you cheat on me?'

'Because it's different with you.'

'Why?'

Tish looked at him, knowing he was demanding that she answer him properly. All the way back from Darlington on the coach she'd been thinking about being with Mo, and why it wasn't the same as being with anyone else. Why it was better, so much better. How the sex was part of it – an important part – but how it wasn't the whole of it. 'Because you love me, and they didn't.'

Still he didn't soften. He kept his eyes on her, his hands shoved deep in his pockets, a clear signal that he was reserving judgement. 'That's not enough, Tish.'

The realisation that he could be about to dump her induced a stomach-shifting rush of panic. It sounded like she was taking him for granted, assuming it was her right to be loved by him, when in reality nothing could be further from the truth. Tish knew how lucky she was to have Mo in her life. That's when it dawned on her what he needed her to say – what she wanted to say. 'And,' she stepped as close to him as Harley would allow, 'because I love you. And I promise that I'll never muck you about, ever. Oh, for God's sake, Harley, get down.' He was such a pain.

And at last Mo smiled, a real smile. 'Good...because I love you too. Not as much as Harley, obviously.' He bent and scratched Harley's head, sending him into paroxysms of joy. 'But as you come as a pair, I suppose I'll have to put up with both of you.'

Chapter 64

THE REQUEST was relayed to Harry by Jim, his key worker. Jim broached it carefully in one of their mentoring sessions. He talked – a lot – about the principles of the restorative justice process, the pros and cons, the list of things that Harry should take time to consider before deciding whether to agree to participate. It was a barrage of words, which Harry was not required to respond to. He knew that Jim's verbal diarrhoea was a technique designed to make him feel less pressurised, less on-the-spot. The officers' treatment of him was not the same as their treatment of the other inmates; his dad had been right about that. It was as if they thought that because he was quiet, polite, with a brain and an ability to speak in coherent sentences, he was different – better somehow – not your commonplace con. He wished they would stop making such a distinction. Prison was supposed to be a punishment. He was no better than the other guys; in many ways, he was worse. None of them, as far as he could tell, had killed anybody.

In reality, the officers' determination to care was one of the biggest pressures of being inside. The consideration of his feelings, the understanding, the kindness, even from a battle-hardened old screw like Jim – who had more tattoos and worse language than many of the inmates – made Harry very uncomfortable. He knew there were concerns that he was losing it: 'going under', to use their term for it. December was apparently the month that saw the highest number of suicide attempts amongst inmates. Hence all this concerted effort to keep him on track, to keep him focused on his studies, to make him socialise, to remind him endlessly that he had his whole life in front of him, after he finished his sentence. It was curiously exhausting.

Jim was still talking. 'You'd best you speak to your dad about it next time you call him. I can talk to him as well, if you want me to. And remember, you're not under any obligation to say yes.'

'What – other than the fact that I killed their daughter!' That shut him up for a few seconds.

'Harry, speak to your dad, please. Take some time to reflect. My advice, for what it's worth, is that there can be benefits from doing it, but you need to be in the right frame of mind; and you've got to be prepared for the fact that they can be very unpredictable sessions. With the best will in the world, no matter how well we all do the groundwork, you don't really know – not until you get into the room – how people are going to react.'

'I've had seven months to "reflect".' That was the problem. All he could do was think. It was time he apologised – inadequate as that might be. 'I want to do it. Get back to them and say I'll do it.'

'I really think—'

Harry stood up. 'I said I'll do it. Please, Jim. Just get the thing organised.'

Chapter 65

BEING BACK into the routine of work, after the barren despair of Christmas, was helping – a bit. The skills required to perform her job came back readily enough and the daily grind filled the days, but it didn't change the way Fran felt. That wasn't a surprise. It was other people who seemed to want her to feel different. A new year, a new start. She knew that was an impossibility.

The opticians' branch where she worked was in the centre of York, so it necessitated getting up, early, getting dressed, smartly, then catching the bus like other folk, and joining the shuffling wodge of bodies heading into their jobs. The whole process could, she discovered, be done on automatic pilot. Even the customer interactions, the sight tests and glaucoma checks, the mindless small talk and complicated lens equations could all be performed competently by the version of Fran that still looked, spoke and behaved like any other rational, professional, middle-aged woman. The other staff were kind, bringing her extra cups of tea, spacing out her appointments, dropping their voices and shutting off any laughter when she went out to the front desk. The part of her that registered such consideration appreciated it, but it didn't really help. If anything, it made her feel more under pressure to put on a good show.

She was sitting in the examination room, staring at her hands, when Eileen knocked softly at the door. Fran composed her face, expecting yet another brew. 'Come in.'

Eileen stuck her head round the door, but didn't enter the room. 'Sorry to disturb you, Fran, but we have a bit of a situation with a young lady in reception. I wouldn't normally bother you, but...' She waited. 'She has a sight test booked, but she's only fourteen and she's come along on her own. I've explained that she needs an adult with her, but she's insisting on being seen.'

Fran stood. 'That's okay. I'll come and speak to her.' Eileen looked relieved.

After the cocooning gloom of the examination room, the shop was uncomfortably bright. Fran's eyes took a moment to adjust. The girl was sitting on the seats by the designer frames display, hunched forward.

Martha.

Fran walked over. Cautious and confused. 'Martha?'

'Lucy!' Martha stared at Fran, challenging her to disagree. Lucy White – the name against the appointment booking.

Eileen was watching the exchange with a puzzled expression.

'Sorry. Yes. *Lucy.*' Fran stumbled over her own inept pretence. 'It's okay, Eileen. I know this young lady. She's a family friend.' Not true. Not any more. 'Do you want to come through, Lucy?' Martha stood and gathered her coat and bag. 'Would you like one of the girls to be present while I conduct your examination?'

Martha looked stricken for a second or two, but she recovered enough to mutter, 'No. Thank you.'

Fran pointed her in the right direction and plastered on a smile. 'Okay. Well, come on through.' Neither of them looked at Eileen as they walked past the desk, both of them acutely aware of their clumsy performances.

Fran closed the door behind them and gestured to the chair that real clients sat in. Martha didn't resist. She climbed up into it and sat clutching her coat to her chest. Fran perched on her stool. 'So?'

Martha was silent for a long time.

Professionalism was all Fran could offer her. 'Have you been having problems with your eyesight?'

Martha blinked. 'No.'

'And yet you want a sight test?' The answer to this was presumably 'No', but after a long pause Martha opted for 'Yes'. Because there seemed no other alternative, Fran went into her usual spiel. 'Okay.' She reached for the glasses and fitted them onto Martha's face. Martha sat like a statue, neither helping nor resisting, as Fran tucked the earpieces into place and adjusted the fit. She slid in the trial lens, dimmed the lights and clicked on the light box. 'Okay, if you could read as much as you can for me, please.'

Martha blinked and started, 'R O K Z D.' She took a breath that sounded shaky and went on, 'K V D R O.' She kept going. 'C H S D N...I think.' This was said in a rush, as if getting it wrong was a crime.

The optician in Fran briefly wondered if there might be an astigmatism in Martha's left eye and was about to reach for the black lens to cover it and begin a thorough check. Then she snapped out of it.

'Martha, why are you really here?' She leant back, demonstrating that the charade was at an end.

Martha slowly took the glasses off. 'I wanted to see you.'

'But why go to all this effort? Why not just come to the house, or text me?'

'Because I wasn't sure you'd speak to me. Not after everything's that's happened.' At least she had some grasp of the gulf that now existed between their families. Martha shuffled in the seat when Fran didn't help her out by saying something. 'And because I didn't want Dad to know.'

Fran stuck to a simple, direct 'Why?'

This finally provoked a flicker of defiance in Martha. 'You know why.'

Fran couldn't be bothered with working out the riddle of Dom and his family. Not any more. She held her silence. Martha fiddled with the glasses. Fran somewhat roughly snatched them out of her hands. They were expensive; she didn't want Martha breaking them.

Under pressure, Martha blurted out, 'I know you're thinking about going to see Harry.' How the hell had she found that out? Martha answered Fran's unspoken question. 'Dad told me that you've applied for a visit. Well,' she paused, compelled to be truthful, 'he didn't actually tell me – I heard him talking to Harry about it. Harry said you could visit him, didn't he?' Fran was taken aback that Martha was so well informed about something that was so intensely private. 'I want to come with you.'

Fran saw that Martha was serious. She was actually asking Fran to take her to the prison to see her brother – as if it was a reasonable request. 'It's not appropriate.' What did Martha think Fran was going to see Harry for? A reunion?

'Please, Fran. Even if it's only for a few minutes. I want to see him in the flesh, to check he's okay. I appreciate that you'd want to talk to him on your own. I just need a few minutes with him.'

'No.' Fran stood up, signalling that their ridiculous conversation was over.

But Martha didn't budge. 'Please. Dad won't take me.'

'That's between you and your dad. I'm not going up there to have a nice, cosy little chat.' She could hear the flint in her voice.

Martha flinched, but didn't back down. 'Please. I can't bear not seeing him. When I talk to Harry on the phone, he sounds so down. It was awful over Christmas. Just awful. I'm worried about him. Really worried about him.'

Fran could see how distressed she was. She understood why. The Westwood household wasn't the only family missing its beating heart. Looking at Martha's pinched, thin little face, Fran could feel the desperation emanating from her, but she felt absolutely no responsibility to alleviate it. 'Martha, there is no way I'm going to take you up to Darlington to see your brother. Not next week or any other time. It's something you need to sort out with your dad. You need to leave. Now.'

Martha looked confused. 'Fran?' She reached out to touch Fran's arm, as if wanting to check that this woman who was so coldly dismissing her was the same person who had always been so warm and open.

Fran instinctively pushed her stool back out of reach. She stood up, walked over to the door and opened it. The sound of the outer shop drifted into the room. There was nothing left to say.

Chapter 66

MARCUS TRIED to cling onto sleep, but it slipped away from him, unconsciousness denied. Regardless, he lay still. Another day lay in wait, but he was in no rush to face it. Better to stay, flat on his stomach, his eyes blind in the pillow. Fran was not next to him. He heard a couple of cars pass the house. He lifted his head. His phone showed 6.40 a.m. He had had a full eight hours' sleep, but he still felt tired out. He rolled onto this back. It was still dark in the bedroom. It took a huge effort to push himself upright. He got out of bed. Fran was in the kitchen. When he entered, she smiled and flicked the kettle on, opened the cupboard and took out his mug. 'Morning.'

'Morning.'

'How did you sleep?'

'Not bad. You?

'Better than last night.'

They weaved around each other, making toast, pouring cereal. The overhead light bounced off the surfaces. Armed with his breakfast, Marcus went to go through to the lounge, on his own.

Fran had other ideas. 'Will you come and sit with me?'

It was an oddly formal invitation. 'Yes, of course.'

They sat opposite each other at the kitchen table, crunching, swallowing, eating breakfast. Fran's silence sat at odds with her request for him to join her. Marcus's mind turned to work, and the day ahead. It took an act of will and disciplined determination to summon up the energy to face a school full of kids. Tuesday was especially bad, given that he had no PPA time. He would have to be 'on' all day.

Fran pushed her bowl aside, dragging his attention back. 'Marcus, I need to talk to you about something, and I want you to hear me out before you say anything.' He could do nothing but nod. 'I've been looking into a service called restorative justice.' She paused, as if waiting for him to react. He didn't. 'It's a scheme they run for the victims of crimes. They arrange meetings with the perpetrators – face-to-face sit-downs – with a moderator present. It's all very safe and well managed...from what I can make out. The meetings are so that everyone directly involved in an incident can talk through what happened and learn from it.'

'And...'

'Well, I approached them...regarding Harry.'

'When?'

She looked uncomfortable. 'Before Christmas. Just to make initial enquiries. It's a non-starter if the perpetrator refuses.'

'And...'

'I've received an email from them, saying Harry has agreed to meet us, if we want to pursue it. I obviously haven't committed us to anything yet.'

Marcus wasn't really surprised. He'd seen what she'd been watching. He'd looked at her search history. What he was angry about was Fran taking him for mug. If it had got to the stage of them approaching Harry, she'd hadn't simply *made initial enquiries*; she must have made a formal application, must have spoken to them, pursued it, provided them with information – all without saying anything to him.

Fran was still talking. 'We can discuss it more tonight. I've got some information I could show you, but given that I've just heard he's said "Yes", I thought I should tell you.'

'Yeah' was all he could manage by way of a response.

She actually squirmed in her seat. 'Marcus? Do you think it's something you would consider? It might really help. Give us a chance to speak to Harry directly. He barely said two words at the hearing. This way, we could talk to him for as long as we need – find out what really happened that night. That's got to be worth pursuing, hasn't it?'

Harry *had* said more than two words at the sentencing. He'd read out a short statement, the paper wavering in his hands, his voice low and distressed, his face so tight it was amazing the words had managed to get through his clenched jaw.

'Marcus?'

He stood up. 'I'll think about it. I've got to get ready for work.'

Upstairs he cleaned his teeth, looking at himself in the bathroom mirror. If the eyes are supposed to be the window to the soul, in his house the blinds were down.

Chapter 67

THREE WEEKS later Harry received the letter confirming the restorative justice meeting. He took it back to his cell. It had been opened and read, of course – that was one of the many personal infringements of serving time. Nothing was private, nothing except your thoughts, and even those they wanted. Up until that point Harry had stoically resisted their attempts to get him to talk – to share – and yet by agreeing to the meeting with Fran and Marcus he had walked straight into the firing line. He slid out the letter. He skipped through the official waffle on the front. Fran and Marcus's questions were on the second page:

The applicant[s] would like the discussion to focus on the following areas:

- The events on the night of the crash, specifically,
  - for you to talk about what happened at the party
  - for you to explain your decision to drink and drive
  - for you to provide a detailed breakdown of exactly what happened after you and the others left Alice Mitcham's house

- to explain why you left Mo Akhtar behind in the car park
- for you to give your explanation of what caused the crash
- for you to describe what you did immediately after the crash
- for you to express your understanding of your responsibility for what happened.
• For you to tell us anything you can about how Jess was that night – before, during and after the crash. What mood she was in. What she said. What she did. Specifically, for you to describe her last few hours of consciousness.
• For you to say what you would do differently.
• For you to demonstrate that you comprehend the impact of your actions on the lives of everyone involved and on the lives of their families and friends.

The questions were what he'd expected, because they were what any parent would want to know – had the right to know – about the death of their child. And the only person who could answer them was Harry.

He put the letter aside, lay down and stared at the ceiling.

Over the course of the next couple of hours he sensed, rather than saw, the screws on duty slow as they passed his cell door. They all looked in, checking on him. At least none of them tried to engage him in conversation. As he lay on his bunk he concentrated on the floaters that drifted across his field of vision. Jess had once gone into a long spiel about them – she'd just done 'eyes' on her biology course. The weird, ghostly shapes were something to do with blood cells and proteins reflecting off the retina. Aware that he wasn't listening, she'd taken it up a notch. She'd announced that in some people they were an indicator of a rare medical condition – she made up some daft name – and that in these people the floaters were actually microscopic creatures that had got inside the eyeball. She claimed that you picked them up from swimming in infected water – he'd just come back from a holiday in Goa at this point – and that, if left untreated, the bacteria could multiply and destroy the person's sight, so that eventually they couldn't even see what was right in front of them. At that point Harry had put his phone down and given Jess the attention she was demanding, and deserved.

He rolled onto his side and wished he could cry, but the sea creatures swirled by, refusing to cooperate.

Chapter 68

FRAN HAD arranged to meet Natalie, her advocate, in the visitors' car park at the prison. Even with the heavy traffic, she was early. She was glad. She needed the time to calm down and compose herself. The drive had been as bad as she'd imagined: lorries whizzing past within centimetres of her car, splattering dirty slush and spray onto her windscreen; impatient drivers flashing at her to move over; the anxiety about coming off at the right junction. It was the furthest she'd driven in ages, in terrible weather – the type of trip no loving husband would make his anxious wife do on her own. But she had made it safely, in one piece, arriving in the right place, in good time. Relieved of the pressure of staring at the road in front of her, she took in her surroundings. The prison was what she was expecting. An ugly main block of a building, surrounded by equally brutal smaller blocks encircled by a chain-link fence.

It had taken months to get to this point; it had taken courage and perseverance, and it had cost her.

Marcus's abandonment of her and Jess was unfathomable. Right up until this morning she'd thought he would have a change of heart and come with her, if not willingly, then at least out of his sense of loyalty. That he was making her face this on her own was…

unforgivable. She knew – and this is what made it seem such a calculated ploy – that he'd banked on his last-minute refusal to drive her up to Darlington in bad weather as the insurmountable hurdle that would get her to cancel. It just went to show how little Marcus knew her any more. How out of touch he was with the steel in her spirit.

He'd signalled his discomfort with the whole idea over the course of the weeks building up to the visit: refusing to watch the videos she queued up for him; skim-reading, at best, the literature she left out on the dining-room table; adding nothing to the list of questions they'd been asked to submit in advance of the trip to Darlington. Every conversation they'd had about it had been the same – Fran's belief that this was an opportunity they couldn't pass up, and Marcus's view that it was a very bad idea. His key concern, and the one he repeated over and over again, was what she thought they would get out of it.

Answers! That's what they would get.

Or that's what she was going to get. Not Marcus. Because he was sixty miles away, at home, hiding from reality.

Natalie's car pulled up alongside hers. Fran reached for her coat and stepped out into the cold wind.

Chapter 69

HARRY CHOSE a pair of jeans and a plain T-shirt from the small pile of clothes in his cupboard. They were badly creased, and neither smelt that fresh. The prison laundry was basic – you were lucky if you even got your own stuff back. The jeans and the top had his name inside them, written in indelible Sharpie by Martha. Every time he put on his clothes the sight of her handwriting hurt. Dressed, and ready as he'd ever be, he sat on his bunk and waited for Jim to come and fetch him.

It had transpired that the restorative justice process required Harry to have a representative who was 'on his side' at the meeting – it couldn't go ahead without one – so in the end he'd been forced to ask his dad. It had been a frosty conversation.

'But I don't understand why you'd consider doing such a thing?' Dom had kept his voice low, despite the cacophony of laughing and arguing around them in the visitors' room.

'I just think I should meet them. Now that they've asked?'

'But it'll be awful.' Dom was remembering the fierce energy of Fran's grief and her anger, when she turned up at the house.

'It's supposed to help.'

'How?'

'By getting it all out in the open.'

Dom made a noise, which was not assent.

Harry tried a different tack, one he thought might have more influence. 'They also said that it looks good, if you do it. It can influence parole decisions.'

Dom glanced around the packed visitors' room. 'By much?'

Harry felt the familiar irritation with his father's binary approach to life – the accountant's measurement of profit and loss – and, out of perversity, he downplayed the value placed on the restorative process. 'Well, there are no guarantees. Besides, that's not why I'm doing it.'

'So, why you are?' Dom's impatience wasn't ill-concealed – it wasn't concealed at all.

Fuck him! It hadn't ever occurred to his father than he might need to talk about what happened; that bottling it all up was screwing with his head. It was like having a migraine that never went away. But Dom had no patience with that sort of nonsense. He didn't do messy emotion. Harry resorted to provoking him, as usual. 'Because I knew it would piss you off.'

Dom's response was a sudden stiffening of his whole body. He snapped upright, making full use of his six-foot-two frame and his gym-honed shoulders. He wasn't so different from the thick-necked steroid boys on the wing. 'Harry. Pack it in.'

Out of the corner of his eye, Harry saw one of the officers catch the whiff of trouble rising from their conversation. His attention locked onto them, ready to intervene. Harry took it down a notch, not out of his respect for his dad, but in order to avoid any grief from the screws. 'It's actually my choice, Dad. You can turn up or you can not. It makes sod-all difference to me. I know how much you hate coming here anyway. I don't want to put another date in your busy schedule. I'm sure one of the screws will step up instead.'

'Now you're being childish,' Dom said. 'I didn't say I wouldn't come. I just want to know what the outcomes are likely to be.'

'Hell knows. That's kinda down to Fran and Marcus.'

'And that's my point.'

'Yes. And?'

'You'll be at their mercy.'

'Yes.' Even while agreeing, they could argue. The officer was still observing them. Body language didn't lie.

'Well, that's not good, is it?' Dom pointed out.

'No. Not good. But that's the point.'

'We're going round in circles. You're going do it with or without me, aren't you?'

To which Harry had answered 'Yeah.'

There was a knock on his cell door. It was Jim. 'You ready, lad?'

Harry stood up. 'Yeah.'

Chapter 70

IT WAS all so ordinary.

A room set up ready for a meeting, with tea, coffee and biscuits laid out on the side, a flipchart in the corner. There were only five chairs in the room, arranged in a somewhat pathetic-looking semicircle. Fran and Natalie took their places, but their presence felt inadequate. The space could easily have accommodated twenty or more. Fran had read that some sessions involved whole communities facing down the perpetrator. She'd pored over the stories of neighbours brought together by their indignation over arson attacks; parents who'd stood side-by-side demanding justice for their murdered offspring; siblings who had fought for years for their day of reckoning, after a parent had been left for dead by a drunk driver. There was an army of victims' families out there, united in their grief and their pursuit of the truth. Today she joined their ranks – while everyone else, including her husband, turned their faces away.

She had never felt more alone.

Chapter 71

HARRY STOOD on the other side of the door. He had never felt more alone.

Jim checked one more time that he was 'happy' to go through with the meeting. He nodded. The escorting officer opened the door and Harry walked through it.

There were chairs, set out in a semi-circle. A window. Three people. One of them Fran. No Marcus. No last-minute appearance by Dom. Mugs. A kettle. A plate of biscuits. Touches of humanity. Everyone standing. A woman with severely cropped dark hair taking drinks orders. The banality of it. Then everyone sitting. Harry opposite Fran, too close. Unable to look at her. Voices. The facilitator woman, 'Kerry Something', welcoming everyone. A calm voice that didn't ease the thudding inside Harry's head or lessen the discomfort of his ribs hitching up and down because there wasn't enough air in his lungs.

The woman was going through the 'rules'. There was no need; he had been told them, many times over. They were expected to stick to the basics of a normal conversation – in the most abnormal of circumstances – *mutual respect, listening, no interrupting, learning from each other's experiences.* It was a mantra designed to make what they were about to do *safe*. It didn't feel safe. Harry had never felt more aware of his body; of the bones in his backside that were making sitting on the plastic chair uncomfortable; of the noise of the air sucking in through his nose and out through his dry mouth; of the crack of his joints as he clenched and unclenched his fists. It was impossible to make himself less present. But there again, that was the point.

Finally the moderator turned to Fran. 'Do you want to get us started, Fran? Bear in mind that you have your prompts, if you need them. And I've got a copy of your questions, should you need me to step in and facilitate at any point.'

There was a silence that was thicker and heavier than anything Harry had ever experienced before. Within that silence was compressed months and months of raw emotion – his and hers. He didn't look at Fran. He couldn't. He looked at the floor, not allowing his gaze to stray beyond the confines of his trainers.

'I want to know what happened?' Fran's voice was clear and steady.

It was what he was expecting, what he had prepared for, but it was impossible to answer nevertheless. His trainers were dirty, stained by the months of walking the halls and yards of the prison. The lace on the left shoe had snapped. He'd had to knot and rethread it, so it was laced up wrongly. They were waiting. Fran was waiting. He was waiting.

'Harry!' Instinctively he looked up and instantly regretted it. 'You have to tell me what happened. That's why I came. You owe me that. You owe Jess that. Tell me what happened.'

She had every right to demand his confession. But still...where was he supposed to begin? He wanted to tell Fran, needed to, but he didn't know how. Panic took over.

He hadn't even been aware of Jim, until he felt the pressure of his hand on his arm. 'Harry. It's okay. Take a breath. There's no rush.' Fran's face said otherwise. 'Why don't you start by telling Mrs

Beaumont about the party? About what you and your friends were doing before the crash. Anything at all. Just to get us going.'

Under pressure, Harry blurted out, 'I only had a couple of drinks.' Fuck. Fuck. Fuck! That wasn't what he'd meant to say. What the fuck had he said that for?

He heard Fran inhale – a short gasp of frustration. He'd disappointed her before, hundreds of times when he was a kid, but he'd never seen her look so disgusted.

What he wanted to start with was: *I am so, so sorry that I took Jess from you. I would do anything to bring her back, if I could. I understand why you hate me. I hate myself. I hurt Jess. I didn't mean to. But I did. I wish – more than anything in the world – that I hadn't, but I did. I loved her, but I treated her like I didn't. I don't know why I did that. I regret it. Really, truly regret it. I never meant to hurt her. But that was the problem. I didn't mean anything enough. I didn't realise until it was too late how much I loved her. I didn't appreciate how happy she made me. I didn't realise that I had to let her know that I loved her by what I did. I was a shit to her that night. And other times. I made her sad. I made her happy as well, some of the time. But I didn't stick to it. I didn't stick to her. Not enough. Not in the way she deserved. She was better than me. And I took what we had and fucked it up.*

He glanced at Fran. The look of disgust on her face was what he deserved.

The moderator stepped in, trying to make up for his false start. 'I think what Fran wants from you, Harry, is a description of the events of the night. Why don't we start with what happened at Alice Mitcham's house? How did you get there?'

A simple question.

So, fucking answer it, the voice in Harry's head screamed. He focused on the broken shoelace. 'I drove to the party.' Everyone sat back a fraction in their chairs – Harry could tell by the readjustment of their feet. He made himself keep going. 'I picked Jake and Tish up from her house, and we went on from there.' He was already forgetting that there were details Fran didn't know, couldn't know – because they had kept things from her. But now was the time for telling her the truth. 'Jess was already at my house. She got ready there.' Fran made another odd noise, a strange, stuttery kind of inward breath, like his words had got stuck in her windpipe. 'Jess had said that she was staying with Gabbie.'

Fran pulled her feet back under her chair, retracting from him. Harry kept his head down; it was the only way he was going to be able to get through this.

'So you lied about Jess's whereabouts that night?' The moderator.

'Yes. We lied. I did tell the police.'

'Go on.'

'We drove to the party.'

'Straight there?' the woman asked.

'No, we called in at The Railway on the way.' They waited. 'I bought a round. Me and Jake had a beer, Tish had a vodka and lemonade and Jess had a cider. We stayed for about an hour. Then we went on to Alice's house.'

'Why did you drive, if you knew you were going to drink?' Fran's voice.

He'd rehearsed this with Jim. 'Because I knew I wasn't going to have more than one or two. I had football in the morning.' Was supposed to have football – that had all gone.

'So you knowingly drank alcohol at the pub and at the party, and then drove. With other people in the car. With Jess in the car,' Fran pushed.

'Yes.'

'How much did you drink?'

It had been a light night. Or what would have been a light night in the dim, distant, pre-accident past. Everyone else had drunk far more. Harry chose not to say that out loud, because it was irrelevant. He was the driver. He should've known better. He did know better. But there were reasons why he'd had another drink. Reasons that didn't bear examining.

'Harry?' They were all waiting.

'A beer at the pub, then a bit more later.' Even that truth was complicated. 'I shared a drink with someone, at the party. Vodka and lime.'

The room went quiet as they listened to him confess what they already knew. His blood alcohol levels had been quoted as part of the evidence against him. Percentage proof that he'd not given a fuck. But he had. He did.

'Do you regret that now?' The woman again, asking the blindingly obvious.

'Yes. Of course. Of course I regret it. Every single day.' He risked another glance up at Fran. Her eyes were closed.

'Tell us about the party?' the moderator prompted.

Confessing about the drinking had been the easy part – comparatively. Now he was into more difficult territory. The untold story of the night. He moved his feet, making sure that his toes were exactly level. Across from him he heard Fran take a series of rapid, shaky breaths, as if she was about to say something. He desperately wanted her to tell him how to control all the emotions smashing through him, how to behave, what to say – like she used to when he was a child. But she didn't. There was a bleak, stony silence. He was going to have to get through this on his own. 'It was busy. There were loads of people from college there, along with some of Alice's mates from work. People were just chilling out, talking, catching up. Everyone was having a good time. *We* were having a good time.'

They had been. It had been relaxed. A good vibe, everyone glad it was the weekend. A release from all the pressure of college work and uni applications, and jobs and relationships, and parents planning their lives out for them. Too much of a release, in hindsight. As always, Jake was the life and soul of the party, making everyone laugh – at least to start with – before his jokes got unfunny and his dancing more and more irritating.

Tish's eyes had tracked them both, flicking from Jake to Harry, making clear the comparison – and the winner. After a while she'd worked her way around the room to Harry, eyes locked on his, smiling, reminding him, provoking him. She'd raised her glass to him, beckoned him over. He'd gone. She'd sipped her drink, passed it to him. He'd hesitated, but not for long. A few sips couldn't do any harm. He'd tasted her lipstick on the rim of the glass. They'd passed the drink back and forth, a silent exchange that was loaded with meaning. The next thing he knew, they were dancing. Her fingernails tracing a line down his biceps, her hips connecting with his, her attention focused on him. Her shoulders bare. Her jeans tight. Muscle-memory stirred.

And where was Jess? Off somewhere else, as usual. When they were out, they made a point of not spending too much time together. It was an unspoken rule. Neither of them wanted anything getting back to their parents. They had agreed to keep their relationship secret, because that was the way it had started – out of the blue, in the dark, when no one else was looking, surprising and slightly embarrassing them both. The secrecy was part of what kept it special. It was also supposed to keep it simple. But because they always acted like they were *just old friends* when they were around other people, Harry sometimes felt that it might as well be true. It had all become a bit of a mess, but it was a mess that he couldn't be bothered unravelling – not on Friday night with the music loud and no one else giving a fuck. God, Tish smelt good.

He broke away from her, abruptly, without an explanation, knowing he should stay away from her, and went in search of Jess.

He found her in the kitchen, holding court, oblivious. He could have left the party and she wouldn't have noticed. She was getting serious about some political shit – again. Climate change, probably. That's what it was, most days. How they were killing the earth with consumerism, and how everything was going to be washed away by the rising seas. Seas that were full of harmful plastic. It was choke-or-drown time, before-the-end-of-the-weekend, judging by her passion. Her face was flushed, her hands weaving and jabbing in the air – 'off on one'. Her nerdy, tree-hugging mates lapping it up. Her idea of fun. Not his.

He remembered standing in the doorway, watching her, and being swamped by a sense of separateness from Jess and everything she was interested in, and feeling tired with having to make an effort – all the time. They were not right together. They were too different.

He headed back into the main room.

The party was heating up. People were paired up or dancing. And there was Tish, leaning against the far wall, watching him. Harry made his way over to her. She smiled. He smiled.

'Look at me! No one else. Just me,' she'd commanded, and he had.

'Look at me!' It was Fran giving the commands now. 'You're here because you're supposed to be prepared to tell the truth. Are you, Harry? Are you going to tell me what really happened that night or are you simply going to sit there?' They all waited. Fran continued to stare at him, refusing to let him off the hook.

He had to get it all out in one gush. 'I behaved like a total prick. I got it on with Tish. At the party. Mo filmed it. He didn't mean to, didn't realise that he had. Still doesn't. He just happened to catch us at it. Jess saw the video on his phone, when we were in McDonald's. Then it all turned to shit. It was all my fault.'

'Harry! Please can you be a little more mindful of your language,' the woman complained.

But Fran was still staring at him, her expression a stiff mixture of anger and pain. 'I'm not bothered what words he uses. Go on.' Her impatience was sharp and unforgiving.

The moderator looked from Fran to Harry and back again, aware that the temperature in the room had sky-rocketed. 'Can you walk it back for us, Harry? Are you saying that Jess and you were in a relationship, and that she caught you...' she struggled to find the right words, 'flirting with Tish?'

Harry made himself hold Fran's gaze. 'I'd been sleeping with Tish, on and off, all the time I was with Jess.' Because he was dumb.

'This is Tish, Jess's friend, who was with Jake? Your best friend?' Fran hammered home his crapness.

'Yes.'

'And you're claiming that you and Jess were in a relationship of some description?' Fran said it as if the thought disgusted her.

This part he had to get right. 'I'm not *claiming* it, Fran. I *was*. We were together. We had been for months.' Fran drew herself up in her seat. Unconsciously he did the same. His relationship with Jess was the one thing he was proud of; not how he'd behaved, but that she had loved him – had thought him worth loving. 'It just happened. Neither of us planned it. One night it all changed between us.' *Be honest. Tell them why.* 'I was upset. I'd had another bust-up with my dad, and Jess came round. We talked, for a long time. And she was so kind. Because that's the way she was.' It was Jess who'd leant over and kissed him and, though he pulled back at first, confused by her coming on to him, he hadn't had to think about it for too long, because he realised she wasn't simply a girl he knew; she was *the* girl – in fact the only person – who knew him better than anyone else.

Although he could see how Fran might struggle with that, because of their history, and because of how efficiently and effectively they'd lied to her – and everyone else – for more than a year. 'We didn't tell anyone at first, because we weren't sure what it was. And we didn't want it to cause any upset. Then it became a habit, keeping it secret.' And if he was truly honest, it had suited him. While he and Jess were a secret, his life could go on as before. Cricket, football, nights out with his mates. And yes, he had to admit to himself, looking 'girlfriend-free' had had one other advantage. Tish.

The woman shifted her focus to Fran. 'Do you want to take a break, Fran?'

She shook her head vehemently. It was only then that it consciously struck Harry that Fran was on her own. No Marcus. This realisation was a shock. Harry couldn't work out what it signified. Marcus with his nerdy hobbies and passions, and his cheery willingness to do stuff for other people, as if it was the most normal thing in the world. Jess's dad. A decent bloke. Happy to bowl endless overs on the beach and drop easy catches to stop a seven-year-old having a meltdown because he was out. Why wasn't he here? Could he not stand the thought of being in the same room as Harry?

'No. I want him to keep going. Go back to the party. I want to hear it all. In order. Why did you leave when you did? What happened with Mo?' Fran asked.

He had suddenly wanted to leave the party and get away from all of them: Tish's demanding availability, Jess's indifference, Jake's pissed-up prat-routine. 'I realised that I was behaving like a dick, so I left Tish and went out into the back garden to get some fresh air.'

'To sober up?'

He didn't rise to it. 'To get some fresh air. After a while, Jess came out and we just sat there.' Looking at the stars. He had felt bad and she'd picked up on his sad vibe. She'd lifted his arm and wriggled underneath it, wanting a cuddle. Not a grope, or a snog, but a cuddle. And he'd obliged. Because one of the things he had learnt from Jess was that no-strings-attached affection was good. 'Mo came out and sat with us, and we talked about...normal stuff. Then I suggested that we go home.'

'Why?'

'Because I'd had enough. I didn't want to stay late. Cos of the match in the morning.' Another disbelieving noise from Fran. 'We went back inside the house to tell Jake, and Tish. But Jake wouldn't come. He was having too much of a good time.'

'He was drunk?'

'Yeah.'

'There was a scene?'

'Not really. I just said if he wasn't gonna come with us, he'd have to get himself home.'

'Witnesses said you lost your temper.'

'Nah. Jake is irritating when he's had a few. It was no different that night.' Except it was, because Tish's eyes had been on him, blazing with questions. In all honesty, Jake's pratting about – banging into people and calling him a *party pooper* – *had* got on Harry's nerves more than usual. His stupidity and gullibility were bloody annoying. *Happy-go-lucky Jake*, his best buddy, for ever, blind to what was going on right in front of his beer, schnapps and weed-goggled eyes. 'Jess and I left. Tish must have said something that got through to Jake, because they followed us out to the car.'

'And then you drove, knowing that you were over the limit?'

He nodded. He couldn't deny it. Couldn't defend it.

The woman chipped in. 'Can you confirm who was in the car at this point.'

'Me and Jess in the front. Tish, Jake and Mo in the back. Mo in the middle.'

'And you drove where?'

'We set off to come home, but on the ring road Jake saw McDonald's and started banging on about wanting something to eat.' They'd all started chanting, 'Burger! Burger!' Post-drinking munchies. 'We pulled in and went inside to order.'

'All of you?' The woman again, wanting to get the facts straight.

Though they knew all this. Harry saying it aloud wasn't going to change anything.

'Yes.'

'What about Jess?' Fran asked.

'Yeah, her as well.'

'No!' she snapped. 'I meant: tell me about Jess. How was she? I want you to tell me everything you can remember about that last hour.'

Harry didn't want to answer that. Couldn't bring himself to. He could still see and hear her, laughing, happy, unaware of the tension between him and Tish, just wanting her veggie burger and fries. 'She was fine. Happy. A bit giddy. She went to sit down with Mo, while we put in the order.' He should have kept his eyes on them. If only he'd seen Mo pass Jess his phone and her start scrolling through it, looking at the pictures from the party. But no, even then he couldn't have realised that his world was about to explode, because he hadn't known what was on Mo's phone. No one did at that point.

Harry went back to concentrating on his trainers. Shame itched at his neck and spread up into his hair, tightening his scalp. 'We waited for our order at the counter. When it came, we went over to the table. That's when I noticed that Jess was quiet, not touching her food. It was like someone had let the air out of her.' Tish had noticed as well, and in contrast she'd got louder, more hyper, more animated. Jake was oblivious, stuffing fries in his mouth and singing snatches of some unidentifiable tune. Mo, maybe sensing the new tension, had gone to the loo. 'Something Tish did upset Jess.' *Way to go: blame Tish.*

'What?' they all asked in unison.

'She came and sat on my knee.' Knowing full well that it was provocative. Tish was mad with him. He could tell by the set of her mouth and the defiance in her eyes. 'Jess reacted. She stood up, grabbed the car keys and Mo's phone and ran out.' And he'd sat there for a few seconds with Tish's arse anchored against his crotch, shocked, but unmoving. 'I turfed Tish off my knee and ran after Jess.'

The woman spoke again, and this time her tone was softer, almost kind. 'Harry, I'm sorry, but it's very difficult for us to hear what you're saying when you've got your head down like that. Could you look up, please?'

He chose the window ledge to the left of Fran's head and fixed his eyes on that. He continued, 'By the time I got outside, she was in the car.' Her face turned away from him.

'How could you?' Jess had said fiercely.

'How could I "what"?' he'd asked. But Harry knew – screwing around with your best mate's girlfriend behind your own girlfriend's back, with one of her best mates.

'You and Tish. Tish!' Jess's voice rose and cracked. 'Well?' She was swallowing down tears as well as anger.

'It meant nothing.'

She shook her head.

What to say next? How much should he confess to? Harry had weighed it up. Not wanting to hurt Jess, or himself, more than necessary. Not wanting to be found out and look bad. Not wanting her to dump him. Not wanting to be the one in the wrong.

Someone had left a Perspex lunch box on the windowsill. Inside it he could see a banana that was going brown. The thought of it made him feel queasy. He could feel them waiting for the rest of the story. 'Jess was upset. She'd seen me and Tish kissing in the video Mo had filmed at the party.'

'Did you deny it?' Fran.

'No.'

Jess had passed him the phone. He'd clicked the arrow on the screen and the video had played. And there – in shaky high-res – was the evidence that damned him. Alice's front room, a sea of bodies, the pulsing disco lights and Jake looming up close to the camera, a big, stupid grin on his face. Just another night out. It could have been any house, any party, any weekend, any group of friends anywhere. The tunes coming through the phone speaker into the dead night air of the car park had sounded tiny, distant. As he watched, Harry spotted a couple, strobed by the lights, leaning against the back wall, not dancing or talking or drinking. A fine-looking couple; the girl in a sparkly top, the lad in a tight T-shirt. A couple who were all over each other.

'No. I didn't deny it.' Because he couldn't, and because he knew that he wouldn't be able to lie to Jess, not to her face. He'd never actually *lied* to her – he'd just not told her the truth. What he did with Tish, occasionally, when one or both of them were drunk or horny or bored, was nothing to do with how he felt about Jess. That was separate. She was never meant to find out – would never have found out – if it hadn't been for Mo.

He went back to the story, wanting to get the telling of it over and done with. 'The others appeared.' Running towards them across the car park. And he'd lost it. Mad at himself, he'd let fly at Mo. 'Mo and I had a row. I blamed him. Unfairly.' Mo. The only one of his 'friends' who'd come to see him in prison and kept coming, despite the cost and the inconvenience. Mo, one of the nicest people Harry knew, and the one who had started it all. 'There was a scuffle.'

'A fight?' The woman asked.

'No. I never hit him.' But he had wanted to.

'Then what happened?'

'Tish started yelling at me.'

'Yelling what?'

'To stop.'

'And did you?'

'Yes.'

'But you still threw Mohir's phone across the car park.' The woman. A stickler for correct details.

300

'I was upset that I'd upset Jess.'

'And while all this was going on, what was my daughter doing?' Fran's voice was forceful, demanding.

'Crying.'

The room went quiet, each of them imagining Jess sitting in the front seat of the car, distraught...because of him.

Harry needed to keep going, to put into words the next twenty minutes of that night – the last point when things could have turned out differently and all their lives could have gone on, maybe even recovered from the mess he'd created. 'I went back to the car. Apologised to Jess for losing my temper. Tried to comfort her, but she said she wanted to go home.' Fran swallowed a sob. 'Tish and Jake got in and we drove off.'

'What about Mo?'

'We left him behind.'

The atmosphere in the car had been poisonous. No one talking except Jake, who was yakking total gibberish. Tish's eyes had drilled into Harry's every time he glanced in the rear-view mirror. Jess had been stony silent, her face turned away.

'Then what happened?'

He'd driven them home, fast, wanting the night to end, for the anger and panic in his gut to subside. Just wanting to get back. To get rid of Tish and her silent accusations. To get shot of Jake and his pissed-up ignorance. To park up on a dark side-street with Jess and try and explain. To make her look at him, so that she would see how sorry he was. For him to get her to understand that Tish meant nothing to him, compared to what he felt for her. To tell Jess how he couldn't cope without her. That he would never do it again. That he loved her.

He never got the chance.

'We were nearly back.'

Maybe that was why she finally turned towards him, her eyes

big, her expression bereft, and asked him, again, 'Harry, how could you?'

And he'd looked at her and felt terrible and trapped and guilty and angry all at the same time. He knew that he owed her an explanation, but he couldn't answer her because there wasn't any good reason why he'd cheated on her. He just had – because he was a selfish prick. It didn't mean he didn't love her. He did. But he didn't say that. He didn't say anything. He'd looked back at the road, heard Jess shout, 'Harry!', saw something flash in front of the car, jerked the wheel and lost control.

'Then the car crashed?' The woman again, stating the horrific obvious.

Harry nodded. He really didn't want to have to describe the rest of it – the knowing that the car had become a missile. That they were going to crash. That there was nothing he could do to stop it.

Then the bang.

The pain.

The blank.

Then the screaming.

No, he couldn't.

Fran was staring at him, her hands balled into fists on her knees. 'So she was heartbroken in the last few moments of her life – because of *you*.'

'Yes. I am so sorry. So very, very sorry. I never meant to hurt anyone, especially not Jess. I loved her.'

There was a second or two of stillness as his confession settled and took root.

He had loved Jess and he had killed her.

Fran slowly got up from her chair and crossed the room towards him. The moderator stretched out her hand – a discouraging or comforting gesture, it was hard to tell. Regardless, Fran ignored it. She stood over Harry, her stomach moving in and out, deep, steadying breaths. Harry tilted his face and looked up at her. She stared at him, her eyes full of tears, drew back her hand and slapped him hard across his face.

Chapter 72

THE FLAT of Fran's palm connected with Harry's face. It stung. She hoped it hurt him more. How dare he?

Kerry, the moderator, leapt out of her seat and put her hands on Fran's arms, pulling her backwards.

How dare she?

Fran swung round, and Kerry let go. This was not in the carefully rehearsed plan, with all its emphasis on mutual understanding and respect.

'Fran, please?' Kerry looked shocked, her face ashen. Fran didn't care. She owed this woman and her colleagues nothing. This had always been about getting something back for Jess; it had never been for Harry's benefit, his rehabilitation, his grasp of the consequences of what he'd done – they were by-products, outcomes that the state wanted, to justify all the time and expense. She didn't care about Harry. Not any more. How could she? How could she accommodate any thoughts about his wrecked life, his grief, his guilt, when she had an ocean of pain inside herself? She had walked into this bleak, bland room for one reason only – to get close to her daughter, by getting close to the person who had taken her away.

But it hadn't worked. The more Harry had talked, the less it had been about Jess. He'd sat there, staring at his feet, dribbling out his self-pity and self-justification, and they'd expected her to just sit there, an audience for his performance. They had nodded and encouraged him, even praised him, as if his ability to string a sentence together was an achievement. *I drank, but not much.* Sympathetic smiles all round. *I drove while drunk, but I'm sorry.* Round of applause. *I lied, or we both did.* Indulgent nods. *I cheated, but it meant nothing.* Good on you for acknowledging the error of your ways. *I broke Jess's heart, but I didn't mean to.* Pat on the arm. *I crashed the car, but it's not my fault.* We understand.

I loved her.

No, you did not! You used her. Humiliated her. Hurt her. Then you killed her.

Fran stood over Harry, watching as red finger marks appeared on his cheek, itching to hit him again. He didn't move. He just sat there with his face raised, accepting his punishment.

Kerry stepped into the impending threat. 'We really need to take a break. Jim, perhaps you could take Harry out for a while? Check that he's okay. I think we all need to take some time to reflect and calm down.'

The officer tapped Harry's arm, prompting him. He got to his feet slowly.

Fran suddenly wanted him to stay put. He'd had his say. She hadn't. She wasn't finished with him. She grabbed his arm. Harry stopped. She felt the muscles in his arm beneath her nails, the strength in him, but also the lack of resistance. His eyes were fearful.

'Fran, this really is totally unacceptable. Please let go of Harry, immediately.' There was no calmness in the moderator now. 'Fran!'

She finally found her voice. 'No! He needs to hear me. He's ripped my life apart. He has to listen.'

Still Harry didn't pull away. Their faces were close. She could see the dark shadows under his eyes, and how pasty and unhealthy his skin looked.

'Fran. I'm not going to ask again. Let him go! If you don't, I will be forced to ask the officers to intervene.'

She could smell him. Deodorant. The taint of stress on his breath. He was taller than her. His shoulders wide. A man.

Harry and Jess. Together. No, no, no! Fran recoiled at the thought and let go. Jim hustled him out. The door was pulled shut behind them.

She didn't listen to the debrief. Didn't drink the tea they fetched her. She might have nodded in response to their considered comments; she couldn't remember. She didn't care any more. When they felt she'd been chastised and sympathised with enough, she was escorted out of the prison through the various locked doors and gates. She found herself outside, standing next to a chronically embarrassed and panicky Natalie, whose lipsticked mouth kept moving. More empty words. Fran waited stoically for her to shut up. It was only when Fran went to her car, got in and shut the door that Natalie's monologue finally ceased.

Natalie stood there, for at least another minute, looking distressed, before she finally shifted her bag onto her other shoulder and turned towards her own car. She would no doubt have to write a detailed report about why the session had gone so badly wrong. It would not go down well with her superiors. A black mark. Fran didn't care.

Fran watched Natalie put her coat and bag in the back of her car, climb in, readjust her seat and her mirror – why would she need to do that? she hadn't shrunk in the past two hours – and finally set off. Her departure was a relief.

It was over. It had been a disaster. Fran felt worse, not better. Months and months of lobbying and planning and preparing for this day, believing that it would change how she felt by changing what she knew. But it hadn't helped. She pushed the car into gear and drove out of the car park, following the satnav instructions that would lead her back onto the A1, to a life made worse by the visit.

Chapter 73

FRAN PUT her foot down and overtook a lorry. She was furious, blindingly, bitterly furious. Restorative justice! There had been nothing restorative about it. It had been corrosive. Poisonous! And as for justice, there'd been no justice in what had happened inside that room. Harry had sat there, hanging his head, wringing his hands – the picture of contrition – spilling out his self-pity and his lies, making it all about him. And Kerry, the moderator, the person who was supposed to be the impartial adjudicator, had nodded and made her sympathetic little noises and comments.

They'd positioned the meeting as Fran's opportunity to get answers, to face Harry with the consequences of his actions, to arrive at closure. In practice, they'd ripped the wound of Jess's death wide open, then expected her to sit and bleed out quietly while he got to talk, and talk, and talk. A confession, at last, of his drinking, his lack of attention, his responsibility for the crash, his disloyalty. All those careful, softly spoken words, with the bleating undertone of himself as the victim.

And it had worked. They had been *sympathetic* to him, angry with her.

They'd wanted a polite, civil, conciliatory meeting that ticked a box and earnt points for the judicial service. Jesus! – she undertook another car that was dawdling along in the outside lane – the meeting would probably help his case, earn Harry extra points for showing remorse. It was all a sham. How dare they blame her for the breakdown of the session? How dare they have the audacity to cut her off, censoring her feelings and her words? So much for the voice of the victim; the only voice that had been heard was his.

Fran drove on, her emotions rolling and roaring inside her.

They didn't get it. Couldn't. They hadn't had their daughter taken from them, broken apart, killed by Harry's arrogance and carelessness. Her fury bounced from him to the liaison team, to Marcus.

Marcus had left her to face the ordeal alone. He'd totally abdicated his responsibilities as a husband and a father. How could he do that? He should've been there at her side. The thought of having to explain to him what had happened, when she got back, was too much. He had no right to know, because he hadn't stepped up. But if she didn't tell him, didn't talk to somebody about it, she feared she would go mad.

She took the exit.

And as for what Harry claimed about his relationship with Jess. She ragged the gears from fifth down to fourth. How dare he? No. Fran couldn't bear to think about it. Not Jess. Not her cool, confident daughter. Jess, whose heart she'd known. No. She would never have had a secret that huge. Harry had been like a brother. Fran had half-raised the boy. No, it wasn't possible. But the idea of them together as a couple swelled and pulsed inside her head, releasing a slew of unwanted images. Harry at the hospital, looking shell-shocked. Harry standing at the back of the chapel at the funeral, his face wet with tears.

The same Harry who had been in their lives for so long that they almost didn't notice him. Eating meals in their kitchen. Horsing around with Jess. Sharing in their good times. Christmas, holidays, family birthdays – a thousand ordinary, happy days.

She crossed the first roundabout. Turned left, then drove over the second, took the right turn.

No. Not Harry. She would've known. Jess told her everything. They were close. Closer than most mothers and daughters. It wasn't possible.

Out of nowhere, there was a little girl.

In the middle of the road!

No. No!

Fran slammed on the brakes. Her leg locked. The car kept going. The child's small face froze – the beginning of a cry – but she didn't move. Fran pressed harder. She was thrown forward, then backwards. The seatbelt sliced through her ribs. Too much momentum coming to a stop much too quickly.

The child had disappeared.

Under the car?

No!

Fran sat, chest heaving, hands gripping the steering wheel, and waited for the screaming to start.

Chapter 74

FRAN HAD never hit him as a child, not that Harry could remember, not even a tap on the hand or on the backside. Her disappointment had been a far more effective reprimand than any other form of punishment. Well, she was beyond disappointed with him now – past caring at all – unless pure disgust was some distorted form of affection. Harry's face buzzed where she'd slapped him. She'd looked at him with such hatred.

He endured the unnecessary trip to see the medic and sat through the meeting debrief with Jim, stoically dry-eyed. They apologised for how the session had gone, even offered him the option of putting in a formal complaint. Harry declined. They got him to say how he felt. He lied and said 'shaken, but okay' and that he was still 'glad to have had the opportunity to say how sorry he was'. He signed his statement and deflected Jim's concern as they walked him back to his cell.

He was relieved to be ignored when he arrived back on the wing, other than a raised eyebrow from Elton, one of the lads in his work group. No one was interested. He went to the dining hall for lunch when summoned, though he didn't eat. When he asked for permission to skip his afternoon work detail, they let him. He went back to his cell and sat on his bunk, listening to the other blokes being chivvied off to their different activities. It took a while, but eventually the wing quietened.

Only then did Harry let it in – the shame. The meeting had been his penance. He'd felt compelled to acknowledge the grief he'd caused; that's why he'd participated in the restorative justice scheme. What he'd been unprepared for was being faced with the reality of how absolutely the accident had screwed up so many lives. Marcus obviously hated him so much that he couldn't bear the thought of being the same room as Harry, and Fran hated him so much that she wanted to hurt him physically. Harry got it. They had loved their daughter, and he had taken her away from them. He'd shattered their lives. But deep down, despite all the counselling to expect anger and not forgiveness, he had secretly hoped the bonds that used to tie them together – all their shared history, Fran's role as his surrogate mum – would count for something. That, and his confession that he really had loved Jess.

It hadn't.

They would never forgive him. Jess could never forgive him. No one could. His dad was right to keep Martha away from him. He deserved to be on his own.

He rolled onto his side and pulled his knees up to his chest, making himself as small as possible. And that's how he stayed, sleepless and silent, as the imprint of Fran's hand on his cheek slowly faded away.

Chapter 75

WHAT DO you do after nearly killing someone?

You sit, shaking, behind the wheel of your car, waiting for the sky to fall in.

When it doesn't, you have to choose what you're going to do next.

The little girl hadn't gone underneath the wheels of Fran's car. She was still in the road. A woman was with her. Fran watched the woman scoop the child up into her arms. She ran over to the pavement, clutching the girl's small body to her chest. Once safely off the road, she dropped to her knees, set the girl on her feet and hugged her tightly.

Thank God!

Fran's heart thudded.

In rapid succession she took in the huddle of the woman and her daughter, the traffic lights – now on green, though she had no intention of moving – the pedestrian crossing, the staring faces of a number of passers-by, the awareness that somehow she was on Staincliffe Road, five minutes away from home. And yet it seemed like only a few minutes ago that she was leaving Darlington. Somehow she had lost an hour of her life.

A car behind her honked once, tentatively, then again, more

loudly. With trembling legs, Fran found first gear and set off very slowly. A little further down the road she saw a space and pulled over. Handbrake on. Three sobs escaped from deep inside her. She looked in her mirror, searching for the woman and her child, but couldn't see them. She unpeeled her hands from the steering wheel. Freed of their anchor, they began to shake. As her heart exploded, she sat perfectly still, waiting for the condemnation that never came. There was no irate witness banging on the window, phone in hand, having already called the police. No shaken, distraught mother running up to the car, tear-stained child in tow, accusing her of nearly killing her daughter. No squad car arriving. No officer breathalysing her, assuming alcohol or drug use, and arresting her.

Nothing.

Just a steady flow of traffic and pedestrians – none of whom paid Fran the slightest bit of attention – and the crashing waves of adrenaline careering around her system. Gradually her racing heart slowed and her breathing found its normal rhythm. She sat with her hands in her lap, aware of her own chemistry working to stabilise her. When the shock finally dissipated, she was left calm, but beached. Body back in sync, brain in limbo. It was as if her head had been banged so hard that everything in it had fallen out. She was blank.

Still nothing happened. Still she didn't move.

The thoughts, when they came, did so slowly, tentatively, creeping rather than rushing to fill the void.

She had nearly killed a child. Someone's daughter.

She hadn't.

But she could have done.

A split second separated her from having destroyed a family. It was as slender, and as huge a difference, as that.

But the terrifying thing was that it hadn't been a moment's inattention on Fran's part; it had been a whole journey. She had driven all the way back from Darlington in a daze. All that way, on the motorway and side-roads, at speed, making decisions, overtaking, changing lanes, stopping at junctions, using roundabouts, reacting or not reacting to traffic lights. None of which she had any memory off. Because…

Because she had been blinded by anger.

For the first time in months, Harry's name entered her head and she didn't clench with rage. Harry. Nothing. Just a coldness. She let it be.

She waited for the next name to enter her head. It was not who she was expecting. It was not Jess. Feelings started to return – a mix of panic, sadness and regret. At last she felt an imperative. Marcus. She must go home. She wanted to be with her husband. She needed to tell him what had happened.

She got out of the car, locked it and walked away. No one stopped her. No one shouted. She was relieved. She walked fast, her brain filling up with memories, words spoken that shouldn't have been, shoulders turned away, hands let go. She got to the end of their street and speeded up, praying he would be there – working from home, sitting at the dining-room table. Why would Marcus be at home on a Friday? Come on, she knew why. Because, it came to her: *he was struggling*. The school was being supportive, stepping him down to four days a week, taking the Curriculum Lead role off him, giving him more preparation time – because *he was struggling*. She'd barely talked to him about it. Hadn't cared enough or, if she was honest, cared at all. What did Marcus's career matter, when Jess was dead? The feelings were overwhelming her now. A floodgate opened. His decision not to go to the prison. The decision that had so incensed her. She'd seen his refusal as a denial of reality, a neglect of his parental duties, 'proof' of his failure as a husband, but it wasn't that he'd not wanted to go; it was that Marcus hadn't been able to – because *he was struggling*.

She opened the front door, wanted to shout his name, but found she couldn't. It was such a long time since she'd thought of him as

'Marcus'. Instead, in her mind, he'd become an obstacle, an adversary, a stranger. Was that how he saw her? She didn't know, because she hadn't cared.

He was sitting, as she expected, at the dining-room table, laptop open, work spread out around him. He looked up when she walked into the room, his face guarded. It stopped her from saying anything. She felt unable to pick out the right place to start, from the welter of thoughts and emotions in her head. Instead she walked across to him and put her hand on the back of his neck, lightly, nervously. He let it rest there for a few seconds, before leaning forward to close his laptop.

Chapter 76

SOMETHING ABOUT her face looked different. Not the expression
– her actual face. It was as if the bones had softened and her features
had blurred. It was Fran, but not Fran. She walked across the room
without saying anything and laid her hands on him. They hadn't
touched each other for so long that the sensation of her fingers on
the back of his neck was strange. Marcus's instinct was to pull away,
but he didn't, not immediately.

They sat opposite each other at the table and he waited for the
fallout, but when Fran finally spoke, it wasn't the tirade he was
expecting. It was a question. A mundane, small, hesitant question.
'Have you managed to get any work done?'

'Some.'

She nodded. Still there was no gush of words and emotion.
Instead she seemed to be holding herself in check. This was new.

He asked, 'So how did it go?'

She shrugged off her coat, buying time. Despite everything, he
was struck once again by how thin she was. 'It wasn't what I thought
it was going to be.'

'Okay.' He said, still wary, waiting for the explosion. 'How?'

'I can't really explain.' She saw his face and hurried into the next sentence. 'Not because I don't want to, but I just can't – not yet. I don't know how to.'

He wasn't surprised that Fran wasn't prepared to tell him what Harry had or hadn't said. They'd long since ceased sharing. They both hugged their own versions of grief to their chests fiercely, protectively. Why share, when the only thing you have is so personal and private that you can't even reveal it to the one person who might begin to understand? Even the facts of their daughter's death – even that information – she still wanted to hoard for herself. He was reduced, as ever, to the inconsequential. 'Was the trip all right?'

She looked at her hands. 'No.'

'Why? What happened?'

She scratched at the palm of her left hand. 'I very nearly caused an accident on the Staincliffe Road. A young woman was using the crossing with her little girl. I didn't see them. I don't think I even saw the crossing. I missed hitting the little girl by this much.' She held up her hands, indicating a narrow margin. 'I could've killed her.'

'Jesus!'

'I've left the car. I couldn't drive it afterwards. I didn't think I should.' Her features seemed to smudge even more. 'Marcus. I'm sorry.' He waited for her to say more. 'I was so angry that I wasn't paying any attention to what I was doing.'

'Because of the meeting?'

'Yes.' She stopped. Thought. 'That, and because Jess is dead.' The honesty of the statement surprised him. 'I've been angry ever since we let her go. So angry that I haven't been able to *be* anything else, *think* about anyone else. And for that I'm sorry.' He reached out across the table and held her hand lightly, committing himself to nothing more than sympathy. 'I want it to be different. And I know, for that to happen, I need to change. And I want to try.'

He nodded. He believed her. Or at least he believed in her desire to change, but not necessarily in her ability to do so. That would take

318

a Herculean effort, and if she felt even a fraction as exhausted as he did, it was unlikely to happen.

As if to prove his point, Fran yawned. A long, body-racking yawn. The accumulation of the long drive, the meeting with Harry, the shock of the near-accident, it seemed to hit her all of a sudden.

'I'm sorry. I'm shot. I really can't think straight.'

'Go and have a rest. We can talk later. This will keep,' Marcus said.

'Are you sure?'

Again a question, a taking on-board of his feelings. It was such a long time since he'd felt like he even existed in her universe that Marcus was surprised and touched. 'Of course. You try and get some sleep, and I'll go and fetch the car. Where are the keys?' The safety of the mundane again.

'In my handbag.'

'Can I get them?'

'Yes, of course.' She levered herself up, using the table for balance. As she passed, she paused for a second or two. It was only as she started the slow climb up to bed that Marcus realised she'd been waiting for him to kiss her.

He found Fran's keyring in her bag, pulled on a sweater, took his own keys from the hook in the hall and headed out.

It was one of those in-between winter days, not particularly cold, not bright, not wet, not much of anything really. As he opened the front gate, he sensed the curtains in their bedroom being pulled across. He had a few hours. Not that he could do much with them. Once again he was waiting for Fran to set the agenda. His own car was parked at the kerb. He stood beside it, thinking, but without arriving at any great insight or reaching any conclusions. After her rest, Fran would tell him her version of what had happened at the prison and he would listen, but he doubted whether it would answer any of his questions. Because he and Fran wanted different resolutions. She wanted to reclaim Jess's death. He wanted to remember her life.

He didn't need – no, it was more than that – he didn't want any more of the horror. The hospital had been bad enough. He had no desire to know every awful detail of the events that put Jess there. What he wanted was to find out everything he could about her living, breathing loveliness: her thoughts and fears, her feelings and passions, her highs and lows and, most of all, her relationship with Harry. He wanted the Jess that he, as her dad, had never got to know – the one glimpsed in the mementoes and photos in her room and in the messages on her phone. But the conversation he needed to have with Harry was not one to be had in a room full of strangers inside a prison, amidst a swirl of anger and recrimination. It was an exchange that required calm and understanding and forgiveness. It was a conversation that might never happen, but he was prepared to wait.

Marcus opened the boot of his car and moved the old picnic blanket aside. The bag was there, wedged at the back, exactly where he'd put it a month ago. A medium-sized, anonymous-looking holdall. It was modestly filled with the essentials: clothes, toiletries, a couple of books, some photos of Jess, her phone. All neatly packed inside, ready for the day he decided that he and Fran had truly run out of road. Ironically, it was the thought of the bag being there that had given him the strength to stay. That wasn't as illogical as it sounded. Planning an escape route had seemed the only sane action he could think of, in response to the sense of claustrophobia that had been building up since the day Jess died. He re-covered the holdall with the rug, slammed the boot and set off to retrieve Fran's car. He should at least hear what Fran had to say.

Chapter 77

MARCUS LET himself back into the house. The car had been where Fran had said. Parked neatly enough – just another vehicle clogging up the streets. It was now outside, slotted in behind his. There were no sounds from upstairs. He settled back at the table and stared at the blocks of colour-coded lessons until his eyes hurt.

When Fran came back downstairs a couple of hours later, a crease mark on her cheek from the pillow, he made them both a sandwich. They ate at the table, spoke about the near-miss, even had a conversation about work. All delaying tactics. It was Fran who eventually broached the meeting, with another peace offering. 'You were right not to come.'

He half-nodded. It wasn't for him to say.

'It was...very difficult.'

'How could it not be?'

There was a brief flash of reaction in her eyes, but it flickered and died. 'What I mean is: I went into it expecting something that was never going to be possible.'

'What?'

She cupped her chin in her hand, as if the weight of her head was unsustainable. 'I wanted to shame Harry. Make him feel awful.

Make him face up to what he's done.'

'And that isn't what happened?'

'Oh no, it did. He was in bits for most of it. Really, genuinely distraught. He knows the damage he's done.' Marcus felt a stir of sympathy for Harry, but said nothing. Fran's face looked raw. 'It was how *I* felt that was the problem. I was furious. The more he talked and the more upset he became, the more incensed I got. I slapped him.'

Marcus was saddened, but not surprised. Before the accident, Fran would never have hit anyone; after Jess's death, Fran wanted to slap everyone.

'I hit him really hard. If they hadn't have stopped me, I'd have hit him again. I was out of control.'

'Because of what Harry was saying?'

She stopped and thought. 'No. I think it was because the more he talked, the more I saw how much he was suffering. And I didn't want to have to deal with that. I went in there thinking he had no right to feel anything other than shame.'

'Is he ashamed?'

'Yes, but it's more than that. He's been broken by it. That's what I hadn't considered. The impact on *him*. And I didn't want to have to think about that – about what it must feel like to be responsible for so much suffering.'

It was the first time in months that Marcus had heard Fran speak about anyone else's feelings other than her own. Perhaps the meeting had had benefits, after all. 'Did he explain why he drank, then drove, that night?' Harry was still guilty of that.

'Yes. He said he didn't mean to.' They both knew that was no defence. She went on, 'He was sorry. Very sorry. I believed him.'

'And all the stuff about leaving Mo behind. What was that really about?'

Fran plucked at the skin on her neck, leaving marks. 'They argued.'

'About?'

'A video Mo filmed at the party.'

'Of?'

'Harry and Tish.'

'Doing what?'

'Kissing.'

Marcus felt totally wrong-footed.

Fran reached for his hand. 'It's a mess. Harry claims he was in a relationship with Jess – had been for over a year – but that at the party he and Tish...had a thing. He confessed it wasn't the first time.'

'The bastard!' Marcus's fantasy of Jess and Harry as Romeo and Juliet crashed. All the messages and presents. They were just a way of getting her to sleep with him.

'Marcus, no!' Fran pleaded. 'I know I've no right to ask you not to be angry. But we can't. You can't. It doesn't help. It only makes things worse.'

Marcus didn't know what to do with the emotions coursing through him. The sense of having swapped places with Fran was disorientating.

'Do you think it could it be true? Could they have been together all that time, without us realising?'

For a second Marcus didn't grasp what Fran was asking. There was only one way to answer her questions. He stood up, went out to the car, grabbed the holdall and brought it back into the room. In his fury he didn't see the shock on Fran's face. He dropped the bag on the floor, rooted through it and fished out Jess's phone. Without a word, he offered her the hand-grenade.

Chapter 78

BY MONDAY lunchtime Fran wanted out of the optician's. She wasn't hungry, but she needed a break from the pressure of having to smile and be professional. The rattled feelings from the showdown with Harry the previous Friday, and everything else that had come out as a result of it, had gradually subsided, leaving her feeling bruised and battered, but – and this was a surprise – somehow changed, for the better. She'd finally started to think about the future and how to tackle it.

At the root of this glimmer of hope was her marriage. As overwhelming as the revelation of Jess's relationship with Harry had been, what had truly rocked her was the realisation that Marcus had been considering leaving her. Even in her shattered state, the sight of that holdall, with his clothes all neatly folded inside, had shocked her. She'd been so scared at the thought that they were done, but she'd been unable to call him out on it. Not only because, at the time, they were groping their way towards an understanding of their daughter's secret life, but also because, deep down, she knew why Marcus had been thinking of walking away.

She'd been unliveable with.

Their marriage was hanging by a thread.

Over the weekend they'd holed themselves up in the house and dragged it all out into the open. Jess's relationship with Harry; their blindness to what had been happening under their noses; their failure as parents; their anger with Harry, with other people and with each other. The sense of despair, the intolerable, unforgettable memories – the terrible weeks in the hospital, Jess's death, the storm of emotions around the organ donation, the grimness of her funeral. They talked about their very different takes on the same events, and their shared fear of what came next. It had been awful and painful, and yet it had also been a relief. For the first time since they'd walked into the ICU and seen Jess lying in that bed – no, for the first time since the knock at the door in the middle of the night – they shared their thoughts and feelings, honestly. All of them, including the dark and ugly ones.

On the Sunday night Fran had sat on the bed and watched as Marcus unpacked the holdall and put his things away where they belonged. Then he'd lifted the bedcovers and they'd crawled underneath and clung to each other until they both, eventually, fell asleep.

Now there was just the small matter of getting on with the rest of their lives.

Hence Fran going into work as normal on Monday morning and conducting seven eye exams by lunchtime before the need to escape and breathe became impossible to ignore. She spotted Martha as soon as she set foot outside the shop. She was sitting on one of the benches on the main concourse. She didn't smile when she saw Fran. Fran walked over and sat down beside her. 'Shouldn't you be in school?' Even now the parental gene wouldn't switch off.

'Yeah, but I wanted to talk to you. Can I? Talk to you?' Martha was nervous. Fran wasn't surprised. She'd hardly been kind the last time.

'Of course.'

'I don't know who else to talk to.' Fran let Martha compose herself. 'I'm really worried about Harry. I know you won't take me to see him. It was wrong of me to ask, after everything that's happened. I'm sorry about that. But I need to try and get up there somehow. And you're the only person my dad listens to.' The fact that she still believed this pained Fran. 'I thought, if you asked him, on my behalf – especially given it was you – he might change his mind and take me with him the next time he goes.'

'Why are you so worried about him?' The image of Harry's dark, shadowed eyes came back to Fran.

'There's something wrong. When we Skyped him last night I knew straight away. Something's happened.'

'What?' She knew, of course. Her visit.

'He wouldn't say, but he looked awful. He had a bruise on his cheek. He said it was just muck from working in the gardens, but I don't believe him. When I tried to get him to talk to me, he got angry and upset at the same time. Then he hung up. He's never done that.'

Fran felt something inside her shift. 'Maybe you caught him at the wrong time.'

Martha looked teary. 'It's always the wrong time, but this was different. I think he's getting bullied.'

'What did your dad say?'

'What he always says, that *Harry is an adult* and *we can't spend our lives worrying about him.*' She gathered herself. 'Fran, I know I can be a bit too emotional about stuff but, I swear, there's something really wrong. Please.'

Fran examined the stirring in her chest and recognised it as sympathy. 'Wait here a minute. I just need to call into work and tell them I'm taking a longer lunch break. Don't move. I'll be right back.'

In the car ride over to Dom's office Fran let Martha talk. It was a flood of repressed worry and loneliness that she recognised all too well. The difference was that she was a fully grown woman with a husband, and this was a fourteen-year-old girl with only an emotionally reticent father at home and a brother in prison. As they neared Dom's offices, Martha grew quiet.

'It'll be okay.'

Martha looked doubtful. 'He won't like being interrupted at work.'

'But he is there today?'

'I think so.'

'So it's worth a try, isn't it?' On impulse, Fran reached over and lightly touched Martha's chin, raising her face.

Dom's surprise was overlaid with confusion.

Fran tried to reassure him. 'We're sorry to turn up unannounced, but this is important. Have you got a few minutes?' He looked dubious. She persisted. 'I promise that I'm not here to cause any trouble.' Not like last time.

He showed them through. It was the first time she'd ever been to Dom's place of work, which was odd really, given how long they'd known each other. Despite the awkwardness of the current situation, Fran couldn't help noticing how neat and streamlined his office was. Very stylish, as you'd expect of Dom, minimal and utterly anonymous. She and Martha sat opposite him, the chrome-and-glass desk between them. She was about to try and explain to him, and to herself, why she was there, but he got in first.

'Why aren't you in school?'

Martha bit her lip, but spoke up. 'Because I decided that speaking to Fran was more important.' Dom's expression radiated disapproval. She bravely faced into it. 'I needed to speak to someone, and you weren't listening.'

'So you went to Fran?' The comment was designed to sting. It did.

'Dom.' Fran drew his attention back to her. 'Please. I really don't want to get between you and Martha. That's not my place. I know that. And I know the last time we spoke, it all got out of hand and things were said that I regret.' Perhaps he didn't regret anything, but she did. She ploughed on. 'And this is going sound strange coming from me, but Martha has told me that Harry wasn't good, when you spoke to him last night.'

Dom flashed Martha a look of complete bafflement, which was understandable. 'I really don't see how Harry's situation, or his mood, is any of your business.' He was restraining himself.

Of course he was right. Fran felt, rather than saw, Martha sag in her seat, which gave her the impetus she needed. 'That's fair enough, Dom. But Martha is very worried about her brother.'

Dom had had enough. 'This really is nothing to do with you. I appreciate your "concern", but Martha shouldn't have got you involved.' He went to stand up. 'I'll drop you back at school, Martha.'

The need to make something – anything – better swept through Fran. Martha shouldn't be the one paying the price. She blurted out, 'She's right to be worried about Harry. He looked...unwell when I saw him.'

Dom sat down. He knew full well what she was talking about, but she pressed home the point.

'The restorative justice meeting was on Friday. It was very difficult, for everyone, but especially for Harry. He got very upset. I think he may need your support, now more than ever.'

Dom looked at her for a beat, then spoke with an exaggerated politeness. 'I'll thank you not to tell me how to take care of my own children, Fran. We're supporting Harry through this as best we can. And let's not forget, it wasn't so long ago that you were the one baying for blood.'

'Dad, please.' Martha sounded utterly miserable.

Dom stood up, took his jacket from the back of his chair and put it on. 'I think it best if you leave, Fran.'

She had tried. She stood up as well. On impulse, she bent and kissed Martha's cheek. Her reward was a brief, intoxicating waft of teenage girl. 'Take care, Martha. I hope Harry is on better form next time you speak to him.' She walked across the slate-grey carpet. Before leaving, she acted on a second, inexplicable impulse. 'When you do talk to him, please can you tell him that I was asking after him.' She left the door open on her way out.

Chapter 79

THE LETTER postmarked HMP Darlington arrived three weeks later. Marcus recognised the handwriting. He left the envelope on the side for them to read together when Fran got back from work. The thought of it nagged at him all day. When he let himself in that evening, he was sorely tempted to rip it open, but he didn't. Promises, made on both sides, were worthless unless they were kept.

Fran didn't even take her coat off when he showed it to her.

The letter was handwritten and short.

To Fran and Marcus,

I hope it's okay for me to write to you. I'll understand if you throw this in the bin. But I wanted to let you know that my dad brought Martha in to see me for the first time yesterday. It was _so_ good to be able to talk to her face-to-face and give her a hug. She told me it was you who convinced my dad to let her come. We're both very grateful.

She also said that you asked after me. I don't understand what that means, or even if it means anything. Anyway, I suppose it doesn't matter. I just wanted to say, 'Thank you.'

I also want to say, again, that I'm <u>so sorry</u>. I know that isn't enough. That they're only words, and saying sorry will never be enough. But I am really sorrier than I can ever say, for everything – for betraying your trust, for behaving so badly and, most of all, for what happened that night.

I don't know what else to say.

Harry

Chapter 80

IT WAS his sister coming to visit that stopped Harry going under.

Seeing Martha, being hugged by her, talking to her, promising her that he was going to be okay, that he could hack the remainder of his sentence, that he would be coming home in one piece and that life would, at some point, get back to normal – all of it had been good for him. It had given him the motivation to keep going.

The fact that it had been Fran who had intervened on his behalf – though incredible – was what gave him hope. He didn't understand what had happened, how Fran could have changed so much since their meeting; but that she obviously had was enough to pull him away from the grasping dark. It was that unexpected splinter of kindness that had given him the confidence to risk sending his letter. He hadn't expected a reply, that would be too much to ask; but maybe he had– deep down – hung on to a tiny shred of belief that if Fran cared enough to help Martha then she might, just, find it within herself to write back to him.

His hope was rewarded a week later. A letter arrived, addressed to him in Marcus's loopy handwriting. Harry took it to his cell to read, conscious of his banging heart.

The letter was much longer than his own pathetic note to them.

Dear Harry,

We received your letter.

We're pleased that you finally got to see Martha. We know she was desperate to see you. We hope the visit put her mind at rest, at least a little. She sent us a thank-you card, which wasn't necessary, but was appreciated.

Knowing what else to write is difficult, but we felt we should.

Firstly, Fran wants to apologise for hitting you. She knows she shouldn't have done that. I should have come to the meeting. That is something I deeply regret. I should've been there for Fran. I gather it was very difficult. Fran has told me what you said, and what she said. There was obviously a lot of anger and sadness in the room.

There still is.

But...however bad the meeting was on the day, it has had some benefits. We thought you should know that, in a strange way, it has helped us.

We know more about what happened now. That's always been a huge frustration for us. Not knowing the chain of events that led up to the crash, and what happened in those last few hours of Jess's life, has been such a source of pain. From that first night in the hospital, and all the way through the legal process, we've been shut out – by the system, by your dad and, worst of all, by you. It felt like it was all about you, not our daughter, and that wasn't right. It caused a lot of anger. We are Jess's parents. We had the right to know everything possible about how she died, and why.

But there's been a lot of hiding the truth, hasn't there, Harry?

We know, now, that you and Jess had some form of a relationship before she died. That you were together obviously came as a shock to us. But it won't come as a surprise to you, will it? Because you and Jess lied to us about it. For months and months! Fran and I want to know why you lied? Why it was such a secret? Why our own daughter didn't confide in us?

We also want to know what you really felt about our daughter. No more lies this time. We want the truth.

Fran says you were very cut-up at the meeting. Is that because you did love Jess? Or is it because you feel guilty about the way you treated her? It's confusing to us how you could've been Jess's boyfriend, yet at the same time have been carrying on with Tish. We want you to explain that to us. If you can.

But, even if you can't, we think it is important for you know – it does matter that you are genuinely sorry for what happened.

Fran and I have talked about everything that has happened a lot these past few weeks.

This is where we've got to.

We believe you regret driving when you'd been drinking.

We know you didn't mean to hurt Jess or the others. But you did, and nothing can ever change that.

We think you cared for Jess, maybe even loved her. Only you know the answer to that. Jess seems to have loved you.

And, finally, that the guilt and the sadness you're feeling are more punishment than any time you'll spend in prison.

We think of you often.

We think of Jess all the time.

Marcus and Fran

Jess seems to have loved you. As much at their words hurt, having Fran and Marcus finally know about, and acknowledge, his relationship with their daughter mattered to Harry. He read the letter five times, before hiding it away in his cupboard, underneath his clothes. At the next opportunity he got, he asked the screws for some writing paper and an envelope.

Chapter 81

THEY FILLED in the application form together online.

After weeks of exchanging letters with Harry, it felt like the right time.

The volume and length of his letters had been a surprise; reading them had been a trial, but, in a peculiar way, it had also been a cathartic experience for both of them, something they shared and discussed and used to help them talk about their own emotions. With each letter exchanged, Harry grew in his willingness to tell them things. He came clean about how his relationship with Jess had shifted from being friends – almost so familiar that they took each other for granted – to something far closer. How Jess had been the trigger, the one to reach out and suggest that she wanted more. He wrote about how both of them had been shy at first, embarrassed, not knowing what 'it' was, but how quickly it had become *the most important thing in their lives.* He wrote about his feelings for their daughter; his reliance on her; his regrets; his sense of their mismatched, but somehow well-suited personalities; and, above all, about his love for her.

Despite the confession of so much subterfuge and deceit, Fran and Marcus found themselves looking forward to Harry's letters, because within each one there were nuggets of Jess tucked inside his words. When they caught themselves laughing one day at a story Harry told, about how Jess had got sucked into a conversation about incontinence with two old ladies on the bus, they'd been shocked and delighted. It was a rare, precious moment – a happy, shiny new anecdote. Some of it was hard to read, the worries that Jess hadn't shared with them about the future, especially her stress about their expectations, but with the arrival of each of Harry's letters they added to the store of knowledge of their girl. Finally, Marcus felt he was completing the jigsaw of his daughter. That he was doing it with Fran was more important than she would ever know.

The online application asked all the basic questions they'd expected. Harry's prisoner number and DOB were top of the list. It was a shock to be reminded that he was still only nineteen; an adult in the eyes of the law, but only a boy really. They whizzed through the form until they came to question nine: *Relationship to Inmate*. Marcus left that one blank. He moved on, filling in their names, ages, address, occupations and the date of the requested visit. It was complete in ten minutes. Then they circled back to question nine. Marcus sat, cursor hovering over the tick boxes. 'What shall I put?'

Fran, sitting beside him, read through the options again. After a brief pause she pointed and Marcus clicked on *Family Friend*.

Chapter 82

THE MOOD on the wing changed whenever anyone was coming up for release. The thought of someone else's imminent freedom brought home the weight of the weeks, months or years that still pressed down on the other inmates. It made for a more charged atmosphere. Of course the men covered up their jealousies and resentments as they always did – with banter. There were a lot of nudge-nudge comments about binge-drinking, shagging and 'all you can eat' carveries. It was good-natured, for the most part, but Harry was still uncomfortable being the focus of their attention. He said his goodbyes quietly, thanked the staff who had helped him with a handshake and left the wing – for the last time – as quickly and unemotionally as possible.

It was a long walk to the holding area on the other side of the jail, where inmates were processed for discharge. The relief of being away from the herd was profound. He was one of six slated for release that day. Leroy he knew. He was a big lad, a bit weird, but nice enough. Kyle, who he'd avoided as much as possible during his sentence, was also there. Kyle was a gang member, with status and anger issues. Ricky was another one of the lads getting out. He'd only done a short stretch, for persistent non-payment of fines. He'd spent most of it in his cell, scared witless. The other two Harry recognised from the dining hall, but he didn't know them by name or crime. The officers were efficient, bored. He was passed a sealed bag with his name and date of admission on the front: 5 June 2018. Twenty months and three days served. It felt so much longer, yet still not enough. There were cubicles. He stepped inside one and pulled the curtain across. Some privacy – another novelty. He sat on the narrow bench, ripped open the seal and slid the contents of the bag out onto his knee.

It was a time-capsule containing his clothes, his wallet, his watch and his phone, which was dead, of course. He stripped off his sweatshirt and sweat-pants – thought about leaving them on the floor, then picked them up, folded them and put the grey pile on the end of the bench. He had no intention of taking them out with him. Then he hesitated. Putting his old clothes on seemed like a big step: backwards. But he had no choice, not unless he was going to head out into the world in his underpants or his prison gear. He could hear the other lads talking, out in the communal area. He was holding things up. He pulled on his trousers – black, smart – and quickly buttoned up his shirt – designer. He shoved the jacket into his bag. He was never going to wear it again. His court appearance jacket, as dictated by his father, chosen to give the impression of an upstanding member of society. Socks on, feet shoved into his shoes. He was glad there wasn't a mirror. He pulled back the curtain.

They signed the forms, agreeing to their different probation terms. They were all, with the exception of Ricky, being discharged on licence. Then they were led down the corridor, through another series of doors to the outside. The actual, proper outside.

There was a path down to the gatehouse. The officer escorting them made lame, tired conversation about the weather. No one answered him. It was a welcome slug of reality to be out in the open, with the wind gusting in their faces, after the perpetual staleness of inside. Through the fence Harry could see the other lads' families and friends. A welcome party of relatives, who had all made the effort to be there to see them released on a blustery February day, in an asphalt car park, just off the A1. When the relatives saw them approaching, they started shouting and cheering. One woman picked up a small child and started waving its arm madly, which made the kid howl with shock and indignation.

One last ID check and they were on the other side. Out.

People rushed forward. One bloke barged into Harry in his rush to embrace his son. He was big, tattooed, crying. Leroy's dad? Harry moved out of the way, embarrassed by such open expressions of emotion. He scanned the crowd and was shocked to realise that his dad had been as good, or as bad, as his word and had not come to collect him. Thankfully, the others were far too wrapped up in their own loved ones to notice that there was no 'welcome wagon' for him. The bastard.

It was cold, but Harry's jacket stayed in his bag. He set off walking, away from the prison, across the car park. There was a bus stop. Limited service. One an hour. They had all been issued with a photocopied sheet with the times on it. Harry had hoped he wouldn't have to use it, but Dom was evidently as stubborn as he prided himself on being. He'd said he had an important work commitment that he couldn't get out of. That must have taken priority. In Dom's world, Harry completing his time and being discharged early, for good behaviour, obviously wasn't something to be celebrated. Another 'life lesson', dealt out with clinical efficiency. That it still hurt – still felt like abandonment – surprised Harry. His capacity to want the one thing his father was incapable of giving him was tragic.

He shouldered his bag and walked on. The chatter and laughter of the other families followed him, carried by the wind. The bus it was, then.

'Harry!' Shocked, and for a moment elated to hear his name being called, Harry turned and scanned the car park. Had his dad had a complete personality transplant and brought Martha as well? 'Harry!' This time there was no uncertainty. It wasn't Martha. Dom's BMW was not one of the cars waiting to ferry him back home. But there was a blue Golf that he didn't recognise, parked at the far corner of the lot. The driver's door was open, and standing next to the car was a woman he did recognise. Fran. He should've been surprised, but he wasn't. It made sense in a peculiar kind of way. He walked towards her.

She looked at him, stretched out her hand to take his bag and said, 'Get in.'

Chapter 83

DOM LOOKED at his watch. If everything had gone to plan, his son would now be a free man.

He would not be there to see it.

Dom's calendar was chock-a-block with back-to-back meetings, a normal day's trading – which just so happened to be Harry's release date. He was aware of the contradiction, but didn't want to dwell on it. He'd agreed to let Fran collect Harry. It was all arranged; no reason to go changing things now. It was saving him time and a round trip to Darlington, in the middle of a busy week. What difference did a few hours make? He'd see Harry at home soon enough. They'd celebrate then. The three of them back together. There was a bottle of fizz in the fridge. It was a sensible solution all round.

Dom had been out of the house and on the road by 6.30 a.m. By 10.30 a.m. he was already on stop two, Kev Walton's dealership over in Wallasey. They were currently going through the sales data – which was good for new cars, but less than impressive on pre-owned and after-sales. Kev was, as always, blaming the poor figures on the economy, which was bollocks; the reality was that he was a lazy bastard: good at selling the new models and special offers, crap at the legwork that went into turning a showroom into a real garage that people came back to. There were at the 'butting heads and egos' stage of the conversation, which Dom normally enjoyed, and won, but today he was only half-listening. An awareness that Kev could sense that he was off his game, and was exploiting it, pissed Dom off.

He pushed his chair away from the desk. 'I need a slash. Back in a minute.'

In the Gents he went into a cubicle, locked the door and sat down: 11.10 a.m. Harry would be on his way home. Dom allowed himself to try and imagine his son's feelings. Relief? Happiness? Excitement about coming home and getting back to normal? Full of plans for what he was going to do? No. Not Harry. He'd be worrying, stressing about the reception that awaited him. Harry had refused to believe Dom when he'd told him that life had moved on and no one really talked about the crash any more – today's news, tomorrow's chip paper.

Dom rested back against the toilet cistern. Through the thin walls he could hear the lads in the office next door working the phones, hustling, chasing up orders and closing down sales, making a good living off their wits, their dubious charms and their cheek. Harry could have wiped the floor with all of them...before the accident, before he'd fallen apart.

Watching someone you love struggle, and not being able to fix it, was awful and so frustrating. Dom had tried – he really had – but Harry had rejected his help and advice time and time again. Look where that had landed him. And every time Dom had hacked all the way up to Darlington to see him, it had been the same – the two of them sitting opposite each other, barely talking or, worse, arguing, surrounded by that collection of no-hopers. The longer it had gone on, the more the stuffing had been knocked out of both of them.

That the change had come in the shape of Fran had hurt Dom, badly. A woman's touch. Could it really be a clichéd as that? Was that what Harry had needed all along? A surrogate mother – even if it was an irate, unstable, grieving woman whose motivations were clouded by the need for reparation. Apparently so. Because Dom had to acknowledge that the turning point had come after the restorative justice meeting. Something had clicked, or snapped, at that meeting – he still did not know what – and as a consequence Fran had changed, and so had Harry. And out of that combustion of emotions had developed a weird, but seemingly important new connection. It was a connection that Dom didn't understand. No matter how often Martha tried to reassure him that Fran's motives were sound, he couldn't totally bring himself to trust what he was seeing. Fran helping the boy who had 'killed' her beloved daughter. It felt wrong.

But there was no denying that since Fran's seeming change of heart, Harry's confidence had slowly started to return. It was as if something deep down inside him had finally woken up and started fighting back.

And if it really had been a 'mother's' attention that Harry had craved all along, where did that leave Dom? Out of the picture, that's where.

Whatever he'd done, it would never have been enough.

He stood up, flushed the loo and unlocked the cubicle. He washed his hands thoroughly, stroked a hand over his bald head, straightened his tie and headed back out to the fray, determined to kick Kev Walton's lazy arse.

Chapter 84

'IT'S GOING to feel really weird, isn't it – him being home?' Mo watched Harley disappear under some bushes, hunting real or imaginary squirrels. 'It's like he's been stuck on pause while everyone else has kept going.' Mo was into his second year at York, and Tish – despite her great A-level results and plenty of uni offers – was in a job she loved, working for the tourism department of the council, earning, spending, travelling, coming home to Mo full of enthusiasm and grand plans: Japan in the summer, then a flat together, by autumn at the latest.

Tish bounced along the path, trying to keep warm. 'Well, that is the point of prison.'

Mo was more reflective. 'Harry's served his time.' He could testify to that. Mo had been true to his word and kept hacking up to Darlington to visit Harry as often as his course and his budget would allow. They were friends, and that's what friends did: stuck around when the going got tough, even when it became complicated. Mo didn't let himself think about Tish and Harry being together. Or, at least, he tried very hard not to. 'Do you feel all right about seeing him again?' he ventured.

Tish hurried on, brisk steps, blowing on her fingers to warm them up. 'Yep. Totally fine.'

Harley reappeared with a beard full of leaves and mud and started dancing around them, demanding attention. Mo threw him an imaginary stick, and Harley was daft enough to hare off after it.

Tish stopped yomping ahead. She fell back into step with Mo, slipped her arm through his and pulled him close to her. 'Hey. Quit worrying, will you? Besides, if you think about it, it's down to Harry and the accident that we're even together.'

'Are you saying you wouldn't have looked at me twice otherwise?' Mo asked, only semi-seriously.

Tish laughed. 'Twice! Not even once!' She pulled him to a stop. Planted a full-on kiss on his cold lips, then thumped him hard on the arm. 'Don't go all "complex" on me about this. It's going to be okay. I promise. Nothing is going to change between us – ever. So stop being such a doofus.'

Mo smiled. 'Thanks for that. Your eloquent expression of affection makes all the difference.'

She laughed. 'Hey, mate. If you want poetry, you'd better find yourself some nerdy chick at uni to wax lyrical over your lovely arse and your tortured soul.' She kissed him again, then ran off across the grass, chasing a barking, bonkers Harley, and Mo raced after her.

Chapter 85

FRAN PULLED over to let a white van past. Harry kept his eyes on the fields blurring by – it was soothingly hypnotic. Perhaps she would keep driving, down the A1, on and on until they ran out of road. Harry wished she would. But of course she didn't. He heard the *tick-tick* of her indicator. They took the exit. He had another twenty minutes, tops, before he was home.

'It'll be all right.' She didn't look at him when she spoke. Kept her eyes on the road. He studied her profile. She was so familiar, and yet she was a completely different person now, just like him.

'Um.' He wasn't convinced by her determinedly positive perspective.

'It will. You being back might raise eyebrows for a day or two, but that'll be it.' She pulled up at the lights. Handbrake on. 'Old Harry' would've been irritated by that – he'd have seen it as typical middle-aged-woman driving.

'Have you heard back from any of the colleges?' She obviously wasn't going to give up on the 'what's next?' questioning.

He wanted to lie to her, but couldn't. 'I haven't put in my application yet.'

'Harry!' She moved off smoothly – first, through second into third. 'You promised.'

'I didn't have time.' His own poor attempt to lighten the mood was ignored.

'You have to. You've got your grades. Otherwise all that study will be a waste.'

He knew what she was thinking. She was thinking of another total waste. Jess would have aced her exams, had her pick of Manchester or Edinburgh or Lancaster, would be well into her second year by now, would have dumped him for someone more her level – just as she should have done. She would be alive and happy and with someone who would have appreciated her and kept her safe.

'Harry!'

'Sorry. All right. I'll think about it.'

'Okay.'

They were close now. Back on his old patch. As Fran drove along the familiar roads, Harry's sense of claustrophobia increased. He'd so wanted to get out, to get away from the insistent noise and unremitting boredom, but the thought of trying to pick up where he'd left off made him feel panicky. Because where he'd been before the crash was in a mess – which is what had led to the tragedy. And if it had been bad back then, why would it be any better now? His relationship with his dad was still crap, his friends had all dumped or forgotten about him, except Mo – he couldn't blame them for that, it's what he'd have done in the same situation – and Jess was gone. He didn't see that he had much of a future left. If it hadn't been for Martha, and Fran and Marcus, he might not have come home at all.

Fran cut into his self-pity by indicating and pulling the car over to the kerb. She parked and turned to face him properly. They were five minutes from home, and three minutes from the ring road.

'Harry. You need to listen to me. It will get better; or at least it will get easier and then it will begin to get better. It's a process. Just like surviving inside was. Being outside is no different. You have to make a positive choice. You have to do the thing in front of you, then the next thing after that, and then the next. And that way it'll slowly start to feel normal. And you've got to let yourself feel normal. It's allowed. Even I've learnt that. And if I can learn something that seemed so impossible and beyond me, then you can. You must. That's your responsibility. And it's not all about you. So stop being so self-obsessed. Martha needs her brother back, and Dom needs his son.'

Fran leant into the back of the car and grabbed her bag. She fished out her phone. 'Can you just give me a minute?' He nodded and watched her compose a text, send it and get a response. She reached to open the car door.

Harry was confused. 'What's going on?'

She ignored his question. 'Come on.'

There was no option but to get out of the car. Fran opened the boot. 'Your choice, Harry.'

He walked to the rear of the car. There were two small bunches of snowdrops, wrapped in damp tissue, lying in the boot. Harry started shaking his head.

Fran looked at him steadily, calmly, kindly. 'Martha helped me pick these this morning from our garden.'

'I can't.'

'Yes you can.'

Chapter 86

IT HURT, being this close to the scene of the crash. It still had the power to upend time and push Fran back into the grief, the sense of loss, the awfulness of their daughter's pointless death. God was still absent from the world, but at least now there was no rage.

It was an accident.

It was a tragedy for them all.

Martha was there with Marcus, waiting for them, as planned. When she spotted her brother she ran, full pelt along the verge, into him. As they hugged, Fran met Marcus's eye. He nodded in greeting, but her husband knew her well enough not to reach out and take her hand. He would hold her later, in the privacy of their home. They would cry together, probably not for the last time, in the house they were no longer selling. They didn't want to get away from their memories of Jess any more; they wanted to hold them as close as possible. And they were crying less, and living more. Marcus was right. It was what Jess would've wanted. Love always, and happiness, at least some of the time.

Standing behind Marcus – hanging back, as if uncertain of their role – were Tish and Mo. They were holding hands. Fran felt a flare of pleasure. They looked right together. Happy. In love. Fran didn't begrudge them that. Not any more. Out of tragedy, et cetera, et cetera. Tish was holding a single white gerbera. Fran approved of her choice.

Martha untangled herself from her brother and took a step backwards, leaving Harry rooted to the spot, the flowers gripped in his hands. Fran knew it was down to her to orchestrate what happened next. But Harry was stuck. She smiled, encouraging him. 'You first.' Harry gathered himself and set off. Everyone fell into step behind him. As they neared the site, his footsteps grew slower. Had it not been for Martha, he would probably have turned round, but she pushed him forward, encouraging and cajoling in equal measure.

Eventually they made it to the spot.

The proposed memorial to commemorate the crash had never been bought. It had never been engraved in the cursive script that Fran had, after weeks of deliberation, eventually chosen. The plaque had never been erected on the rebuilt wall of the factory. Never been photographed by the local press. Never been shared on social media. And as a result, it had never become a shrine. After Fran had come back to her senses, she realised she didn't want Jess commemorated for her death. She didn't want their daughter held up to the community as a memento mori – a grim warning of the risks of growing up and having a life. Yes, Jess was dead, but before her death she had been full of life and love, and that was how Fran and Marcus wanted to remember their daughter. Or at least that was how they were going to try and remember her.

Fran pulled herself back to the task in hand. They were all looking to her for their cues. Chief mourner. The mother without her daughter. The one who had lost the most. And yet that wasn't true. They had all lost. She knew that now. Felt it. It was this knowledge that had saved Fran. Her grief had been soaringly, destructively egotistical. It had cut her off from everyone, and everything, that

351

mattered. But the only thing that made grief bearable was company. The meeting with Harry had had the desired effect, but not in the way she'd imagined. It had made her recognise that her grief was not unique. The crash had smashed into all their lives, causing damage and pain in ways that she couldn't deny and couldn't ignore. The truth was they were all connected by the crash, and by Jess. That legacy of friendship, affection and love had to be honoured, not discarded. She had needed these people to help her feel anything other than bitterness and anger. Just as Harry – and Marcus and Martha – needed her to navigate their loss and their debilitating sadness. Being alone was simply not an option.

Martha, having got her brother as far as she could, stepped away. They all waited. Fran put her hand in the small of Harry's back. She could feel the tension in him. His body was rigid with memories that were worse than her own, and as deeply felt.

'She loved you. You loved her.' Gently she pushed Harry forward. 'It was an accident.'

Because it was. A dreadful, life-changing accident, which had taken Jess and shattered the rest of them.

Harry hung his head. 'I'm so sorry.'

'I know.'

One more nudge and he managed to move. He walked the small distance to the spot slowly, watched by them all, forgiven by them all.

The traffic flowed by and the cold sun shone, and life went on as normal as Harry knelt and finally laid down his guilt.

Chapter 87

PETE WAS decorating. Claire had been dropping hints about the bedroom needing freshening up for a while. Finally, in a direct move Pete had been unable to ignore, she'd left a paint chart, with the circled options, on the kitchen table. It had made him smile. Many things about Claire made him smile. Her laugh; her robust views on...well, most things; the way she walked as if there was a fire somewhere that she needed to put out; her open-hearted kindness; her Yorkshire puddings. The radio was on, the windows open, fresh air mingled with the paint fumes. Pete was happy, pleased with his efforts. She'd been right – the room had needed an overhaul.

He got up and arched his back. Time for a brew. A last bit of cutting-in, then the room would be finished. It would be dry by the morning. Blind up, furniture back in, new bed linen on. All ready for Thursday. They had a long weekend together planned. It was amazing how time that used to drag now zoomed by.

Tea brewed, Pete decided to reward himself for his labours with ten minutes outside. He opened the front door, intending to sit on the wall. The back yard was in shade in the afternoon and, cold as it was, he wanted the sun on his face.

He saw them straight away.

It was such a long time since anyone had visited the spot that Pete was taken aback. He succeeded in not remembering the crash and the aftermath – most of the time. Things had changed so much for the better for him since that night that he'd been able to file it away in a locked drawer inside his head. He hadn't spoken to Claire about what had happened, he hadn't wanted to. He knew it was probably stupid, but he didn't want to take the risk of her associating his little house with anything bad, or him with anything so dark. Deep down, he knew that if he did speak to her about it, she would be sympathetic; that was her nature – she might even be a little bit proud of him. But he didn't want to nix their developing relationship with something so horrible.

Pete watched the people across the road with a tightness in his throat.

It was a small gathering. Not like the crowds that had congregated on the verge in the weeks after the girl's death. The sight of them had upset Pete at the time. The clusters of teenagers sprawling on the grass, playing sad songs, hugging each other and drinking, had been a very visible reminder of what had happened – and the consequences of it. The drinking in particular had bothered him. How they could pass round a bottle at the very spot where the consequences of drink-driving had been so spectacularly and terribly demonstrated, was beyond him. He'd been relieved when the vigils had dwindled and eventually stopped; pleased when the council removed the mound of dead floral tributes. He wanted the road to be just the ring road. His house, just a house. Himself, just a bloke who lived in a house near the ring road.

Pete stood in his now-tidy front garden – Claire's influence again – feeling trapped by the sudden appearance of the mourners. He didn't touch his tea. It didn't seem right. He wanted to go back inside, but felt compelled to stay. Because, for all his practised avoidance of dwelling on the accident, he was intimately connected to it and, therefore, indirectly, to these people, whoever they were. Thankfully, due to the distance and the steady stream of cars, they could have no idea that once again he was playing his part as witness.

For an awful moment it struck Pete that he couldn't remember the name of the girl who had died. He could see her face: the flawless skin, the trendy dark glasses, the blonde, almost-white hair. A face full of energy and life, and potential. Photos of her had been everywhere after her death. On TV, online, on the placards the kids brought with them to the vigils. But her name. No. He couldn't retrieve it.

The night of the crash he hadn't seen her face, just the back of her head. That night her hair hadn't been blonde, it had been black.

Pete suddenly felt cold.

It came to him. She'd been called Jessica. Jess. This had to be her family. It must be an anniversary of sorts. Or perhaps it would have been her birthday – if she'd survived. Jesus! He couldn't begin to imagine.

The younger man went forward to lay his flowers first, his steps slow, his head hung low. When he knelt down, Pete had a strong, very clear flashback of the driver kneeling by the wreckage of the car. His name Pete hadn't forgotten: Harry Westwood. Pete didn't want the images in his head, but that was how memory worked, against your will, defying time and intention. He concentrated on the family on the other side of the ring road, the victims of the tragedy. For them, the past would always be part of their present. The lad stayed on his knees for a long time. He only got to his feet when the older woman touched his shoulder, summoning him back to the group. The older man and the young girl laid their flowers next, then a young couple, Jess's friends presumably. A little way off, a bald man in a sharp suit looked on – an observer, not a participant.

As the quiet ritual took place and the traffic flowed past, Pete stayed put, paying his respects. After the flowers were laid and the silent prayers said, the group closed in on themselves, exchanging hugs. Pete looked away. This was, after all, private grief despite the very public location. When he looked back, they had broken apart and started to walk away along the verge, all except the mother and the son. They stood close together, their arms around each other.

Pete had seen and felt enough.

He turned and headed back inside his house. Just as he was about to pull the door closed, he heard the blare of a car horn. His heart thudded. There was a screech of brakes. He looked up, but the traffic was flowing normally. The mother and son and the observing man were gone. He saw a flash of black-and-white streak through his garden gate.

Cleo shot past his legs into the house.

There went another of her nine lives.

THIRTY-TWO DAYS AFTER THE ACCIDENT

PERHAPS THERE was a God after all.

The call they'd hoped for, prayed for, feared would never happen, finally came on the morning of Wednesday 3 April. Angela didn't recognise the number when it popped up on her phone. Of course she didn't; they'd never phoned her before. She listened carefully as Heather, their link worker, told her that a donor had been found. Five very small, simple words. It was, apparently, an excellent match. The surgical team was being contacted as they spoke. The transplant was a definite 'go'.

After the call ended, Angela gave herself a few minutes to digest the news. It was happening. Becky would be in surgery before the day was out. Her diseased, failing heart was going to be taken out and replaced with a healthy one.

They had found a donor.

Two years on the register was a lifetime to wait for something that was such a long shot. It was a percentages game with dwindling odds, but their number had finally come up. Becky's life would be transformed. She could – no, she *would* – live. And live well: without pain, without the debilitating constriction of her floundering, insufficient heart. She would be healthy and happy, at last. She would have a normal life.

They had found a donor.

It was the best possible news – for them.

Angela sat on the bottom stair and allowed the shadow of that donor, and their family, to come and sit down next to her.

Someone had died. Someone young. Someone loved. Someone who had had their whole life ahead of them – until it was snatched away. Somewhere there was a mother, a father, a brother, a sister mourning an unbearable loss. And in the midst of that devastation they'd had the humanity, and bravery, to say 'Yes'. They had honoured the death of their loved one with the gift of life for a complete stranger.

The enormity of it flooded through Angela.

She sat in their narrow, silent hall and rode the waves of emotion, trying hard not to drown in the joy and the sadness.

When she felt stable enough, she rang Noel.

They were a team. That's how they got through stuff. They stuck together, no matter what. They took it in turns being chief cheerleader when Becky had had enough and couldn't face yet another necessary procedure or drugs regime change, with all the attendant side-effects. They shared the time off work, the sleeplessness, the anger, the endless hope-peddling and the despair-denial. They had stomped and stamped and jumped on the right side of the scales for their daughter, determined to balance out the dragging weight of her chronic heart condition, for so long that it had become a way of life. No more.

They had found a donor.

Noel shouted, actually shouted with excitement, when she told him the news. Then he burst into tears. The sound of his colleagues cheering and whooping in the background very nearly tipped Angela over the edge herself, but there was no time for that. They needed to get to the hospital. Between snotty, manly sobs, Noel said he'd get home as soon as he could. They would wake Becky and tell her the news together.

The last thing Angela said to Noel was to drive carefully.

He promised that he would.

Questions for Book Clubs

'Any observations you want to make about the young man?'

Pete paused and gave the officer's question about 'the state' of the driver real thought.

They were all young. It was late. The girl was wearing party clothes. They'd probably been drinking. Two girls, two boys. Testosterone swirling. The temptation of an empty road. A Seat Leon – the 'go-to car' for boy racers.

He opened his eyes and shook his head. 'No.'

He'd been young himself once, a lifetime ago.

1. Is Pete, the witness, right? Is the only 'crime' in the novel that of being young and foolish?
2. Which character did you sympathise with most, and why?
3. Who did you dislike, and why?
4. Where is happiness/comfort to be found in the book?
5. What, or who, 'saves' Fran from her all-consuming grief?
6. What does the book have to say about justice? Is it different for different people? Would you ever consider going through the restorative justice process?
7. What good comes out of the tragedy?
8. Could you, or would you, make the same decision Fran and Marcus do with regard to organ donation, if it was someone you loved?

The traffic flowed by and the cold sun shone, and life went on as normal as Harry knelt and finally laid down his guilt.

9. Should Harry be 'allowed' to lay down his guilt?
10. Did you find the ending hopeful or sad?

Acknowledgements

Acknowledgments are odd things to write. I never know who reads them, other than family members and aspiring writers seeking out the names of agents and publishers.

But here goes…

If you want a good agent who knows the industry inside out and backwards and will, occasionally – when it is most needed – give you the advice and momentum to keep going, then Judith Murray at Greene and Heaton is an excellent choice.

If you are seeking a publisher who treats you like a real person and takes care over every book they publish, then Corvus/Atlantic are the guys to approach. *One Split Second* has been greatly improved by the editorial skills of Sarah Hodgson, Publishing Director, at Corvus. We are on the same wavelength when it comes to telling stories. I hope this book is the start of a long, happy working relationship. The manuscript was professionally 'cleaned' by my copy-editor, Mandy Greenfield. She purged it of a sea of redundant 'that's' and pointed out that I had failed, in one instance, to count to six correctly! Lastly and importantly, this book will only find its way into the hands of readers and onto their Kindles through the efforts of Poppy, Clive, Kirsty, Jamie, and the rest of the sales and marketing team at Corvus. Thank you to you all.

But it's important to acknowledge that I wouldn't have been commissioned to write *One Split Second* if people hadn't bought my first two books. They did so because of the efforts of book bloggers, online book clubs, book shops and the many readers who were kind enough, and motivated enough, to write a review. Thank you to everyone who bothered!

I have also been 'lucky' in my life to spend time with a range of people involved in the NHS, police, criminal justice and prison systems – both professionals and participants. I hope my time with these individuals is reflected in this story.

The personal bit is always about family and friends. In my case, my nearest and dearest love me, cheer me on and leave me alone when I'm writing, fretting and thinking. I don't think you can ask for more than that. It is, after all, my obsession, not theirs.

Then there is Kath Burrow, who has, once again, supported me in the writing of this book. She will get a name check for as long as she can bear to keep reading rough drafts of my books and having conversations about characters who do not exist – though they feel real to me.

Finally, I want to end with a plea for us all to discuss the issue of organ donation with the people we love. Organ donation transforms lives, and not just those of the recipients.

https://www.organdonation.nhs.uk